FIRE WORLD

Also by Chris d'Lacey

The Last Dragon Chronicles
The Fire Within
Icefire
Fire Star
The Fire Eternal
Dark Fire

The Dragons of Wayward Crescent
Gruffen
Gauge

FIRE WORLD

CHRIS D'LACEY

ORCHARD BOOKS ◆ NEW YORK
AN IMPRINT OF SCHOLASTIC INC.

for Angelo Rinaldi

Thanks, as always, to Lisa and Jody, and everyone involved in touring me through North America. If I tried to remember you all I'd come unstuck, but I can't forget Sheila Marie, who was always on the end of a phone when I needed her. Emily, Ann, and Edie, my wonderful media escorts. Elliot and Kevin, the alligator dudes. Rachael and her Reading Rockets at WETA, and Barb Langridge at ABookandaHug.

Nearer to home, thanks to Catherine for her patience, support, and ongoing belief. (Mr. Henry would surely love you as his own.)

And last but not least, a big thanks to the tireless Agent Ed, Rod Duncan and his camera, everyone at LWC, and Jay — who keeps it all going.

Hrrr . . .

PART ONE
WHICH HAS ITS
BEGINNINGS IN THE
STRØMBERG CENTER
FOR AUMA THERAPY
NOVEMBER 3, 031

1.

Professor Merriman. Eliza. Please, come in."

Counselor Strømberg stood at the doorway of his office and swept a welcoming hand into the room. He was a tall, well-built man with pastel blue eyes and shoulder-length fair hair. He nodded at Eliza as she went past, noted her look of concern, but said nothing. He shook hands with Harlan and guided him toward one of the two aumatic chairs positioned in front of the helegas screen on the far wall. A gradient of soft pink colors was playing across it. In the corner nearest to Eliza, a tall *frondulus*, with bell-shaped flowers of variegated colors, was suspended from the ceiling. Eliza ran a knuckle down the twisting stem of the plant and smiled when the flowers opened a little. She came and sat down beside Harlan.

Strømberg positioned himself behind a kidney-shaped

desk and placed his hand on the v:com terminal. "Lara, could you bring David in for me, please?"

A moment later another door opened. A petite young nurse in a pale yellow uniform walked in with a boy of some twelve years. Strands of his nut-brown hair were almost digging into his dark blue eyes. "Mom," he said, going straight to Eliza. She swept one half of her stunning red hair behind her ear so they could touch cheeks in the standard Co:pern:ican fashion.

"You look great," Harlan said, patting the boy's arm. "Have you been OK here?"

Dad, all I've done is sleep, David "said," extending his thoughts to everyone present.

They all laughed and Strømberg said, "Thank you, Lara."

The nurse waved to David and left the room.

Eliza gently tugged her son's sleeve. He was still wearing the blue gown and pants of the auma center. They suited him rather well. "I've told you before, when you're in society it's polite to speak, not commingle."

"Ah, that's my doing," Strømberg said, coming to the boy's aid right away. "I've been encouraging David these past three days to use his mind to commingle or imagineer as much as he likes. It helps us to measure the full extent of his fain."

No worries on that score, Harlan Merriman thought. His son's ability to materialize objects just by thinking about them was unparalleled, in his experience. "So, how's the therapy progressing? Did you discover anything — about the dreams?"

I don't remember any dreams, David commingled.

Strømberg came in quickly again. "David is fit and well. A very intelligent and interesting young man. He's flown through every test we've thrown at him and kept us all amused with his abilities. We'll be sorry to see him leave. As you know, he's been filmed in our sleep laboratory and we have recorded evidence of the disturbances you observed at home."

Have you? David commingled. *Sorry, I mean,* "Have you?"

"Yes," said Strømberg. "And that would support the theory that you're . . . imagineering in your sleep, though why you don't remember it is still a mystery. For that reason, David, I want to continue your therapy so that we can get this resolved properly. It won't be here though. I need to move you to another facility."

"Oh," said Eliza, who'd assumed he was coming home with them that night. The sensors embedded within her chair immediately registered a change in the auma envelope surrounding its occupant. Strømberg, looking at the readings on a monitor only he could see, moved a dial on his com:puter. Accordingly, Eliza's shoulders lifted and her pretty facial muscles relaxed.

Will it be more sleep? David commingled.

"No," said Strømberg, swinging in his chair. "This will be an altogether different adventure."

Harlan sat forward to ask more about it but Strømberg was quick to speak again. A little *too* quick, Harlan thought. Had he been deliberately cut off?

What Strømberg said was this: "There are the usual tedious formalities, which will be of no interest to you, David. Why don't you go and challenge Lara to another game of Flyng while we sort this out? She'll be eager to get her revenge, I'm sure. You can see Mom and Dad again before they leave."

"OK," David said. He smiled at his parents and scooted from the room.

Eliza's gaze trailed after him. Before anyone else could speak she said, "Listen, do you need me for this?" She waved a hand at Strømberg's desk. "If

David's staying in therapy for now, I'd prefer to spend some time with him rather than with filing answers into a com:puter. Is that all right, Harlan?"

"Yes," he said, getting a nod from the counselor.

"Have as much time as you like," said Strømberg, gesturing toward the door that David had gone through.

"Thank you," she said. She pressed Harlan's shoulder and left.

"So," Harlan said, as the door closed behind her, "what do I have to do?"

"I want you to watch something," Strømberg said. A note of seriousness had suddenly crept into his voice. He moved his hand across the com:puter's neural interface. An image of David, asleep in a single bed, appeared upon the helegas screen. A prompt flashed once and read PAUSE. "I'm rather pleased Eliza isn't with us. I don't think she would have coped with this very easily."

Harlan narrowed his gaze. "What exactly have you filmed, Counselor?"

"Something extraordinary," Strømberg replied. And he switched the com:puter to PLAY.

2.

The footage is brief, but dramatic," said Strømberg. "David slept peacefully for most of the night, with no abnormal spikes in his consciousness. This segment was recorded some six hours in, close to the break of dawn."

Harlan turned his eyes fully to the screen. For the first few frames, David lay on his back with his hands tucked under his therma:sol sheet. Then, just as if a pin had been stuck into his foot, his head twitched away from the camera and came violently back, making an audible *whack* against his pillow. He drew up his knees. His back arched slightly. His hands began to push the sheet away.

Suddenly, the screen flashed as if a light had popped. At the same time, David jerked up in bed with his jaws wide open and his lips curled back. Two of his teeth seemed slightly extended. His eyes, normally so placid and round, slanted sideward and briefly changed color from their usual deep blue to a strong shade of brown. With both hands he clawed wildly at the space in front of him, though nothing appeared to be occupying that space. And out of his throat came an uncommon noise. A roar, not unlike the sound of an engine.

In a moment, it was done. David sank back onto his pillow with a *thump* that almost buried his face. The only indication of stress was a trace of saliva running down his jaw. Whatever force had animated him had just as quickly left him.

Strømberg paused the film. "These were the only abnormalities we captured. After this, David slept peacefully with no other conflicts."

Harlan Merriman stood up and stepped toward the screen, tilting his head to examine David's features. "Have you recorded morphing like this before?"

"No."

Harlan looked puzzled. "But what could be happening within his fain to make his eyes change color and his teeth grow like that? And what was that noise he made? It looked as if he was fighting something. How could he possibly be *fighting* something?"

Strømberg raised a hand. "Sit down. There's more to see." He reset the film clip to its beginning, but this time David was pictured the opposite way around. "This is the view from a second camera. When I run the sequence, you'll see exactly what you saw from camera one. But I want you to look beyond David to the window behind him. Concentrate your attention there." He gave a command and the film replayed.

Harlan watched closely. The window next to David's bed was darkened by a set of vertical blinds. But as the recording reached the point where the boy's body jerked up, a series of brightly glowing objects appeared in blotches behind the slats. The objects swelled in size then slipped through the slats in lines of colored light. Strømberg paused the film. "Any guesses?"

"The only things I know of that move as rapidly as that are firebirds."

"Correct," said Strømberg. The film ran in reverse, back to the moment where the colors had materialized. "Here it is again, nine times slower than normal speed. Watch carefully."

And Harlan did. This time, as the colors slipped through the blinds, it was possible to see them re-expand into the familiar long-tailed shapes of the creatures that inhabited every part of Co:pern:ica. Firebirds. Four of them. Green, cream colored, sky blue, and red. They flew to David's bed and hovered in the region of his flashing hands. It was then that Harlan witnessed something even more extraordinary. Just in front of David, over an area approximately two feet long, the air was rippling in a vertical line, as if the fabric of the universe was being torn apart.

"In the name of Co:pern:ica, what's that?" Harlan muttered, and watched in fascination as the fire-birds went about sealing the rift with bursts of the white-colored fire that was sometimes seen to issue from their nostrils. When it was done, they went back the way they'd come. Only one, the green one, a kindly-looking creature with a yellow plume of feathers sprouting up between its ears, stopped to hover in front of David. As the boy fell back to his pillow, the crea-ture touched its feet to David's forehead and zipped away. The film ended.

"What just happened there?" Harlan gasped.

Strømberg ran a hand through his long fair hair. "I don't know," he answered truthfully. "But I'm bound by the nature of my work to tell you that these pictures would be of great interest to the Higher."

"You're going to *report* him?"

"It's my duty to note anomalies like this."

"But he's a child. He's barely twelve spins old. He'll be sent to the Dead Lands. We'll never see him again."

The counselor gave a solemn nod. "This is only an initial assessment, but it's my belief that your son is a rare ec:centric."

Harlan buried his hands inside his pockets and let his worried gaze drift back to the screen.

The image of David remained there for a moment before Strømberg hit a button and cleared it. "He could be a danger to us all," he said.

3.

No, no, no." Harlan turned away, shaking his head. "David is a kind, good-natured child. I'm telling you, he's no threat to the Higher."

Strømberg spoke to the com:puter. "Project Forty-Two. Load and hold." A violet light flashed and a few lines of text scrolled out across the screen. "And what makes you say that?"

Without turning to face him, Harlan replied, "He materializes nothing more than any of us would. Yes, he can be surprising sometimes. But children often are when they're learning to develop their fain. You don't need me to tell you this."

Strømberg, legs crossed, let his chair swing. "Give me an example."

"Of his constructs?"

"Yes. Anything unusual — or surprising, as you put it."

Harlan came and sat down again, perching on the lip of one of the aumatic chairs. Strømberg switched its correctors off. "All right. Recently he imagineered a katt. I know there's nothing odd about that, but this katt was different from any I've ever seen before."

"In what way?"

"It was imperfect."

Strømberg lifted his fingers off the chair arm. "Go on."

"It has a small piece missing from its left ear."

"Has? You haven't corrected the flaw?"

Harlan pressed his lips together and sighed. "Eliza pointed it out to him. But when she offered to help him fix it or produce another katt, he refused. We assumed at first that he hadn't understood the template properly, but it soon became clear that he'd introduced the flaw deliberately. It gave Boon — that's what he named the katt — 'character,' he said."

Counselor Strømberg raised an eyebrow. "Interesting choice of word. Have you gone into this with him?"

Harlan shook his head.

"And he does this kind of thing . . . how often?"

"Look, Counselor —"

"Thorren," said Strømberg. "I'd be happier if you called me Thorren. I think we might be seeing quite a lot of each other and formal assignations will soon become tiring." He placed his hands on the table and adopted a calm, professional tone. "I understand that you feel you're betraying David by giving me information like this. But the laws of my profession are quite straightforward. The Higher expect me to thoroughly investigate cases of this nature and keep an active register of innovative anomalies. They also expect an honest testimony from the subject concerned or those involved with the said subject. Honesty is beauty, and beauty is perfection. Perfection maintains the Grand Design. Anything that attempts to challenge that continuity could be damaging to our shared consciousness. This is why ec:centrics, even one as young as David, have to be monitored and, if necessary, resolved. That is the Co:pern:ican way. However, there is a great deal of flexibility in these cases and it is left to the integrity of the counselor involved as to what action is to be taken."

Harlan looked up.

"Everything you've told me," Strømberg said, "confirms that David is aberrant. The film of his disturbed sleep patterns supports this."

Harlan felt his auma wane. So far, little had been said about the film. How much "aberrance" did Strømberg need to condemn David to the Dead Lands, or even de:construction? Very little, Harlan suspected. And yet the thoughtful look in the counselor's eyes suggested that he was not about to follow standard procedures. And so it proved to be when he said, "I *will* need to log a report of these disturbances — but so far, the only two people who have seen what camera two has seen are you and me."

"Are you suggesting we hide this?"

Strømberg pursed his lips. "I will report what was seen from camera one. If it comes to the attention of the Higher and they choose to send in another investigator, that will be another matter."

"Why?" asked Harlan. "Why would you do that? Why would a distinguished auma therapist put his career at risk for the sake of my son?"

Strømberg shook his head. "I don't know," he said plainly (and with shining honesty, Harlan thought). "Your son intrigues me — possibly because he's *your* son."

"You're interested in my work?"

Strømberg nodded. "Not long ago, I attended your lecture at the Ragnar Institute. I found your concept of thought frameworks very illuminating, particularly the way you hinted at the suggestion that what we imagineer on Co:pern:ica might also be happening, with slight variations, in an infinite number of parallel universes. It was the word 'variations' that gripped me most. It made me wonder what we'd be like if we all existed on another world, in a slightly different guise. You, me, Eliza — David." With that, he swung his chair toward the helegas screen. "My com:puters were able to record a great deal of data about the rift that appeared over David's body — co:ordinates and other physical factors. Like me, you must be wondering what it was and what caused it. As David's counselor, I have the authority to call in any expertise I require to resolve his case. I'm calling in you, his father. The file I recorded, along with the film, will be downloaded to a secure server at your laboratory. It's simply labeled 'Project Forty-Two.' In any correspondence, that's how you'll refer to it. I want you to analyze Project Forty-Two and find out what happened while your son was sleeping. Report your findings to me, and only to me. Meanwhile, I'm going to be conducting some research of my own — from a different angle."

"The firebirds?"

Strømberg nodded. "The greatest mystery on Co:pern:ica just got a little more puzzling, don't you think? Why did these creatures that we all take for granted come to David's aid? Because I have no doubt that they did. Did he call them? Or were they watching him, perhaps?"

"And how were they able to seal that rift?"

"Indeed," said Strømberg. "Now, as I said earlier, I need to send David away for a while. It will seem suspicious if I don't. Often in these cases it helps to place the subject in a completely neutral environment."

"You're preparing a construct for him?"

"Not a construct — a reality," Thorren Strømberg said. "I'm sending David to a librarium."

4.

A *librarium?*"

Eliza's face was so filled with shock that Harlan swiftly imagineered a rose. He put the violet-colored flower straight into her hand and was relieved to see its auma:scents begin to calm her as they rose visibly toward her nose and mouth. Bizarre, he thought, as he stroked her arm, to have seen (and felt) such a variety of emotions in the space of one hour. He put out a thought for a taxicar and one was there before he'd framed his reply. "We have no choice," he said. "If we resist Strømberg's therapy, he will have to refer David directly to the Higher. We're not going to lose our son, Eliza."

He drew her into the taxicar and spoke their destination: Pod 24, The Crescent Way. Bushley. The doors closed and the taxicar sped into the night.

Eliza sat heavily back into her seat, putting out the thought for no incidental music, film, or color. For once, she just wanted to talk. "What good can it do to send him to a place stacked high with books? He'll be so bored his fain will just . . . shrivel."

"I rather think that's the point," said Harlan. "Strømberg is pretty sure David's an ec:centric. His fain is hyperactive, to the point where his constructs are turning against him. Hence the bad dreams. Strømberg believes that a spell in the librarium will calm him down. The curator is a very good man, he says." He unfolded a piece of paper and handed it to her.

"Mr. Henry?"

"He and Strømberg are related — distantly. We're to collect David tomorrow and take him to the librarium ourselves. Mr. Henry will be expecting us."

The taxicar swished along the Bushley clearway. Through its transparent shell, Eliza could see a narrow river, lit by a series of hanging lights. She loved the river and its arched bridge made of stone. Sometimes she thought she could imagineer feathered creatures swimming in pairs on the surface of the water, maybe even bathing in its swell. But they were always just shadows, tricks of the light. The only creatures on Co:pern:ica were firebirds and katts. Neither of them, she was sure, liked to get wet. She folded the paper and handed it back. "How long will he have to stay there?"

"Until the curator is satisfied that David is resolved."

"Will we be able to visit him?"

"No."

Eliza brought the rose up to her mouth. Its colors had seeped into the flesh of her wrist. She squeezed her eyes shut. When she opened them again, a distinct redness was forming in their corners. "How can they change what we imagineered, Harlan? David is a construct of our commingled love. If they alter him, if they dampen him down, aren't they denying us what we wanted? Aren't they tampering with *our* combined fain, just as much as his?"

Harlan switched seats so that he could face her directly. "I'm just as dismayed as you are," he said. "But I believe that Counselor Strømberg is acting in our best interests. He and I have agreed" — and here he chose his words carefully, covering his thoughts about Project Forty-Two — "to liaise closely with Mr. Henry about David's progress. Hopefully, he won't be away from us for long. I'll commingle with him tomorrow and make him understand that this really is just an adventure. Something we've all done once. And . . . I thought we might arrange a treat for his return."

Eliza looked up. She read in her husband's face what was clear in his mind. "A child? You think it's the right time for us to apply for another?"

"Yes, I do," Harlan said. "The girl we've always wanted. A sister for David."

"Penelope," Eliza said, brightening up.

Harlan Merriman took his wife's hand in his. "Penny," he said. "I like 'Penny.'"

5.

The next day, November 4, 031, Harlan and Eliza took a taxicar back to the therapy center to pick up David. The three were then whisked away on a journey that was going to change all their lives. The only address Harlan gave was "the Bushley librarium." He knew of no other and the taxicar did not require further clarification.

Eliza remained silent throughout the journey, leaving Harlan to entertain David. The boy was on his feet for most of the way, imagineering an escort for them. He described to his father what he could see through the shell of the taxicar: a small fleet of golden-colored rocket vehicles guiding them to their glorious destination. Harlan joined in the game, extending his fain to construct pilots for the vehicles. Square-chinned men in astro:nautic uniforms who saluted David as they flew past, all of them wearing *The Crescent Way* badges.

Pity, then, Eliza thought, that their journey's end did not live up to its stately approach. When she stepped out of the taxicar, she shuddered. They were in a wilderness. A calm and pleasant wilderness of green fields speckled with white, violet, and yellow daisies that swung back and forth on the gentlest of breezes (all maintained, she imagined, on low-level diligence from the Higher). No pods or other buildings on any horizon. Just fields and sky and flowers and clouds.

And the librarium.

It rose out of the flowers like a great gray monolith. A single tall building with an uncountable number of floors. The upper floors were lost in wisps of cloud and the whole structure seemed to be bending backward as though it had reached a critical mass and was ready to topple over at any moment. Fine red sand (or something like it) was raining down from the joints in the brickwork and being taken away in skirts on the breeze. At ground level there was just one door. It was made of wood (unusually) and was twice Harlan's height. It was already halfway open, despite the fact that a small sign badly attached to the door frame invited visitors to R NG THE BE L. Harlan moved forward to do just that and stepped on something that had spilled out of the doorway. It was a large-format book. He reached down and picked it up. It must have been thirty spins since he'd seen one. He smoothed a film of the red sand off the glossy cover and handed it to Eliza.

"*The Art of Baking Cakes,*" she read.

Harlan shrugged. "Welcome to the librarium."

Eliza opened the pages and looked at several of the ancient digi:grafs. "Why do we keep this stuff? I could easily imagineer anything in this. I don't understand what use this is to anyone."

"Historical value," Harlan said. He took the book from her and flipped through its pages. He showed a digi:graf of a chocolate gateau to David. The boy's eyes lit up and he quickly imagineered a miniature version. He gave it to his mother.

Eliza smiled and de:constructed it. "Bad for your purity of vision," she said.

"I think books are rather quaint," said Harlan. "And they're real, of course, not constructs." He closed the book and laid it back in the doorway. "Our ancestors would have relied on these things."

Eliza shook her head and looked up at the building. "Is this *real*, do you think?"

Harlan touched the brickwork, feeling its roughness, though that in itself was no proof of authenticity; anyone on Co:pern:ica could imagineer a brick. "Yes," he said. "I'd be surprised if anyone had enough in their fain to put up something as large as this and still be able to maintain it."

Eliza sighed and put her hands on David's shoulders, pulling him back toward her a little. "Why would Strømberg send him to a relic like this?"

"Well, let's begin the process of finding out." This time, Harlan did press the bell. The sign above it tilted and clattered to the ground.

Surprisingly, the bell did work. But rather than making one distinct sound that would normally have soaked through the heart of the building, rooms began to light up at random, each one making a variant of a ring or a clang or a trill or a whistle (even a buzz, Harlan thought). For the first time, he realized there were no coverings of any kind on the windows. No ultra:plex panes to keep in warmth, just a few wooden shutters half-open here and there.

"This could take forever," Eliza tutted as the noises went on and on and on. She crossed her arms and frowned.

All of a sudden, David pointed to a window about eight levels up. An emerald green firebird had just appeared on the sill. It made the strange *rrrh*ing noise the creatures often did, popped its eyes slightly, and went back into the room. The librarium "bell" stopped.

For a moment, all the visitors could hear was the swish of the breeze and the gentle rustle of sand falling among the flowers. Then a head appeared through the window where the firebird had been. A young girl. No older than David. Her hair was the color of night. And though a lot of it was falling in straggles around her face, half-hiding most of the defining bone structure, it was impossible not to see the wild beauty in her shining eyes.

"Yes?" she said curtly.

"We're here to see Mr. Henry," said Harlan.

"He's sleeping," said the girl.

"Through that racket?" Eliza muttered.

The wild eyes immediately picked her out. "Who are you?"

Eliza tapped her foot. "I don't think I like your impertinence," she said, extending her fain to touch the girl's auma and register her official displeasure.

The girl smirked and put a curl of her hair into her mouth. "None of that fain stuff's welcome here. And Mr. Henry doesn't like people who try it. Who's he?" She tilted her chin at David.

"He's our son," said Harlan. "He has an appointment. Now go and fetch Mr. Henry or I'll come in there and find him myself."

At this, the girl hooted with laughter. "Yeah? And how many spins of Co:pern:ica have you got?"

"That's it, we're leaving," Eliza said. "Harlan, get a car." She tapped David's shoulder.

But David stayed exactly where he was, staring up at the girl and smiling. And before his mother could speak again, the boy did something quite amazing. He imagineered a bubble on the palm of his hand and blew it gently into the air. Up it floated, to the eighth level, where it stopped and hovered right in front of the girl.

"What's this?" she said, thrown for the first time.

From the ground, David showed her what she should do with it: Prod (gently), with the tip of a finger.

The girl studied the floating sphere, fascinated by the way its flimsy outer surface seemed to change color if she tilted her head. She frowned at David, then prodded the thing. It immediately burst. The girl gasped and put out a hand to catch what she thought was a glimmer of light. She gasped again when she saw what she'd really caught. "Water," she said. "You made a raindrop float."

"Harlan?" Eliza said, glancing sideways at her husband. "What just happened? How did he do that?"

"I don't know," Harlan whispered, though there was no denying what he had seen. His son had changed the property of a droplet of water and made it lighter than air. Somehow, he'd challenged the force of G:ravity.

A clatter of feet on stairs made the professor look toward the door. The girl heaved it open, cursing as she spilled a whole stack of books into the foyer behind her. She stepped outside wearing a jet-black dress that splayed out in large puffy pleats around her knees and a pair of black-and-white ankle boots, one of which was unlaced. She went right up to David and looked him in the eye. The children were, as it happened, precisely the same height. "Speak," she said.

Eliza tutted at the girl's arrogance. "He doesn't like to," she said. "He prefers to commingle."

"Not allowed here," the girl said to David, shaking her head and making her feral hair cascade across her shoulders. "Mr. Henry likes words. Tell me your name."

"David," he said.

Both parents raised an eyebrow.

The girl smiled. She looked at her wetted hand and used it to shake David's. "I'm Rosa," she said. "This is my librarium, and *you* can come in."

6.

Y*our* librarium?" Harlan said.

Rosa bobbed her head. "OK," she drawled, "spare me the pedantry." (Which made Harlan laugh and Eliza frown.) "It might as well be mine." She crouched down and picked a daisy. "I've been here for eight or nine spins at least."

"Nine spins?" said Eliza, sounding alarmed. (A "spin" was a term used to describe the flat rotation of Co:pern:ica around its fire star. Sometimes people called it a "year.")

Harlan touched her arm. "Why were you brought here, Rosa?"

"My family didn't want me," she said with a shrug. She threw the flower aside and took David's hand. "Come on, I've got lots to show you." They were almost through the librarium door when Eliza called out, "David?"

He turned and let go of Rosa's hand. Although displays of affection were uncommon on Co:pern:ica, he nevertheless came back and put his arms around his mother.

"You won't forget us?" she said, unsure of how to hold him.

David gave her a puzzled look. "It's an adventure, isn't it?" He turned to his father.

Harlan was looking at the discarded daisy, lying in the grass, its life juice steadily seeping away. If this place had been a construct, the Higher would have fixed the daisy by now. He glanced up at the silent building and nodded. "Yes, a proper adventure," he muttered. And with that he waved good-bye to his son, drew Eliza into the taxicar, and took her away.

"Hey. New boy." Rosa was at one of the ground-floor windows. She had her elbows on the sill and her chin in her hands. "Cover your eyes and count to ten."

"Why?"

"After ten, you can come in and find me. And remember, you're not allowed to extend your fain. If you do, I'll know and I'll punish you."

32

"Erm, how?"

The dark eyes rolled. "I won't talk to you for three whole days."

And this is a bad thing? David thought, extending his fain so she might commingle if she wanted to.

She stuck out her tongue. *Yes,* she replied.

So you can *commingle, then?*

"Yes, but it's *not* allowed," she said. "It hurts me anyway. And I won't do it again or Mr. Henry will be mad. Eyes. Cover. The full ten, OK? Runcey will be watching. He's my best friend. He'll know if you cheat." She pointed to the firebird in the next window along. He was sitting with his green wings folded back and a slightly faraway look on his face.

David shrugged and covered his eyes.

After a not-so-generous "ten," he looked up and saw that Rosa and the firebird were both gone. Quickly, he ran inside the librarium, where he soon discovered that speed of movement was of little advantage and a positive hazard. Books of all sizes and colors, some glossy backed, some dull and plain, some open, some not, were stacked and strewn in piles of varying height (including singly) across the floor of the foyer and again up the dark, uneven-looking stairs.

Picking his way through them, he turned to his right and headed for the room he thought Rosa had spoken from. She wasn't there, but the scene was exactly the same as in the foyer, except the walls were also laden with books, so many that the shelves were bowing with their weight. As he stumbled across the room, almost losing his footing on something called *Flamenco Guitar Made Easy*, David found himself on the threshold of two more doorways, at right angles to each other. He took the one he thought would lead him deeper into the building, convinced that Rosa would be hiding in the heart of it. She wasn't. In total, he visited eleven more rooms. And the only difference between any of them was that some had windows and some did not. And in one he found a chair that rocked, and in another an old-fashioned easel. In the twelfth room he thought to glance out of the window and realized, to his surprise, that the daisy horizon was shrinking. In other words he'd actually been going upward, though he'd had no sense whatsoever of climbing.

"Fed up yet?"

He whipped around. There she was. Leaning against a doorway, grinning.

"I thought I'd be kind," she said, looking at her fingernails. "It takes forever if you don't know what you're doing. The librarium is kind of . . . spatially arranged. I'll teach you if you're going to be here for a while. Did you find a bathroom?"

David shook his head.

"Clothing closet?" she asked a little hopefully, clearly not happy with the pants, shirt, and tie he was wearing.

"Just books," David said. "Hundreds of them."

"Two million, four hundred and eighty-two thousand, and sixty-three to be precise." She grinned like a katt.

David nodded. It was a tall, tall building. "What do you do here?"

"Store books," she said with a shrug. "It's my job to put them in order. I'll show you." She stepped into the room, picked up a book from a heap on the floor, and examined its spine. "We do them by author. Duncan," she read out. "This can go before" — she scanned the shelves — "Essinger." She reached up on tiptoe and attempted to push the book into a space too small for it. So she created a space instead. "This Ringrose shouldn't be here," she said, and pulled the book before the Essinger out of its slot, replacing it with her Duncan. The Ringrose she simply dropped onto the floor. "I'll do that one another time. I wonder if Mr. Henry is going to ask you to order them, too. You do know your alph, don't you?" And circling David with her hands behind her back she chanted, "A B C D E F—"

"G," David said.

He looked up and saw the firebird prick his ears. Along his iridescent neck, several of his feathers shimmered bloodred and orange.

Rosa came to a halt in front of David. Her pupils dilated as she tilted her head and looked into his eyes. "Why were you sent here?"

"To have an adventure," David said, desperately wanting to add, in thought, *You heard what my father said outside.* But he obeyed the librarium rules and felt that the building had warmed to him because of it.

None of this was lost on Rosa. "You sense it, don't you?" A hint of excitement glittered in her eyes. She looked to her right, drawing David's attention to a shelf just above eye level, one of the few that still had a little space on it. Its books had fallen sideways. Only one, at the open end, was standing upright and free. But only for a moment. David saw it wobble, then lean and fall against the book beside it. Nothing had touched it, and he had certainly not imagineered it, and there was not enough wind in the room to cause it. "How . . . ?" he asked. But by then Rosa had switched her gaze again, beyond him, to the open window.

"*Hhh!*" she gasped. "Rain!"

She was there in two secs. Her feet picked out the spaces between the books so fast that she crossed the floor like a ghost.

"Come and look!" she beckoned him, bouncing on her toes.

David joined her. They were at least twelve floors up, looking west of the taxicar route but still seeing nothing more than green grass and daisies. A rainbow was arcing through the cloudy sky.

"They love this," she said.

"The flowers?"

"*Mmm.*"

And though it was hard to tell from this height, David thought he could sense them stretching their stems and widening their petals. Their colors had changed. From yellow to pink, from white to pale blue.

Here and there, orange. He put his hand through the window and turned it, enjoying the caress of the raindrops on his skin. "The rain brings everything together," she whispered.

David glanced at her, not sure what she meant. "What made the book fall over?" he asked.

She turned to him and placed her hand on his heart. As the warmth from it seeped into his shirt, she said, "Before we had fain, before we were able to imagineer, we built worlds in our heads with words, David. Those words are all here, in these books, in these rooms. The words moved the book. This building is *alive*."

7.

Hmph, well, everything is *alive*, child."

Rosa and David turned to see a tall and slightly frail old man putting a book onto a shelf on the far side of the room. He was dressed in very simple clothing: loose baggy pants, a shirt with the cuffs rolled back, and a waistcoat that had a thread or two undone at the buttonholes. His hair, what there was of it, rose in faint gray wisps around his ears. Liverish-colored spots could be seen on his scalp. He seemed kindly enough, though the overlarge, black-rimmed spex he wore added a note of austerity to his face. And one of his teeth was chipped.

"This is Mr. Henry," Rosa said to David.

"*Mmm,*" went Mr. Henry, and continued with his lecture. "Nothing in the universe is ever still, you see. But some things appear more still than others.

Everything has auma, from a humble splint of wood to the raindrops falling past that window. Auma is life. And life is never static. It changes and evolves. It *grows*. You must be David?"

"Yes," said the boy.

"Welcome to the librarium. Rosa has shown you how to get around?"

"Not really. Can someone tell me where the bathroom is, please?"

Mr. Henry extended a hand in the direction of the room next door. "Through there, perhaps?"

David aimed a worried look at Rosa. "I came in that way. I didn't see one."

"OK, I cheated a bit." She blushed. "You're allowed to use your fain to sense your way around. You have to tune your auma to the building to do it. If you want a bathroom, for instance, you put the thought out and the librarium will guide you through the quickest route to one. I've found nine so far, but I think they move around. Go on" — she nudged him sideways — "before you wet your pants. Oh, and find something a bit more interesting to wear. You look a bit . . . retro, if you know what I mean?"

"All right, that's quite enough teasing," said Mr. Henry. He brushed a little dust off David's shoulder. "Join us in my study when you're done."

"Your study? Where is that?"

Rosa tapped her head.

Think it. Right.

"Runcey will go with you, till you're used to it," she said.

David looked at the perky little firebird. He spread his wings and fluttered to a shelf by the door.

"And be polite," Rosa said, following Mr. Henry out of the room. "The librarium doesn't like it if you're disrespectful."

David rested his hand on the nearest row of books. *Bathroom,* he thought, adding *please* into the mix. He let his auma dissolve into the books and immediately felt the slightest of tugs, as if the molecules in the skin of his chest had been magnetized to those in the air in front of him. The librarium had recognized his request and responded. He strode forward through the door Mr. Henry had pointed to and felt Runcey's soft claws alight on his shoulder. Confident he wasn't going to need the bird's guidance, he marched through two more doors, up a flight of stairs, down a dark and tilting corridor, and stepped into ... a broom closet.

Rrrh! went Runcey. The creature landed on an upturned bucket, shaking his head in a gesture of despair. He spread his wings in a kind of meditative arc.

"You're telling me to think more clearly?"

Runcey did not seem to understand this. But in a further attempt to be helpful, he rummaged through several books (even here, among the brooms, they had found a ledge or two), flipping them open and tossing them aside until he found one with an illustration. He showed this to David and circled a wing over it.

"You want me to make a picture? In my head?"

Rrrh! went the bird.

David smiled. He understood now where he'd gone wrong. He'd been sloppy in his intent. The librarium must have heard "broom" instead of "bathroom." So he closed his eyes and carefully refined his thoughts, picturing a tub and a cistern and a sink. Within twenty seconds, he was there.

He applied the same tech:nique to "wardrobe" and burst through a door into a closet full of shirts and sweaters (making Runcey wince). But he was learning quickly, and by the time he'd strolled into Mr. Henry's study, wearing blue jeans, boots like Rosa's, and a plain khaki combat jacket over a maroon T-shirt, he'd also found a bedroom (a hammock slung between two bookshelves) and a room with kitchen implements hooked on to a wall. He was, he thought, beginning to get the hang of it.

"Wow," said Rosa, sitting cross-legged on a large cushion. "Look at you. All ready for action, or what?"

David had been quietly wondering about this, his course of action, his grand adventure. He ignored Rosa's jibes and spoke up boldly. "Mr. Henry, I really like the librarium. But what am I actually doing here? When does my adventure begin?"

Mr. Henry thought about the question carefully. He poked around in the drawers of a desk and found several blunt-nosed pens of different colors. He took them to a flipchart and exposed a large sheet of plain white paper.

David's mouth fell open in surprise. Was the old man actually going to *write* something? In these days of :coms, no one ever did that.

But Mr. Henry, as Rosa had rightly said, liked words. Without further ado he inscribed one in bright red capitals on the lower part of the paper: "ORDER."

"Order?" asked David.

Mr. Henry circled it (twice). "Essential in a librarium, boy."

"I already put the books in order," Rosa piped.

"*Hmm,*" said Mr. Henry. "But it's time to move onto another level, child. We're double-handed now. Have to make use of the new pair of hands." He drew a curved arrow away from "ORDER" and wrote a new word, in blue this time: "GENRE." "Who knows what that means?"

Rosa's hand shot up like a daisy stalk. "It means a type of something."

"Correct," said Mr. Henry. "Imagine the *greater* order we would have if we put the books together not just by author but by type."

Rosa's big brown eyes almost popped from her head.

"Won't that take a long time?" asked David.

"Oh, yes," said Mr. Henry. "A very long time."

"But won't we get . . . erm, bored?" David said. Boredom was a concept so alien on Co:pern:ica that he'd struggled for a second or two to find the word.

But Mr. Henry understood the concept well. "Not if you both do this," he said. And he drew another line to another circled word.

"Read?" said David.

Mr. Henry smiled. "Read the books, David. Read them as you go."

"All of them?" asked Rosa. She didn't seem fazed.

"Any that appeal to you," Mr. Henry said.

"But won't that take even *longer*?" asked David.

Mr. Henry smiled again and completed the triangle on his chart. "Think of the worlds you will enter, David. Think of the knowledge you will gain, the enjoyment to be had. This is your adventure — to soak up the librarium and see what you become."

"Is this what my father wants of me?"

Mr. Henry lifted his chin and stared at the boy for a long, long moment. "This is what the *librarium* wants of you," he said. "You may begin."

8.

Two days after leaving his son at the Bushley librarium, Harlan Merriman received a high-priority e:com to his office at the Ragnar Institute for Realism in Phys:ics. The sender was Thorren Strømberg. The message was short:

Harlan. Here is the data from Project Forty-Two. I will be interested to know what your analysis reveals. I can be contacted at any time through the usual channels. I hardly need remind you of the sensitivity of this information. Use all security measures you deem necessary to protect it. By the way, I received a message from the curator of the librarium to say that David is settling in well. No further sleep disorders reported. Will keep you updated. Best regards, TS.

Harlan sent back a message of acknowledgment before copying all the files to an encrypted micro:pen. Then, dimming the office lights, he sat back in his chair and ran the films again.

He was on his second playthrough of the view from camera two when a voice behind him said, "Goodness, is that David?"

Harlan stopped the film at once. A younger man, a little overweight for his height, but with an open, pleasant disposition, was standing just inside the office door. He was dressed in black pants and a plain white shirt. His name was Bernard Brotherton, Harlan's tech:nical assistant.

"I'm sorry, Professor, should I leave?" He had guessed from the look on Harlan's face that he had walked in on something quite private.

Harlan shook his head. "No, Bernard. Come in. I want to show you something." He ran both films again.

Bernard was practically speechless. "That's extraordinary," he said, so stunned by what he'd seen that he only managed to place a knee on the seat of the chair next to his boss.

Harlan said, "I need to be sure I can trust you, Bernard."

Bernard shook his head in slight confusion. The blue of the com:puter's helegas screen glinted off the bald patch spreading through his hair. "Trust?" he asked.

"I know it's a concept we've largely forgotten about. But this is not the kind of thing you see every day. David's been experiencing severe sleep problems. He's been diagnosed ec:centric. His counselor has sent him to a librarium for observation. Outside of official sources, I don't want this known."

"But they've given you the films?"

Harlan explained what he'd been asked to do. "I want to run this through SETH," he said, tapping a folder labeled SPATIAL ENIGMAS AND TIME HORIZONS.

Bernard rubbed his chin for a moment, taking off several flakes of skin. He reached for the com:puter's neural pad and advanced the film, pausing it when the rift appeared. "That certainly looks like a spatial enigma. But isn't it equally possible that David has imagineered all of this, even the facial changes? We've all heard stories about how potent the dream state can be." Before Harlan could offer a reply, Bernard let the film run on for twenty secs and pointed to the screen to support his argument. "It's the firebirds that make me think it's a construct. Why would they come and fix everything? We all love them and have our fanciful theories about them, but there isn't a single piece of research that points to them having the level of intelligence necessary to seal a rift like that."

"But to some degree that's the problem," said Harlan. "The definition of ec:centricity is the ability to imagineer outside the framework of the Higher's Grand Design. The very fact that David visualizes firebirds rescuing him from an unknown threat indicates he's reaching way beyond the limits of the Co:pern:ican Stencilla. I want to believe you're right, Bernard, because if you're not, what we're seeing on these films is real." He swung his chair sideways and spoke a few words of command to the com:puter. Several strings of code ran out across the screen. "These files were recorded by David's counselor. They contain the pro:dimensional co:ordinates of what you saw in the films. I want you to load them into the SETH program, using every probability filter available. It might be several days before we have a result, but I'm pretty sure SETH will confirm that what we're investigating is a time horizon."

Bernard closed his eyes momentarily. His face, in this state, resembled the full moon. He sat back and placed one hand behind his head, clutching at hairs that were no longer present. "And then?"

A :com light flickered on the wall in front of them. A video message from Eliza Merriman. Harlan placed it on hold. "We'll deal with that when we know." He handed Bernard the encrypted pen. "Everything you need is on there."

Bernard nodded. "I'll get on it right away."

"Good man," said Harlan, and clapped him on the shoulder. The tech:nician left the room.

"Eliza," Harlan said. Her face appeared in the small :com window.

"Sorry to interrupt you at work, but I thought you'd like to know that I've made an appointment with an Aunt. She wants to come over tonight. Is that all right?"

"That was quick," Harlan replied. "Is it the same one we had for David?"

"No. I did ask for Aunt Agnes, but she wasn't available. They assure me this one is very efficient."

"Good," said Harlan, looking pleased. "I'm hoping David will be out of the librarium very soon, so efficiency is exactly what we need if we're going to surprise him with a little sister." He smiled and imagineered a picture of their son with a baby in his arms. Eliza smiled back. "What's her name, this Aunt, in case she gets there before I arrive?"

"Gwyneth," said Eliza. "Her name is Aunt Gwyneth."

9.

By the time Harlan Merriman had returned home that night, the Aunt whom Eliza had spoken of was already at the pod. They were in the gardenaria with Boon, admiring Eliza's latest construct: a rockery, which she'd populated with a dazzling array of small green plants, many with intricate leaf structures. It was a beautiful composition. A real feat of imagineering. Something that could not fail to impress even the harshest of Aunts. As he watched them chatting from the kitchen window, Harlan saw the Aunt crouch down beside a group of plants near to the ground. This was some achievement, for the woman was dressed in a tight-fitting two-piece suit, and the skirt was all but clamping her knees together. He watched her shoo Boon away, then circle her hand over the place where the katt had been sitting. Eliza's placid gaze changed in an instant.

She was clearly unhappy about what the Aunt had done. But by the time the woman had raised herself, Eliza had fixed a gracious smile to her face. Quick to realize she could use his support, Harlan loaded up a tray with three tall glasses and filled them with a sparkling white juice. Then he strolled into the gardenaria, speaking a greeting. The Aunt turned to face him. She was older than he'd been expecting, with a sharpness in her eyes that their first Aunt, Agnes, had not possessed. Next to the Higher itself, the Aunts were the most powerful group on Co:pern:ica. This one bore her authority like a mask. It was etched deep into the lines of her face. Even her silver-peppered hair, pulled into a bundle at the base of her neck (a recognized trademark of her profession), looked brittle, like it would crack if it were touched. He felt her fain probing his, and knew that he must not resist. She was, by the nature of her business, allowed to do this, and Harlan, although he did not approve of this most invasive manner of commingling, gave himself up to her. She could not read his mind, but she could measure his general auma in an instant. It was important for her to sense that he was happy in her presence. Any show of disrespect might influence her decision to grant them permission to imagineer the daughter they wanted. And that would break Eliza's heart.

"Harlan," Eliza said, "this is Aunt Gwyneth."

He bowed his head and offered up the tray. "Thank you for agreeing to such an early appointment. A drink, Aunt Gwyneth? We find this whiteberry construct very refreshing."

The woman lifted her chin and looked, almost suspiciously, at the glasses. "I do not like anything *fizzy*."

"Well, I can —" Harlan began.

Eliza held up a hand and said, "We've already had an herbal tea, Harlan. Aunt Gwyneth has been here for a little while."

"Oh, I see. Forgive me," he said. "I was, erm, caught up with something at work."

"You lecture in Realism, I understand?" The woman's fain reached out again, like fingertips pressing at the flesh around his ears.

"That is one aspect of what I do," said Harlan. And feeling somehow vulnerable with both hands occupied, he de:constructed the tray of drinks and said, "Shall we go inside?"

Aunt Gwyneth turned on her stocky little heels. "I prefer the gardenaria. I like the freshness of the air."

Eliza saw an opportunity to gather ground in this. "Harlan, look what Aunt Gwyneth has done. She's added a new construct to the rockery."

Harlan glanced down. "Is that . . . fungus?" he said. Growing out between the rocks were three short stalks with large gray caps.

"Very knowledgeable, Professor," Aunt Gwyneth said, purring at the same low level as Boon. (The katt by now had padded away and was playing with a piece of tweedy fluff that he'd managed to imagineer — the same blue color, Harlan noticed, as Aunt Gwyneth's suit.) "Fungal constructs are quite a rarity these days."

Rarity? thought Harlan, trying hard to keep his fain at bay. "I thought they'd been —"

"Limited?"

"Yes."

"Not to us."

Harlan gave a respectful nod. Aunts had a vast catalogue of constructs to call upon, though how anything with the poor nutritional value of *mushrooms* (was that what they were called?) could be helpful to anyone was beyond him. He looked up at Aunt Gwyneth and sensed she was reveling in a minor victory. Her fatuous smile reminded him of a wet line drawn across a steamed-up mirror.

"So, may we talk about the prospect of a daughter?" He moved forward and took Eliza's hand. "We've completed our application to the Higher and believe we are favorably placed to bring a new child onto Co:pern:ica. We have her image and her auma traits fixed. We merely ask for your guidance and approval, to help us bring together this happy —"

"Tell me about your son," said the Aunt, cutting him off without a glance. She was staring instead at two orange-colored firebirds, which were perched in Eliza's cherrylea tree, hiding themselves in the thick of the leaves.

"Oh. Well, David . . . ," Eliza began, but this was just the topic she and Harlan had been fearing, and she found herself unable to go on.

Harlan patted her hand. A gesture that suggested that he should do the talking. Drawing down calm into his auma, he said, "We imagineered David over twelve spins ago. He's been a model son."

"It says in my report that he's ec:centric, Professor."

Harlan laced his fingers together. The woman was thorough. He must choose his words with care. "It's . . . true that he's been exhibiting some minor sleep distur-bances, but —"

"When did these terrors begin?"

"Well, I'd hardly describe them as —"

"It is not your place to teach me what I know! Answer the question, Professor."

"Some months ago," he said, curbing the desire to snap. Was this a test? Was this woman deliberately trying to provoke him?

"And how does he describe the dreams?"

"He doesn't. He appears to forget everything by the morning. We're not sure why."

The Aunt closed her eyes. "Who is his counselor?"

"Thorren Strømberg."

The corners of the woman's mouth twitched into a sneer.

"You disapprove of him?" asked Harlan.

"I have heard he is very able," said the Aunt, "though his methods are considered 'questionable' by some."

"In what way?" asked Eliza, looking concerned. "We took David to him in good faith, Aunt. We only want what's best for our —"

"It is of no matter," Aunt Gwyneth muttered. She flapped a hand, startling the firebirds out of the tree. They fluttered away and landed on the slanting roof of the pod. Her sober gaze traveled with them and stayed there. "I wish to ask you a question, Eliza. You put in your application that you would like your daughter to inherit the demeanor of those creatures. Why was that?"

Once again, Eliza seemed a little lost for words. "I . . . I find them . . . graceful," she said.

Harlan came in again before she could flounder. "Eliza has always had a strong affinity with the firebirds. They're regular visitors to her gardenaria. They seem at ease here. We think if we could reproduce that same mutual fondness, that level of attraction in our daughter, then —"

"Do you talk to them, Eliza?"

"*What?*" said Harlan.

"My question was intended for your *wife*," hissed the Aunt.

Once again, Harlan composed himself. He bowed and took a step back.

"Well, I *do* talk to them," Eliza said, playing with a corkscrewing strand of her hair. "They seem to enjoy the sound of my voice, especially if . . ."

Aunt Gwyneth stared at her, probing her fain. "Go on."

". . . especially if I sing," Eliza said. She looked down at her feet as if she were ashamed. "It's more a kind of humming, really. Don't ask me why. It just feels natural. They like it and it seems to attract them. But I don't converse with them. That would be silly."

Aunt Gwyneth tapped her manicured fingers together. Her nails, Harlan noticed, were completely black. "Have you ever attempted to commingle with their fain?"

"Aunt Gwyneth, is this really —?"

"Professor, be silent!"

Now it was Eliza's turn to signal to her husband that she was confident enough to deal with the questions. "Yes," she said boldly. "Haven't we all at some time?" *With no success,* she added into her fain, though the sentence hardly needed to be raised. No one had ever linked into the firebirds' consciousnesses. No one. Not even an Aunt.

Aunt Gwyneth made her own kind of humming noise. She strolled down the gardenaria a way, stopping to admire a bright yellow rose. "I cannot approve your application," she said.

Eliza covered her mouth. She looked at Harlan, who immediately placed himself within Aunt Gwyneth's line of sight. "Why?" he demanded.

Aunt Gwyneth brushed past him.

"*Why?*" he said again, grabbing her arm.

"Harlan, what are you doing?!" Eliza gasped.

Aunt Gwyneth whipped around and confronted the professor. Her eyes were wide and violet and blazing. "How *dare* you touch me or question my authority? I could have you banished to the Dead Lands for less. The imagineering of a child is a selfless act that must benefit and support the continuity of the Design and the welfare of all Co:pern:ica. You have already constructed one ec:centric and I am not convinced you won't do so again." Harlan reeled as her fain powered into him. He stumbled back, clutching at the sides of his head.

Eliza immediately rushed to his aid. "Aunt, please stop this. Harlan means no harm. He's a good man. Believe me. He's simply disappointed. We've wanted a daughter for so long now."

"Yet you only decide to call in an Aunt when your dysfunctional son has been removed to a librarium."

"I . . ." Eliza felt the heat in her eyes. "No, it's not like that. Penny is not a replacement for David. I love him dearly. He . . ."

Aunt Gwyneth raised a hand. "Enough," she said. "My decision is made. I cannot grant approval for a daughter at this time." She glanced down. Boon was pawing plaintively at Harlan's leg. One of the firebirds had landed on a fence post and seemed to be carefully observing the situation. The other had flown away. Aunt Gwyneth pressed her hands together and went on another of her little walks. "Your husband will recover in a moment. When he does, he will be aware that I have branded him with a warning. This is not something to be taken lightly. His temperament is partially the reason for your son's ec:centricity and should have been dealt with by your first Aunt. But it is not the entire reason your son now finds himself removed from the Design. You are responsible, too, Eliza Merriman."

"Me? Are you saying my auma is flawed?"

Aunt Gwyneth turned. Her eyes were glowing violet. "No, quite the opposite. There is a purity in you that I rarely observe in other applicants. As such, I am prepared to offer you an arrangement. You will have the daughter you desire, but first you will come away with me — for training."

"Training?" said Eliza. "Training? In what?"

"In *this*, of course," Aunt Gwyneth said. She ran a hand down her body. "I have chosen you as an aspirant. You are to become an Aunt."

10.

In the librarium, time seemed nonexistent. True, there were always days and nights. The windows darkened and lightened again. The daisies closed and the daisies opened. A moon rose occasionally. A soft rain fell. Co:pern:ica spun around its yawning fire star. But to David and Rosa, this changing scenery was just something that occurred outside their frame of reference. All that mattered, to them, was books.

Now that there were two putting the librarium in order, the building hummed with the spirit of competition. And yet it rarely observed David and Rosa in the same room for long. For each child had their own ideas of organization, and what this generally translated to was a frantic crossing of paths, not a selfless joining of forces. Several times a day — nay, *dozens* of times a day — one child would sweep past the other, usually with books stacked up to their chins, en route to whichever shelf was occupying them. Their snippets of conversation would go something like this:

"I've done forty-seven *L*'s this morning."

"I bet you didn't know there are twenty-four books about cushions." (Thirty-eight, as it happened; David still had a way to go with that subject.)

"My shelves are so tidy you'd *faint* if you saw them."

"My archaeology collection is going to *fill* two rooms."

On top of this there were the reading exchanges. For when the pair of them was finally too exhausted to sort or stack, they would sit down as Mr. Henry had suggested and actually *read* a text (usually with food in their hands, for their days had no timetable and there was no insistence on formal meals). Rosa was quicker at reading than David and could whip through as many as two hundred pages in a single afternoon. But what David lacked in speed he made up for in depth. He also liked to walk as he read, mainly because Mr. Henry did it. Many a time David had poked his head into a room and seen the old man sailing through it with a book in his hand, spouting the words (some-times David followed him, just for fun, though the building seemed to know it and would eventually steer him off course). Once in a while, the curator would call both children to his study and inquire about their progress. And it was usually David who gained the most credit when the darts of factual information were flying.

This was Rosa, for instance: "In our history, there were these things called 'pi:anos' that were, like, polished wooden boxes on legs. They had these parts called 'keys' — which sort of looked like teeth — and when you hit the keys with your fingers they made a sound. People used to play them and make music come out of them, which is weird, but there you go."

"And what made you read about pi:anos?" asked Mr. Henry.

"I was doing some *S*'s," Rosa said. "I found a book written by this man called Steinerway. I thought it looked interesting."

"Excellent," Mr. Henry said. "You might also look out for Petrov, Graveau, Beckstein, and Frazioli. All of them famous for making these instruments. And how about you, David? What have you been reading lately?"

"I know about the music pi:anos made," he answered.

"Typical," said Rosa, sounding trumped. She flicked a piece of her sandwich at him.

"I've been gathering books about composers," said the boy.

"What's a composer?" Rosa asked Mr. Henry.

"Think of them as people who imagineered music for the masses."

"Oh," said the girl. She didn't seem impressed.

"I read about a man called Shopan," said David, "who composed melodies so beautiful — on the pi:ano — that people thought he had captured them from the wind."

Rosa looked through the window at the stationary clouds. No melodies there today.

Mr. Henry encouraged David to continue.

"People talked in strange ways about the music he wrote, saying it was as light as the air, or as easy on the ears as sleep is on the eyes. They said it was like poetry. What's poetry, Mr. Henry? I've looked for it, but I can't find any."

Mr. Henry studied the boy carefully. "It's an ancient, lyrical form of writing."

David thought back to the flipchart Mr. Henry had used on his first day here. Writing again. "Where is it? Can I see some?"

Mr. Henry smiled. "It's on the upper floors, David."

"The upper floors?" said Rosa. A slight gasp escaped her mouth.

David sat up at once. "I've been meaning to ask about that. I've tried to go there, to the top of the librarium, but I never get farther than —"

"Floor Forty-Two." Rosa looked at him and shrugged. "It's right. I've counted the windows. You can't count upward above Forty-Two because of the clouds. I bet Runcey knows, though. I've seen him flying up there." She sent a stream of tongue clicks across the room.

The firebird, sitting by the window, preening, turned his head and went *rrrh?*

"Why can't *we* go up there?" David asked the curator.

Mr. Henry pushed his glasses back farther up his nose. "You will," he said, "when everything is in order."

"What's it like up there?" asked Rosa. "What can you see if you stand on the roof?"

Mr. Henry looked at his helpers in turn. "Everything," he said. "All the world can be seen from the roof of the librarium."

This extraordinary, if somewhat metaphorical, notion almost sent both youngsters scuttling back to their shelves that instant. For the incentive in Mr. Henry's statement was clear: Whoever completed their labors first would probably be the one who made it at least as far as Floor Forty-Three. And what an achievement *that* would be.

But he told them the next day must be a rest day. From now on, there would be one in every seven, he said. They should go out. Walk. Enjoy the daisy fields. Chase around. Play. Be tiresome children. Make a nuisance of themselves. (He meant these last two jokingly, of course.) If they wanted to be helpful, the water butts were low.

Water! Rosa sat up brightly. "Tomorrow morning, first light." She elbowed David in the ribs.

"What are we doing?" he asked.

"Getting water, of course!"

Of course. Everything was obvious if you lived in Rosa's head.

But he was ready, bright and early, at dawn the next morning, with a backpack of food (mainly cookies) on his back, leaning against the wall outside her room when she emerged. She was surprised to see him, but pleased, he thought. She'd changed her clothing: new white boots, pretty yellow dress. He looked her up and down, not sure if he should comment. She folded her arms as if to say, *And what do you think* you're *staring at?* He wanted to reply but his tongue was in knots. She knew it, and was soon in command again. "Better tie your laces up." She sniffed.

Laces? Wasn't he wearing slip-on shoes? Stupidly, he looked down to check. The next thing he knew she'd pushed him over and gone running for the fields.

He caught up with her by a circular wall in an area where the daisies were a lovely violet color. He threw down the backpack and played a game of this way and that before she stumbled and he finally got hold of her.

"*Agh!*" she squealed.

With one heave he threw her onto his shoulder. And though she pummeled his back with her fists, she knew there was no escape.

"What is this place?" he said. The circular wall was several feet in diameter. Above it was a V-shaped roof and a pulley. Suspended from the pulley was a bucket on a rope. Below the bucket was a deep, dark hole.

"It's a well, of course. Now, put me down."

"Dunno. It looks deep."

"I don't mean in the *hole*!"

"Hole?" he said, pitching forward a little.

"*Agh!*" she squealed again. "What are you *doing*?"

"Tripped on my laces."

"Oh, fun-nee."

"What's down there?" he asked.

"Water, stupid. Be careful, will you? This is my best dress."

"It's just a dress," he said. "You'll dry out."

"NOOOOO!" she screamed, as he made to let her go.

Instead, he brought her down with a bump on the wall, keeping his hands firmly around her waist (for safety's sake, he later said). She threw her hands around the back of his neck (in case she lost her balance, *she* later said). She shook her hair from her face and glared at him with her smoky brown eyes. "Do you hate me?" she asked, pouting her lips.

"Probably," he said.

She stuck out her tongue and called him a liar.

In return, he pressed his fingers to her waist. She screeched with laughter and tried, with both hands, to slap his chest. He caught her and held her until she was still. She stuck out her tongue again. "Don't know what to do now, do you?" she said.

And that was true, he didn't. He looked at her fingertips, roughened by years of handling books, and let his thumb glide across them.

He was sure he felt her tremble.

"You don't really hate me — do you?" she asked.

He made a show of thinking about it, but eventually shook his head.

She cocked her head. "Do you love me, then?"

"Probably," he said, just as Runcey landed on the roof of the well.

"Well, I'm spoken for." She laughed, and blew the firebird a kiss. He responded, as usual, with a puzzled little *rrrh?*

She struggled free and flopped down with her back to the wall. "We forgot the buckets."

"Buckets?" David said.

"To carry the water. To the librarium."

"Oh. Right. Shall I go back?"

"Only if you never want to see me again."

He chewed on that a moment, but only for a moment. Then he sat with his shoulder pressed against hers, pleased that she didn't try to move away. He opened the backpack and took out the cookies. Runcey fluttered to the ground in front of them.

All of a sudden Rosa said brightly, "I'm going to make you a daisy chain." She sat forward and picked a handful of daisies, plucking them close to the ground to preserve the lengths of their bright green stalks. For the next ten minits she made David sit back-to-back with her, so he couldn't see what she was doing and steal the "secret" of how a daisy chain was made. Content enough to share a cookie with Runcey and enjoy the warmth of the sun on his face, he obeyed. In the distance, the tall shape of Mr. Henry could be seen strolling the walls of the librarium, completely lost in a book. David closed his eyes. Not quite an *adventure*, a day like this, but very pleasant all the same. As he sat there, with Runcey taking crumbs from his hand and Rosa tutting ceaselessly about her creation, thoughts of home began to flash through his mind. How, he wondered, were his parents and Boon? Why was it they didn't come to see him here? Fortunately, any threat of despondency was soon dashed by Rosa's energetic shuffling. She showed him the circle of flowers. He readily deduced that it was simply made by splitting stalks and carefully inserting neighboring ones into them, but he oohed and aahed in suitable fashion and was genuinely moved when she slipped the chain over his hand and wrist. It was the first real gift he'd ever been given.

He wore it the next day when they went back to work. By now both children were building up their catalogues and making small, but visible, impacts on the clutter. The librarium buzzed in tune to their industry. But there was one minor flaw in this endeavor that neither of them had yet worked out, though it was about to be uncovered with dramatic consequences.

Midmorning, as Rosa went flashing by en route to a room, David crowed that his collection of books on aviation history was almost complete.

"I found this on Floor Twenty-Nine," he said. He held up a large, rather weighty book that had a photograph of a biwinged air:plane on the cover.

Rosa skidded to a halt. "Let me look at that," she said.

Caught a little off guard, David gave it to her. Air:planes had not existed on Co:pern:ica since the origins of global taxicars, but they were still talked about fondly in some quarters. David imagined therefore that Rosa was simply attracted to the beauty of the obsolete machines. But it was not the plane she was after at all. It was the author.

"Nyremann," she whispered, measuring the width of the spine. "I've got a space on my *N* shelf in Transport for this. Thanks, David. Bye." She even had the temerity to plant a light kiss on his cheek as she ran.

"Hey!" he called out. "You can't have that. It'll leave a gap in *my* collection. Rosa?!" And off he went, charging after her again.

And so began the fateful chase that led them to the window on Floor Thirty-One, where Rosa, by then out of breath and out of options, knew she could run no more.

"Hand it over," David said. He was nearly exhausted, too, but had saved enough energy to come striding, almost manfully, across the floor.

Rosa raised the book high. "Make you a deal."

"What deal?" he puffed.

Her mouth curled into a mischievous grin. "A race," she panted. "Whoever gets to it first gets to keep it. Agreed?"

David looked at the window and guessed her intent. "No," he said.

But her arm came down and she hurled the book out. Almost immediately, they both heard a dreadful *thump*.

"Uh, what was that?" Rosa said.

Both children thrust their heads out of the window. Far below, the book was lying among the daisies.

Poking out from underneath it was an emerald green wing.

11.

Runcey!" Rosa gasped.

"He's hurt," said David, turning away at once. "Fetch Mr. Henry. I'm going down to see."

Rosa just stood there, pale and mortified.

David stopped at the door to the room and looked back. "It was an accident," he said, softening her auma with a huge slab of kindness. For in a world where everyone could create what they needed, what else but an accident would cause any kind of harm? Even so, Runcey's situation looked desperate and there was no time to waste. "Find Mr. Henry," David repeated. And he dashed downstairs, asking the librarium to guide him to the ground floor by the quickest possible route.

It was warm outside, the clouds nearly absent, the daisy fields still. Barring one small area of soiled pages and displaced feathers, all was well. "Runcey," David whispered as he knelt. He lifted the book and put it aside. The firebird was flat on his back with his wings splayed out and his toes curled up. His delicate eyes were closed. His wonderful ear tufts were limp and askew.

In all his youthful time on Co:pern:ica, this was the closest David had come to actually handling a firebird. His mother had often desired to tame them, but he could not recall her, or anyone else for that matter, ever picking one up. But that was precisely what he did now. Sliding his hands underneath the bird's wings, taking care to center them under Runcey's shoulders where the bones, he thought, were probably strongest, he lifted him out of the daisies. Straightaway the left wing tried to flop back. It was weaker than the other one, presumably broken. There was a trickle of green fluid from the left ear as well. And patches of the breast were sore and grazed. To David's greater dismay, the tiny spray of feathers that normally sprouted up from the top of Runcey's head were all laid flat. He tilted his ear toward the bird's beak. Not a breath of air was traveling through the nostrils. Runcey's chances of survival seemed bleak.

Despair and anger raced through David's mind. If only he hadn't chased after Rosa. If only he'd let her have the book. If only Runcey hadn't flown by the window. If. If. If. The painful stabs of guilt went on. But as their composite effect turned into sorrow, it was his body, not his fain, that was first to respond. Heat prickled the corner of his eye. Astonishingly, a droplet of *water* bloomed out and settled precariously on his cheek. David felt the wetness forming but made no attempt to touch it or dry it. By then he was simply consumed with the need to do what he could to save Runcey's life. He squeezed his eyes shut and extended his fain, hoping to commingle with the creature's auma. The result was a little odd. Like anyone who had ever attempted this before, David couldn't link into the firebird's consciousness. What he did feel, though, was a tremendous warmth seeping into his hands. It spread swiftly up his arms and circled in the pectoral muscles of his chest, as if it were seeking out his thumping heart. The teardrop struggled to the edge of his chin. *Live* was the intent he put into his fain.

Live.

Suddenly, there was a *whoosh* of air above his head and a fearsome squawk announced the arrival of another firebird. David, his focus broken, jerked back. The new bird was twice the size of Runcey. It was a deep red color with a purple frill around its neck. There was savagery in its eyes and rage in its auma. All the warmth David had felt in his chest suddenly turned to a dreadful chill. He knew without having to commingle or speak that the creature judged him responsible for Runcey's fall. Without another sound, it swept forward and gripped Runcey in its claws and took off for the upper floors of the librarium, but not before it had made its mark on the boy. As it closed in, it opened its jaws and sent forth a jet of fire, so white-hot that it could only be described by the thermal patterns in the air around it. The fire should have struck David full in the chest. Instead, a blinding flash of light filled the space between them, as if something had jumped in and cushioned the flame. It only lasted a sec. Long enough for the firebird to leave with Runcey and David to fall back, barely conscious. By then, Rosa was close enough to catch him but not near enough to be dazzled by the light. Mr. Henry was right behind her.

"What's it done to him?" she cried, clamping David's forehead. The boy lay limply against her shoulder. "Why did it attack him? They just don't *do* that."

"Go inside, quickly," Mr. Henry said. Leaning forward, he picked up the boy. David was frothing lightly at the mouth. A large portion of his favorite maroon T-shirt was bleached and some of the threads were torn. Mr. Henry chewed his lip and looked up toward the clouds. Every window that was visible above Floor Thirty-Five was occupied by at least one firebird. They stared at Mr. Henry. Mr. Henry stared at them. When he went inside the building, they did, too.

Only one — a pretty, cream-colored creature with apricot tufts around its ears — dropped down and landed among the daisies. It was smaller than the bird that had come to claim Runcey and not nearly as frightful. It poddled around thoughtfully on its long, feathered legs, stopping now and then to drum its claws, as if it were assessing the situation. It looked upward at the window the book had come through, then at ground level and the damaged flowers. Suddenly, the lines of its eye sockets twitched. It tilted its head. It had spotted something. Lifting its long, spectacular tail feathers, it walked a few paces and peered at the ground. There among the squashed and bent-back flowers was a joined-up ring of violet-colored daisies. At its center was a tiny, glittering object. Extending one foot, the bird scooped the thing up as best it could (such a nuisance, not to have paws), then turned away from the librarium to observe the item in a better light. What it saw made all of its feathers stiffen. It had found David's teardrop, preserved and made whole by the energy condensed and captured inside it: the glowing white flame of a firebird.

12.

Mr. Henry carried David inside to a room that Rosa had never seen before. There were books in there, of course, but not nearly as many, and they were all surprisingly tidy. None lay on the floor or in piles, for instance. And although there were gaps to be filled on the shelves, there was a certain neatness about their arrangement, which suggested that someone (Mr. Henry, she supposed) had gathered them together with care, with love.

But for once, books didn't dominate the room. Over by the window, bathed in a slanting cone of light, was a proper single bed. Rosa hummed in envy when she saw it. She and David normally slept in hammocks or on the floor (or occasionally on a shelf if they were very tired). Mr. Henry laid David down on the mattress, supporting the boy's head with a shallow pillow.

To Rosa's surprise the curator imagineered a blanket, which he flowed across David's body. A glass of water appeared beside the boy as well. And a small lamp. Rosa gulped and put her hands behind her back. For Mr. Henry to be using his fain, the situation, she guessed, was serious.

"Is he going to die?" She was standing in the center of the room looking on. Her auma was overflowing with guilt.

The curator slid back one of David's eyelids. Despite the brilliance of the firebird's flame, the pupils were massively swollen. "His breathing is normal but his auma is in stasis. It's impossible to say if the effect is permanent. I will need to seek advice. I'm going to my office to make a v:com. I may have to leave the building for a time." He parted David's hair and stood up to leave. "Stay with him, child. You are excused from your duties in the librarium today."

Rosa looked at David's body and shivered. "But . . . what should I do?"

The curator paused and took something from his waistcoat pocket. Rosa's pupils almost grew to the size of David's. Mr. Henry owned a *watch*. A ticking thing, with (what were they called?), oh, yes, "hands." She'd never seen one before, not even imagineered, but knew what they were from books she'd come across on the subject. (Timepieces. What a quaint idea.) Mr. Henry looked at the watch, pouted his lips, and snapped it shut. "Read to him, Rosa. That's all you have to do."

"Even if he can't hear?"

"He can hear," said Mr. Henry. And in three quick strides he was out of the room.

So Rosa went to the shelves in search of something. Though what was suitable in these circumstances wasn't really clear. Instinct, as always, would have to be her guide. The librarium, she told herself, would not let her down.

The first titles she examined, however, were dull to the point of knuckle-gnawing blandness. Who else but Mr. Henry would keep a whole shelf of books... about books? Most were to do with the layout of librariums, though the buildings were referred to by another name: "libraries." Rosa could not understand this. The pictures of the "libraries" were much like her present surroundings (internally, at least), though the Bushley librarium, as far as she knew, did not possess movable shelves (called "trolleys") — an intriguing idea that she thought she would take up with Mr. Henry when the curator next invited them into his study.

Things did not improve on the next shelf along. Here she found a whole collection of books that appeared to be just about the use of words. "Dictionaries," they were called. They varied in thickness and density of writing, but all had one thing in common: The entries, in bold type, were in perfect alph order. She tingled with envy to see such a thing and felt inspired to rush back to her work right away. A slight groan from David's lips reminded her that her duty — this day — was to him.

She slid the dictionary back onto its shelf. Fascinating as David would undoubtably find it, it didn't lend itself to fluid reading. She glanced across the room. On the shelves opposite were several rows of books with jazzy spines. She yanked one out. It was about something called "pool."

Rosa drew her head back, as if she had just smelled something unsavory. She opened the book with one finger. The pages were old and brown and wavy. They made a slight crackling sound as they parted. The book fell open at a picture of a well-dressed man with neatly combed hair, bending across a high green table, pointing a long thin stick at a cluster of colored balls.

What on Co:pern:ica . . . ?

Another groan from David brought her to attention. Whatever this pool thing was, it was going to have to do. She plonked herself down on the bed beside the boy. His eyelids were flickering, but decidedly closed. Rosa gulped and reopened the book, somewhere in the middle, at a section called Tech:nique.

"The striking of the cue ball," she read aloud, *"is what determines good positional play. It is not just a question of studying angles. Knowing where to hit the white, and with what degree of pressure or follow-through, is what separates the professional player from the amateur."*

That was as far as her reading got. She was about to close the book and look for something a little less dreary, when she glanced down and noticed the daisy chain was missing from David's wrist. She gasped and jumped up. He must have lost it outside, during the attack. Anxious not to leave him, she headed for the window, hoping she could lean out and spot it. She was just a few paces from the light when there came a heavy fluttering of wings and the recess was occupied by the silhouette of a firebird.

"MR. HENRY!" Rosa screamed for the curator at the top of her voice. But the old man did not come running and the firebird by now had swooped inside to perch squarely on the headboard, right above David's pillow. It was the same red bird that had flamed the boy earlier. It stared down at him and twisted its prominent beak.

"Get away!" Rosa yelled, and hurled the pool book at it.

She missed — practically by the width of the bed — but the firebird had set its sights away from David anyway and was already flying toward the nearest shelf of books.

Unbalanced by her throw, Rosa lost sight of the creature for a moment. The clattering sound of books raining down upon the floor quickly identified its whereabouts. To her astonishment, the bird was going along the uppermost shelves, clawing the contents off them as if it intended to destroy the whole collection. It was certainly disrupting the order Mr. Henry had so fondly created. Rosa leaped to her feet and stormed across the floor, balling her fists, her shoelaces trailing.

"What are you *doing*?" she screamed. "What's *wrong* with you? Stop it! Stop it! You *horrible* thing. What have we done to deserve *this*?"

Then the most extraordinary thing happened. The firebird did stop throwing down the books and hovered by one in particular. A glowing white light emerged from its eyes and strobed the spine for a couple of moments. Then it stretched its hooked claws forward and appeared to *select* the book from the shelf. It flew back with it toward the bed and dropped it, with reasonable care, on David's chest. *Rrrh*, it went. Grumpy, but mildly apologetic. It tapped the book twice with its beak, then flew for the window and was gone.

Rosa stumbled across the floor. Her thoughts, like her hair, were in total disarray. She lifted the book off David's chest. On its cover was a picture of a flaming firebird, though it looked like no variant of one she'd ever seen. Fearsome. Wild-eyed. Terrifying. And *scaly*. Her auma struggled to cope with the image. She switched her gaze to the titling instead and read the three words across the top of the cover: *Creatures of*

Mythology. The one word across the bottom she spoke aloud. It was unfamiliar to her and the pronunciation, she would later come to learn, was incorrect: *"Drar . . . gones,"* she breathed.

    Dragons.

13.

Just seven days after her dramatic visit to the Merrimans' home, Aunt Gwyneth returned to take Eliza away. Seven days was the standard time allotted for couples to resolve their commingled auma in the knowledge of an enforced separation. Even so, when the moment came, Harlan struggled to physically let go of his wife and had to be admonished again by the Aunt. Such outrageous displays of emotion, she snapped, would see *him* condemned to a counselor as well. He would then be on file. And what would that do for his future with Eliza?

"How exasperating," Bernard Brotherton said, when Harlan told the tech:nician about it the next morning. "To be chosen as an Aunt is a great honor, but the timing is dreadful for both of you. How long will she be away?"

"Who can say?" said Harlan, looking distant, looking lost. Some aspirants were taken for three or four months; some for as long as Co:pern:ica took to complete a full spin. He sighed and smoothed his fingers around the contours of his face. "Any progress on Project Forty-Two?"

Bernard swung around and faced his com:puter. "Well, there the news will be more to your liking. It's been a challenge, but I have achieved a breakthrough. Those co:ordinates you gave me are like nothing I've ever seen before. I had to recalibrate SETH to accept them. You were right; they do describe a time horizon, but it's a far more complex event than the shimmer we saw on the film. Macro Forty-Two," he said to the machine.

The com:puter quickly uploaded a series of routines, then paused, awaiting further input. Bernard's fingers hovered over the neural control pad. "I ordered SETH to run a simulation of the rift that appeared during David's sleep, based on the data sets from Strømberg's recording. The results are quite impressive. I've slowed the sim down substantially to give you an impression of its physical composition." He tapped the pad. The com:puter screen quickly drew a vertical "rip," which appeared to be made up of a limitless number of helical strands, orbiting around a common core.

Harlan sat forward, his steepled fingers pressed up against his mouth. "Excellent," he muttered. "Did you do the 3-D?"

"*Mmm.*" Bernard's fingers flowed across the pad. The screen responded by turning the simulation on its end. At first the two scientists seemed to be looking at a solid hexagonal structure. But as Bernard zoomed in, the screen became filled with a series of fuzzy dots, indicating there were spaces between the individual strands.

Harlan put on a pair of spex. "What's the resolution of this?"

"Subatomic. Notice anything?"

Harlan studied the image and shrugged. "The strands are shimmering, but there's bound to be a high degree of electro:magnetic force between them."

"Oh, it's far better than that," said Bernard. "Watch what happens if I apply a single color to a small group of strands." His hands moved over the pad again. He paused the simulation and pointed to a region of red dots at the top left of the structure. "This is a still, of course.

But look at the red in active mode." He ran the program again. Instead of staying where they were, the red dots began to flash in different areas of the rift.

Harlan Merriman breathed in sharply.

"Thought that would excite you," Bernard said. "The sim always maintains its structure. But when you run a fine trace on the strand trajectories you discover that individual strands are popping in and out at light speed — but they never come back in the same locations. They're moving, Prof. Swapping places. What you're looking at there is not one rip —"

"But an infinite number of possible rips," Harlan said quietly.

Bernard nodded. "I've revised my previous opinion, by the way. Even if David is ec:centric, I don't believe that anyone on Co:pern:ica could imagineer something of this complexity."

"Then what does that say about the firebirds? How could they *possibly* be involved in this?"

Bernard parted his hands. "How are they able to pass through our constructs? How did they evolve on Co:pern:ica in the first place? Where do the feathery little critters go at night? I don't know. Let's stick with the phys:ics for now. Do you want to see the really spooky bit?" Harlan switched his gaze sideways. The tech:nician was chewing his lip. "Here's a full-color sim from the normal view." Without waiting for permission, Bernard uploaded another series of routines. Immediately, the rift was fizzing with energy, almost sparkling around its perimeter and tips. Every third sec or so, as if a small current had been passed along its length, a changing gradient of color rolled from top to bottom, then bounced back again.

"It's beautiful," Harlan said. "Can we go into it?"

Bernard nodded again. "It's fractal, but it doesn't obey any of the known systems or processes. Watch what happens if I push into the core." Using the pad, he sent a small cursor into the pattern. The rift responded as if it had been punched. There was a blooming of color in all directions. And yet, wherever the cursor moved, there remained an image of the rift.

Harlan Merriman opened his mouth and out came one small word. "Wow."

"It self-replicates," Bernard said. "In any number of simultaneous dimensions."

"And the spooky bit?"

Bernard swallowed hard. "Although the spatial possibilities are infinite, the time point, wherever you set the cursor, is fixed. In other words, what turned up in David's dream was not a little ripple in the envelope of space. More like . . ."

"A portal," Harlan said, pushing back his chair. "So if you or I — or David — had stepped into that rift, we would not have traveled through time, we'd have passed into a different dimension, but in the same time frame as the one we'd left behind."

"That's how I read it," Bernard said, a little shakily. "But the portal, by its nature, must operate both ways. So given David's reaction in the film, one can only conclude that whatever created that rift was looking for him — not the other way around. It sounds ridiculous, but based on the evidence we have, it would appear that something was trying to contact your son. Something from another *world*."

14.

The taxicar that came to take Eliza Merriman and Aunt Gwyneth away was like none that Eliza had ever seen before. It was roughly the same size and elliptical shape as the standard carriages, but its outer skin was grimy and badly dented (in several places), as if it had been involved in a number of collisions. Aunt Gwyneth assured her new charge there was no need for concern, but did add that the journey might be a little "bumpy."

Where exactly are we going? Eliza commingled.

Back to the beginning, the Aunt replied cryptically. *Back to the beginning.*

Bumpy the journey certainly was. Chilly. Tedious. Miserably long. The cabin light flickered all the way. The seal nearest to Eliza's head whistled as though it would split at any moment and suck her into some awful void. The chair she was riding on wobbled persistently. Every now and then the whole taxicar would drop through the sky so fast that the organs of the body felt as if they'd been pinned to the roof.

Aunt Gwyneth *slept* through it all.

Finally, the thing did come to a halt. Even then, the doors refused to open. A well-aimed kick from Aunt Gwyneth's sturdy heels soon remedied that. A slab of air came in as the Aunt stepped out. Dampness. Coarse soil. Ferocity in the wind. All of these conditions registered with Eliza before she had put a foot outside. But nothing could prepare her for the wilderness she was about to encounter. Aunt Gwyneth snapped her fingers and the taxicar zipped away. It was a dot on the horizon before Eliza could measure the extent of the isolation the two women now found themselves in. All around them was nothing but barren land. Grassed and dark green, going to black. In the sky were thunderclouds and every threat of cold. Hope perished in Eliza's heart.

"Where are we?" She shuddered.

"You *know* where we are."

The Dead Lands. Eliza shook her head in confusion. "Why have you brought me here?"

"To learn, my dear."

Eliza clamped her arms and looked all around her. *What could anyone learn in a place like this?* She shivered and tried to imagineer a sweater. There was no response.

"Once, there was a civilization in these lands. Buildings. Rivers. Trees. . . . Creatures. All dead, because of what we became."

Eliza wasn't listening. "What's wrong with my fain?" Her failure to produce a sweater had now been compounded by her failure to imagineer a pair of gloves. She cupped her hands and tried to construct a button: the first thing any child on Co:pern:ica was taught. Even this most simple of acts was beyond her.

The Aunt turned and gripped her powerfully by the wrists. "Your fain is useless here. What would you do if I told you that you could never imagineer again? That you were here to plant a seed? To give something back?"

The wind blew through Eliza's hair, holding up its strands like precious red jewels. "Take me home," she said, shaken by the look in the old woman's eyes. Some kind of madness had enveloped the Aunt, underpinned by a look of angry desolation.

"This *is* your home," Aunt Gwyneth sneered. "It's where you came from. It's where the very soul of this world resides. Here. Still clinging to this dying earth." She dug in a heel and twisted it hard, churning up a divot of squelching mud. "*This* is what you will learn, Eliza Merriman. This is what you will take back to your pod and your precious gardenaria. When you appreciate the truth about this land, I will grant you a daughter."

"You're making me uncomfortable," Eliza said. The Aunt's grip was actually causing her pain.

The old woman relented and let her go. "Do you know how old I am?"

"No. Does it matter?"

Aunt Gwyneth gave a quiet snort. "I have seen things you would not believe."

"Yes, I imagine you have," said Eliza. "And I'm sorry that my ignorance of the Dead Lands offends you. But I'm willing to accept whatever knowledge you can offer me. Especially if it means I can make Harlan happy. A daughter is something he's always wanted.

What is it that you want me to do?" She folded her arms and waited.

Aunt Gwyneth circled her slowly. "Tell me about your parents."

"My —?" Eliza was suddenly thrown by this. "I . . . why?"

"It's not for you to question. Answer me, girl."

"I can't. I . . . I don't remember my parents."

"You do," Aunt Gwyneth said from behind her.

Eliza turned her face to the sky. The clouds, she thought, were moving toward her, as if they were eager to hear her story. "I don't. I have no memories of childhood. I'm an abandoned construct. I remember nothing before my twenty-eighth spin. When I met Harlan, I was an empty shell. He took me in, loved me, married me without question. I have no idea who imagineered me, or why so old, or why they orphaned me. Why are you making me say what I'm sure you already know? Why are you making me . . ."

"Suffer?" said the Aunt.

Eliza looked away.

"You need to reach inside yourself. To do that, you must *feel*."

"Feel?" Eliza's pretty face screwed into a ball. "You

100

know very well that the Higher put an end to all that . . ."

" 'Soul-searching'?" The Aunt examined her fingernails, as if they were suddenly the answer to everything. "That was what people called it in the past. The inner search for meaning. But you know this, don't you, Eliza? I can read it in your auma. You've tried it, haven't you? You question your parentage constantly, tormenting yourself because you cannot resolve it. But you don't have the courage to examine the doubts. Question the doubts, child. Only then will you be able to deal with the truth."

"What are you doing?" Eliza said. The Aunt had spread her fingers and was pointing them, rootlike, at the ground. Wisps were beginning to rise around her feet, emerging from the soil like coils of smoke. Eliza gasped as two of them twined together and formed themselves into the shape of an animal. Long, floppy ears and a rounded body. Roughly the size of Boon, but not a katt. Her eyes darted to another wisp. A tiny buzzing creature was flying around an even wispier flower. And then . . .

The next apparition stopped her breathing. She knew what it was. She even had a name for it. The word was in her head as if it had been there all her life, simply stored away for safekeeping. She stepped forward for a closer look, but the ghostly contours shook its wedge of tail feathers and waddled off before dispersing. "Duck." It was a *duck*. The very creature she'd fantasized about but never seen on the river. She sank to her knees, feeling the softness of the earth where it supported her. Slowly, she put her hands into the mist, trying to gather the threads of it in. But it was the mist that soon had control of her. It wrapped itself around her arms and tried to pull her down. The force of it made her cry out. But with one snap of Aunt Gwyneth's fingers the mist retracted into the soil. Eliza looked up to see the Aunt looking down. In what appeared to be an act of genuine kindness, the woman laid a hand on Eliza's forehead and moved a lock of red hair out of her eyes.

"You did have a childhood," she said.

Eliza by now was shaking uncontrollably. "How? How do you know this?"

Aunt Gwyneth hunkered down. Her eyes were a stunning violet color. "I know, because you spent it with me."

15.

Teeth gritted, Eliza struggled to her feet. "No," she said, crossing her hands several times. "Why are you mocking me like this? If I'd met you before, I would have recognized you. And this mist. These forms. Are they some kind of . . . advanced imagineering? Some trickery to measure my worthiness for motherhood? If I'm flawed beyond redemption, please just tell me."

Aunt Gwyneth straightened her skirt as she rose. "In the days before we had fain," she said, bringing her wrinkled fingertips together, "people would have used the word 'magick' to describe what you just saw. Are you familiar with this term?"

"No," Eliza said abruptly.

The Aunt gave a supercilious sniff. "'Magick' was an art form used by charlatans skilled in deception to make the impossible appear to be plausible. It was considered 'entertaining' by some. Nowadays, we have no need for such amateurism. We simply materialize whatever we require. But, oh, the price we have paid for it."

Eliza's head swept back and forth. "I don't understand what you're talking about."

"You recognized a rabbit, a bumblebee, and a duck. Tell me if these names mean anything to you?"

Eliza sighed and covered her eyes. The smell of damp earth was on her hands. "Duck," she muttered. "I've found myself trying to picture them."

Aunt Gwyneth nodded. "Good. In time, you will recognize more. These creatures were not my constructs, Eliza. They were *your* memories, given limited reality by your residual association with this place."

"Aunt, I've never *been* here before! And this 'place' just tried to kill me!"

"No, girl. It was trying to reclaim you."

"Oh!" Eliza threw up her hands. Her eyes were almost as dark as the clouds. She turned and stared intently at the horizon. "Are you saying I spent a childhood *here*?"

"Yes."

"Then why don't I remember it?"

"Because you were not meant to. It was erased just days before your fifth spin. You were then re-formed by the Higher to become the woman that Harlan Merriman would marry."

"Are you implying that Harlan and I were deliberately brought together by the Higher?"

"That is immaterial."

"Not to me." There was an uneasy pause. When it became clear that the Aunt would not be drawn further on this matter, Eliza said, "Very well. I was re-formed. For what reason? Was I ec:centric, like David?"

Again, Aunt Gwyneth chose to hold her tongue.

"Tell me," Eliza insisted, having the courage to shake the old woman. "Did I do something wrong? Did I threaten the Design?"

"*Yes.*" Aunt Gwyneth's voice was brittle. "Yes, but through no fault of your own. You were given up to the Higher when it became clear that you'd inherited . . . your father's anomaly."

Eliza reared back. "This is not from one of your reports, is it? You *knew* him, didn't you? You *knew* my father." Her gaze narrowed. The Aunt's face was as rigid as stone.

"He was an out:kast," she said eventually. "The very worst kind of ec:centric."

"Why don't I know him?" Eliza pressed. "What became of him? Is he still alive?" She thought of David, in the librarium. In her father's time (and just how old would her father have been?) the counselors and Aunts might not have been so generous as to send a potentially dangerous individual to a place of relative safety.

But just as Aunt Gwyneth was about to give an answer she flicked her head to one side and said, "I am being summoned." Her sober expression faded to a glint of amused curiosity. "Well, well. How interesting."

Eliza could hear nothing of the Aunt's communication, and with her fain disabled could detect no thoughts in the ether either. "We're leaving?" she said, looking for a taxicar. None was coming.

"*I* am leaving," Aunt Gwyneth said, brushing down the sleeves of her jacket. "It seems I'm required — by Thorren Strømberg."

"Strømberg?" Eliza stepped forward again. "Is it to do with David? Is there something wrong?"

Aunt Gwyneth pulled on a pair of white gloves. There appeared to be elec:trodes running down the finger seams. On the palms was a strange-looking mark, made up of three ragged but unconnected lines. "What you will discover here will shape your future. Go carefully, Eliza. It may be some time before I return."

"Wait. You can't abandon me! Where will I sleep? What will I eat? You haven't explained about my father. And what about my training? And the daughter you promised?"

"An Aunt," the agent of the Higher cut in, "must learn to cope with any adversity. Your training starts here. Alone, in the Dead Lands." And right before Eliza's eyes, Aunt Gwyneth spread her arms and the mist rose up once more and surrounded her. Blue flashes lit up her gloves and she was drawn away swiftly, as if she were nothing but a feather on the wind.

For twenty paces, Eliza gave chase. Failing breath and the loss of a shoe finally brought her stomping to a halt. She hung her head as the solitude closed in, then limped back and retrieved the shoe. It was soaked and reeked of something . . . unwholesome. With a hostility she barely knew she possessed she set herself to hurl it far away and go barefoot across the grass. (Where to though? *Where?*) But before the rage had her in its sway, something else had conquered her auma. She paused and looked at the dirt on the shoe. Smoky wisps were rising out of it again. With her free hand, she scraped some mud off the sole and rolled it through the ends of her fingers. Strangely, it did not smear. And the more she rolled, the more permanent and workable the stuff became, until she had a ball of it on her palm. It sat there, gray and shiny and smooth. It was then she recalled a name for it.

"Clay."

16.

Voices. Mr. Henry and someone new. Rosa pushed the dragon book under her arm, blew a kiss to David, and hurried from the room. She paused inside the doorway of the next room along and hid herself there, to listen.

"Good grief," she heard Mr. Henry splutter. He had stumbled against the mess of books. And though the cause of it was no real fault of hers, Rosa felt a mild rush of guilt nevertheless.

"This is unusual?" the visitor asked. There was a jocular note in his smooth, deep voice. A kind voice. Maybe with a tribal twang. Rosa liked it, and thought she might like the man, too, but she wasn't going to show her face just yet.

"This is one of *my* rooms," Mr. Henry muttered, his manner implying that *they* were always tidy. "I don't quite understand what's happened. I left Rosa here, looking after David. I asked her to read to him, not trash the place."

Now Rosa couldn't resist a look. Poking her face around the edge of the door frame, she caught sight of the visitor. A tall man with stunning fair hair. He was looking at the upper shelves. "Do you have a ladder to reach those?"

Mr. Henry nodded. "Yes, but it's hidden." To Rosa's astonishment, he struck a small square on a tall dividing panel between the shelves and it turned on itself to reveal a ladder.

"Perhaps she found it?" the stranger suggested.

Mr. Henry shook his head. "She's been here for nine spins and has never worked it out."

"Then maybe she had help?"

Rosa craned her neck a little farther around the door. She gulped when she saw that the visitor had crouched down and picked up a bright red firebird feather. He twiddled it in his fingers. "Is this from the one that attacked David?"

Mr. Henry looked on, concerned. "Yes, it could be. I'd better go and search for her, Thorren. If it was here, she's probably run from it, fearing it would injure her."

"No, wait." The visitor pressed his hand to the floor, almost making the wooden boards creak. "If she was hurt, the building would surely know it. I can't detect anything."

"Could they have taken her, then? The birds?"

Thorren drummed his fingers on the boards. "No, the girl left of her own accord. I think she's gone in search of something."

Rosa gulped again as she saw Mr. Henry stoop down and run his gaze across the fallen books. How long would it be, she wondered, before he discovered the one that was missing? She withdrew the dragon book and glanced at its cover. Did she really want to read a book so . . . sinister? Wouldn't it be easier to give herself up? Tell them what had happened? Let Mr. Henry and this visitor take charge? She balled a fist. No. She must be brave. This was between her and David and the firebirds. Whatever mysteries this book contained were going to be theirs to unravel.

Hearing footsteps again, she prepared to run. But the sound was falling away and she realized that the visitor had simply crossed the floor to go to look at David.

"I've summoned an Aunt," he said.

Mr. Henry took a sharp breath.

"I know you don't like them, Charles —"

"They have a blatant disregard for my work," the curator grumbled.

"— but I'm required by law to bring one in. He may have injuries we can't detect. If so, only an Aunt can aid him. Have you noticed any recurrence of his dreams?"

Dreams? Rosa clutched the dragon book to her.

"He's been calm," said Mr. Henry. "An absolute model of efficiency and goodness. He's adapted to the building as if he were born here."

"And his fain?"

"Haven't seen him use it. He's competitive with the girl, but never reaches for his fain to better himself. He and the girl are very close, by the way."

Rosa heard the other man suppress a quiet chuckle. "And how far has he got — with the books?"

Mr. Henry drew another breath, but this one was longer and more considered. "He's reached Forty-Two.

But they all do that. You really think he can break through to the upper floors?"

Thorren Strømberg took a moment to reply. "There's something odd about this boy that I've not come across in other ec:centrics—his ongoing relationship with the firebirds, for one thing. And the range and power of his fain are extraordinary. Then there's the time rift, of course."

Time rift? Rosa mouthed.

"Any progress with that?" Mr. Henry asked.

Once again Strømberg paused before replying. "His father fed the co:ordinates I gave him into a specialized com:puter program. It predicted a multidimensional portal."

"What kind of portal? Where to?" said Mr. Henry. (Rosa by now was biting down on her knuckles to keep herself quiet.)

"Anywhere, Charles. That's the point. Think of a revolving door that can turn faster than the speed of light and deliver you into an infinite number of places. That's what appeared during David's dream and that's what the firebirds came to shut down. What the data doesn't definitively show is whether David created the rift himself or whether it came via some external source. But in answer to your previous question: Yes, I'm confident that David possesses the ability to find a way into the upper floors, but we may yet solve the mystery ourselves if he doesn't."

By now, Rosa's heart was thumping so loudly that she had begun to back away from the door, lest either man should hear the pounding. But she did not want to leave until she'd heard Thorren Strømberg complete his statement. Mr. Henry was the first to speak.

The curator said, "Surely you're not thinking about *using* the portal?"

"It's a gem too sweet to resist," Thorren answered. "The boy's father believes he can replicate it — in his laboratory, under controlled conditions."

"And you think it might take you to the roof of the librarium?"

"Well beyond that, Charles."

"But the danger must be immense? Who would dare to go through a thing like that?"

"That has yet to be decided," Strømberg said.

But in Rosa's mind, he was shading the truth. He'd send David through the portal. She was sure of it. David would be made to face the danger. At that point, she picked up her skirt tails and ran. She said, with profound intent to the librarium, *Take me to where I can't be found, so I can read this book quickly from cover to cover.* She was sure that the dragon book would tell her something — why else would the firebird have singled it out?

Through room after room after room she flashed, her mind buzzing repeatedly with everything she'd heard. Dreams. Portals. Upper floors. David. Dreams. Portals. Upper floors —

"Ow!"

With a thump, she came to a sudden halt and staggered back, rubbing the tip of her nose. Her toes hurt, too. And one knee. She couldn't believe it. She had run into something! A mistake she hadn't made since her very first day in the librarium. But when she looked up to see what the obstacle was, she realized it wasn't a mistake at all. She was at the end of a darkened corridor. In front of her was a closed wooden door.

It looked old and quite impenetrable. (How on Co:pern:ica had she not found *this* before?) And although it wasn't labeled, Rosa knew in her heart that this was the entrance to Floor Forty-Three. She squeezed her hand around the hexagonal doorknob. It was made of burnished metal and coated with dust. She took a deep breath and gave the knob a twist. It responded with a weary degree of resistance, but only went a quarter turn then stopped. Breath held, she pushed her weight forward. The door did not open.

"Please," she said, pressing her shoulder against it. *Thump. Thump.* Still it would not budge. Reaching up, she banged it with the palm of her hand. "Please," she begged it, "you've got to let me in."

And as she spoke those words, a powerful hand came to cover hers. Rosa screamed and jumped around. A dark silhouette stood in front of her. Not Mr. Henry. Nor the visitor, Strømberg. A woman, fierce and frightful.

An Aunt.

17.

"Well, well. What have we here?" the woman said.

"Who are you? What do you want?" Rosa snapped. She pulled the dragon book flat to her body and folded both her arms across it.

"Impertinent whelp. I could have you de:constructed for an outburst like that."

Rosa smirked and tried to push past her, saying, "Like to see you try."

The Aunt stopped her and threw her back against the door with a force that belied her wiry frame. Without a hint of warning she reached out and pinched Rosa's earlobe, forcing a fingernail into the flesh.

"*Agh!*" the girl cried, and slewed away in pain.

"So, you're human," drawled the Aunt, rubbing blood off her fingertips.

"What's it to *you?*"

"I am an AUNT!" the woman roared. "And you will obey me or face the consequences. I could order your re:moval from this cozy existence in the time it would take to wipe my fingers clean." She grabbed Rosa's chin and turned the girl to face her. The black centers of her eyes drilled into Rosa's soul. "You are that most pathetic of objects: a natural-born child with limited fain." Rosa gasped as she felt the Aunt's thoughtwaves probing her. "You are the progeny of misguided parents who wanted to believe that it was right to take a retrograde step from the Grand Design. Let me guess . . . they abandoned you here when they realized it was too much for them to bear, seeing their cute little human *project* unable to cope with children far more talented. And when you wanted what you could not imagineer you became temperamental — and a burden to them." She squeezed Rosa's cheeks, making the child wince. "And this," she continued, pressing her thumb against the tear rolling down Rosa's face, "would have been the pinnacle of their embarrassment." She leaned forward until their noses were almost touching. "Believe me, child, re:gressives like you are not wanted outside institutions like this. So if you wish to stay here, you will do my bidding. My name is Aunt Gwyneth. Now, show me the respect I deserve."

With that, she let Rosa go.

The girl sniffed and wiped her nose on her sleeve. "I'm sorry."

"I'm sorry, *what?*"

"I'm sorry, Aunt Gwyneth." And Rosa bowed politely as she was expected to do.

The Aunt cast her gaze down. "What is that you're hiding?"

"Just a book."

"Let me see it." Aunt Gwyneth snatched it up. Immediately, her breath was like shattered glass. "Where did you get this?"

Rosa spread her arms. "Here," she said, sounding credibly innocent. "I found it downstairs." She didn't want to tell the story behind it, and withholding the truth from an Aunt was dangerous, but the way the old woman had reacted to the cover had ignited a deep curiosity in Rosa and a strange desire to protect the book. So she took a chance and asked, "What is a drargone, Aunt?"

"Dragon," said Aunt Gwyneth, paging slowly. "The correct pronunciation is dragon."

Rosa nodded, taking this in. "Why do they look like fi —"

"They are a myth," said the Aunt, snapping the book shut. "They do not exist. They are a wicked invention, and even you, a wretched excuse for a girl, will not sully her auma with such perversity."

"No, Aunt. Sorry." A wicked invention? Limited though it might be, Rosa's fain flared. "Have you come to see David?"

"Yes. What is beyond this door?" The old woman's cruel eyes were scanning the obstruction.

Rosa did her best to shrug the question off. "I'll take you to him. I know the quickest routes."

"Stay where you are. I know how to find the boy."

"Then, erm, what are you doing on this floor, with me?"

"I detected a powerful auma surge and the building drew me here."

"Thanks," Rosa said beneath her breath to the walls.

With an ill-mannered tug, the Aunt bundled her out of the way. She, too, tried the handle. Once again the door failed to open. "Where is the key to this?"

"I don't know," Rosa said. "There isn't a lock."

"There is always a lock," Aunt Gwyneth rumbled, implying that there must be a key as well. "I ask you again, what is beyond this door?"

Rosa sighed and tossed her hair. "The upper floors — where the firebirds nest."

This made the Aunt suck in a breath as if someone had pulled a string to her lungs. "What were you doing here?"

"Trying to get in," Rosa said truthfully — then compounded it with a lie. "I come here every day, but the door is never open." She chewed her lip and glanced at the dragon book. "Shall I put that back where it belongs?" She held out a hopeful hand.

Aunt Gwyneth filled it with shattered dreams. "You are never to touch this book again. Now, walk in front of me, where I can *watch* you. It's time to go to David."

Not surprisingly, it took a lot less time for Aunt Gwyneth to find David than it had for Rosa to find the locked door. Mr. Henry and Thorren Strømberg both bowed to the Aunt as she glided in.

A rough hand between the shoulder blades propelled Rosa forward, almost making her trip on the books still strewn across the floor. "I found this, loitering upstairs."

Rosa thought she saw the blond-haired visitor smile.

"She was in pursuit of *dragons*."

The old woman held the book out for Mr. Henry, but it was Thorren Strømberg who took it from her. He touched his fingers to the cover and said, "And did you find them, Rosa?"

Rosa saw the Aunt bristle. "No, sir," she said.

The blond man nodded. He handed the book sideways to Mr. Henry (who seemed to examine it for damage, Rosa thought). "Strange creatures, don't you think?"

"Enough," the Aunt said. "You would do well to remember, Counselor Strømberg, that to encourage disruptive thinking is a crime against the Grand Design. A dangerous practice, in my presence."

Once again, Strømberg bowed to her. "Far be it from me to challenge your authority. By asking such a question I seek not to encourage but merely to search for possible flaws."

"I'm not *flawed*," Rosa piped up. "I just like books."

"Be quiet," snapped the Aunt. She moved toward David and looked down at his face. He was still lost in (peaceful) sleep. "Books," she muttered, as if she'd just cut her finger on the edge of a page. She cast her imperious gaze around the shelves. "I have long believed this building could be used for something far more meaningful than harboring *antiquities*."

Rosa saw Mr. Henry grinding his teeth. His face was trembling with anger. She had never seen rage in the old man before and it frightened (and slightly excited) her. Thorren Strømberg came to the curator's aid. Putting out a comforting hand he said, "One mustn't forget, Aunt Gwyneth, that the librarium is a recognized firebird aerie and therefore protected by the Grand Design."

"Aerie." Another new word. Rosa looked at the Aunt and saw her spine stiffen. It was clear that the old bag hated the firebirds just as much as she did the books. She was learning a lot today.

"So this is David Merriman," Aunt Gwyneth said.

Rosa raised her eyebrows. "Merriman?" she hooted. What kind of a name was that?

"Get *rid* of that irritating child," said the Aunt, batting a stiff hand back through the air.

"No way," Rosa hissed. "I'm not leaving David."

Aunt Gwyneth whipped around. "I will cut you into slices and press you between the pages of your books if you do not get out of this room, girl."

"Perhaps," Thorren Strømberg interceded, "it would be better if Rosa stayed. She was nearest to David when the firebird attacked. She might have information that will help your diagnosis."

Aunt Gwyneth's nostrils flared.

Strømberg took this as a positive sign. "Rosa, you will be quiet until one of us asks you to speak. Or you will be sent out. Is that understood?"

"Yes, sir," she muttered.

The counselor gave her the faintest of nods, then turned back to the Aunt. "Yes, this is David. I called for you because I know you've had contact with his parents. It seemed sensible to keep some kind of continuity."

"A wise choice in any circumstance," Aunt Gwyneth said, with such an air of superiority that Rosa wanted to gag. "Now, what happened to the boy?"

"He was flamed by a firebird, yet appears to have suffered no external injuries. A strange flash was observed at the point of the attack. Mr. Henry believes that something either deflected or absorbed the bird's fire. Whatever the cause, we fear it may have left the boy blind."

Aunt Gwyneth took this in and studied the patient carefully. She reached inside the jacket of her suit and drew out a small instrument. It looked to Rosa like that odd thing, a *pen*. (Mr. Henry kept a few in a display case in his study.) Certainly, when the Aunt touched her thumb to one end, something sharp like a nib extruded from the other. Leaning forward, Rosa saw it was a tip of green light. It began to buzz at increasingly higher frequencies as Aunt Gwyneth brought it closer to David's head. She inserted it into his ear. Right away, his physical features disappeared and all that could be seen was a halo of light in the shape of a boy.

Is that...? Rosa mouthed, and was fortunately seen by Strømberg, who said, "This is a sight that never ceases to amaze me. Auma, in its purest state."

"Be silent," said Aunt Gwyneth. "Let me do my work." And to Rosa's horror, the old woman plunged her hands into David's auma, sweeping it around as if she were searching for a prize in a game of lucky dip.

Although she knew nothing of this diagnostic process (a high form of commingling, she would later come to learn) Rosa was relieved to see great waves of violet sweeping David's auma wherever the Aunt's black-and-white, bony hands traveled. Violet, children of Co:pern:ica were taught, was the color of truth. Only one area of David's body did not resolve itself in that shade, and that was the deep, deep blue of his heart. Aunt Gwyneth hovered there for the longest time, her fingers moving like strips of paper in the blades of a fan. When she finally withdrew, Rosa kept her worried gaze fixed on the heart. She watched it pulsing right up to the point in which the Aunt removed the probe from David's ear and his body reappeared on the bed as before.

"He is physically perfect," the Aunt reported. "As good as the day he was constructed. He isn't blind — but he *is* seeing things."

"Dreaming?" Strømberg asked.

"Deeply."

"Is he calm?"

The Aunt nodded. "He is in a recurring alpha wave."

A twitch of relief pulled at Strømberg's mouth. "Do you know when he might wake?"

Aunt Gwyneth shook her head. "He is in an unusual form of stasis, brought on by a strong melancholia."

"What does that mean?" Rosa couldn't help herself. Bravely, she stepped forward and picked up David's hand.

"It means he's sad," said Mr. Henry, stepping forward, too. He moved his jaw from side to side, the way he sometimes did when he was musing in his study. "He was trying to save a firebird when he was attacked. It fell a great distance. It was probably dead. He would have been moved by that."

"His fain is not resolving it," Aunt Gwyneth said.

"So mend him," said Rosa.

"I just tried," said the Aunt, with steel in her voice. Her eyes scanned David's body again. "The boy is ec:centric and emotionally flawed. He is beyond the help of an Aunt. His situation must be reported to the Higher."

"And your recommendation would be?" said Strømberg.

Aunt Gwyneth raised her chin. "De:construction," she said.

18.

N O!" screamed Rosa, looking at the faces of all three adults. "You can't do that. I won't let you hurt him."

"Get this child out of my *sight*," said Aunt Gwyneth, with such a degree of vehemence that a shower of spittle sprayed across Rosa's dress.

"Rosa, come with me." Mr. Henry gripped her arm.

"No!" she cried again, freeing herself. "How can you stand there and let her say this?"

"Rosanna, go to a rest room. Now."

The girl planted her feet. "I'm *not leaving David*."

Then thunder rose in Mr. Henry's chest and blood boiled in the veins of his face. "GO!" he bellowed, clenching his fists — not to strike her, Rosa was sure about that, but simply to try to get a grasp on his emotions. She'd never seen him so expressly disturbed. (And he'd never used her name in full before.) Nevertheless, she stared at him in utter betrayal. He calmed himself and spoke in a gentler tone, as if asking her to pardon this dreadful outburst. But by then the hurt could be seen in her eyes. She shook her hair wildly and ran from the room.

Charles Henry dragged a handkerchief out of his pocket and wiped it across his gibbering mouth. "Whatever's to be done, do it quickly," he said. "I want no part of it."

"Nothing is to be done," said Strømberg.

Aunt Gwyneth turned on him at once. "You would defy my ruling?"

Strømberg picked up a book and put it back onto a shelf (in no particular place). "No, Aunt. I support your ruling; this incident must be reported to the Higher. But as David's approved counselor I will be expected to submit an assessment of his case, and my recommendation would be that he is kept in the librarium and watched."

Aunt Gwyneth snorted her displeasure. "For what reason?"

"Until this day, no one in the history of Co:pern:ica

has ever been rendered melancholic by a firebird. I find that intriguing. I believe the Higher will, too. They will want me to study the boy."

"Poppycock," the old woman sneered. (Mr. Henry raised an eyebrow at the use of this word and found his glance drawn toward his dictionary shelf.)

Unfazed, Strømberg put his hands into his pockets and idly continued to stare at the books. "Then, of course, there is your professional reputation to consider."

"What?" said the Aunt. A tiny sprig of hair jumped out of her bun.

"I understand from Harlan Merriman that you've accepted the boy's mother for training?"

"What has that got to do with it?"

Strømberg turned to face her. "Would it not be considered odd — anomalous, even — that an aspirant, chosen by you, had recently had a child de:constructed? Hardly the ideal qualification for Aunthood."

Aunt Gwyneth took a step forward. She seemed to grow in height as she sought to meet Thorren Strømberg's eye. "You are treading a dangerous line, Counselor. Do not think to interfere with my business."

"It's my business to advise people," Strømberg said frankly. "In my opinion, the facts are very plain. It's up to you what you do with them, *Aunt*."

Her gaze slanted sideways to David. "The boy might never wake up."

"Then what threat can he be?"

Aunt Gwyneth breathed in deeply. "Very well," she said, waving a hand. "You may keep your 'therapy' intact. But I will be back to see this boy again. If his melancholia worsens or his terrors return, that will be an end to it." And with one more skewed look at David Merriman, she strode out of the room, kicking a book across the floor as she departed.

Mr. Henry sighed with relief. "Thank you," he whispered, patting Strømberg's arm.

"We must go carefully now," Thorren Strømberg told him. "That encounter will have prickled her spine. I may not always find a winning argument against her."

"What do you want me to do?"

"Exactly what I told her. You must monitor the boy."

"Do you think he will recover?"

Strømberg considered the question carefully. "I hope so. I think he's got a lot more to show us."

"His parents, will they be informed of his condition?"

"The mother may learn through the Aunt, but I'd rather keep it from his father, for now. Telling him gains us nothing. He's already accepted that the boy is out of bounds while in our care. I don't want him losing focus, not with his research at such a critical stage."

Mr. Henry nodded. "What about this?" He held up the dragon book.

"I'll take that. I need to talk to Rosa. Where will I find her?"

Charles Henry pointed to the nearest window. "Outside, in her favorite place — the fields."

Rosa was sitting cross-legged among the daisies, with her back to the librarium, her hair dancing in the breeze. She did not take her gaze away from the horizon when Thorren Strømberg came and crouched beside her. Speaking quietly he said, "I'm sorry you had to go through that. Aunt Gwyneth has gone. David is staying in the librarium."

The girl swallowed hard and closed her eyes. When

she opened them again, the lashes were wet. She noticed Strømberg looking and said, "I suppose you think I'm a freak as well, don't you?"

Strømberg shook his head. "Very few of my ideas coincide with Aunt Gwyneth's."

Rosa's face grew dark with loathing. "I hate that woman — if she is a woman."

"Oh, yes, she's human," the counselor said. "She would have had emotions once, but her fain overpowered them long ago. She's not all bad, Rosa. She's in the business of producing perfect offspring for perfect parents in a perfect world. You're always going to be an irritation to her kind."

The girl picked a daisy and twiddled it in her fingers. "Will David be OK?" *How could any world be perfect without him?*

"I'm not sure," Strømberg answered truthfully. "If he stays melancholic, he *will* fade away." He saw her shoulders drop and he pressed on quickly. "What happened, Rosa — in the room, before you ran? How did you come to have this?"

She looked at the dragon book in his hands. "The red firebird came. It picked it off a shelf and dropped it on David."

133

"To hurt him?"

Lips tight, she shook her head. "It looked sort of . . . sorry for what it had done."

"So the book was a gift?"

"I don't know," she said.

Strømberg thought about this for a moment. He ran his hand across the tops of the daisies, enjoying the sensation of their petals on his skin.

"Do you know how to get into the upper floors?" Rosa asked.

"No," said Strømberg. "You've found the door, haven't you — to Floor Forty-Three?"

Rosa looked away, but immediately confessed. "I was trying to get through it when 'Aunty' turned up. She said there'd be a key, but I couldn't find a lock."

Strømberg stared at the horizon and smiled. "Nothing is straightforward in the librarium, Rosa. You of all people should know that. Aunt Gwyneth is correct; there will be a key. We just don't know what it is — or where to find it. Maybe the book is a clue."

At that moment it started to rain. A single droplet of water landed with a *splat* on the picture of the dragon. Rosa clutched at her upper arms and shuddered. "Come inside," Strømberg said, cutting short her next intended question. "I must leave here soon and I've more to show you." He stood up and offered his hand. She looked hesitantly at it and he added, softly, "Some interesting things — in other books you've not seen."

She thought about this for a moment, then gripped his hand and raised herself up. He set off toward the librarium. He was three or four paces ahead when he realized she wasn't following. He looked back to see her standing in the rain, her wet hair clinging to her pretty face. Her eyes were busily scanning the ground. "Rosa? Have you lost something?"

She shook her head. She wasn't going to tell him, but the daisy chain bracelet was nowhere to be found. That, in its way, was as crushing as the thought that David might not wake. "Did the fire go inside him?" she whispered. "Did David absorb it through his tears?"

Strømberg glanced at the dragon book again. A raindrop had run beneath the eye of the creature depicted on the cover, making it look as if it were crying. "No," he said. "Aunt Gwyneth would have found it."

"Then what happened? What was the flash I saw?"

"I don't know," said Strømberg. And he walked away without another word.

19.

Back in the room where David lay, Mr. Henry had already begun the process of restoring his spilled books to their proper places. He was halfway up the once-hidden ladder when Strømberg and Rosa came in.

"Charles, I'd like to show Rosa something *special* about dragons. Could you find me an appropriate text?"

The curator stopped what he was doing. His eyebrows rose to a point well above the frame of his spex. At first, Rosa thought he was going to refuse. But instead he leaned sideways and the ladder slid with his weight (and his intent). It not only traveled three feet horizontally but up two shelves as well.

Wow, thought Rosa. Where was *that* when she and David were at their most industrious?

Once again Mr. Henry pressed a button some-where and what looked to be an ordinary shelf of books revolved to display a hidden one. On it was a large old book, held together by some kind of stiff brown binding. Mr. Henry stepped down off the ladder with it. Blowing dust off the cover, he said, "This is the rarest and most valuable book in the building." He handed it to Strømberg, but his gaze was on Rosa. "I hope you know what you're doing, Thorren."

Strømberg said, "Sit down, Rosa." With a sweep of his hand he imagineered a table and three upright chairs.

Rosa tutted (even though she was secretly impressed at the speed and power of the blond man's fain) and pulled out a chair at the side of the table from which she could still see David. The boy slept on like a statue, barely breathing.

Strømberg sat down beside her but put the old book aside temporarily. Instead, he held up the glossy one again, showing the cover of the roaring dragon.

"What *are* those horrible things?" Rosa asked.

"Good question," said Strømberg. "No one really knows."

"Then why have we got books about them?"

Mr. Henry joined them at the table. He took off his spex and polished them on the corner of his jacket. "Thorren, are you sure it's right for her to hear this?"

Thorren Strømberg merely said, "Do you know what a 'myth' is, Rosa?"

"Sort of," she replied. She remembered Aunt Gwyneth using the word just before her chilling warning: *You are never to touch this book again.* Part of her was willing to accept the Aunt's caution. The roughness and terrifying size of the creatures, compared to the mountainous landscape they were pictured in, really did frighten her. But they were strangely compelling, too.

"It's a word we use to describe a phenomenon that has no foundation or basis in truth, and yet is somehow strong enough to survive in our consciousness."

"It's not in mine," said Rosa, nodding at the dragon.

"Yes, it is," said Strømberg. "It's merely been suppressed."

Mr. Henry rubbed a hand across his forehead and sighed.

"Charles, bring me something on zo:ology, would you?"

"No, Thorren. She's not ready for that."

"Animals, Charles."

"Are you insane?" The old man looked up sternly. "She'll be in the boy's state before you know it." He jutted a finger at David.

For a moment, there was stalemate. Rosa, unsure of what to do, remained quiet. Everything seemed to rest with Mr. Henry. Finally, the curator scraped back his chair and again struck one of the panels between the shelves. It opened on a dark, cubicle-shaped cupboard. Inside the cupboard was a small book, hardly any bigger than a man's hand. Mr. Henry brought it over and placed it on the table. *A Comprehensive Field Guide to Small Mammals.*

Strømberg picked it up and flicked through a few pages. They were stiff and difficult to hold in place. He found what he was looking for and showed it to the girl.

"A katt?" she said. "It looks a bit fierce. Why are the letters wrong?"

"It's a wild cat," said Strømberg, "and the spelling is correct. Try this." He flipped to another page. There was an image of the most extraordinary little creature Rosa had ever seen. It had fur like a katt, but its hairs were just a series of short gray spikes. Two slightly bulging eyes were positioned on the sides of its mischievous-looking face. It was sitting upright, on the branch of a tree, balanced by a bushy tail that curled right over its back.

"That's a squirrel," said Strømberg.

Rosa shook her head, confused.

"One more," he said, "then this goes away." And he showed her a picture of something long and sleek on the bank of a river. The book labeled it an "otter."

"Thorren, that's enough," Mr. Henry said grimly. He took the book out of Strømberg's hands and dropped it into his pocket.

Strømberg leaned back against his chair and said, "All the creatures in that book existed once, Rosa, including the habitats you saw them in."

"They're beautiful," she said. "What happened to them?"

"They died out — as our fain evolved."

"How? Why?"

"That's a mystery many people have tried to unravel, me included. We have physical evidence, in a place

141

called the Dead Lands, that squirrels, cats, otters, and thousands more species like them once roamed Co:pern:ica. But they're not there now. Interestingly, there is nothing to suggest that dragons were *ever* among us, except for precious books like these. Yet I can tell you, without exception, they are in the auma of every child I have ever counseled. Somehow, even though we're not aware of it, we collectively believe in dragons and no one, not even an Aunt, can say why."

Rosa shuddered and turned up her nose. "Are we all flawed?" she asked.

"Possibly," Strømberg said. "But I think there's a much more intriguing answer still waiting to be uncovered. And this building might be at the heart of it."

Rosa looked at Mr. Henry. The old man was holding his breath.

Strømberg pushed the dragon book aside and opened the one from the secret shelf. Rosa cast her gaze across the page. All she could see was a pattern of fading ink marks that made no sense to her. She placed her hands in her lap and waited. Strømberg turned another page. "We are sitting underneath the largest firebird aerie on

Co:pern:ica, and yet we know nothing about it. Many people — learned people, like Mr. Henry and myself — have attempted to reach the upper floors to study the birds' habitat, but with little success. Interest in the birds has gradually dwindled. Most Co:pern:icans now accept them as nothing more than a colorful aspect of the Grand Design. But they don't know about this." He ran his finger around a corner of the binding. "Do you know who found this book, Rosa?"

She shook her head.

"You did."

"*Me?* How?"

"It was on your first day," Mr. Henry said. "You were running around like a month-old kitt-katt and hit your head on the post at the foot of the stairs."

"I remember that," she said. "It's the only time I've done it. Well . . ." (She didn't mention that day's encounter with the door to Forty-Three.) "After that you taught me how to move with the building. So how did . . . ?" She turned her head and stared at the secret cubicle.

"Yes," said Mr. Henry. "You opened a hidden compartment at the foot of the stairs and in it was . . . that."

She looked up at Strømberg.

"We believe this book holds the truth," he said. "We believe that firebirds and dragons are connected. If we can make sense of that link, we think we will unlock the secrets of Co:pern:ica — possibly the entire universe."

Rosa leaned forward and glanced at the page. "With a load of smudges?"

Strømberg laughed politely. "I agree at first glance it does appear quite indecipherable. But this is a book, remember. These marks are a language. Almost certainly an ancient language. Long forgotten by us. Probably never used by us."

"Who's the author?" Rosa asked. Without waiting for permission she closed the book and looked at the cover. "There's nothing on it."

Strømberg turned it over. "You read this book from right to left."

And there, in what she'd once heard Mr. Henry describe as "gothic script," Rosa saw a title. *"The Book of Ag . . . a . . ."*

"Agawin," Thorren Strømberg said.

Agawin. Rosa repeated it to herself. The name had an interesting chime. "Who's he?"

"I'm hoping you and David will find out."

She looked worriedly at the boy. His condition hadn't changed. "How?"

"Through your work, that's all. Through patience, diligence — and faith. I don't believe it was coincidence that brought you two together or that made you discover the location of this book or that made the firebirds point you in the direction of dragons. I think they want answers just as much as we do. I want you to change your intention, Rosa. From now on, when you're putting the books into order, ask the librarium for something else. Ask for guidance about this author and for the means to translate this text."

Rosa blew a short breath. *No pressure,* she thought. "What language *is* it? Do you know?"

Strømberg bobbed his head. "Well, it only ever appears in other books about dragons. So . . . Charles, do you want to tell her?"

Mr. Henry cleared his throat. "We believe it's evidence of their existence, Rosa. We don't know, of course, how the creatures would describe it, but we like to call it 'dragontongue.'"

20.

At the same time that the rain had begun to fall on Rosa outside the Bushley librarium, it was falling on Eliza in the Dead Lands, too. It was the final irony, she thought. Abandoned, lost, endangered by *memories* (if Aunt Gwyneth was to be believed), and now getting soaked as well. The only thing that seemed to make sense to her was the piece of clay in her hands. As the rain came down and droplets ran off its smooth gray surface, Eliza let her fingers instinctively work it, using what she needed of the rain to help her. Slowly, an object came together in her hands, though it seemed to possess no useful shape. It wasn't even circular, more . . . what was the word she'd heard Harlan use to describe graf:ical data of unequal distribution? "Lopsided." That was it. The thing was lopsided. Fatter, more globular at one end than the other. Imbalanced, but somehow perfect for it. And once she'd settled on the basic shape, it seemed right to her to want to make dents, or *pits*, all over its surface, until each pit had a smooth finish she could only describe as . . . She squeezed her eyes shut. Her equilibrium rocked. Her fain-free mind was working so fast that her head literally shook as she tried to identify the unfamiliar images flashing through it. All around her she could feel the Dead Lands responding, pulling at her senses, wanting what she knew. Her thumb passed over the object again, re-examining its textured surface. And suddenly, the word she was seeking came to her. "Planished." The surface of the object was *planished*.

At that moment, something began to happen with the rain. Suddenly, it wasn't just falling anymore, but sweeping across her from any number of different angles. It was bulging and swirling and slapping at her sides as if she had somehow offended the clouds and they were bent on driving her away from underneath them. Each fresh eddy was accompanied by a terrifying sizzling noise and an unmistakable flare of heat. The effect was so pronounced that as the pressure of air around her body increased, it soon became clear that it was not really water striking Eliza's arms as she raised them, but vaporized water. Steam.

Amazingly, she felt no pain. Only terror. As she began to look about her, not for rabbits and ducks upon the surface of the land, but for something *large* in the howling skies, she noticed a monster banking through the storm. *Monster.* A word most Co:pern:icans had long forgotten. But there it was, in a muddling, vaporous form. A creature so hideously beautiful that its improbable existence would have torn apart the mind of anyone who looked upon it unprepared — unless they already had a memory of the beast. Somewhere in Eliza Merriman's consciousness she was able to put a name to the wraith. *Dragon.* She was seeing a dragon.

And not just one.

The ghostly images of a dozen or more crossed one another time after time. Now and then, she would catch a glimpse of an eye. Jewel-like. Complex. All-knowing. Magnificent. Wings shaped like the edges of holly leaves, so dark that they tented out the light as they approached. Tails, supple and immensely strong; a single flick would have the creatures swapping direction or rolling on their backs at any moment. Claws like the talons of firebirds, but ten times, twenty times bigger than theirs and with danger oozing from every tip. Fire that exploded a million raindrops and caused the air around them to bend to its will.

Dragons.

Eliza stumbled back and forth, trying to make sense of it. There was no time to think if they might be attacking her or how she might defend herself or where she might *go*. All she could do was experience them. On and on and on they came. Swooping, glaring, showing off their power. Until, in time, the bizarre thought struck her that the real enigma here was *she*, and not they. At that point some unforeseen confidence rose inside her and she reached up her hands and cried, "I AM ELIZA!"

Immediately, the creatures ceased their strafing. The rain settled back into vertical patterns and the dragons hovered in a dome-shaped arrangement around her.

"WHAT DO YOU WANT?" she called out. She swept around, staring at these ghosts in turn, until one of them put itself forth as a leader.

It was smaller than the rest, and there was something about its slimly built frame that made Eliza shudder to her core. Its body was more like the size of a man's. Less scaly. Definitely boned (there was next to no covering at the ribs). But the notion of a man with the face of a dragon and the wings of a bird (a gigantic bird), was not something her auma could cope with. She looked away rather than look it in the eye.

Eliza, hold up your hands, it said.

The voice was in her head. A growling, primitive sound that reminded her of the roar that David had sometimes made during his dreams.

Shaking wildly, she turned and faced the thing. "What are you?" she whispered.

The eyes, she could swear, despite their strange triangular slant, were those of a man.

Your hands, it said again.

And so Eliza raised her hands in the shape of a cup. Only then did it occur to her that the object she had molded was still within them. A burst of white light suddenly engulfed it. The shock wave traveled through Eliza's arms and onward to every extremity of her body. Her knees buckled and her breath expired. For a blink of time her constructed heart stopped. She collapsed unconscious, onto the Dead Lands. The object she had made from clay rolled from her hands.

When the firebirds found her, she was still in a heap. Six of them came. Three were dispatched into the skies above to either keep watch or to trace elements of the ethereal activity that had drawn them to this place. One, a green-and-orange beauty not unlike Runcey, attended to Eliza's auma and general body warmth. The red bird responsible for the attack on David stood guard.

The last to arrive was the cream-colored bird with the apricot tufts that had visited the daisy fields outside the librarium. As before, it occupied itself just strolling around, investigating the scene. At one point, it hopped onto Eliza's shoulder and was immediately shooed off by its red companion. There was an element of good fortune about this dismissal. For when the cream bird landed on the earth again, it stumbled across a jewel every bit as impressive as the flame it had found embedded in a teardrop outside the aerie. And it was not just its eye ridges it lifted when it saw it. Every feather on its body stood on end. It let out such a startled *rrrh!* that the red firebird gave an irritated squawk and poddled over to see what all the fuss was about.

The two birds gulped and looked at each other. There in the dying grass was something never before seen outside the aeries.

An egg.

21.

Two days after his chat with Rosa, Thorren Strømberg arrived at the Ragnar Institute to meet Harlan Merriman and Bernard Brotherton. He was immediately escorted to a secluded ground-floor laboratory and into a square, windowless room. In the center of the room was a piece of apparatus that resembled a large horseshoe (although horses were long extinct, the symbol associated with them was not; a common irony on Co:pern:ica). The apparatus was serviced on either side by two dormant com:puters. In front of the "shoe," as Bernard called it, was a dark observation screen. It was behind here that Thorren Strømberg was directed while Brotherton set about priming the device.

"So innocuous a setup," the counselor said. A number of lights flickered on around the shoe, coating the ceiling in a warm blue haze.

Harlan nodded. "Less than four dec:ades ago, the equipment you see here would have taken up the entire institute, and more. Developments in molecular tech:nology have enabled us to not only reduce the size of the hardware, but vastly increase the speed of our research. This inoffensive piece of gear is close to creating dark matter. One day, in this very room, we will make — and analyze — the glue that binds our universe together."

"And today?"

"Today we find out what tore it apart, briefly, in your clinic."

Strømberg gazed through his reflection on the screen. The blue lights were now chasing each other around the shoe and a thin, distinct hum had risen from it. "Do you have clearance for this, Harlan?"

The professor turned his gaze to a screen at his right, adjusting the position of a crosshair marker. "It's my job to investigate spatial enigmas."

"That's not what I asked. Is it safe?"

Harlan Merriman pushed his tongue between his lips. "Since I last spoke to you, Bernard has run over a thousand simulations. The rifts produced by them have all been stable. The only means of activating a rift is by direct physical intervention."

"Stepping through?"

Harlan smiled. "Don't worry, Counselor. This is just a test. In transference terms, it couldn't tele:port your outgoing breath, let alone your body. Bernard, how're we doing?"

Brotherton walked in front of the device and made a final check on the second console. White coat. Balding head. Drainpipe pants. *The caricature of a scientist,* Strømberg thought. "Another minit," the tech:nician said.

Harlan primed his com:puter. "How's David?" he asked, flicking switches. "You said you were going to visit him soon."

"I did," Counselor Strømberg replied. Keeping his auma even he said, "He was sleeping soundly all the time I was there."

"No more dreams?"

"Apparently not."

Harlan nodded silently.

"You look disappointed."

Harlan shook his head. "I can't help thinking that

if David was able to access his dreams, there wouldn't be a need for what we're doing here."

"Are you having second thoughts about the procedure? It's not too late to abandon this."

"This is science," Harlan replied. "As long as we have a need for answers, there will always be a need for procedures, Thorren."

Bernard joined them at the observation area. "All set," he said, with a nervous breath.

Harlan laced his fingers together and stretched them. "Well, gentlemen. Let's see if we can find out what bothered my son. Ready?"

Strømberg and Brotherton nodded.

"Then behold the universe in microcosm."

And he lowered his hand toward the controls.

In that same time frame, in the Dead Lands, Aunt Gwyneth had returned to find a trail of stones where Eliza had been, each of them dropped ten paces apart. The trail stretched over the nearest rise. And even when the Aunt had crested that, the stones continued well into the distance. Far ahead, but still within walking range, the old woman could see a small and dreary group of hills. From the way their contours caught the light, she knew there would be caves among their slopes. And that was not all. When she poked her disagreeable nose into the air, the elemental scent of wood smoke entered them. From then on, her new aspirant became of far greater interest.

Eliza had learned to light a fire.

With her ability to move quickly, Aunt Gwyneth was at the end of the trail in barely the time it took to imagineer it. Her sudden appearance drew several fingers of smoke from the fire and sent a pother of cinders flying into the cavemouth. Eliza was not visible right away, but the products of her time spent waiting were. On every rock that bouldered the cave sat a sculpture of a dragon, made from clay. Each was no bigger than the size of a fist. And though there was no color or life in them, their snarling jaws and grasping talons were enough to make the Aunt grit her teeth in disgust. All the sculptures were pointed toward the cave approach, guardians of the slope she was standing on.

But that was not all.

"What heresy is this?" the Aunt hissed, and cast her glance farther, beyond the fire.

Eliza, surrounded by miniature dragons, was sitting cross-legged just inside the cave, her red hair falling into her lap. "I'm sorry, Aunt. I had no need of you," she said. "I found out by myself what my family's anomaly was." And she held out the bundle she'd been cradling in her arms.

It was a baby girl.

Simultaneously, on a floor of the librarium not visited by humans for countless spins, the cream-colored firebird — Aurielle was her name — was pacing the length of a relic left behind by those same humans: a polished oak dining table. In the center of the table were two wide-necked candlesticks. On top of one stick, still perfectly intact and possessing more than enough buoyancy to keep it upright, was the flame of the firebird Azkiar, preserved in the teardrop of the boy, David. On the second stick sat an even greater conundrum: the egg, made from the clay of Co:pern:ica. Lying on the table between the sticks was the circle of violet-colored daisies that Aurielle had picked up with the teardrop, purely because its beauty intrigued her and its auma spoke of love.

A tear.

An egg.

A circle of daisies.

And a lot of kerfuffle.

What did all of this mean?

From a nest of dust and feathers on the bookshelf opposite (there were many such nests on the upper floors), a tired voice went *rrrrrrh*.

Aurielle stopped walking and looked across the room to see Azkiar jiggling his tail.

Would she please stop pacing? he begged her. The scratch of her claws was setting his ear tufts on edge.

Rrrh, she went back. It was all right for him. All he did was fly about and make a nuisance of himself. He didn't have to make *sense* of things.

Blowing dust motes out of her nostrils, the female firebird opened her wings and fluttered to her perch: a high mound of books at the far end of the table. It was not the most reliable, as perches went (books slid away if she landed too hard, or someone — not thinking of any red bird in particular — decided to pull one out of the stack), but it faced the wall upon which the great tapestry hung. In Aurielle's opinion, there was no better post in the entire aerie.

She looked at the woven picture and sighed. The

tapestry was so beautiful, with its wide green hills and its dragons flying gracefully around the valley. And yet so menacing, too. It seemed to tell the story of a great battle — "Isenfier" as Aurielle knew it. Emerging from the tallest hill was a dark apparition, which firebirds through the centuries had labeled the "Shadow of Ix." It towered over the humans on the cloth. And everyone or everything pictured beneath it was shying away in fear, especially the white, horned horse and the dragons flying nearest its center. Only the kneeling child, who held a small dragon in her hands, seemed unafraid. A faint white halo lay around the girl, marking her out as a savior, perhaps. As for the dragon. Well, that was the biggest conundrum of all. Aurielle was very familiar with dragons as a breed. They were pictured all around the aerie (if you knew where to look). But the dragon in the hands of the girl was different. Spiky. Green. Slightly comical, really. And if the scale was correct, smaller than a firebird. And yet it had *paws* — an unmerited improvement on firebird anatomy that always made her huff in envy.

But how, she wondered, had the tapestry gotten here? When, and by whom? Why had firebirds always protected it?

And what did it *mean*?

Suddenly, her thoughts were interrupted by a squawk from the window.

A blue firebird, Aubrey, was calling urgently for help.

Azkiar was off his shelf in a moment.

Rrrh! said Aubrey. *Portal. Come.* And he shimmered his feathers and entered light speed, which would take him to Harlan Merriman's time rip in less than a sec.

But as Aurielle and Azkiar prepared to follow, there was a jolt and the whole world turned. The last thing Aurielle remembered of it was the sound of two identical clatters and a white flare behind her. Just as if two candlesticks had fallen over and whatever was upon them had come together in one small but significant fusion of light. . . .

Rosa and Mr. Henry would feel the jolt as well. The whole of Co:pern:ica would. For Rosa it would come after two more days of putting books in order and renewing her intent, none of which would bring her any closer to unlocking the door to Floor Forty-Three. Mr. Henry (or rather Thorren Strømberg) had over-ruled Aunt Gwyneth and allowed her to keep the glossy dragon book, which she had read from cover to cover when Strømberg had gone, and reread to David a dozen times already. Despite her early uncertainty she now regarded it as a wonderful treasure, with many excellent illustrations and several vivid accounts of how dragons had lived (and died). But the remedy wasn't working. Nothing was working. The door remained locked. The mysteries of Agawin stayed unresolved. And David, despite the occasional twitch of an eyelid, continued to sleep.

But Rosa did not lose faith. She had become a minor expert in "dragon:ology" by now. She knew their anatomy, their habitats, their spiritual significance (though some of the concepts confused her), and their legends. There was also a possible clue to why the red firebird had singled out the book. One of its pages showed a dragon in "hibernation." She'd had to run this term past Mr. Henry and his reference books before she understood that it meant a kind of deep sleep. More importantly, a short paragraph later in the book described how a dragon's fire could induce a prolonged "stasis," which usually wore off over a period of time. How much time the book didn't say. But it was encouraging all the same. Mr. Henry praised Rosa's diligence and passed the information on to Counselor Strømberg, who sent an e:com saying, *Excellent. Keep watch.* There was a little more to the e:com than that. It was, in fact, quite a detailed composition on the possible pheno:typic associations between firebirds and dragons. But all of that was kept from Rosa (and Aunt Gwyneth), whose only real interest was David anyway.

There *was* something else she was working on though, quite possibly the most intriguing thing of all about dragons, and that was their language. Thorren Strømberg had told the truth when he had said that the symbols in *The Book of Agawin* could be found elsewhere. They were in her book. One little squiggle in the right-hand corner of every page. At first glance, every squiggle looked the same. But a careful page-by-page examination showed that none were completely identical. They were arranged in slightly different places, too — always within the same triangle of white just near the page number, but definitely spaced apart.

Rosa went to sleep with those marks in her mind. She saw them as she turned the pages in her dreams. What was it about them? Why were they important?

Did they *have* any real importance? Maybe Thorren Strømberg had got it wrong. Maybe the author of the book was playing games.

Then, on the morning that Harlan Merriman was about to conduct his spatial experiment with the horizons of time, Rosa found her answer. She was sitting beside David with the book in her lap when Runcey landed in the window space.

"Oh," she gasped. Her heartbeat doubled. The bird looked fit and well.

He poddled to the inner lip of the window and cast his kind eye down at the boy.

Rosa laced her fingers into a bundle and brought them up to the level of her chin. "Can you wake him?" she whispered.

The firebird looked at the book she was holding.

And Rosa, thinking back to the day of the accident, suddenly felt guilty for having it. She said, "I'm sorry you were hurt. It was all my fault. But . . . the red one gave me this. Look, Runcey."

And with that she did something she had not done before. She ran her thumb across the edge of the pages and flicked through them. She was searching for the picture of the hibernating dragon, but as her gaze fell upon the corner of the book something quite extraordinary happened. In the short time it took for sixty-four pages to roll past her thumb, the marks came together as one symbol. Three ragged lines. Parallel, not connected.

There was a click. The symbol not only seemed to leap from the book but its meaning entered Rosa's head as well. *Sometimes.*

Sometimes, she thought, *the rain will fall or the sun will shine.*

Sometimes, David will wake or David will dream.

Sometimes, the door will be closed or the door will be open. . . .

Sometimes.

"Mr. Henry!" she cried out. "I know how to read dragontongue! I —"

That was the point at which the world jolted.

Everything went dark. Co:pern:ica turned. And Rosa passed out.

She came to on the floor of the room. Her chair had spilled over and Runcey had gone.

But time had passed, and David was stirring.

She went to him at once. Kneeling beside him, she gripped his hand. His face was turned to the window. She spoke his name and he turned her way.

Then came the shock that neither was expecting.

"David?" she said again.

"Rosa?" he replied. He sounded just as puzzled as she was.

She let go of his hand and ran to the only reflective surface in the room — a brass plate that titled the dictionary shelf. In the brass she saw a beautiful young woman, with large dark eyes and long dark hair.

David pushed himself onto his elbows. "How long have I been asleep?"

Rosa ran her fingers over her face. "At a guess, about . . . eight spins." She gulped.

PART TWO
WHICH HAS ITS
BEGINNINGS ON
FLOOR FORTY-THREE OF
THE BUSHLEY LIBRARIUM
MARCH 7, 032

1.

Eh? How did *that* happen?" David peered at his hands as if the answer might be written in secret on his palms. "How could I have slept for *eight spins*?!"

"You kind of did and you didn't," Rosa said. "A few minits ago, we were both kids. Then there was this . . . time quake or something and suddenly we're all grown up — and you're awake."

"Time quake?"

"Or something. I don't know."

David patted his head and face. Hair. Longer hair. Wavy. Thicker. Parted in the center, almost down to his shoulders. He swung his feet off the bed. "What caused it?"

"I don't know."

"Something here? In the librarium?"

"I don't know."

"Is it just us, or —?"

"You know, I think I preferred you asleep," she cut in. "I realize you must be feeling all kinds of bright and sparkly right now, but just . . . slow down, OK? I have no idea what caused the time jump. All I was doing before it was . . ." She picked up the dragon book from the floor.

David launched an inquisitive frown. "What's that?"

"A book — about dragons."

"About *what*?"

"Drag — Oh, David, just trust me. A lot of things happened while you were sleeping." She came over and sat beside him. "I know this must be weird for you. It is for me, too. But don't drive me crazy with questions yet. I'll tell you everything when it's time, I promise. Right now, I need a moment to make sense of something."

He nodded and cast his gaze over the book. "Are they firebirds — in armor? Warbirds or something?"

"No. They're *dragons*. And they're actually very spiritual."

"With jaws like that?"

"David, will you just shut up and listen! The firebirds *gave* me this book. Well, actually, one of them dropped it on you. I didn't know why until just before the quake. I found a door to Floor Forty-Three. Do you remember . . . about the upper floors and stuff?"

"I think so. You've been up to the roof?"

"No. The door is locked, but the key to it is in this book — I think. Come on, I'll show you. I want to try it." She bounced to her feet.

"Wait. Where's Mr. Henry?"

"Don't know. Haven't seen him."

"Well, shouldn't we go and find him? He could contact my dad. He knows about time."

"Later," Rosa insisted. "This is exciting." She tapped the book. "Come on, we'll try the door, then surprise Mr. Henry with it."

David stood up (a little unsteadily) and looked at his reflection as Rosa had done. "Wow," he said, turning his face left and right. "How has this *happened*? That's amazing."

"Not the adjective I would have used," she said. "But you'll do."

At the end of the corridor on Floor Forty-Two, the door was just as locked as ever.

"No keyhole," David said.

"Yeah, I kinda spotted that," Rosa said. "I think it opens with a command."

David struck a commanding pose. "Open!" he shouted, with his arms extended.

Rosa dropped her shoulders. "A *special* command, idiot. Sleep hasn't improved you, has it? You're basically still a boy in a man's body."

"Yeah, and what are you?"

She tossed her hair to one side and chose not to answer. "Stand back. Let me have a go." She placed a hand upon the door and spread her fingers. "Sometimes," she whispered.

To her dismay, nothing happened.

"Was that it?" David said.

Rosa stood away, sighing. "I don't understand. It should have worked. It was so strong in my mind when I turned the pages." She banged her fist lightly on the door.

"Have you tried that?"

"Tried what?"

"That — knocking."

She swung around, anger blazing in her eyes. "Will you please take this seriously! I sat by you for ages while you were asleep, never knowing if you were going to die or not. So just — what are you gawping at?" His gaze was roaming all over her face.

"You're really pretty, aren't you? Especially when you're angry."

She gulped, then whacked him in the chest with the book. "Concentrate, will you? On the *door*. Look, if you flick through the pages of the book, it makes a symbol come alive in one corner. I'm sure it means 'sometimes' in dragon language. I thought it would get us in if I said it. I was wrong. Let's go and ask Mr. Henry."

"Wait." He caught her arm. "Show me the symbol."

"Don't know if I dare," she said, tucking her hair behind one ear.

"Why not?"

"For all I know, it was me that caused the time quake."

"With a symbol?"

She pointed to the dragon on the cover of the book. "These creatures are powerful, David."

"Maybe it's the *symbol* that opens the door?"

With a sigh, she thrust the book at him. "All right. You try it. But if I end up wrinkled and old, you're history."

He smiled and opened the book.

"There," she said, pointing out the marks. "Flick fast. See what comes into your head when it appears."

And so, David turned the pages as Rosa had done. Once again, the three-lined symbol appeared. It seemed to float off the pages as the ink marks came together.

Rosa, her breath held, looked at the door. Nothing. And, thankfully, she hadn't aged a day. "Did you get a meaning?"

David stared at the symbol. "Yes," he said. And he spoke it, deep in his throat: *Rrrh!*

With a centuries-old creak, the door to Floor Forty-Three finally clicked open.

2.

The same could be said of Rosa's mouth, though that *fell* open rather than clicked open. "How did you do that? You made a noise like a firebird."

"I heard it in my head when I saw the symbol."

"The firebirds talk *dragontongue*?"

"Don't know," he said, lifting his shoulders. "I just heard the noise. And a different translation. 'Sometimes' is the nearest we can get to it in Co:pern:ican. It really means 'all things that are possible are probable.' And it's . . . *big*."

"Big?" she prompted him, becoming impatient. She glanced at the door, barely open a crack. It was moving slightly as if a breeze were blowing from the other side.

Like you could imagineer a universe by saying it, he

thought. But instead he said this: "It sounded like Runcey with a sore throat. Is he . . . ?"

"Runcey's fine," Rosa sighed. "And much as I love this idle chitchat, can we do it another time, please?" She gestured toward the door.

"OK, go on. I'll follow you in."

"Uh-uh," she said, clutching her arms. "You first."

"Why should *I* go first? You're the one who's insisting on doing the exploring."

"It might be dangerous."

"My point exactly!"

"Oh, David, just . . . open the door." She put herself behind him and shoved.

Warily, he gripped the old brass handle and opened the door just wide enough to poke his head around it.

"What can you see?"

He waved her quiet. "Bones. The bones of a thousand dragons."

"*Whaaat?*"

He pulled his head back. "Oh, and some books."

With one big push, he swung the door open.

He wasn't lying (about the books). Rosa stepped

past (having whacked him again) into a room full of written wonder. It smelled of dust and paper and wood, of sunlight on wood, of the settlement of age. It was enormous, ten times the size of any room she'd seen on the lower floors. Strangely, the shelves were set within the body of the room and could be accessed from either side, it seemed. Dozens of them, placed at angles, like a maze. All of them neatly arranged with books.

"Wow," Rosa said, trailing her fingers over a few spines.

David, following just a few steps behind her, was reading the names of the authors. "They're in order," he muttered.

"This is amazing," Rosa said, taking no notice. "Why do you think it's been hidden from us?" She disappeared from view around the end of a shelf.

"Rosa, we should stay together," he warned her. They were used to the peculiarities of the floors they knew. But this was different. There was something strange about these books. David could feel them pulling him in all directions, whispering, as if they were begging to be read. He ran to catch up, but Rosa was several shelves ahead already and all he saw was a swish of her skirt. He doubled his pace and called out again. His voice, lifted by the space around him, drifted into the high ceiling. Looking up, he saw patterns in the ancient plaster. A system of stars. Planets. A universe. Flying long and flat among the stars were dragons.

With a bump, he found Rosa again.

"Watch where you're going," she tutted. She flicked her hair off her shoulder and showed him a book. "These are weird. I can't make out their genre."

He took it from her as she walked away. *Alicia in a Land of Wonder*. Inside was the normal printed text, but here and there were drawings of grotesque people in even more grotesque clothing, plus what appeared to be pictures of animals, though the only one David faintly recognized was a katt with an oversized, hideous grin. "Did you read any of this?"

"No," Rosa said, scanning the shelves higher up.

"It's got amazing auma. Do you think anyone will miss it?"

Before Rosa could respond, their attention was drawn by a clanking sound farther down the room. A firebird had landed on a large metal sign suspended by two long chains from the ceiling. It let out a shrill *rrrh!*

"Oh, no," Rosa gasped. "That's the red one that attacked you. Run!"

"Wait," David said, but she had already gone. With a *whoosh*, the bird took off, leaving the sign swinging and the chains creaking. The last thing David became aware of before he ran off in pursuit of Rosa was the lettering on the sign, beating its rhythm against his eyes:

FICTION

3.

The red firebird, Azkiar, swooped low over David's head and landed on a shelf, displacing multiple clouds of dust. Unsure whether to run or confront it, David found himself stumbling down unexplored lanes between the shelves. He was going to be lost, very quickly, he knew. But at least he was drawing the bird away from Rosa. If she could make it to the door, she would be free to bring help. And what was the worst that could happen: more sleep?

When he turned down a lane that ended in a wall, he realized that question would soon have an answer. He skidded to a halt and looked back. Azkiar had landed on the uppermost shelf at the far end of the lane. David backed up until the wall stopped him. He was half-concealed in shadow and could see the bird's sharp eyes adjusting to the light. Making hardly a sound, it opened its wings and glided closer, crossing to the shelves on the opposite side. Now it was just four sections away — twenty paces at most.

Books. They were David's only defense. He hated the idea of using them as missiles, but what other choice did he have? He was still holding on to *Alicia in a Land of Wonder*, but that was quite small as literary weapons went. He grabbed another one of better weight and turned to face the bird. "Stay back. I don't want to hurt you. I mean no harm here. I . . . I like books." And how hypocritical was that, with four hundred pages of something by the author Steven Kinge ready to be launched from the end of his arm?

Azkiar fluttered across the lane once more. *Too close,* David thought. He hurled the Kinge.

Before he could grab for another, he bore witness to one of the most dramatic and distressing events of his life. As the book flew foward, Azkiar unlatched his jaw and let forth a burst of orange fire. It engulfed the book while it was still in midair and turned it into a crackling fireball. A small corner of the spine, not instantly consumed, fell to the floor and jumped around painfully as the flames fizzled out. Black leaves edged with bright red cinders drifted in flurries over the shelves. A small part of the librarium had been destroyed. All around him, David could sense the building's sorrow. He could almost hear pages folding in grief.

"What do you want?" he shouted.

Azkiar responded by leaving the shelves and hovering in the air in front of David. The bird's ear tufts were up and glowing scarlet, the frills around his neck like spikes of steel. There was anger and passion in his unwavering gaze. The kind of look that said trespassers were definitely not welcome. David took a deep breath. He had nothing but his honesty with which to shield himself now. He stepped forward, out of the shadows.

He braced himself for a burst of fire, but it did not happen. Instead, a subtle change occurred in the firebird's expression. It tipped its beak down and swiveled its eyes forward. Those eyes grew very round indeed and blinked several times before settling to a stare. Whatever mech:anism governed the way they took in light extended to its maximum, making the eyeballs shine like mirrors — until David could see himself reflected in them, playing back like a pin-sized movie.

Was he imagineering this or did the bird look puzzled?

"Please," he tried again. "I mean you no harm. Let me go and I'll —"

He never got the chance to complete his sentence. With incredible versatility of movement, the firebird rose up and simply flew away.

"OK," David muttered, blowing with relief. He had no idea why the bird had let him go. But it had, and he needed to be out of there — fast. He crouched down and touched what was left of the Kinge, to offer it what little compassion he could. Reminded that he still had the strange *Alicia*, he glanced at the cover again. For the first time in months (spins, even?) he extended his auma and let it commingle with the auma of the book. To his amazement, it seemed to reach right into him. It was ready to forgive. And it wanted to be read. So definite. Almost like a dying request. He slipped it into his jacket pocket, then tip-toed to the end of the lane and looked around the shelves for signs of more firebirds — or Rosa. Why, he wondered, had she not come to his aid? Maybe she was lost? Or hiding somewhere? He called her name. It floated like a living thing among the shelves. When he followed it, it brought him back to the doorway and Floor Forty-Two.

Closing the door, he hurried through the known part of the librarium, asking it to take him straight to Rosa. Four connecting rooms later, he arrived at the threshold of Mr. Henry's study.

Rosa was there, kneeling beside Mr. Henry's chair. The curator himself was sitting in the chair, with his head lolling forward onto his chest.

"Rosa?" David said. She glanced up as he stepped in.

She was weeping, and looked as if she had been for a while. Only now did David see that she was clutching one of Mr. Henry's hands. His other hand was hanging limply. "He's dead," she sobbed. "He aged as well. I found him like this. He's gone, David."

"I'm so sorry," said a voice from the door.

David whipped around. *"Dad?"*

Harlan Merriman stepped into the light. "I came here immediately, to make sure you were safe." He placed a hand on his son's face, running his thumb along the perfect cheekbone. "Oh, David. What have I done to you . . . ?"

"You know about the time quake?" David asked.

Harlan looked bleakly at Mr. Henry. "I caused it," he said. "A failed experiment."

"Can it be reversed?" Rosa said tearfully.

Harlan shook his head.

"There must be *something* you can do?" she begged.

"There is," said Harlan, his expression fixed. "I can give myself up to the Higher."

4.

No, this can't be happening," Rosa said. She sat back against the swivel chair, burying her face.

Harlan looked at David and said, "You need to leave here. Now. And take Rosa with you. It won't be long before Mr. Henry's death is noticed. Any diminution in the universal auma triggers the inception of the Re:movers — programmed constructs who deal with death and bodies and criminals. They don't ask questions, David."

"I'm not leaving," Rosa said.

Harlan bit his lip. "The Aunts will come as well."

"Aunts?" David queried. He, of course, had no experience of them.

"It doesn't matter," said Harlan, gripping his son's arm and drawing him a step or two away from Rosa.

"There isn't much time. And I must speak to you —
privately."

"What happened?" Rosa growled. "What did
you *do*?"

"David?" Harlan said quietly to him.

David looked into his father's eyes. "I'm staying
with Rosa. This is where we belong. Anything you say,
you say to both of us, Dad."

Harlan ran his gaze around the study walls. "Very
well." He sighed, rubbing his hand across his mouth.
"You've both been affected by the time shift. It's only
right that you should both know why." He walked
across to Rosa and touched her shoulder. "I really am
genuinely sorry."

Shuddering, she drew her knees up to her chin. And
though she couldn't bring herself to look at Harlan's
face, she nodded gently to acknowledge his remorse.

"I was running an experiment in my lab," he said,
"trying to recreate a peculiar rift in the fabric of space
that had been observed during your dreams."

"My dreams?" said David.

Rosa put her hair behind her ears and listened
closely.

Perching on the corner of Mr. Henry's desk, Harlan went on, "It showed up on a film Counselor Strømberg made of you sleeping. You were never able to recall what you'd dreamed about, remember? Rifts like that are not supposed to happen, not in a carefully controlled world like Co:pern:ica. So you were confined here by Strømberg while we tried to work out whether you were the cause of it. You suffer from a condition called 'ec:centricity,' David. It means that you can imagineer outside the limits of the Grand Design, even though you may not be aware of it. The librarium is considered a neutral environment. The plan was to keep you here to calm you down, so you wouldn't draw unnecessary attention to yourself while we carried out our investigations."

"And what did you find?" Rosa asked bitterly. "It had better be important 'cause it's just killed Mr. Henry."

Harlan nodded. "The rift came from another dimension."

"What?" said David.

"I was looking for the source of it," Harlan said, "because I wanted to protect you — and, who knows, the rest of Co:pern:ica, too. Unfortunately, we generated a temporal distortion and this is the result: Everyone connected to the project has aged. Fascinating for you, myself, and Rosa. Tragic for poor Mr. Henry."

"Taxicar," David said, glancing through the window. Four men in black suits had just stepped out of it.

Rosa scrambled to her feet and looked out. "We could hide," she said. "We know lots of places. And we can get into the upper floors."

"I can't hide," said Harlan. "I have to take responsibility for what happened here."

"What will they do to you?" David asked.

"I'll be banished — to the Dead Lands. They'll send me somewhere I can't be found."

"But that will mean . . ."

"That this will be the last time we'll see each other, yes."

"They're coming in," reported Rosa.

"Dad, let us hide you."

"No," said Harlan. "That would make you culpable — both of you. They'll track me down eventually, wherever I go."

"What about the rift? Tell me what else you found."

"I hear footsteps," said Rosa. She went and stood by Mr. Henry, and turned to face the door.

"Dad, the rift," David said, with more urgency now. "What else did you discover? If I didn't cause it, what did?"

Harlan stepped forward and pressed a micro:pen into David's palm. "Something stronger than you," he whispered. And he threw his arms around his son and hugged him tightly, just as the first of the suits walked in.

"Stand away," said the man. "You will separate. Now."

David parted from his father and stood beside Rosa. The knuckles of her free hand brushed against his. He gripped her hand lightly, never taking his eyes off the four Re:movers. They had the same kind of auma readings as machines — low, with no emotional oscillation. They were also perfect clones of one another, right down to the level of the hair on their foreheads. The only way they could be told apart was by the patterns on their ties. Crosshatched. Pinstriped. Plain black. And spotted.

Spotted (the Re:mover who had spoken) walked across to Mr. Henry. He passed a handheld scanner over the body. It responded with a terminal-sounding beep. "Death, by natural causes," he said.

"Not quite," said a new and more cynical voice.

To Rosa's horror, Aunt Gwyneth sailed into the room.

The Re:movers, David noticed, immediately stood aside, apparently awaiting orders from this woman. "Who are you?" he said coldly.

Aunt Gwyneth saw Rosa's hand in his. "Oh, I'm sure your charming . . . companion will bring you up to speed eventually, David. For now, you will be silent while I do my work. This room is overcrowded," she snapped at the Re:movers. "Take the body to the taxicar."

In one fluid movement, Spotted Tie lifted Mr. Henry from his chair, threw the curator over his shoulder, and carried him out of the room.

Rosa covered her mouth.

"As for this one." Aunt Gwyneth turned to Harlan. "He has been keeping secrets from us." She put a jet-black fingernail on Harlan's cheek, drawing it down his neck as she circled behind him. "Where is Thorren Strømberg, Professor?"

"I don't know," he said, trying not to gulp.

"We have the tech:nician Brotherton," she said, dragging the fingernail oh so slowly, pressing it into the soft pit of flesh behind Harlan's right ear. (David saw his father wince.) "Please, don't make this difficult. I don't want to humiliate you in front of your son. I ask you again, where is Strømberg?"

"I don't know," Harlan repeated quietly.

Aunt Gwyneth stepped away from him and set her spine straight. "Check the boy's palms."

"What?" said Rosa. Why the sudden interest in David?

The pinstriped Re:mover stepped in front of him. "You will show me your hands."

"He's innocent," snapped Harlan. "Leave him alone."

"Do it," Aunt Gwyneth said, rounding on David. "Your father passed you something before I came in. It's written all over his neural pathways."

The Re:mover raised his scanner in a threatening gesture.

David had no choice but to open his hands. In the palm where his father had placed a micro:pen was a golden ring. "My father knew his fate," David said to the Aunt. "So he wanted me to have this . . . ongoing symbol of love for my mother." He saw his father give the faintest of nods.

"Please, Aunt Gwyneth, don't take it," Harlan pleaded. "Let Eliza have something to remember me by."

Aunt Gwyneth breathed in sharply. "Arrest him," she said, sweeping a hand toward Harlan.

David closed his hand around the ring once more.

Plain Tie stepped forward. He scanned Harlan's eyes. "You are identified as Harlan Arthur Merriman. Arrested on the authority of an Aunt. Have you anything to say?"

Harlan stared deep into the old woman's eyes. She *was* somewhat older than the last time they'd met. And that troubled him deeply. Whatever the outcome of this, she was going to be somewhere at the heart of it. Why, he wished, thinking of Mr. Henry, could this dreadful woman not have died instead?

"Have you anything to say?" the Re:mover repeated.

Aunt Gwyneth put her mouth within spitting distance of Harlan's ear. "What a pity," she whispered, with cruel intent written through her auma, "that you will never have a chance to see your daughter."

"My . . . ? How? What have you done?" Harlan floundered.

"Take him," Aunt Gwyneth commanded.

"Dad? What's the matter? What did she say to you?" David stepped forward, only for Crosshatched and Pinstriped to move to intercept. With a shock of pain, David fell back as Pinstriped placed a hand on his chest to restrain him.

In an instant, David imagineered the Re:mover across the far side of the room. The man-machine flew across Mr. Henry's desk, knocking over a globe and a small com:screen before crashing into the shelving behind it. Crosshatched was about to go the same way when Aunt Gwyneth cried, "Enough!" and turned her powerful eyes on David. He sank to his knees in agony. The throbbing inside his head was horrendous, as if she had put a fork into his brain and twisted it twice before pinning him down. "Very impressive," she growled. "Use your fain like that once more and I will have you de:constructed, cell by cell." She scowled at Pinstriped, who was getting to his feet (readjusting his tie). "You will be committed for reprogramming. Now, take this criminal away."

And with that, Harlan Merriman was hauled from the room.

As though to add insult to injury, Aunt Gwyneth cracked her knuckles (a quite hideous sound), then came around the study desk and sat in the curator's green swivel chair. She rocked it back and forth with very little relish. One by one, she opened the drawers of the desk and closed them without disturbing the contents. She picked up a book of something called "crosswords" and dropped it into the trash can in disgust. At last, she spoke. "Rosanna — so much more elegant than Rosa, don't you think? You don't mind me using it, do you?"

It was a question intended to be answered, but Rosa preferred to keep her silence.

"I thought not," said the Aunt. "Rosanna it is. Listen closely, my dear. There are going to be some changes in the running of this building, now that your beloved curator has gone." She clicked her fingers. Two identical Aunts walked into the room. Both were dressed in the manner of Aunt Gwyneth: gray two-piece suits, plain black shoes. Like the Re:movers, they both wore ties. Maroon bow ties against white collared blouses. The tie of the woman on the right was at a slightly crooked angle. She kept adjusting it, as though it were a constant embarrassment. It was the only way to tell the two of them apart.

"Who are you people?" David said. He was recovered again now and on his feet.

Aunt Gwyneth said, rather haughtily, "We are what brought you into being, David. And we will decide your fate. Rosanna, meet Aunts Primrose and Petunia. They are not clones. They are that rare commodity, twins. They will be your keepers during the period of re:assessment."

"Keepers?" Rosa's eyes darted over the women.

"You do want company, don't you?"

"I've *got* company, thanks."

Aunt Gwyneth swung her chair. "If you're referring to David, I'm afraid you're mistaken. His time here is done. He is going home." She raised a finger to shut Rosa up. "At his mother's request, I might add. Tell me, David, what good-hearted boy could possibly refuse? Especially now that you have a sister as well."

"Sister?" he said.

"Penelope. Quite a sparky creation. Artificially aged to eight and a half by your father's dangerous, unauthorized experiment. She is eager to meet her unkempt, if really rather handsome, brother. I took the trouble to order you a taxicar. It's right outside. Don't keep it waiting."

"David?" Rosa said. She ran across the room and plunged into his arms.

He stared at Aunt Gwyneth over Rosa's shoulder. "What do you mean by 're:assessment'? What's going to happen to the building if I go?"

"The Aunts will survey it and make a report. A new curator will then be appointed. That is the law, David."

For a moment, he thought about it. "All right, but I'm taking Rosa with me."

Rosa stepped back a little, gripping his forearms. "No. Our place is here, taking care of the books. It's what Mr. Henry would have wanted."

"How touching," Aunt Gwyneth said, without any hint of warmth or sincerity. "David, let me see if I can make your decision easier." She sat back, steepling her fingers. "Oh, yes. Rosanna *can't* leave here. She was committed by her parents and they must give permission for her re:moval. That is also the law. The trouble is, her parents are dead."

"What?" said Rosa.

"Well . . ." Aunt Gwyneth twirled a hand. "They voluntarily left for the Dead Lands. That's as good as dead. Which means you are officially an orphan, my dear. That puts you under my jurisdiction. And as I can't afford to have you trailing around after me or interfering with my work, I've decided that this building will house you — for life. So there's your predicament, David. Rosanna stays here. You must choose between her or your mother."

David took a shuddering breath.

"Don't leave me," said Rosa. "Please, don't go."

"I'll come back," he said, pulling her hands off his arms.

"No," she begged him. "The building needs us. You can't just leave behind everything we've done." The Aunt called Petunia stepped forward and held her.

"I promise, I'll come back," he said to Rosa again. And with one last glance at her beautiful eyes, he moved toward the door. He was right on the threshold when she cried out bitterly: "If you go, I won't *want* you back!"

David paused as if a cold spear had passed through his heart. He closed his hand tight around the golden ring, and reimagineered it to its proper shape. Clutching his father's micro:pen, he walked out without another word.

"I do believe it's going to rain," said Aunt Gwyneth.

And she swung her chair toward the window and smiled.

5.

Meanwhile, upstairs on Floor One Hundred and Eight, a very different kind of meeting was taking place. In the time it had taken David Merriman to hurry downstairs and learn of the death of Mr. Henry, the red firebird, Azkiar, had flown with great haste to Aurielle's room, to inform her, first and foremost, that he'd encountered humans on Floor Forty-Three and . . . Well, he was out of breath before he could deliver the next part of his story and by then Aurielle was flapping her wings in a dire panic and immediately suggesting they sound the alarm and wake the flock. Azkiar sighed. He hopped from foot to foot and fluffed his feathers. Why did Aurielle *never* listen to him all the way through? And she called *him* impatient? He fluttered to her book perch and raised his eyes to the *Tapestry of Isenfier*. Looking at it now made his heart skip a beat. With a snort, he turned his gaze back to the table where Aurielle was still hopping about. There was no need for defensive action, he assured her, because he'd seen the man leave and close the door behind him (he'd tracked back, silently, just to be sure). *Man?* Aurielle's ear tufts widened. Once again Azkiar started to explain and once again the cream bird interrupted him. *The curator?* she asked, paddling her feet. *The curator has discovered the code?* At that point Azkiar almost wished he'd just gone to his nest and slept for a spin. *It was the boy that Rosa calls David,* he said. *Except he isn't a boy anymore. He's grown.*

Now, although this information was undoubtedly of great magnitude, it was not the principal ingredient of Azkiar's report. But before he could get to the *vital* disclosure, Aurielle had turned aside yet again and started doing her pacing thing. She tottered toward the center of the table, feeling the creaks in the joints of her knees. They had not been so good since the onset of the jolt, which supported her belief that she'd aged because of it. She had spotted signs of aging in Azkiar, too. The slightly graying fringes at the tips of his ear tufts. The general lack of shine in his normally glossy feathers. If what he was saying about David was accurate, there was no doubt that a time shift had occurred. But what had caused it? And what did it mean? She paused by the candlesticks, now righted again. Between them, in the traditional nest of sticks where a firebird would place a hatching egg, was the egg that Aurielle had found in the Dead Lands. Since the jolt, it had grown to three times its size and was clearly going to open before long. The tear she had picked up among the daisies had disappeared during the confusion, but Aurielle was certain it had merged with the egg. What else could explain the changes in the clay? The egg had grown a shell, like a firebird egg, the only anatomical difference being that instead of bright colors pulsing around the skin there was a plain white glow coming off the surface. Whatever was inside, it wasn't a firebird. But for now, Aurielle was saying nothing about that.

Azkiar gave an impatient squawk. "Mmm, yes," Aurielle muttered, aware that he needed some kind of response. Quickly, she settled on a course of action. She must meditate on his discovery, she said, which was not the answer Azkiar was waiting for. To her alarm, he flew down to the table and chased her twice around the candlesticks. Meditate? How many hours and spins had she wasted, brooding over this woven cloth, bending his ear tufts with her theories? He collared her against a high-backed chair. Downstairs was visible proof that the tapestry actually *meant* something. If she didn't believe him, she should go and investigate the humans herself. Aurielle gulped and tightened up the muscles of her beak, drawing her beak slightly away from his. Yes, she could do that, she said, but then in a timid voice she added that she still didn't *quite* understand what he was getting at? All right, a human had triggered the door, but that in itself didn't mean very much. Azkiar sighed and turned away. *It's not the door,* he said. *It's David, the man. I've seen him before — and so have you.*

And therein lay the nub of the puzzle. For when Aurielle rightly suggested that Azkiar's senses were becoming addled because she had not been present on Floor Forty-Three when he had encountered the grown-up David, Azkiar twirled his glowing ear tufts and pointed a wing at the *Tapestry of Isenfier*. And at last he was able to finish his report and tell her why he had backed away quickly when he'd cornered David in the fiction department. He pointed to two of the pictured humans: a man, cradling a woman in his arms. *Them,* he said to the stunned Aurielle, *They were the humans I saw on Floor Forty-Three.* They *are David and Rosa.*

6.

I thought you'd be taller."

"*Hmph,*" said David. "Well, I'm quite a lot bigger than you."

"I'm only *nine.*"

"Eight and a bit, actually. I *am* tall anyway. I'm over six feet."

"And very handsome," Eliza Merriman said. She stopped what she was doing and came to sit down at the kitchen table.

"I've got longer hair than you," Penelope said. She pulled a strand of her blond curls down toward her shoulder.

David tilted his head and let his wavy hair fall. "Yes, but mine does that without help."

"Well, mine's springy!" the girl said furiously.

"All right," said Eliza. "It's not a competition. I love

you both — just the way you are. Hair, height, shoe size . . . temperament."

"My shoes are size four."

"Thank you. Duly noted. Look, why don't you make your brother feel at home by making him a nice cup of tea?"

"Make?" said David. The verb was unusual on Co:pern:ica.

His mother waved him silent.

"OK, I'll put the kettle on," Penelope said. Even more unusual.

"Yes, Penny, put the kettle on," her mother echoed, almost singing the words.

The little girl jumped up and ran to the sink.

"She doesn't imagineer very well," said Eliza, keeping her voice low so the child wouldn't hear. "Her fain is there, but she hasn't had the chance to learn how to use it, probably because of the aging process — and the way she was born. We'll talk about it later, when we're alone. Just indulge her for now — and don't mention Harlan."

"She doesn't know about Dad?"

"No. And I want to keep it that way for now."

"Are we having cake as well, Mommy?"

"The best," Eliza said, sending Penelope scurrying to the fridge.

"Oh, Boon!" the girl tutted, almost knocking the katt sideways as she yanked the door open. "Get out of the way!"

Boon muttered and righted his course. He spent a sec or two imperiously licking his tail, then jumped up and settled on David's lap as if his owner had never been away.

"Hey, Penny?" David said, stroking Boon's head. He ran his thumb inside the shell of the imperfect ear.

"Yes?"

"I brought you a present from the librarium."

"Did you?"

"*Mmm.* It's in my room."

"Where? On the bed?"

"I'm not saying. You've got to find it."

Penny put the kettle down and was gone in a flash.

"Well, there goes your cup of tea," Eliza said.

"It's all right, it was deliberate — so we can talk."

Eliza glanced down the arm of the pod that led to David's room. "Don't be silly. She'll be back at any moment."

"No, she won't." He grinned. "I'm moving her present around until I need her to find it."

"You can do that? From a distance?" Eliza stared at him in wonder. "Your father always said you would reinvent the rules of imagineering."

"I need to find him, Mom."

She looked away, trying to resolve her hurt. "David, he killed someone. It was all over the t:com news. If you go after him, I'll lose you both."

David rested his fingers against Boon's neck. "Mr. Henry's death was an accident. Dad made a mistake, but he's not a criminal. Did he explain to you why he was running the experiment?"

Eliza shook her head. "Harlan rarely discussed his work. I'm not even sure I want to know. Eight years of life with my children are gone. I can't forgive him for that. Besides, I wasn't around when he was planning the experiment. I was taken from here, to be trained as an Aunt. I was in the Dead Lands when all this was happening."

"An Aunt? You couldn't become an Aunt in a million spins."

"*Hmm*, truer than you think. According to the one who took me in, I'm too 'wild' to learn their ways. She canceled my program and sent me home. I'm just so relieved that she let me keep Penny. I'm effectively under house arrest, here. I'm being monitored by her. She could turn up at any moment, day or night. If she comes calling, you must give her access. I mean that. No confrontations, OK? Her name is —"

"Aunt Gwyneth."

Eliza looked up. "How did you know?"

"I met her at the librarium. She's the one who exiled Dad. Sounds like she's got a finger in everything."

"She's an Aunt Su:perior. A very powerful influence."

"I don't trust her," David said. He picked up a banafruit and started to peel it.

"David, that kind of talk is going to get you into trouble."

"I can read it in her auma, Mom. The woman's not right."

Once again, Eliza looked away, pained. "I hear what you're saying and I know I should feel great anger toward her. She's torn our family apart, after all. But there was a moment in the Dead Lands when I sensed she had genuine compassion for me."

"Why, because of Penny?"

"No, not Penny. And that's another story anyway. Aunt Gwyneth wasn't there when Penny was born. Neither was your father. I constructed Penny without Harlan's auma — or the patronage of the Aunt. Your sister was birthed from an egg."

"An *egg*?"

"Shush. She's got ears the size of your librarium. I don't understand how this could happen either. Aunt Gwyneth had a few spiky words for it, but I'm not going to repeat them here. You must promise me you won't say a word of this to Penny."

"Of course not. But an egg? Like a firebird, you mean? You found a firebird's egg and imagineered a girl inside it?"

"No. I *made* an egg. Physically. From this." She opened a drawer and plopped a chunk of earth wrapped in paper on the table. "It's called 'clay.' I brought it back from the Dead Lands. David, I saw things in that place. Things way outside the Grand Design. Animals like Boon, different from Boon. And incredible flying creatures."

"Dragons?" he asked, suddenly becoming still.

"Yes." She looked stunned. "You know about dragons?"

He thought back to Rosa and her book. Rosa: What must she be feeling at this moment? "I learned a little in the librarium. Tell me what happened."

Eliza raised her shoulders. "There isn't much to say. One moment I was totally alone in the wilderness and the next, dragons had appeared in the skies all around me. They were transparent, almost ghostly, but they felt very real. I had a powerful instinctive memory of them. That's how I knew what they were. After that, it gets a bit fuzzy, but one of them, a really strange-looking creature, skinny and bony and not nearly as thickly scaled as the rest, guided me to a cave — to shelter. That's where I began to work with the clay. As well as the egg, I made figures of the dragons I'd seen. Aunt Gwyneth destroyed them all before we left. I was lucky to smuggle this lump of clay out."

David pressed his thumb to it, leaving a dent.

"There's something else you should know. They did something, David. The dragons, I mean. They were partly responsible for Penny's birth. One night, I left the egg in a nest of dead wood at the mouth of the cave. A dragon spirit came down and immersed it in flame. It tripled in size and glowed for two days, too hot to go near. As it cooled, it cracked open. And there she was. This tiny human child. Beautiful. Fully formed. And completely unblemished — apart from one thing."

"And what was that?"

Eliza picked at her fingers for a moment. "She had a small dragon's tail."

Tail? David mouthed. He felt his gaze being pulled toward his room. "And is it . . . ?"

"No. It shriveled away almost immediately. It seemed to be absorbed inside her."

"So she's part dragon? She has their auma?"

"Yes. It's possible I do, too. And you know what? The idea fills me with joy. They are amazing creatures. I felt more alive among them than I ever have before."

David finally took a bite of his banafruit, though he seemed to have lost the will to chew. "How did Aunt Gwyneth react?"

"She doesn't know — about the dragon auma. I was planning to tell her. But after she destroyed the sculptures I thought it would be too dangerous."

David nodded. That was a reasonable assumption. "Why destroy the sculptures? I don't understand that."

"She called them a heresy against the Design. And yet I'm convinced she believes in dragons."

"She must have had her suspicions about Penny?"

Eliza nodded. "She almost collapsed when she saw her. The feeling I had was . . . what's that old word? Envious."

"Surely Aunts can have a child like anyone else?"

"Not one like your sister."

"Got it!" cried a voice.

David sat back, tutting. In the midst of the conversation he had let his concentration slip. Penny was pounding back toward the kitchen. He cleared his thoughts and said, "Dad's com:puter. Is it still in his study?"

"Yes, but it's useless. Wiped, I think. The Re:movers came and . . ."

"That's OK," David said, raising his hand.

Penny ran in, breathless. She plonked *Alicia in a Land of Wonder* on the table. "What is it?" she asked.

"A book," David said. "You read it and . . . pictures come into your head."

"What's reading?" Penelope looked blankly at her mother.

David pushed Boon off his lap and stood up. "I'll teach you," he said. He picked up the book and tapped

213

Penny on the head with it. "I'll read it *to* you. Tonight. At bedtime. Would you like that, little sister?"

"Read it now!" she said excitedly.

"Not now," said David. "Too many things to do."

"Oh! Like *what*?"

David smiled and tousled her hair. *Com:puter. Micro:pen. Answers*, he was thinking.

He put the last of the banafruit into his mouth and made his way to his father's study.

7.

Harlan Merriman's private room was just as David had remembered it: pale blue walls (plain, for calmness, his father always said), vertical blinds (half open) at the window, a purple *frondulus* to add a sweet breath of contrast to the blue, a desk in the center of the wood-effect floor. A model of minimalism, the study had always been neat and uncluttered, though the ornamental constructs that usually decorated the alcove shelves were gone — possibly taken by the Re:movers, more likely faded away. A material construct, if uncared for or left untended for a while, would eventually begin to disassemble, and the fain required to make it would be returned to the Higher. An individual's power to imagineer could quickly diminish in this way. In extreme cases it could be lost for good. For that reason, shrewd Co:pern:icans did not create excessive

215

possessions, but managed their fain at comfortable levels and learned only to construct what they needed, when they needed it. A true appreciation of the world around them was one of the greatest Co:pern:ican virtues. Harlan had been a wise exponent of the practice, but had always liked to gather real artifacts, too. David picked up a light gray pebble, the only thing left lying on the shelves. It was shaped like a cloud and had yellow striations across its surface. There was no telling where his father had found it, but that was just part of Harlan's enigma. David dropped it into his pocket, exchanging it for the micro:pen. He went and sat in his father's chair.

"Begin," he said.

The com:screen pinged to life.

"Explore."

The com:puter reported no software available. Wiped, as Eliza had said.

David inserted the pen. It was recognized immediately. As data poured into the molecular drive, he tapped his knees in appreciation. His father, forward-thinking as ever, had downloaded all the run:time software the com:puter needed onto the pen. It wasn't long before the machine was up to full efficiency. As it reached that status, a window opened and Harlan Merriman's face appeared on the screen.

"One to one," David said. The sound of Harlan's voice would now be digitally reshaped so that it fell only within David's envelope of hearing.

In a whisper, the image of his father said, "David, if you're watching this, then I managed to reach you before they tracked me down. I didn't have long to make this :com, so if I've missed anything or I'm repeating what I've already told you, forgive me.

"There are two films on the drive. One is of you in a sleep facility at Thorren Strømberg's therapy center. We took you there when you were twelve spins old because you were experiencing nightmares you couldn't recall the next day. You were sent to the librarium on Thorren's advice. He did it to protect you. He's a good man, David. Trustworthy. Clever. He's gone into hiding to avoid the Aunts. He didn't betray me; I asked him to do this because he was present when the second film was shot. That was done at my lab, where we were trying to recreate the conditions of your dreams. You'll know about the time distortion by now. I haven't had time to analyze the footage, but I believe that whatever caused the quake is not of this world.

You possess extraordinary talents, David. Something, somewhere, knows it and wants to track you down. I don't know why. Watch the film — I can hardly stop you now — but if anything becomes apparent, I beg you not to attempt anything. Find Strømberg. Show him. Take it to the Higher. And please, don't come looking for me. They'll send me to the Dead Lands. You could spend an eternity trying to find me. I want you instead to take care of your mother. But most of all, take care of yourself."

The window closed. Without waiting for a verbal command, the com:puter began to play the film *Project Forty-Two*. David sat forward. For the first time he saw what his father had seen — the disturbed sleep, the rift, the firebirds coming. But what made him tilt forward on the edge of his chair was the sight of himself morphing into . . .

"Reverse twenty secs," he said. "Replay till command."

The section played over and over. David sat back again, shaking his head. What was happening to him? What was he becoming? What kind of creature had curving yellow teeth and brown eyes that slanted back like that? And what was that creature attempting to fight? A burst of laughter distracted his thoughts. Glancing sideways, he saw Penny in the garden, playing with Boon. Penny, who looked just as human as he did. If his sister had dragon auma inside her, was it possible that he had something unusual as well? *I saw things in that place. Things way outside the Grand Design. Animals like Boon, different from Boon.* His mother's words tripped through his head again. What if the animal he'd become in his dreams was once alive and well in the Dead Lands? He swung his chair back to the screen again. "Stop. Next film." The com:puter cleared the image. Up instead came the darker environment of Harlan Merriman's laboratory. David recognized his father and Thorren Strømberg and guessed that the third man was Bernard Brotherton, the tech:nician who had visited his father at home several times. The camera was pointed at the horseshoe of lights, giving roughly the same view that the scientists had from their observation platform. Their conversation was hard to pick out, but David heard his father make a bold announcement before he activated the horseshoe device. *Behold the universe in microcosm.*

At first, there was nothing. No obvious effect. Then the airspace circumscribed by the frame of the shoe began to stretch and fold, and crackling bolts of elec:trical energy emerged from nodes all around its inner surface. Where they met, at the center of the airspace, a vertical shimmering line appeared, just like the one in David's dream. The two scientists briefly congratulated each other. Then David saw Bernard Brotherton turn to the panel of controls beside him and say something back to Harlan. The tech:nician shook his head. He sounded troubled. But Harlan half-raised a hand, clearly indicating that the procedure was not to be halted yet. Strømberg was pointing to the shimmer at the same time, which was bulging as though it were about to split open. Suddenly, a firebird came into the picture. It had flown through the construct that was the laboratory wall and had positioned itself right behind the horseshoe. It wasn't one that David recognized, but it had clearly come to do the same job as before: seal up the shimmer and go. He saw his father leave the observation platform, frantically waving his hands in an effort to stop the bird interrupting. The bird widened its nostrils and produced a jet of fire. An unseen wave of energy was expelled from the shimmer in all directions. The result was dramatic. The firebird and all three men were catapulted as far from the pulse as the walls of the laboratory would allow. Likewise, the horseshoe and the com:puters controlling it were torn apart or smashed against anything solid. The shimmer disappeared to a fine point, as if it had been sucked into a hole in space. A sec later, the camera flickered and gave out. The film stopped.

But there was something, just before the end of it, that aroused David's curiosity and made him call again for a slower replay. He thought he had seen a blemish on the film. A small blip of blackness just before the pulse. A camera glitch perhaps? He asked the com:puter to zoom in and play back the end sequence, showing it in single frames. Over the course of five of those frames he noticed a strange sequence of events. The firebird's flame, far from being blown well away from the shimmer, had been sucked right into it and something else had emerged in its place. It looked like a puff of black smoke, nothing more. Further zooming proved no help. And even when David lassoed the "smoke" with a drawing tool, isolated it from its background, and asked the com:puter to analyze the structure, the software had no answers for him.

And yet a possible answer was about to emerge from a most unlikely source. As David swung back in his chair, tapping his toes and pondering what he'd seen, there was a knock at the window. It was Penny, of course. She was cupping her face and trying to stare through the half-open blinds. Not wanting her to see the images he'd found, David thought about blanking the screen, but decided instead to tease her a little by reimagineering the blinds in a different position. As she moved to try to find a clearer view, he partially frosted the glass.

Her fist came up and she knocked again. In a muffled voice she shouted, "David, come here. I've got something to show you."

"Busy," he shouted back. He blanked the screen anyway. "Close down," he said to the com:puter.

"Boon chased a firebird! Look, it dropped this."

David glanced at the waving hand. In it was a feather. A pure black feather. Puzzled, he rose up and opened the window.

Penny waggled the feather proudly. "It was on the fence. Boon jumped for it and it flew away."

David glanced around the gardenaria. Everything was calm. "A black firebird?"

"Yes!"

"Did you see where it went?"

She shook her head. "It was fast." She let him take the feather. "Good, isn't it?"

David nodded. "It's very interesting, Penny."

"I'm going to put it under my pillow."

"Put what under your pillow?" Eliza had just stepped into the gardenaria.

"My feather," said Penny, taking it back.

Her mother's face crumpled up in a frown. "Where did you get that?"

"From a firebird, silly," Penny said a little rudely, annoyed at having to repeat herself.

"But there are no black firebirds on Co:pern:ica." Eliza looked blankly at her daughter.

"There are now," David muttered. And he closed the window.

And Penny shrugged happily and ran to her room.

8.

Although he would have liked to dwell a while longer on why a black firebird had appeared in the gardenaria (or indeed appeared at all), David abandoned the mystery just then in favor of reintroducing himself to some kind of home life. He spent the rest of that day with his mother and Penny, either walking in the woodland constructs near their pod, or playing with Boon, or looking through dozens of digi:grafs of himself when he was Penny's age (carefully sifted to avoid shots of Harlan). Only when Penny's bedtime came around did he get the chance to speak to his mother again privately. And it was she who began the conversation.

"You're troubled, aren't you?"

They were in the gardenaria, under the setting sun, imagineering possibilities for Eliza's rockery. The horrible fungus Aunt Gwyneth had introduced had been not-so-mysteriously de:constructed. In its place Eliza had tried a variety of rocks, any number of different plants, a few ornaments, and a hanging light, though none of them seemed to fit her overall concept. Eventually, David solved the conundrum by imagineering a small arched door at the base of the stones, which, he said, would give Boon the impression that something actually lived in the mound. Hours of fun could be had, he suggested, watching Boon waiting for the door to open.

Eliza punched his arm in jest. "You are horrible to that katt. All the same, it's a sweet idea. Thank you." She pulled him closer and kissed his cheek. "You haven't answered my question: What's bothering you?"

"I've seen a film that was taken during my time at the therapy center."

"Film . . . ? How?"

"Dad gave me a micro:pen when he was arrested. Don't worry, it's in a safe place."

Eliza nodded. She crouched down and tended the flowers. "What was on this film?"

"Me, turning into some kind of animal." He described it for her. "I don't know what it is or what it means, but there are only two places that might hold the answers. And as you'll disapprove of me going to the Dead Lands, it will have to be the librarium. I need to go back there, Mom."

"So soon?"

David shrugged and ran his hand over Boon (who had just stretched out near the rockery door). "In a day or two maybe. It never really occurred to me until now that I could use the books as a resource. And I feel very bad about walking out on Rosa."

"The brash girl? Is she still there?"

"*Mmm.* Not much of a girl anymore. She's very . . . well, grown-up, I suppose. When I left the librarium I had to get out quickly and keep my auma detached, in case Aunt Gwyneth found the micro:pen. I couldn't tell Rosa. She was pretty hurt, Mom."

"You like her, don't you?"

"Hard not to, really."

"Will you bring her here?"

David sighed and pulled a flower stalk through his fingers. "She's not allowed to leave the librarium."

"Is she going to take over from Mr. Henry?"

"I don't know. She'd be the obvious choice."

"Hey!" a voice called.

David turned and saw Penny at her bedroom window.

"Are you coming?" she shouted.

"In a minit," he shouted back. He rubbed his mother's arm. "Look, I don't have to stay away long. I just want to find out what I can about the dream and make sure Rosa's all right."

Eliza gave him a knowing smile. "You'll stay," she said. "You miss her already." She reached over and pushed her hand through his hair, helping it fall toward his shoulder. "You're everything I ever expected of you, David. If you care for this girl, I'd want you to do your best for her. But be a good brother to Penny as well. She's going to miss you just as much."

He took hold of his mother's hand and kissed it. "I'll stay until I've finished the book."

"Books — whatever happened to them?" she mused. "What is it, again, this thing you're going to read to her?"

He rose up and took a step toward the house. "A story — from Floor Forty-Three."

When he got to the bedroom, Penny was sitting up in bed in her pajamas, the book already open in her hands.

"I've been looking at the pictures," she said excitedly. "There's a girl in it. She looks like me."

"That's Alicia. She doesn't look a bit like you. She's got more hair, for a start."

"Mine will *grow*. What's she wearing? Over her dress?"

David took the book from her and turned it around. "I think it's called a 'pinafore.'"

"I like it," Penny said. "She wears ankle boots as well."

"She does," said David, remembering someone else who was never seen out of them. He sat down on the edge of the mattress and turned to the first page of text. "Right. Are you ready?"

"Yes!"

"*Chapter one.*"

"What's that?"

"What's what?"

"Chapter one."

David flicked his eyes sideways. "Chapter one is the start of the story. Books are split up into chunks, called 'chapters.'"

"Oh. When will I see the pictures in my head?"

"When you stop asking questions, and listen."

"OK," she chirped, and set her shoulders straight.

"Chapter one. Alicia was in a bad mood —"

"Why?"

David paused and drummed his fingers over the page. "Well, if she's anything like me, she gets annoyed at people who interrupt while she's trying to *read*."

"Sorry," Penny whispered, pulling in her lips. "Is Alicia reading to someone, then?"

Stay calm, thought David. *She'll get used to it in a minit.* He read on a few lines and summarized the text. "No. She's fed up because her sister won't play a game with her and now she's wondering whether to chase a white rabbit across a field."

"What's a rabbit?"

OK, that is *a fair question,* he thought. He turned the book around and showed her a black-and-white illustration of a rabbit in a waistcoat looking at a pocket-watch.

"I've never seen a rabbit before."

"No, me neither," he said. Were they imagineered? he wondered. Or did they actually exist at the time the book was written? If so — what happened to them?

"I like its ears," said Penny. "What's it doing?"

"Checking the time."

"Doesn't it have a :com?"

David shook his head. "The book is very old. In those days, people carried devices called 'watches' and read the time from them." He remembered Mr. Henry doing just that, and once again that reminded him, poignantly, of Rosa. He read a little more. *"Odd though it was to see a rabbit with a timepiece, Alicia decided that she would give chase. She dashed across the field and was just in time to see the rabbit skid to a halt beside two doors in the side of a grassy hill."*

"Show me!" Penny cried.

"There isn't an illustration for that," David said. "The idea is you see it in your mind."

Penny drew her eyes down into a frown.

"I can see it," he said. "The doors are made of panels, some of which have holes that you can't quite see through. And they don't have handles but they do have knockers shaped like . . ."

"Like what?" Penny prompted.

Like dragons, David wanted to say, though there was nothing about them in the book.

"Show me," Penny said again, sitting forward.

"I just told you, there aren't any pictures for this."

"Show me *your* pictures. Mom says you imagineer really well."

David thought about it. "OK, that could work. But you have to join in."

Penny sat up, knocking her fists together. "Are we going to commingle?"

"Well, we can try."

"Great!" She closed her eyes and started to hum.

"Penny, what are you doing?"

"Commingling," she said.

"You don't have to hum." He laughed. "You just need to focus your fain. Watch." And right before his sister's eyes, a perfect image of a worried white rabbit floated into view.

"*Hhh!*" Penny gasped.

"This is what makes reading fun," said David. "Building pictures in here." He tapped the side of her head. "You don't need much fain to keep them there, just patience and the right words to guide you. See if you can imagineer Alicia."

"OK," she said. Her eyebrows came together in a knot of concentration.

The result made David smile. Floating beside the rabbit now were a pair of boots, minus a body. The rabbit stared down at them and jumped in surprise. David glanced at the book. That piece of action wasn't described in the text. Interestingly, his imagineered character was acting on its own behalf.

"Did it work?" said Penny. Her eyes blinked open. Right away, her shoulders sagged in disappointment.

"You only got the boots because that's what you most desired," David said. "Think about Alicia — all of her. She doesn't have to be like she is in the book. It's how you picture her yourself that matters."

So Penny tried again. After a stuttering start, Alicia's body grew upward out of her footwear. Penny had constructed her the way she was drawn, except for one thing: the color of her hair.

"Well done," David said (adding in an arm that Penny had missed). "Why the red hair?" The white rabbit, he noticed, had picked up a few strands to admire it.

"When I grow up I want hair like Mom's." Penny's, at the moment, was a grainy blond.

David nodded and imagineered the rest of the scene: the doors in the hill; more hills fading to nothing behind them. "'Oh dear,'" he read, in the character of the rabbit. (It began to hop about in front of the doors.)

" 'I'm late! I'm late! And I don't know which door I'm supposed to take!' "

Penny giggled. "Is Alicia going to help him?"

"*Mmm,*" said David, reading on. "*Alicia stepped forward. She spoke politely, with her hands behind her back. 'Why don't you take this door?' she said, pointing to the one on the left. Rather helpfully, a sign appeared upon it saying 'THIS.' "*

"I can see it." Penny laughed. It was hanging off the knocker by a piece of string.

David ran his finger down the text and continued. "*The rabbit, who was still in a fluster, patted his brow with a handkerchief. 'Are you sure you don't mean that door?' he asked, aiming his paw at the door on the right. A sign saying 'THAT' had now appeared there. 'No, I'm quite sure I meant* that *door,' Alicia said, still pointing to her original choice. The rabbit danced from foot to foot. 'But that's THIS,' he argued, scratching his nose. 'I don't think you know what you mean at all. You don't know your THIS from your THAT in my opinion.' Hearing this (or was it that?), Alicia stamped her foot. 'Oh!' she exclaimed. 'I've had quite enough of this — or do I mean that?' And to simplify matters, she marched up to both doors and turned the signs over. Immediately, the doors disappeared."*

"Hhh!" gasped Penny, watching them go. "Now what's going to happen? The rabbit can't get in without a door."

"'Now look what you've done!'" David read on. *"The rabbit was furious. His whiskery white cheeks were growing quite pink."*

"He's crossing his ears, look," Penny said, laughing.

"'Now we'll have to use the OTHER door,' the rabbit said. 'And I don't know WHERE that goes to.' Alicia played with a strand of her hair. 'Where is the other door?' she asked. The rabbit started to run again. 'On the OTHER side of the hill, of course.'"

Penny clapped as the rabbit hurried up the hill and over it. Once again, Alicia went in pursuit. But as they began to come down the other side, the plain grass gave way to clustered stones with fine plants growing in between them. The characters stumbled to the bottom and looked back at the slope as they dusted themselves off. Penny sat up in surprise. "That's Mom's rockery," she said.

Not only that, David noticed, but Alicia and the rabbit were standing in front of the arched door he had imagineered there. He closed the book softly.

"Are we finished?" asked Penny.

"This part isn't in the book," said David. "Shall we see what happens if we open the door?"

"Yes," said Penny, breathy with excitement.

So, after a bit of polite bowing and a few "After you's" and "No, after you's," Alicia stepped forward and opened the door. Into the rockery the characters went. Immediately, they slipped and lost their footing and both began to tumble down a deep, dark well (it made Penny feel a little queasy to watch it). After what seemed like a very long fall, they landed with a bump (thankfully not a splash, for the well was perfectly dry) at the end of a rather spooky-looking tunnel. Neither character was hurt, and the rabbit had already set off at tremendous speed toward a window at the far end of the tunnel. Alicia ran after him as fast as her boots would take her. She caught up very quickly but did not overtake him, and for a time it seemed there was no time at all, and that the characters were running but not really moving. Then, whether it was a jolt of David's imagination or whether it was real or whether this land of new wonders they had entered had finally decided to make itself known to them, Alicia and the rabbit arrived at the window and peered through it.

Penny and David leaned forward instinctively, to see what their characters could see. It was a bedroom, not at all unlike their mother's, but the common features (the bed, the wardrobes, etc.) were something of a blur in the background. Alicia and the rabbit were focused instead on a dressing table right in front of them. They were standing behind the table, looking through its mirror.

"Look . . . ," said Penny, her mouth falling open. She pointed, just like Alicia was doing.

On the table were three small creatures, all of which seemed to be solid sculptures, though David suspected they were actually quite real. Two of them were dragons, quite kindly looking and nothing like the pictures he'd seen in the books or on the ceilings of the librarium, though definitely cast in the dragon image. They had their eyes closed and were holding paws, as if they were waiting for something to happen. And yet, intriguing as these sculptures were, it was the third one that raised David's pulse rate a little. Standing just in front of the dragons was an elegant creature he had never seen before and yet he somehow felt he ought to recognize. In general body shape it was not unlike Boon, though its legs and neck were very much longer and its head was far more graceful than the katt's. The creature was white all over and did not have a blade of hair upon it, except for a mane down the back of its neck and an equally impressive tail. What really drew David's attention, however, was the twisting horn that grew straight out of the animal's forehead. He could see a familiar pattern on it — a wavy three-lined mark, spiraling outward from its base and repeating all the way up to the tip. He jerked back with a sudden realization. It was the code he'd used in the librarium to open the door to Floor Forty-Three, the one that translated in dragontongue as "sometimes."

"Where is this?" said Penny. "What are we looking at?"

"Another world," David muttered, thinking about the time rift and his father's words about other dimensions and a force too powerful for David to control. Then, as if a conduit had somehow opened, the image of the black firebird entered his mind and he felt a tremendous pressure in his head. He fell sideways, holding his hands to his temples. The book slid off his lap and clattered to the floor. His body began to shake as if it were no longer his to control.

In that instant, Penny screamed.

Alicia and the rabbit had both turned around and were peering back down the tunnel. Even though the light was poor, something could be seen flying at tremendous speed toward them. Bare teeth. Fearsome talons. A savage eye, perhaps. There was no real time for detail. The thing was coming with an awful screech and clearly intended to do them harm.

"David, stop it!" Penny wailed. She was backing up against her headboard as Alicia was backing up against the mirror.

Then, in a scene that truly was something from a land of wonder, the white horned creature tilted its head and a bolt of violet light passed through the mirror. It struck not the beast, but the shuddering rabbit. Right away, the rabbit fell down and turned himself into something new. A strapping white animal with thickset paws and a body so burly that it almost filled the width of the tunnel. He reared up and flashed his paws at the attacker, which hovered to a halt in front of this creation, spitting and hissing and fearful and *dark*. And there the chapter ended and the pictures went away.

For the door to Penny's room had suddenly burst open and David had been pulled off the bed onto the floor, with a pair of strong hands cradled around his head.

"Let it go. Let it go," the intruder was saying.

And Penny was squealing, "Who are you? Who are you?"

And then Eliza Merriman was there as well, with calming gestures and reassuring words. "Penny, it's all right. He won't harm David. He's a friend."

And the man held doggedly on to her brother until the convulsions had ceased and he was still. Only then did the stranger speak to the girl. "Forgive me, Penny. I had no time to introduce myself."

"Who *are* you?" she said again, drawing up her blanket.

"I'm a counselor — and an outlaw," he said with great charm. "My name is Thorren Strømberg."

9.

As a result of the incident in Penny's room, David once again fell into a deep, slow sleep, which this time lasted for approximately two days. He awoke, peacefully, in his bedroom, with his anxious mother in a chair at his side and Boon purring softly on the bed, at his feet.

Eliza was over him at once, feeling his forehead and gripping his hands. "Oh, thank goodness. Are you all right? How do you feel? I've been so worried."

"I feel fine," he said, though he looked a little bleary. He pushed himself upright against a stack of pillows. His mother immediately imagineered another.

"How long have I been . . . ?"

"Two days." She poured a glass of water. He drank it down in one swallow.

"Where's Penny?"

"Upstairs."

"She OK?"

"She's fine. Just a little shaken by what she saw. How much do you remember?"

David frowned and shook his head. "I was reading. That's it. Everything else is . . . a blur."

"Well, Penny remembers," his mother said. "But she refuses to talk about it to anyone but you. Were you aware that Counselor Strømberg was here?"

"Strømberg? How?"

"He'd been tracking the movements of the firebird you saw."

"The black one?"

"Yes. He burst in when he heard Penny screaming. It was he who calmed your auma and carried you to bed. He helped Penny, too, before he left."

"Is he coming back?"

"No. Not here. He says it's too dangerous for him to stay in one place for too long. He wants you to meet him on Bushley Common."

"When?"

"Any evening. Just turn up. He'll find you, he says."

David glanced at the sky. Still light, but the dusk was closing in. He threw off his covers and swept out of bed.

"David, wait."

He paused, one sock half on.

"Please think about this. They might be watching you."

"The Aunts?"

"Them or their agents. If you go to meet Strømberg, you'll be aiding a fugitive. That might be all they're waiting for — enough reason to send you the way of your father."

David continued to dress. "If I don't go, I'll never know what this is all about."

Eliza gripped his arm and made him look at her. "It's about them keeping control. That's the way it's always been. The Higher. The Aunts. The Grand Design. Your ec:centricity frightens them."

"Then that's how I'll defend myself from them," he said. And he pulled on his other sock.

Ten minits later he was in the kitchen when Penny came in and leaned back against the door frame. She was wearing a pair of new red boots.

"Like them?" she asked, stretching out a foot. "Mom imagineered them while you were asleep."

"They suit you," he said. Laces untied, just like Rosa's. His heart pinged.

Penny held his gaze a moment and waited. "You don't remember, do you?"

"Remember what?"

She marched across the floor and dropped *Alicia in the Land of Wonder* on the table.

He blinked a couple of times and picked it up. *Oh, yes. The book. Alicia wore boots.*

Penny pulled out a chair. She sat down with one foot tucked beneath her. "You were reading this to me and showing me the characters having an adventure. Alicia and the rabbit went down a tunnel and looked through a mirror at another world."

"There were dragons," David muttered, beginning to remember.

"There were lots of things," Penny said. "Were you the rabbit?"

"Sorry?"

"I was being Alicia. Were *you* being the rabbit?"

"Probably," he said, not sure where this was going.

"In that case, you were this as well." From her (pinafore) pocket, she unfolded a piece of paper and smoothed it out on her knee. She put it on the table for him to see. "That's what the rabbit turned into."

David picked it up and carried it around the kitchen. "You drew this?"

"Yes."

"Have you shown it to Mom?"

"Of course not, silly. What *is* that creature? I've looked, but it's not in the book."

"I don't know," he said quietly, folding the paper. Even though the drawing was childish and sketchy, there was enough basic detail to convince him that this was what he'd almost morphed into in the therapy center. "Can I keep this, Penny?"

She nodded. "If I can keep the book."

"Are you sure you want to?"

"Mom says you're going away. She says she'll finish the story with me. I don't think her version will be *quite* as scary as yours."

"No, it won't," he said, and tousled her hair. "I'm sorry I frightened you. Look after Mom for me. I have to go."

But as he turned toward the door she suddenly said, "I don't want this anymore."

He stopped and looked back. She had put her black feather down on the table and was slowly pushing it toward him. "In the tunnel, you were fighting something."

"The firebird you saw?"

She lifted her shoulders. "It was like a firebird, but ugly. Horrible."

David picked up the feather and drew it through his fingers, feeling its sleekness against his skin. "I'll look out for it," he said. "And so will Boon." The katt had just jumped onto Penny's lap.

David looked at her, waiting for an explanation. "That's two things protecting us, then," she said.

"Mom's going to make us a dragon."

Bushley Common was one of only three places in the district surrounding the Merrimans' home that was still considered "real" (sometimes called "natural"). It was a long, sprawling piece of grassland, broken up by walkways and clusters of trees. Although it was a beautiful, undisturbed place, most citizens of Co:pern:ica Central avoided it. It was generally believed that to be seen walking in the "undeveloped" countryside was indicative of a desire to think introspectively. And that could attract the attentions of an Aunt. Or worse, a Re:mover.

So it seemed an odd place for a rendezvous, at first. But a plentiful amount of open space meant that conversations would not be overheard. And there was time enough to see any agents approaching. With those thoughts in mind, David chose a bench in the center of the common, shaded by one small tree. It was raining lightly and a mist was descending in grubby gray patches, but visibility was still good. He sat down and waited.

The first thing to approach him though was not Thorren Strømberg, but a rather bedraggled black-and-white katt. Herein lay a peculiar irony. It was illegal to imagineer any structure upon the common, yet it was home to many stray katts. They survived by procuring the attention of passersby. One kind sweep of the hand could keep a katt constructed for several days, though many perished due to the sheer lack of visitors. This one was bold enough to find its way onto David's lap and soak up enough fuss to keep it maintained for another spin at least. David was idly tuning in to its grateful purr when footsteps along the path to his right announced the arrival of Thorren Strømberg. The counselor sat down without looking at him. "How are you?" he asked.

"Wide awake," said David, glancing over both shoulders. No sign of anyone behind them.

Strømberg noticed the katt and smiled. "I'm glad to hear it." He uncapped a bottle of water and drank. For a man on the run, he looked in good shape.

"Do you have any news about my father?"

The shock of blond hair moved freely in denial. "Once you're in the Dead Lands, you're pretty much cut off."

"Will he survive there?"

Strømberg gave a confident nod. "Knowing your father, he'll probably thrive. It's only the clever ones, those who question the way we live, who are sent into the wilderness. Some say it's a better, more natural way of life, though few are brought back to tell the tale. You hear rumors now and then that an uprising might spring from there, but the real unease is developing here."

"What do you mean?"

"This is a failing society, David. I could talk all day about the negative aspects of imagineering, how it's left

247

our minds lazy and stripped us of all sense of pride and ambition — but that's not the real issue. There's a whisper spreading among those who know that the Aunts are plotting to overthrow the Higher."

David narrowed his gaze. "But no one really knows what the Higher are, do they? I was always taught that their fain is so powerful that they can cloak themselves and still maintain the Design. How can you conquer what you can't find?"

Strømberg ran his thumb down the katt's right ear. "Listen to me carefully, and don't repeat this to anyone else: Mr. Henry believed that the Higher are based in the Bushley librarium. He thought they might operate through the firebirds."

"What?" David leaned so far forward that the katt was almost squashed against his knees. It hissed (rather loudly) but didn't jump off.

"I know it sounds odd," Strømberg said, looking off into the middle distance. "But I've seen enough in that building to convince me it's plausible. It's a place of great mystery, that no one on Co:pern:ica has managed to resolve — until now."

David threw him a quizzical look.

"I saw the storybook you were reading to Penny. That could only have come from the upper floors. Mr. Henry and I have been trying to get up there for twenty spins or more. You managed it in a matter of weeks. How?"

David steepled his fingers just below his nose. There were katt hairs on them. He blew them aside. "There was a code in a dragon book Rosa showed me."

"The one that was dropped on your chest while you slept?"

"You know about that?"

"Yes. From Rosa. Tell me about the code."

"When you flicked through the corners of the book it formed a sign. When I saw it, I could read it — in dragontongue. *Ow!*" David glared at the katt. For some reason, it had just dug its claws into his thigh. He unhooked the offending paw and said, "We only got as far as Floor Forty-Three before the firebird that flamed me chased us out. I took the storybook as proof for Mr. Henry. The rest you probably know."

Strømberg rocked forward on the bench a little. When he spoke again his voice was bristling with urgency. "I want you to go back to the librarium as soon as you can and ask Rosa to show you *The Book of Agawin*. It's hidden. But she'll know where to find it."

"Agawin? What's that?"

"There's no time to explain. The book is full of symbols. Read them if you can, then send for me. And, David, be careful. That book is the oldest thing in the building. We think it might tell the whole history of Co:pern:ica — and of dragons."

It was growing cold now and the mist was thickening. David thrust his hands into his jacket pockets and found Penny's "gifts" in them. He took out the drawing. "What do you make of that?"

Strømberg ran his fingers over the paper. "Where did you get this?"

"From Penny. She drew it. I was imagineering story characters for her and my adopted character turned into that creature. It was fighting a grotesque version of whatever dropped this." He brought out the feather.

Strømberg turned it between his hands. "I saw a black firebird flying away from the debris of your father's experiment. I traced it here on a hunch that it might be looking for you. You're saying it broke into your consciousness — a firebird?"

David nodded. "Dad left me a film of what happened in the lab. I studied it carefully on his com:puter. I think something came through the time rift. Something with powerful fain that invaded a normal-colored firebird and turned it black."

"Then we must be careful," Strømberg said. "If that's correct, we're dealing with an unknown threat as well as the Aunts. There's no time to lose. Get to the librarium — tonight, if you can. Hide there if you need to. And find that book."

"What about you?"

"Don't worry about me. I won't be far away. When you need me, I'll be there. Just use your fain." The counselor stood up and offered his hand.

David shook it firmly. "Is there any chance you can find out where they took my father?"

"I'll work on it," Strømberg promised. "Go carefully, David." And with that he pulled up his collar and walked into the mist.

As David watched him go, he thought about calling a taxicar. But remembering he shouldn't use his fain on the common, he stood up, placed the katt on the bench, and got ready to walk in the opposite direction.

He had taken only two short strides when he was stopped by a tiny *meow*. The katt had settled in a moody huddle with its paws tucked underneath itself, staring straight ahead in that odd glazed fashion so familiar to their kind. The ends of its fur were glistening with moisture.

"Sorry," David said. "Can't take you with me. You won't be appreciated where I'm going." He waved good-bye and set off along the path.

With a soft thump of paws the katt jumped down and trotted up beside him.

"No," David said. He picked it up and carried it back to the bench. "You *mustn't* follow me. You'll frighten the birds. You have to stay here. Behave." He plonked it down again and wagged a finger, then hurried off at twice his previous pace.

He was swallowed up in the mist before the katt moved again. "Well, of course I'll frighten the birds," it said. But by then David was out of earshot. And the katt had morphed into its true shape.

The Aunt Su:perior.

Gwyneth.

10.

Around the same time that David was meeting Penny and trying to settle in again at home, Rosa was discovering the harsh reality of life in the Bushley librarium without him. Her keepers, the twin Aunts Primrose and Petunia, took not a shred of interest in her and didn't care if she organized the books or not. What mattered to them was cleanliness. For this reason, they did want the books picked up, but only so the floors could be cleared for scrubbing. Within hours of David's departure, Rosa found herself down on her knees with a bucket of water and a dirty brush, preparing a room that the Aunts could sleep in. She was made to go over it three times at least, until Aunt Primrose was satisfied. As if that wasn't enough, she complained endlessly about the cold. There were shutters on some of the windows, of course, but Mr. Henry had never wanted them closed, and neither David nor Rosa had ever experienced what the curator affectionately called "goose bumps" on their skin. (Strangely, they never did question the etymology of this word.) But Aunt Primrose was different. On the first day, she imagineered a thick gray coat and a scarf that wrapped three times around her neck and overflowed down her starchy back. Maroon gloves came next, to match her crooked bow tie. Then a hat with button-down flaps for the ears. And she insisted that the window of the room be blocked. Not closed. Blocked. To Rosa's annoyance there were no shutters on the window in the room they had chosen, the one that she had so diligently cleaned. Yet when she offered to prepare the Aunts a better room, one with tight-fitting shutters and a lovely view of the daisy fields, which even had a southerly aspect to it (to pick up the heat of the sun in the mornings), they refused and said they would stay where they were, near the ground floor, well away from "those irritating birds." And when Rosa rather rashly stamped her foot and asked, "What, pray, should I block the window with?" the twins exchanged a wicked smile. "The books," they said in chilling unison. "The books."

With no choice but to do as she was told, Rosa set

about piling books into the window space to form a barrier against the wind. (This also shut out the light, though both Aunts favored imagineered lighting anyway.) With every book she added, Rosa could feel the building resisting. It would move slightly and make the books topple, just as she was completing a stack. Or when she turned her back in search of a book she was sure would fit into a particular space, she would return to find the dimensions of the hole compressed. Only when she cried out, "Stop it! Stop it! I don't want this any more than you do!" did it give in and let her complete her task. Even then there were gaps and the Aunts complained of drafts. "I can't help that," Rosa protested. The books alone were never going to make for a perfect fit. But Aunt Primrose had a most hideous solution. The nasty old woman did no more than snatch up a book, tear out several pages, and stuff the gaps at the window with crumpled paper. Rosa ran from the room in tears, the Aunts' laughter chasing her through the building.

In time, the twins did tire of such cruelty and began to leave Rosa to her own devices. She could be alone, she was told, but she could not hide. This she knew all too well, of course. She remembered the ease with which Aunt Gwyneth had tracked her down that time on Floor Forty-Two.

Oh, Floor Forty-Two. On several occasions, Rosa had stood outside the door there, trying in vain to replicate the dragontongue David had used to open it. If there was any kind of sanctuary from this madness, it was going to be found higher up the building, surely? But the door just would not open for her. And fearful that the Aunts would catch her there and quiz her and maybe breach the upper floors themselves (the idea simply mortified her), she gave up and confined herself to her own company. Hours she spent, barefoot in a window recess, knees drawn up to her elegant chin, staring helplessly at the horizon, always wondering if she dared run away, not knowing where she would go to if she did, knowing in her heart that the building needed her, remembering her happiness when she was twelve, remembering Mr. Henry and the undemanding joy of ordering the books, remembering the rain that had ceased to fall ever since David had gone away.

She tried very hard not to think about David.

It truly was a miserable time, compounded by the feeling that even Runcey had deserted her. She had not seen the lovely green firebird for days and had started to wonder if the birds had actually abandoned the aerie following the death of Mr. Henry. But this was not so. Unbeknownst to Rosa, Runcey *had* been to see her. What's more, he had not come alone. Aleron (to give him his proper name), along with Aurielle and the grumpy Azkiar, had visited her hammock one night during sleep. They were there to verify Azkiar's claim that an image of Rosa was stitched on the *Tapestry of Isenfier.*

By the light of the strong Co:pern:ican moon, they had examined and measured and recorded her face. When Aurielle saw the changes in Rosa, she was stunned. Yet, she was not convinced. For of the two humans shown on that part of the tapestry, the woman's features were the harder to distinguish. In the picture, "David and Rosa" were kneeling and he was holding her head to his chest, protecting her from the Shadow of Ix. Only half the woman's face could truly be seen. But the hair, the eyes, the shape of the head, the long slender arms. It did look like a positive match. There was only one problem. *The mark,* Aurielle said to the other two birds. *She doesn't have the sign of Agawin on her arm.* In the tapestry, the three-lined mark (the one Rosa had discovered in the dragon book) was clearly visible on the girl's arm. It was one of the most potent signs on the whole picture. For it not to be present on Rosa's skin left serious holes in Azkiar's theory. Azkiar puffed his feathers out and said Aurielle was simply making excuses. The humans had gotten through the door, he reminded her. But Aurielle refused to be swayed. *The girl is inconclusive,* she said. *The only way to be sure is to check on the grown-up David as well.*

But that would not be easy now that David had left. Yes, they could seek him out well enough; few humans (construct or real) possessed an auma trail like his. But if they went to him, together, in a less secure environment, it might cause problems. Aurielle drummed her claws in annoyance. *Why,* she wanted to know, *was the boy dismissed from the building in the first place when the books had clearly warmed to him so?* Aleron, who'd been carefully observing the situation downstairs, said it was the work of Aunts, two of whom had been installed in place of the old curator. Azkiar made a sound like Aurielle's knee joints. He didn't like Aunts. He'd crossed paths with them before. *They're going to be trouble,* he said. Aurielle, looking at the moon through Rosa's window, agreed. Over the last few days it had not been difficult to sense a decline in the general intensity of auma in the aerie. Some of it was due to the loss of the curator, though his spirit still floated over the daisies. But there was also a crippling moodiness present that seemed to be leaching right out of the stones. And in all this time, the rain had not fallen. And that was very wrong indeed.

Aurielle folded her wings and assessed the situation. A mysterious time shift, two intriguing humans, and an egg that was not of the firebirds' making. And still no one had seen Aubrey. She glanced at the sleeping Rosa. And here was plausible evidence that the story of the Isenfier tapestry was unfolding. Something must be done. Guidance must be sought. There was nothing else for it.

She must speak with the Higher.

11.

Up a hundred floors she flew that night. A hundred? Well, that was just a token number. No firebird had ever really taken the trouble to measure how many floors there were between the designated cutoff point for humans and the great glass dome at the top of the librarium. The count would not have meant much anyway. For to reach the roof (and this is what humans did not understand) it was not so much a question of how far one traveled, more of how much one needed to get there.

So it came to pass that after *some* time, Aurielle set down on the circular balcony that ran around the whole circumference of the dome. The dome was surrounded by thick clouds, as always, but the air was calm with no hint of a chill. This close in, it was easy to spot an open window, which was the only requirement necessary for a firebird to gain entry. Aurielle selected one and flew straight in, pulling it closed as tradition dictated. (Such an annoying task when all you had was feet!) But it was the custom and that was all that mattered. Before she'd finished fixing the latch, a hushed voice swept into the center of her mind. "Hello, Aurielle," it said.

It always made her feathers shake, the nature of that voice. Despite the dizzy height she was at, there was nothing particularly "lofty" about it. It was gentle and caring and really rather welcoming. She had tried to describe it to Azkiar once (who had always shied away from coming up here for fear that he'd pass out in the watery air and kill a thousand daisies in his plummet back to the ground). Like a wind from another world, she called it, because no matter where she hovered or tumbled or flew she could always hear the voice, all around her, like a whisper.

Yet she had never seen what produced it.

(*That*, she suspected, was the *real* reason Azkiar never went near the roof.)

Apart from the billions of tiny fire stars that twinkled on and off, off and on, in the dome, only once had Aurielle seen *anything* here. Strangely, that had been on the last occasion when she'd gone to report on the time rift the firebirds had sealed above David. As she'd entered through her chosen window, she had seen what she'd thought was a length of ribbon, twisting and curling in the glittering space. But when she'd followed its movements closely, she had seen that it was, in fact, some kind of object, shaped like a slender tube. The only thing she could equate it to was a fragment of bone. It was half the span of her knees to her toes and etched with a number of unusual marks. As it twitched it produced three uniform contrails, which eerily reminded her of the ancient symbol that opened the door to Floor Forty-Three. But what would a piece of *bone* be doing here? She had asked herself that many times of late. It made no sense. No sense at all.

She was thinking of this when the voice of the Higher invited her to join them. Spreading her glorious cream-colored wings, she closed her eyes and launched herself toward the stars, into the sensory matrix the Higher called the Is. To be in the Is was just like flying without wings. (In fact, spreading her wings had no effect on her movements, it simply felt more natural to do it.) She knew she would never fall within the Is, but simply float where the power of the Higher wished to take her. The more she let go of what she knew about flight, the better the experience became.

In the Is, there was no need for speech (though the movement of the mouth, like the movement of the wings, always felt more appropriate). All Aurielle had to do to communicate was *be*. For the Higher knew precisely what was in her mind from the very first moment she entered the dome. They knew what she'd discovered on the floors downstairs. They knew of her concerns about the future of the books. They acknowledged her excitement about the *Tapestry of Isenfier*. And in that one full moment of knowing, they also considered all the probable outcomes that might arise from those discoveries and concerns. And this is how they responded to her: "Aurielle, what will be, *will* be."

With a *whoosh*, they swept her to the top of the dome as her concentration lapsed into fragments of worry. "Do not be concerned by these developments," they soothed her. "The Higher will always seek order in the aerie. When there is order in the aerie, there is order in the world. Whatever actions you take to aid our task will always be correct. This is a result of your purity of spirit."

There was a time shift, she commingled, relaxing a little.

The Higher let her spiral down within the Is. "We are aware of this," they said. "You were not at fault. We allowed it to happen."

Aurielle felt herself roll. "May I know why?"

There was a pause. They let her glide for a moment. "Isenfier is upon us," they said.

Whoosh! That made poor Aurielle plummet as her mind grew heavy with a daisy field of questions. Once again the Is was there to support her. As she calmed, she rose again.

"She is coming," they said.

"She?" said Aurielle.

"You are tending Her closely."

The egg on the table.

"Yes," said the Higher, reading her thoughts. "She will lead you to Isenfier. David will prepare the way."

"Then it's him?" said Aurielle, thinking of the tapestry.

"Aurielle, you always knew," they said.

Aurielle gulped. She found herself floating motionless now. Yes, in her heart, she had always believed that the boy was special. Trust your intuitions, the Higher had always taught her. Intuitions, they said, were the future calling.

Daringly, she opened her eyes. The strange fragment of bone was dancing about her, looping her body in figures of eight, wrapping her in its lengthy trails. The sun was shining through a parting in the clouds, making all the fire stars dance. And the rain was falling. The *rain* was back, making a rainbow over the dome. Suddenly, Aurielle knew what she must do. "I must find him," she said. "I must drive out the Aunts and bring David back."

"He will be the new curator," they said.

The rainbow illuminated Aurielle's heart. She soared. Courage flooded her breast. She would need it, for the Higher's next words were a caution: "We have only one warning."

Oh. Aurielle faltered a little.

"Beware the thread," they whispered.

Thread? she commingled.

"Of time," they said. "The thread of time."

Aurielle twitched her ear tufts a little. "But the birds are the guardians of time," she said. Hadn't this always been so?

"That is your vulnerability," they warned her. "But only She can decide the final outcome."

She. There was a pause. The fire stars blinked. "Is She like us? A bird — from an egg?"

"She is what you see on the tapestry," they said.

A girl, dressed in white.

"Yes," said the Higher.

"And you?" Aurielle asked rather boldly. She had floated this question in her mind many times and the Higher had always let it do that — float. Now Aurielle pressed for an answer. At last the Higher replied with one.

"We are Fain," they said.

Aurielle drew a breath and looked all about her. Pure fain? No physical body?

"We are everything — and no thing," the Higher whispered.

The piece of bone twitched as it whipped past her face. It was starting to make her go cross-eyed now. "This is some *thing*." But what exactly?

The Higher paused before replying. "This is your possible future," they said.

"My . . . ?" *I'm going to be a piece of bone?* she thought.

266

"This is an agent of the universe," they said.

Oh, thought Aurielle. *That is better.*

"This is not its true form."

"May I see its true form?"

There was a humming sound within the Is. "It can only be a moment, a shimmer in time. It will be here but not here. Seen but not seen."

"I understand," said Aurielle. A glimpse was all she wanted.

A glimpse was all she got. Right before her eyes, the "bone" stopped moving and physically changed shape. It happened so quickly that she almost sneezed and blew the apparition to the far side of the dome. But there, so faintly trans:lucent that it was almost lost among the pulsing stars, Aurielle saw a hint of how her kind would evolve. Not into larger birds. Not even into dragons. But a creature somewhere between the two. The image was there in a blink and gone. She barely had time to take it all in. But the one thing she couldn't fail to notice was a feature she had always envied in dragons. A physiological improvement on the firebird anatomy that filled her with the greatest excitement ever. She paddled her feet in the Is and was joyous.

Someday, firebirds were going to have *paws.*

12.

One thing Aleron had not explained to Aurielle during their conversation about Rosa was how the Aunts were treating the books. Thankfully, he had not been there to witness Aunt Primrose savagely tearing out random pages, but he had found the shocking results of her wickedness when he'd flown by the blocked-up window space. What a terrible thing it was for a caring firebird to register the distress of ripped-up words, crumpled in their paper, dying and forgotten. He'd found a ball of that paper lying on the ground at the edge of the daisy bed and had straightened it out as best he could. But it was never going to be as clean and sharp as the day the words had been put onto the page. There, in those wrinkles, was the sadness of the aerie in microcosm. Aleron had burned it, to relieve it of its suffering, and blown the ashes over the daisy fields.

One shred of paper, at least, was at peace. But the books could not tolerate much more stress.

Rosa had been coming to that same conclusion. She, too, was not immune to the sadness around her, but had so far sat back and done nothing about it. But as time went by and the librarium's mourning seemed to be growing worse, she began to wonder what the Aunts were up to. To her relief, they had not gone around the building wrecking shelves or tearing down books. She was grateful for that, but she was still suspicious. They had practically ignored her since that first day of scrubbing and had kept themselves confined to the room she had cleaned. What, then, was the nature of their "re:assessment"? What could they assess from one small part of a building as huge as this?

On the third day, curiosity got the better of her and she crept downstairs to investigate. Most rooms in the librarium had no doors, and those that did were rarely closed. The Aunts' door was not only closed but had a large KEEP OUT sign hanging off the doorknob. For the first time, it occurred to Rosa that the blocking of the window had nothing to do with drafts or cold. The Aunts just did not want to be seen. She stooped down and put her eye to the keyhole. It was stuffed with paper. She raised her fist to knock, then thought better of it; if they were this keen on secrecy, they weren't going to let her in on a whim. Politeness was not an option. But how could she, a girl with no fain, possibly distract two powerful Aunts?

She took the problem to her hammock that night. As she tossed and turned between half sleep and worry, her mind seemed to fly around the walls of the librarium as if she were spinning on a carousel of books. For the first time in her life, she realized she was dreaming. Or was it that the building was leading her somewhere? It had done this many times in her waking life, but that had always been in response to her intent. This time the intent seemed to be that of the building. And so it proved to be. In the middle of the night, with the moon outside her window, she woke with a start, swung out of her hammock, and started to run. She arrived breathless in a room on Floor Eleven and skirted the shelves, almost tearing down the books until she found the volume she was looking for — the title the building had put into her mind: *The Properties of Mushrooms*.

Mushrooms. She had heard Mr. Henry say something disparaging about these things once. How they were prisoners of the dark and grew in damp corners in the muggy cellars beneath the librarium, only fit for consumption by *Aunts*, who couldn't get enough of the horrid things, apparently. Rosa had been very young at the time and had not understood this little rant, but she *had* taken note of it. Aunts liked mushrooms. And now here she was with a strange book about them and two scheming Aunts in a room downstairs. But what did the building want her to do? A sudden breeze swept through the room, rapidly turning the pages of the book. Three firebirds (Aleron being one) had just flown in. They looked at Rosa and she at them. "You, too, huh?" she said, knowing full well they'd been drawn here, as she had. She glanced at the open book. On the page was a glossy digi:graf of a basket made from woven grass. In it was a number of strange gray objects with spongy stalks and purple spots on their rounded caps. Rosa read the caption beneath. *Purple-spotted mushrooms are edible, but will induce drowsiness if eaten in quantity.* She smiled and patted the librarium wall. Suddenly, a plan had formed in her mind.

"These. Where will I find some?" she said. She turned the book around and showed it to the birds. They looked at one another and exchanged a few *rrrh*s. "Tonight," she said, tapping it. "It has to be tonight."

The following morning, Rosa returned to the Aunts' room carrying a tray. On it was a pie, oozing tails of steam from a cross in the center of its pastry crust. Beside the pie were two large spoons.

She knocked the door.

Predictably, a voice said, "Go away."

"It's Rosa, Aunts."

"We know who it is."

"I'm sorry for my absence. I want to make it up to you."

"We don't need you. We're busy in here."

"I thought you might be hungry. I've cooked something for you."

"Go *away*, girl. We can imagineer anything we want."

Rosa chewed her lip. Not for the first time, she wondered about the wisdom of what she was doing. If it all went wrong, the consequences would be dire. She steadied herself. She must be brave. "It's mushrooms, real ones, baked in a pie."

There was silence on the other side of the door. "Mushrooms?" said a voice. One Aunt to the other.

"They grow . . . erm . . . at the back of the librarium. I've had some myself. They're very —"

The door whipped open a crack.

"— tasty."

Aunt Petunia's dark gaze scanned the tray. "It is a pie," she hissed back over her shoulder.

"I can smell it," said Primrose.

Aunt Petunia's nose began to twitch. Rosa could swear that the old woman's bow tie was trying to spin.

"Bring it in," said Primrose.

"Not you," said Petunia, extending a forbidding hand toward Rosa. "Give me the tray and be gone from here, girl. You can pick it up later and then clean the dish — twice."

Rosa held the tray out. "Do you need any help? What exactly are you doing in there, Aunt?"

"None of your business," the old woman snapped. And she snatched up the tray and forced the door shut.

Rosa stared at the blank brown door for a moment. That hadn't gone quite the way she'd hoped, but the Aunts had taken the bait nevertheless. She wiped her palms, one across the other. "Enjoy," she whispered with a smug little grin. And gathering her skirts about her knees, she went and sat primly on the stairs.

In the shadows behind her, the firebirds waited.

For several minutes they listened to the greedy clink of spoons. Then there came a loud, rather crude spell of burping. Then a brief spell of silence. Then the most hideous, labored snoring, so potent that it made a loose board on the stairway hum.

"I think that's done the trick," Rosa said, jumping up. "OK, guys, how do we get in?"

If she was expecting that the birds would speak some kind of dragontongue and open the door in the way David had done upstairs, she was wrong. This one was locked by a regular key. The only way in was via the outside window. Aleron reached it first and began to pluck out the pieces of paper. But this was all taking too long for Azkiar. With a loud and impatient *RRRH!* he ordered Aleron out of the way, then launched himself, feetfirst, at the wall of books. He hit them at tremendous speed. With a bang, they collapsed inward.

Rosa ran forward and cleared the remainder, then climbed through the window and into the room.

The Aunts were laid out in the middle of the floor, each with a spoon in hand. The pie dish was on its side and empty. Apart from that, there seemed to be nothing amiss. The books were mostly in place on the shelves. And though they'd been moved around or laid down flat, they did not appear to be damaged in any way.

"What are they doing?" Rosa muttered to herself. It occurred to her then that the Aunts might have simply been *reading* the books and that she had misjudged their intentions horribly. If that was the case, oh, what a trial she had to look forward to. Knocking out a pair of Aunts for no reason was sure to see her banished to the Dead Lands for life.

Rrrh, went a voice across the room. Aurielle had landed on a bed in the corner, where she had found some kind of device. Rosa made her way over, stepping across the legs of both Aunts to get there. (Azkiar and Aleron were perched on the Aunts' chests, guarding the women, their ear tufts lifting every time the Aunts snored.)

Aurielle nudged the device with her beak. It was a

thin flat pad, about half the size of a standard book cover. It had a sleek black screen, which appeared to have a number of thumbprints on its surface. Flashing lights were jumping back and forth across the bottom, as if the device were waiting for an input. Rosa had never troubled herself with elec:tronics and hadn't sent a single :com in her life. Even so, she picked up the pad and pressed her finger to a likely area of the screen. It lit up at once. A message invited her to SCAN OBJECT. She looked at Aurielle. The firebird frowned. *Object?* thought Rosa. *What object?* And then it struck her: the books, of course. She picked one off the bed and slowly brought it into contact with the pad. To her horror, the pad came alive. Numbers. Lights. Menus. Colors. They all appeared on the screen at once. At its center was a window more active than the rest. And though the data stream was moving far too quickly to gauge what it was, Rosa was sure that the device was uploading the contents of the book. A great wave of anger rose inside her. But worse was to come. For that was not the end of the process. Suddenly, the pad gave a little beep and a new question appeared on the screen:

Auma rating: 72% efficient. Absorb?

Rosa pulled the book away in an instant. The device immediately asked if she wanted to cancel the procedure. She screamed and hurled it across the room, then ran to the nearest shelf of books. She pulled one down and opened it. For one moment nothing happened. But as she tilted the book, the periods, the commas, the question marks, and eventually the words themselves all began to slip from their places on the page until they were falling like ash around her feet.

"No," she wailed. She sank to her knees, clutching the book to her heart.

They were dead, all of them. She knew it at once. Their auma taken. Their power destroyed.

Rrrh! went Azkiar, urgent and loud.

Rosa looked tearfully over her shoulder. The Aunts were waking. She narrowed her gaze.

Good.

13.

Aunt Petunia came around to find Rosa sitting astride her chest.

"OK, here's the drill," said the girl. "Don't try to move or use your fain. Your sister is laid out right beside you, but she's got a nice big angry firebird perched on top of her to keep her company. I've seen him in action. Believe me, he's mean. I'm sure you know they're immune to your tricks. One hint of imagineering and he'll turn poor Primrose to ash. Are we clear?"

"You will die for this," Aunt Petunia growled, fury reddening her swollen cheeks. "Primrose, dear, are you all right?"

"Shoes," the twin Aunt squeaked.

"Shoes?" Petunia rolled her eyes sideways. She was slightly surprised to see her sister's feet, not her head, beside her. What's more, the feet were bare. "What deplorable villainy is this?"

Rosa gripped the Aunt's chin and pulled her back. "I hope you won't have to find out. Now, what exactly are you doing in this room?"

"It's none of your business," Petunia snapped.

Rosa curled her lip. "Runcey," she said, and sent him a tongue click.

The green firebird stepped forward. In his beak was a feather, plucked from his tail.

"What's that thing doing?" Aunt Petunia said, anxiously rolling her eyes again.

On a nod from Rosa, the firebird dipped his head and dragged the feather over Primrose's feet.

Aunt Primrose screeched. Her bare toes danced. Her feet clapped together like shutters in a storm. Even Aunt Petunia made an O with her mouth and let out a kind of whistling noise.

"Oh, yes, of course, you're twins," Rosa said. "You feel each other's discomfort, don't you?" She leaned down and looked Aunt Petunia dead in the eye. "Confess and I'll let you leave. Or twinny here feels my feathered friend's wrath. It's probably worse if he turns the feather around and scratches the skin with the point of the shaft."

"Confess!" cried Primrose.

"Be silent, Primrose. I'll deal with this." Petunia tightened her immaculate eyebrows. "You've nothing to gain by threatening us, girl."

"Oh, really?" said Rosa. In a flash, she had snatched up Petunia's bow tie. To her amusement, it was held in place by elastic. She pulled it as far from the neck as it would stretch. "This is my home. These books are my family. I'm not going to see your kind destroy them."

"Not the tie," Aunt Petunia begged.

"What's she doing?" echoed Primrose. "What is the wicked girl doing with your tie?"

"Don't make me let go of this," Rosa warned. For good measure, she twisted it once.

"All right!" Aunt Petunia's gray eyes bulged.

Rosa relaxed and let the tie sag back, only letting go when it was just off the neck. It snapped, making both Aunts gurgle. "I strongly advise you to speak the truth."

"You were *told* the truth," Aunt Petunia said. "We were sent to assess the building. That's it."

"You were sent to steal its auma. Why?"

"What use is all that auma here?" piped Primrose.

"Shut up, Primrose!"

"It's all right for you," the twin called out. "You've still got your shoes and socks."

"Well?" said Rosa, threatening to play with the tie again.

"Primrose is right," Petunia said. "This building is an untapped auma source. It has infinitely more than any other structure on Co:pern:ica. Its energy is wasted. The Aunts could put it to much better use."

"One Aunt, you mean."

Petunia wiggled her nose. "Are you implying something about Aunt Gwyneth?"

"You trust her?"

"Of course. She's an Aunt Su:perior."

"She's a vile witch."

"*You* —"

"Ah, ah." Rosa wagged a warning finger.

Suddenly, Primrose started to sniff. "What's that . . . GHASTLY smell?"

Rosa glanced over her shoulder at Azkiar. "I believe he's just urinated on you, Aunt."

"Ugh!" cried both the sisters at once. Aunt Petunia scraped her nails on the floor.

"Tell me about the pad," said Rosa. Across the room, Aurielle was standing over the device, consumed in concentration. She kept picking up one of her feet now and then as if she were thinking of touching the screen. Despite the impact it had suffered from the throw, it was still blinking steadily.

Aunt Petunia sneered. "A simpleton like you couldn't hope to understand the complexity of its functions."

"Wrong answer," said Rosa. She clicked her tongue.

"No!" Aunt Primrose wailed. Her heels beat a loud tattoo on the floor.

"All right, stop this!" Petunia growled. "I'll tell you what you want to know."

Rosa clicked again and Aleron backed off.

"The pad absorbs auma and stores it in cumulative energy cells."

"Again, in Rosa-speak, if it's not too much *trouble*."

"It takes the power of each book and adds it to the last."

"How many have you done?"

Aunt Petunia breathed in. "This room is almost complete."

Rosa allowed herself a glance at the shelves. "What happens to the auma you've gathered?"

"That is for the Aunt Su:perior to decide."

"I bet it is," Rosa said, gritting her teeth. "Tell me how you reverse the process."

"You can't," shouted Primrose.

"Be quiet, Primrose. I'm *concentrating*."

There was something not right about that remark, but Rosa rather foolishly let it pass. "Is she lying?" she snarled. The woman stared deep into Rosa's eyes, as if she were scanning her for some kind of weakness. "I said, is she *lying*?" Rosa demanded. And grasping not only the tie but the collar, she lifted Aunt Petunia's head off the floor.

"No," the Aunt snapped. "The books have only low-level consciousness. They're not able to accept a contrary input. They would return as nonsense, a jumble of marks. I should warn you, girl, the pad is extremely dangerous. Think about that before you do something foolish."

Rosa glanced at Aurielle again. The firebird was cautiously tapping the screen. "I'll take my chances," she said. "What can be done with the auma that's stored?"

That *stare* again.

Rosa tightened her grip.

"It can only be transferred."

"To what?"

"To anything — if you know what you're doing."

"What does Aunt Gwyneth want with it?"

Aunt Petunia closed her eyes.

"Answer me, you freak. What would she do with the auma from this building?"

Aunt Petunia's eyes flickered open. Her face had a strangely confident look. "She'd use it to take control, I imagine. So the Aunts could rule over all Co:pern:ica, without being bound by limits — or the Higher." She flicked her gaze sideways. From the direction of the window a voice said, "Rosa?"

"David?" Rosa gasped, and turned to look.

That was her undoing.

In the moment it took to realize she'd been tricked, Rosa's hold on Aunt Petunia was gone. With a strength well beyond the composition of her body, the old woman shifted her weight and threw Rosa across the floor, into a space between two shelves. At exactly the same moment, guided by her twin's tele:pathic impulse, Aunt Primrose raised her hands and stabbed her fingernails into the soft tissue under Azkiar's beak. The red firebird squawked in rage. He lifted off and let out a bolt of fire. It missed Aunt Primrose (she'd been quick to roll away) but swallowed up one of the books. The book exploded in a shower of ceiling-high sparks, igniting a therma:sol sheet on the bed. Within seconds, the bed was a raft of fire.

Aurielle, watching this, had difficult choices. Azkiar wounded. Rosa winded. The threat of fire raging through the aerie, already too wild for three birds to contain. *Rrrh!* she cried urgently to Aleron. But the green firebird was already flying. With a *whoosh* he was through the window, away to bring help from the rest of the flock.

Suddenly, Aurielle found herself caged. The bars had simply appeared from nowhere. It took her just a fraction of a sec to realize it was a temporary construct, created by one of the Aunts. As such it had no control over her. But to be able to pass through it and therefore escape, she needed to lock her geo:centric sensors onto a stationary part of the image. Rather cleverly, the twins had made the bars revolve. And the cage itself was turning in the opposite direction from the bars. It was impossible to get a fix. Aurielle looked in hope at

Azkiar. But he was likewise trapped. Aunt Primrose had made certain he would suffer by wrapping his head in a tight metal helmet that clamped his beak shut and clanked loudly every time he crashed against the bars.

Their only chance was Rosa. She was on her feet, clutching her ribs low down. In one hand she held the auma pad. She saw Aunt Petunia's eyes flick to it. "Let the birds go or this gets toasted."

Aunt Petunia smiled.

"I mean it," Rosa shouted, finding it hard to breathe through the heat.

Aunt Primrose came to stand beside her sister. Behind them, a lick of flame roared up the wall, igniting another column of books. Eerily, they both held out a hand.

"Never," said Rosa, and hurled the pad over them. It was half a sec away from hitting the bed when it stopped in midair and rose again. The twins had captured it, using their fain.

Rosa screamed and launched herself at them.

Sadly, her petulance was short-lived and foolish. Aunt Petunia, always the quicker of the pair, grasped the girl's forearm and used her momentum to twist her to her knees. At the same time she gouged three scars into her flesh, drawing up three hot streams of blood.

For Rosa, the pain was horrendous. Her mouth opened, but she fainted in absolute silence.

"Oh, dearest, how could you?" Primrose said. "Now you've got her blood on the ruff of your sleeve. You'll have to imagineer a brand-new blouse."

"Shall I finish her?"

The auma pad dropped into Primrose's hands. "I think the fire will do that. Time we were going."

Aunt Petunia let go of Rosa's arm. The girl slumped to a heap on the floor. But just when it seemed that the balance of power was firmly with the Aunts, the auma pad started beeping loudly.

"What's that?" said Petunia, focusing her irritated gaze on the device.

"I . . . I don't understand," her sister stammered.

"What don't you understand?" Petunia said impatiently.

Aunt Primrose ran her thumbs across the screen. "The pad's been set to discharge."

"Impossible. Only an Aunt could know the encryption code for that."

"I'm telling you, Petunia, it's about to unload every shred of auma we've gathered. And I can't override it."

Aunt Petunia stiffened her spine. "Have you betrayed me, Primrose?"

"Of course not, Twin."

"Then how has it been primed?"

"Dear, I don't *know*."

"Well, the girl couldn't do it."

"Then it has to be . . ." Both Aunts stared suspiciously at Aurielle.

"That's ridiculous," said Petunia. "Give it to me." She made a move to snatch the pad from her sister's grasp.

Primrose held it out to one side. "Why should you have it?"

"Because I'm senior."

"One micro:sec between our births doesn't make you any better than me!"

"But I am, dear Primrose. I'm perfect. I'm Petunia. *You* can't even set your tie straight."

"You want the auma for yourself. Well, you shan't have it!"

"I shall!"

"You shan't!"

And for once, Aunt Primrose was absolutely right. With a burst of light as powerful as the flames around them, the pad lit up and a visible ribbon of violet energy flowed out of it. But it did not go to either of the squabbling Aunts. It flew around them both and in between the cages and dissolved into the wound on Rosa's arm. Her head jerked violently as if something had bitten her. And though she did not wake, the wound began to burn with a blue-white flame.

"What have you done?" coughed Primrose, backing away.

"What do you mean, what have I done?"

"Look at her arm, at the marks you gouged. You've branded her with the symbol of Agawin."

Aunt Petunia shook her head in fear and confusion.

Primrose let the auma pad fall from her hand. "Run, dear," she said. "We've got to run away." She hurried to the door, pulling her sister with her. Such was their haste that her foot struck the auma pad and knocked it under the burning bed. But it mattered not to the Aunts anymore. They had failed. The only thing now was escape. Primrose opened the door and dragged her sister out.

Almost immediately, two things happened. The cages surrounding Aurielle and Azkiar de:constructed as quickly as they'd formed. Both birds were now free, but too dizzy to fly. To Aurielle's relief, she heard wingbeats through the crackling flames. She looked up expecting to see a host of firebirds coming through the window to quench the fire. But only one had landed on the sill. Her heart rate tripled and her ear tufts rose. *Aubrey?* she said. The bird in the window had its features, but there was something horribly wrong about it. There was no color in the feathers. No kindness in the eyes. And why was there a line of fresh green blood congealing around the ruff of the neck?

Suddenly, it twisted its head to one side, clearly aware of something coming. Only then did Aurielle see that it was carrying an item in its beak. It looked as if it might be a nesting twig, but she was too far away to be sure. The bird was gone before she could decide. And after two or three secs of empty sky, David Merriman scrabbled through the window.

"Rosa!" he yelled. He came powering across the floor, using his arm to shield his face from the flames. He didn't even look at Azkiar and Aurielle as he dropped to his knees to lift Rosa up. But the two firebirds were busy in their own right by then, barking orders at the twenty or so more that had just flown into the room. David turned, with Rosa in his arms, to see the fire being consumed by a host of brightly colored birds.

When it was done and the birds were settled, on any (cool) perch they could find, David looked at them all and spoke the only word of dragontongue he knew. "Sometimes." Every bird sat up, their ear tufts raised. One by one they set their gaze on Aurielle, who spread her wings and hovered in front of the humans. She replied, in her own form of dragontongue. And though David did not understand her little *rrrh* he knew from its tone it was a kindness, a greeting. He nodded at Aurielle and she at him.

Welcome back, David, the firebird had said.

Now the librarium was his.

Part Three

WHICH HAS ITS

BEGINNINGS ON THE

ISLE OF ALAVON,

A LONG-FORGOTTEN AREA

OF THE DEAD LANDS

ALSO MARCH 7, 032

1.

Harlan Merriman and Bernard Brotherton were transported to the Dead Lands, at night, by penal taxi-car. They were escorted there by two Re:movers (Pinstriped and Plain). The prisoners were not allowed any possessions, only the minimal clothes they were dressed in. And though neither man was formally bound, the Re:movers ordered them to sit with their hands clearly visible on their knees. All speech was forbidden. The use of fain, the prisoners were warned, would be considered a grave violation of the terms of their re:moval from the Grand Design. When Bernard rather foolishly asked, "What *terms*?" he was rewarded with a bolt of charge from a scanner. The shock of it left his four limbs shaking and froth bubbling from the corners of his mouth. Harlan, careful not to show any form of dissent, gathered the wounded tech:nician in his arms. The Re:movers let this pass. It was the only concession they made to either captive throughout the remainder of the journey.

When the taxicar finally slowed to a halt, the doors opened with a crisp *whoosh* and the man-machines stepped out in perfect synchrony. They ordered the prisoners to move. The scientists stumbled down a short metal ramp, onto a dark, desolate, odorless wilderness very similar to that which Eliza Merriman had encountered. The land was mostly flat in all directions and barely seemed able to sustain a blade of grass. Here and there, thanks to the few rays of moonlight finding outlets through the clouds, a rough cast of stone could be seen jutting out of the sterile surface. There was no sign of water, certainly no food. Nothing on any horizon but the promise of loneliness.

Bernard began to shiver. It was cold here. Very cold. Nothing like the carefully controlled environments either man was used to in Co:pern:ica Central.

Pinstriped spoke. "Harlan Merriman, Bernard Brotherton, your citizenship of Co:pern:ica is revoked. You will remain in the Dead Lands until you expire by any means. This is by order of an Aunt Su:perior. This is the will of the Higher."

With that, the Re:movers climbed into their taxicar and were gone.

Bernard dropped to his knees, sinking his bones into the gluey earth.

"Come on," Harlan said, touching him gently on the shoulder. "We have to go."

"Where to?" Bernard begged, throwing his arms wide. "Look around you, Harlan. Everywhere leads to nowhere. We're doomed."

"You've heard the stories," Harlan said. "There are communities here. People survive. If we stay where we are, the cold will kill us. We must walk, Bernard. It's our only chance."

The tech:nician dropped his stubby hands flat against his thighs. "In which direction? We can't even use our fain to guide us."

"I'd say our best bet lies that way." Harlan nodded at something shimmering in the distance.

Bernard squinted for a focal point. "Are they . . . *torches?*" he whispered, gathering hope into his voice. He scrabbled to his feet for a better look. Away to their right, on one of the rolling parts of the landscape, several specks of light were dancing in the darkness.

"Let's find out," said Harlan. And he began to pick his way across the turf to meet them.

"What if they're hostile?" Bernard stood his ground. There were many rumors about life in the Dead Lands. Not all of them were kind.

"There's little point in running," Harlan replied. "They'll catch us if we try. Whoever they are, they're used to this terrain; we're not."

"We could wait. Lie low. Assess them as they pass."

Harlan flicked his eyes toward the lights again. "They're heading this way. They know we're here. They probably saw the taxicar or monitored its flare."

"Then I suppose our fate is sealed." Bernard sighed. And without another word, he fell into step behind his colleague.

It wasn't long before the approaching lights began to illuminate the shapes of men. There were six in total, but three were carrying two torches each. Harlan found this reassuring. It suggested to him that these people were used to taxicar drops and had brought extra torches for newcomers to hold. As the group drew close, a youngish man at the head of the party doused a failing torch in a puddle of water. The sudden fizzle made Bernard jump. The young man quickly put him at ease. "Friends, we mean you no harm." He signaled to a shaggy-haired member of the group, who stepped forward with two bundles of clothing. All the men were wearing shin-length robes, tied at the waist by a short brown cord. "I recommend you undress," the young man said.

Harlan, not questioning, took off his jacket.

"Leave it on the ground," said the man with the clothing.

"Why? What's the point of this?" Bernard demanded.

The young man stabbed his torch into the ground, took a robe, and let it fall open in his hands. "This will be considerably warmer, trust me. Regular clothing offers little protection to you here, and it will deteriorate quickly."

"And it's probably full of tracers," a man with broken spex put in.

"To monitor our movements?" Bernard asked.

The young man looked at him kindly. "No, friend, to take bets on how long you survive." He offered the robe up. This time, Bernard took it.

"You'll also need these." An older man with cheek-bones as prominent as his nose stepped forward. He handed Harlan a pair of sandals. They were basic and fairly shapeless, with a toe post between the big toe and the next. "Traveling the marshland is tiring without them. They will help to spread your weight and keep you balanced. In the morning, we'll find you a better fit."

Lastly, the young man gave Harlan a torch. Harlan received it well. There was something oddly comforting about the weight of the wood and the scent of fire in his nostrils. "Who are you?" he asked.

"Renegades, like you," the young man replied. "Left here by a dying society that wrongly believes we were the cause of its ailments. My name is Mathew Lefarr and we are the Followers of Agawin. Let me lead you to our shelter. We can talk along the way."

He signaled to the shaggy-haired man, who put his torch to the bundle of clothing. When the fire had taken, the group moved off in the direction from which Harlan had first seen the lights. "Agawin?" he asked, having to work to keep pace with Lefarr's trained stride. "I've heard that name before, but I don't recall where. Is he the leader of your tribe?"

Lefarr considered the question for a moment. "What's your name?" he asked quietly.

"Harlan Merriman."

"And your companion?"

"Bernard Brotherton."

"Colleagues or friends?"

"Both," said Harlan, looking back. Bernard was relaxed now and moving freely, aided by the man who had given out the sandals. "We are scientists — were scientists — from the Institute for Realism in Phys:ics."

"At what level?"

"Professor. Bernard was my tech:nician."

Lefarr nodded, taking this in. "Do you know where you are, Professor? Did the Aunts or Re:movers tell you where you'd be dropped?"

"The Dead Lands. That's all they said."

"The Dead Lands are vast," Lefarr explained. "You are in a sector called Alavon, which we believe was once home to the seer, Agawin, whose legend we follow."

Harlan glanced around him. This dreadful, inhospitable place offered little promise of "home" to anyone. Even so he said, "Sounds like an interesting story."

"You will learn more of it in time," Mathew said.

They slogged on for another few paces. Despite the cold he could feel in all his extremities (the toes were probably the worst), Harlan could detect his body warmth building and feel it being retained by the fabric of his robe. "How do you know the name of this region? I'd always assumed that everything outside of Central was uncharted."

A frail smile broke across Mathew's face. "The Dead Lands were mapped many spins ago."

"Oh? How do you know that?"

Lefarr looked sideways at him. "It's the reason I'm here." He took a larger step over a pool of water, urging Harlan to copy what he did. "Take care. The ground here is very boggy. It can suck a man down in a single draw. Go in too far and we have no way of pulling you out. Don't talk, just follow. Till we reach the higher levels."

Harlan looked up. Now that his eyes had adjusted to the darkness, the contours of the land were easier to see. Some two hundred paces ahead the ground curved up in a gentle, extended slope. The men behind Harlan were preparing for the climb by organizing themselves into single file. At the risk of annoying his host he asked, "What's over the ridge?"

"History," said Lefarr. "Now concentrate and follow."

The next fifty paces were some of the longest of Harlan's life. Twice he was stopped by shouts from behind when one or other of the men — thankfully not Bernard — lost their footing and had to be rescued by their companions. Lefarr, who seemed to cope better than any with the treacherous conditions, went back on both occasions to offer his help. If he wasn't a leader, he deserved to be. That made Harlan think again about the origins of the name Agawin. It was reverberating around his skull like an echo, yet he could not put a time or a memory to it. An answer lay over the ridge, perhaps? That intriguing promise, as much as the threat of submersion in the marsh, sharpened his attention for the last part of the trek. The slope was reached without further incident, and by the time they could walk and talk again at leisure, Harlan's mind had drifted back to the latter part of his conversation. "You said you were involved with the mapping of this area. Are you a scientist as well? Did you work for the Geo:grafical Institute?"

"Not exactly," Lefarr replied. "I used to make t:coms for the broadcast networks. I had a promising career, a reputation for being thorough. One day, I was assigned to a top secret project whose object was to quash an uncomfortable belief that was gaining strength among the citizens of Co:pern:ica."

"Something to do with Agawin?"

"No. It ended here, with Agawin, but it began with the Grand Design." Lefarr extended a hand to help Harlan over a crumbling rock. "A covert poll, arranged by the Aunts, indicated that over sixty percent of the citizens of Central felt their lives were 'missing' something. I was given the job of finding out what. During my research, I heard the name Agawin for the first time. It ignited something in me that I never knew existed: a crushing desire to step into the past, to understand where I had come from. This feeling of insecurity, for want of a better phrase, was the root of the problem in Central. So I began to ask questions I wasn't supposed to ask. All of them turned my investigations here. I'd heard rumors that the Dead Lands were very far from dead and were beginning to spontaneously regenerate. But when I sought permission to explore beyond Central, to my amazement the Aunts denied it. So I went to the Geo:grafical Institute — which, as you know, is controlled by the Aunts — looking for evidence."

"You broke in?"

"At the time, it seemed like a worthy thing to do. They caught me, of course, and sent me here, to a region where they send all the worst — or depending how you look at it, the best — offenders. This party of men are some of the finest minds to come out of Central. You may not think so yet, but you're in excellent company." He crested the ridge and pointed with his torch, releasing a shower of cinders from its tip. "Welcome to the Dead Lands' best-kept secret. This is the Isle of Alavon."

Some way ahead, about three times farther than the distance they'd walked, a small and almost symmetrical hill was rising from the base of a natural valley. "That's amazing," said Harlan, shaking his head in wonder. "I'd always assumed the Dead Lands were flat. Do you live on the hill?"

One of the approaching men said, "We keep to the lowlands around it."

But on the peak, Harlan could see a small tower — or maybe the ruins of one. Pointing to it he asked, "Is that inhabited?"

"No," said Lefarr. "Not anymore."

Bernard drew up alongside. Out of breath, but

equally transfixed, he panted, "Wind." He laughed. "Actual wind, in my hair."

"What there is of it," one of the tribe joked.

They all laughed, including Bernard. "I haven't felt this for years," he said. "Real air blowing through my lungs." He opened his mouth and took a deep breath in.

"And it's fresh," said Mathew. "Not like the filtered environments in Central."

"It's beautiful," said Harlan, "in a rather grotesque kind of way. How do you men survive here?"

The six Followers looked at one another as if they weren't entirely willing to give up the answer. Once again, it was left to Lefarr. "Look carefully at the hill. Tell me what you see."

Harlan studied it in detail. Dawn was beginning to break across the valley. In the gathering light it was possible to see that the mound was composed of three or four tiers of earth, defined by upwardly spiraling terraces. At first there seemed nothing remarkable about them. But as the light began to flood the lower slopes, Harlan's gaze was drawn to a shoulder of land near the foot of the hill — and something rather peculiar on it. He stepped forward to be sure his eyes weren't deceiving him. "Color," he said.

"Crops," said Mathew. The men around him placed a hand across their hearts.

In among the blackness lay a field of green.

2.

"Firebird!" one of the men shouted suddenly.

Harlan let his gaze run across the skyline and quickly picked out the familiar shape. The bird was circling toward the valley floor, barely moving its bright orange wings. It tipped a little as it caught the sunlight, resembling a soaring ball of flame.

Two of the Followers dropped their torches and began to sprint down the hill. The other three looked to Lefarr for guidance.

"What's happening?" asked Harlan.

Lefarr, who'd been carrying a small backpack made from the same rough cloth as his robe, let it fall to the ground. He threw his torch aside. "Do you run, Harlan?"

Bernard looked at Lefarr in horror. "You're not hunting it, surely? It's illegal to take the life of a firebird."

Mathew Lefarr grunted quietly. "In the Dead Lands, Bernard, we make our own rules." He nodded at two of the remaining men, who quickly went in pursuit of their friends. To the other man he said, "Roderic, will you stay and guide Bernard to the Shelter?"

"I will," said Roderic. He was the man with the cheekbones. The oldest of the group by far.

"Harlan?" said Lefarr, inviting him to come.

Harlan took a deep breath. He had no idea what was being asked of him, but there was only one way to find out. New world, new rules, as Lefarr had said. "I need to see this," he said to his worried-looking colleague. And kicking off his sandals as the other men had done, he charged down the hill after Mathew and the others.

By the time they were all on level ground, with the Isle of Alavon standing huge beside them, the men had spread out and each was turning his face to the sky. The bird was coming down, but it was hard to say where. Several times it changed direction, which had the men pointing, predicting new landings, and running toward their next best guess.

Lefarr, however, had a different strategy. As a puffing Harlan Merriman appeared at his side, he said,

"Conserve your energy, Professor. This one intends to play with us a while. My advice: Pick an area and stick to it."

Harlan spoke, doubled over, with his hands on his knees. "What happens when it comes down?"

"The first one to catch it, claims it."

"And then?"

Lefarr didn't answer. He was engaged in a dialogue with another group of men who'd come sprinting toward him, eager to join the hunt. Harlan heard his name reported to the newcomers, but noted no animosity among them. Curiosity afforded them each a single glance, but their clear priority was the bird. Harlan could still just see it, a dark slit against the glaring orange sunrise. "How many of you — in the tribe?" he panted.

"Twenty-two," Lefarr answered. "Including you and Bernard."

"All men?"

"In this area, yes."

To Harlan's left, a wild shout went up.

"It's dropping," said Lefarr. "Now we must be swift. Good luck, Harlan. From this moment on, it's every man for himself."

"Wait," Harlan cried. "What exactly am I supposed to do?" But Lefarr was heading back toward the ridge, where he and any one of four other men were the likeliest candidates to catch the bird. It was flying at little more than twice head height, but still leading them on a merry dance. Just when it looked as if it might come down in favor of a man with bright red hair, it swerved away and plummeted to earth out of Harlan's sight. He heard a chorus of brief, excited cries, before the group of men came abruptly to a halt. Their collective stillness was a clear indication that the creature had been captured. But even Harlan was surprised when he saw the victor.

The bird was in the arms of Bernard Brotherton.

"Get back!" Bernard shouted to the assembled gathering. "You're not going to kill it! I won't let you harm it!"

Mathew Lefarr spread his hands wide to tell the other men to be silent and calm. He stepped toward Bernard in a nonaggressive manner. "Bernard," he said, "the bird came here to die. None of us ever intended to kill it."

"Then why did you chase it?"

"Friend, you must not let it struggle," said a man.

Bernard gulped and eased the tightness of his grip. The bird laid its orange head against his chest, letting its dark red ear tufts fold.

"Kneel with it," Lefarr said. "Let it face the earth."

"Why?"

"Bernard," said Harlan, stepping forward. "This is their way. Do as he says."

"The bird has only moments to live," said Lefarr. "Hold it, Bernard. As its captor, that is your honor and your privilege. But it needs to face the land."

And so Bernard Brotherton dropped to his knees with the heartbeat of a firebird fading against his trembling palm. He arranged its head in the crook of his arm and let it see the dead soil all around it. The bird blinked and gave up a grateful *rrrh*. And as it closed its hooded eyes for the very last time, it shuddered and produced a single tear. Inside the tear burned a violet flame. The tear ran down the firebird's beak and dripped onto the blackened earth.

Instantly, as if a pebble had been dropped into a pool of water, a great burst of energy swept across the dirt. The ground Harlan was standing on was purged with a strange white fire before its color settled back to a rich shade of brown. But that was not the end of it. Suddenly, a host of bright green shoots began to push up from the energized soil.

One of the men knelt down to examine them. "Corn," he said. He looked joyously at Lefarr.

Mathew went up and touched Bernard on the shoulder. "It's done," he said quietly. "Lay the bird down."

Shaking and confused, Bernard did as he was told and nestled the body among the new plants. In a matter of moments, the bird's molecular structure had collapsed and it had faded from view to become one with the soil it had brought to life.

"This field of crops now belongs to you," said Lefarr. "All we ask is that you tend it wisely and be aware of the needs of the men around you." He stood aside and invited the other men closer. One by one they shook Bernard's hand and thanked him for what he had done.

Last to approach was Harlan Merriman. He crouched down and looked his technician in the eye. "Well, Bernard. Welcome to the tribe."

"What is this place?" Bernard whispered. He was still kneeling, still overcome.

Harlan extended a hand to help him up. "This is Alavon," he said. "Our new life."

3.

It was at least half a day before Harlan and Bernard were ready to speak with Lefarr again. At the suggestion of a senior man, Hugo Abbot, the newcomers were escorted to a suitable dwelling place where they were encouraged to rest. The Shelter, as the tribe described their settlement, was little more than a small collection of huts on one side of the hill, put together from dried earth and woven grasses. When Harlan set eyes upon his new accommodation, the luxury of a self-adjusting pneumatic bed was soon a distant fantasy for him, but after the tiring slog across the marsh it wasn't difficult to find several hours of welcome sleep on the rough bedding provided.

He woke to the warmth of a crackling fire and the humid atmosphere of steam rising from a bubbling pot. Every joint in his back ached, more so as he pushed himself upright. Roderic, the man who had stayed with Bernard on the summit of the ridge, handed him a ceramic dish filled with a pale, uninviting broth.

"I'm sorry, it's the best there is."

Harlan manufactured a grateful smile. He glanced at the broth. There was some kind of loose peel floating on the surface.

"Potato," Roderic said, guessing at the coming question. He pressed a clutch of bread into Harlan's hand and encouraged him to try it. It clung to the teeth and was completely saltless, but otherwise palatable.

"You have flour?" Harlan asked.

Roderic turned away to stir the pot. "A bird gifted us a field of wheat. So, yes, we make bread when we're able to."

"How do you bake it?"

"We found we could construct a tolerable oven by cutting a rectangular hole into an earthen embankment. We heat it with hot rocks. It's an art, getting the timings right. I've been cursed more than once for giving the tribe a bad gut. The small flecks of dark material you can taste are wild berries. They are coated in natural yeast, which helps the bread to rise and gives it flavor."

"And the water?"

"From a spring in the hillside."

Harlan brought the spring-water broth to his mouth. One sip nearly took away the back of his throat. He retched a little and had to spit out.

"Don't worry, you get used to it," a familiar voice said. Lefarr swept in and sat cross-legged on a pile of loose cloths, the same material the robes and blankets were made from. "What we lack in seasoning, we make up for in nutrition."

Harlan wiped his lip. He'd need a lot more convincing of that, he thought. But the growing threat of hunger persuaded him to take another swig, which this time he swallowed. "Where did you find the dish?" And the cooking pot, for that matter? The potatoes, he assumed, were another "blessing" (as he'd heard one of the men say) from a dying firebird.

"We go out regularly in teams of four, searching, collecting up what we can. Sometimes when we're digging the crops, we come across gems like the cooking pot."

"Then there's really stuff out there?"

A smile played across Mathew's face. "I told you, this place is not as dead as its name implies. The Aunts provide us with cloth, but no food. They are well aware that with enough ingenuity and determination a tribe can survive here — just. By handing us the responsibility of scraping together our meager existence they can claim they're not condemning us to outright starvation, which eases their questionable conscience and keeps them within the law. But hundreds do die here, Harlan."

A weary groan from the bundle of blankets in the corner announced that Bernard, at least, was still alive. Roderic moved across the floor to attend to him.

"Do the Aunts know about the crops and the firebirds?"

"If they do, they've done nothing to stop it," said Lefarr.

"Has it always happened?"

"No," said Lefarr. "Roderic can tell you more about it than I."

Harlan looked at the kindly old man. The skin on his cheeks was painfully thin, his facial muscles all but stretched to their limit. He was hardly the best advertisement for his own cooking, but his small gray eyes were quick and lively, and if what Lefarr had said about the collection of minds here was accurate, even a bag of bones like him was not to be underestimated. "The crops are a recent development," said Roderic as he welcomed Bernard awake, "though it's never been uncommon to see firebirds circling overhead, leaving food or helpful implements."

"This was dropped by one," said Lefarr, taking a needle from a pouch pocket stitched across the front of his robe.

Harlan nodded. He'd been wondering how the clothing had been put together. He pinched at his robe and sniffed an armpit. The odor from it wasn't good.

"It's rumored that they aid the sick," Roderic added, "though we, on the Isle, have never seen any evidence of that." He handed Bernard a dish of broth. "The kind of event you witnessed in the valley began when one of our tribe, a man called Hugo Abbot, whom you met yesterday, was exploring the region and saw a distressed bird come down in the field beside him. One of its wings had got entangled in a small piece of netting that Hugo had found. Unbeknownst to Hugo, the net had blown away on the wind, into the flight path of the bird. Hugo was able to tear away the net, but in its struggles the bird had put the wing out of joint. It was in anguish and ready to give up its life. But Hugo steadied it as best he could and brought it to the Shelter, where another of our men, Terance Humbey —"

"A medic in Central," Lefarr put in.

"— was able to tend it. The bird gave a terrible cry of suffering as Terance reset the wing. The poor creature went painfully limp, and at first we thought it had died of shock. But Terance detected a trace of air in its nostrils and he stayed with it until it duly came around. By then he had strapped the wing and settled the bird in a makeshift cage. It awoke blowing plumes of fire, spitting its red-hot embers at us as if we were its mortal enemy. Hugo bravely knelt down and spoke to it. Perhaps it was his gentle tone of voice or the fact that the bird simply recognized its rescuer, but it allowed him to put his hands up close and take the cage apart. There the bird stood, glorious in its bright yellow plumage, with its ear tufts raised like orange twigs. It looked at us all in turn, then began to peck at the binding on its wing. Terance followed Hugo's example and knelt down also. Gently, so as not to startle the creature, he unwrapped the bindings and set the thing free. It took to the sky in a flash of feathers, rolling and tumbling as though it was flying for the very first time. We clapped and cheered and wished it well. Before it left to go back to wherever it had come from, it hovered above us with its wings spread apart and the sun forming an aura around it. It was a wonderful sight to behold. Two days later, the first one came to add its fire to the Isle. Since then, others have done the same. The result, as you saw, is extraordinary."

Lefarr stood up. "I've called a gathering," he said. "Whenever new men arrive we come together to introduce ourselves and exchange knowledge. Roderic will show you what to do with your dishes. I'll be waiting outside."

"Mathew?"

Lefarr turned to look at Bernard. The tech:nician looked weary, but was otherwise OK.

"What does one do about . . . the soup that isn't absorbed?"

Lefarr laughed out loud. "One thing we're not short of is ground to bury waste in. Roderic will take you to a designated field. When you're ready, join us."

The twenty-two Followers of Agawin assembled in an open space between the huts. Many of them were sitting on parts of old trees they had presumably dragged there. How far, Harlan wondered, did their explorations take them? He had seen no sign of trees the night before. Bernard was guided to a spare block of wood and Harlan to a boulder that must have required the shoulders of the strongest men to move it. Lefarr sat opposite, winding his limbs around a ragged trunk that seemed to have footholds specially carved out for him.

"Friends," he announced, "we welcome to the tribe Harlan Merriman, once a Professor of Phys:ics, and his colleague, Bernard Brotherton, from that same line of work."

The men looked at Harlan keenly.

"In a moment," Lefarr went on, "I will ask you both to explain why you were sent here. But first, let us introduce ourselves to you. On my left is Hugo Abbot, whom you have already heard about."

"Welcome," said Hugo. He nodded his nearly bald head. Two slim wedges of dark brown hair sat like crowns just above his ears. He wore round-rimmed spex, though only the left side lens was present. "I was sent here for openly speaking my opinions of the Aunts and advocating a return to natural births." He turned to a square-chinned man at his left, whose jaw was red with shaving marks. Whatever cutting implement the firebirds might have gifted him, it wasn't slick or intended for human skin. The whole tribe, except two, had facial hair.

"Welcome," he said, thick and nasal. "My name is Colm Fellowes. I am an engineer. I used to imagineer and tune Re:movers. I was sent here for making them deliberately malfunction when my wife was taken for Aunthood against her wishes."

That raised a small cheer. And so it went on, all around the circle. One man after another, telling of their rebellion against the Higher or the Grand Design. Harlan's confession of his experiment gone wrong stimulated many questions and prompted a long discussion about the properties of time and the possible role of the firebirds in it. Finally, Lefarr said to the new men, "Is there anything you would like to ask of us?"

"Yes," said Harlan. "I'm interested in the tower." He pointed over his shoulder to the hill, rising like a moody giant in the background.

"Does the path take you to it?" Bernard asked. From his position he could see the hill clearly. He nodded at a faint brown line winding across the elevated ground.

"The tower is a sacred place," said Hugo. "It's all that remains of the dwelling place of Agawin."

Harlan swiveled on his boulder, cupping his hands above his eyes. "Can we go up there?"

Lefarr glanced around the circle. He leaned close to Hugo Abbot and spoke in a whisper. Hugo gave the faintest of nods. "It is every man's right to make the climb," said Mathew, "but I should warn you, there are dangers."

Bernard's questioning gaze shifted back to the hillside. The sun was sitting just behind the summit. "It isn't high. Surely we're not likely to fall?"

One of the men, Thomas Spilo, gave out a short grunt.

Mathew raised a hand before others could respond. "Men have been changed by the experience, Bernard. The tower, as Hugo said, is a spiritual place."

Another of the men muttered something and for a second time Mathew overrode it. "We will climb the Isle today, before dark. Myself, Colm Fellowes, Harlan, and Bernard."

"Why 'Isle,' not 'hill'?" Harlan asked. He couldn't wait to get started.

Colm Fellowes replied, "Alavon was once surrounded by water. When the Great Re:duction began, it drained to leave the marsh you crossed."

"Re:duction?" Bernard said, looking around the circle.

"You've never wondered how these lands earned their name?" said Lefarr.

Bernard concentrated inwardly for a moment. "Weren't we all taught that the elemental forces — 'nature' I believe they were called — simply fell into collapse when humans gathered in Co:pern:ica Central?"

One or two of the men began to shuffle their feet.

"I'm afraid that's not correct," Hugo Abbot said. "Mathew, tell them what you discovered in the Geo:grafical Institute."

Lefarr waited for Harlan to look at him, then said, "As I'm sure you know, all living things have auma, from the smallest blade of grass to the largest hill. Once, this land was rich with it. Every stone, every granule of soil, every creature that burrowed through or lived in the soil or ran across its surface or swam in its pools of life-giving water, every tree or flower that sprouted from the land and drank in the rain that fell from the clouds — all of these things had natural auma, linked together in a collective consciousness called Gai:a, and shared with us, the most privileged, intelligent life-form on the planet. And do you know what we did with that privilege, when we eventually discovered how our minds were connected to this extraordinary resource? We slowly sucked the consciousness out of the earth and all of its creatures and all of its plants, and we took it to ourselves and we used it to enhance our fain. Before we knew what we were doing, the plants and the creatures were fading from view and the land had become *dark*. We took it all, Bernard. We re:duced it to nothing but a barren wilderness where hardly a memory of its beautiful, boundless diversity survives."

"But why? For what purpose?" Bernard said, wringing his hands in a belated show of guilt.

"For the purpose of 'a better way of life,'" said Hugo.

"For the purpose of imagineering," said Lefarr.

4.

In essence, we are farmers," Colm Fellowes was saying, as he prepared Harlan and Bernard for their trek to the summit of the Isle of Alavon. He tossed a sandal aside from the pile he'd been working through and chose one with a wider base for Bernard's left foot. "We miss our wives and our children, of course, but what we have here we are rightly proud of. There is not a man among us who would not defend Alavon to his death." He tapped Bernard's ankle as he found a good fit. "That pair will serve you well when we reach the stiffest part of the climb. They won't be entirely comfortable, but they will keep the calluses and blisters down. Harlan, you seem ill at ease."

Harlan snapped a dead twig and let the pieces fall. "I was thinking about the greenery," he said. Earlier, he had accompanied Colm and Bernard to

Brotherton Field, as it was now known, where Colm had offered Bernard useful advice on what help he could expect from the rest of the tribe, what tools were available to work the new crops (which, after their amazing first flourish, were now dormantly soaking up the heat of the sun), and the best way to carry water to the field, with which to irrigate the fledgling plants.

"The greenery?" Colm repeated.

"After what I learned at the meeting this morning, it fills me with an odd kind of sadness to see it."

"But the plants are our lifeline," Colm said, frowning.

Bernard raised a hand in a gesture of explanation. "I think I know what Harlan's getting at," he said, walking in circles to test his new footwear. "It was the study of plants, in particular the efficiency with which they converted light to energy in the photo:synthetic process, that indirectly led to a greater understanding of the laws of quan:tum mech:anics and the relationship between light, perception, and consciousness — and hence the ability to imagineer."

"But that was afterward," said Harlan, staring grimly at the hill.

"Afterward? I don't understand," Colm said. He pulled on a backpack and whistled to Lefarr.

"Bernard is talking about the way we fine-tuned our imagineering once we discovered we were capable of it. But how we made the breakthrough is still a mystery. We have always been able to travel in our minds, to think freely, to dream of better things. We can still do it here, in a place where our fain is useless, and I find that strangely liberating. But what was it that initiated the profound leap in consciousness that ultimately enabled us to make stable constructs of our thoughts? And was it worth it, if it left Co:pern:ica like this?"

Colm Fellowes shrugged. "How did the universe evolve from a cloud of gas? What defines the way a seed, once watered, divides into leaf and stem? How does a firebird's tear replenish the earth? Maybe some questions are too big to answer — and therefore better left alone." He turned and checked the position of the sun. "We should leave. The journey isn't long but it *is* hard and we need to reach the ruins before nightfall. Keep drinking from your vessels. If your breathing becomes difficult, signal me or Mathew. The air grows thinner toward the peak."

"How?" asked Bernard. "It can't be high enough to register a significant change of atmosphere?"

Colm Fellowes looked at them both in turn. "You can ponder that mystery along the way. Trust me, it's better to think than to talk."

From a nearby hut, Lefarr and the medic, Terance Humbey, came to join them. After a further check of provisions and a few more words of advice from Terance, the party made its way to the rising ground. Men working singly in the fields to either side leaned on their improvised hoes and watched them go.

"Why are they so solemn?" Bernard whispered to Lefarr.

"They fear we may not come back," he replied.

That stopped Harlan before he'd struck the path. "Why?" he asked directly. "What are you keeping from us?"

"We should tell them, Mat," Colm Fellowes said, the ground almost cracking with the weight of his stride. He stopped and took it upon himself anyway. "Men have been known to go mad up there. They say the ruins are haunted."

"By Agawin?"

Fellowes glanced back at Lefarr and said, "Some

329

travelers have returned from the Isle with a tale —
about a flying beast many times bigger than any firebird.
They say it guards the tower, though none of us have
seen it from the settlement below. They say its fire can
steal the air from within a man's lungs."

"Roderic attaches a name to it," said Mathew. "He
was a scholar of history once. He identifies this creature by the anonymous term 'dragon.'"

Bernard gulped and loosened the neck of his robe.
"A fire-breathing creature bigger than a *bird*?"

"You may both turn back if you wish," Mathew
said.

And what kind of choice is that? thought Harlan.
He pressed on, dropping in behind Colm Fellowes.
"Have either of you ever encountered this 'dragon'?"

"We have both felt its presence," Mathew said.

"With respect, that tells me nothing."

Colm Fellowes tightened his lip. He nudged a few
pebbles to one side of the path. "You will have the
opportunity to test your skepticism when we stand at
the doorway to the tower, Professor."

"If it's ruined, what is there to see?" said Bernard,
adopting Colm's example of avoiding the stones; they
felt like small explosions on the soles of the feet.

"At the center of the tower is a dais," said Lefarr, "made from the same gray stone as the building. It rises to about the midheight of a man and is circular, equidistant with the walls of the tower. Carved around the edges of its flat, upper surface are symbols no one has been able to interpret. At its center is an image."

Bernard paused to quench his thirst. His slightly bloated cheeks were already beginning to glow with the first signs of perspiration. "Of the beast that haunts the place?"

Lefarr stopped and opened his own water vessel. "No. The figure of a man in the creature's image."

"A man — with wings and fire?"

"And is *that* Agawin?" Harlan said.

"We believe so," said Mathew.

"The Followers say the dais is his tomb," Colm added.

Bernard's lips made a gentle smacking sound as he wiped them dry of water.

"There has never been a successful excavation," said Lefarr, in anticipation of the scientists' next question.

"But there have been attempts?" Harlan pressed him.

Mathew capped his water vessel with a firm thump. "There won't be one today," was all he said. And at that moment, it began to rain.

Bernard instinctively reached for a hood. Not finding one attached to his robe, he accepted it, as Colm and Mathew had done, and let the water run where it would.

"Tread carefully now," Mathew advised them. "The rain is refreshing but it makes the way slippery. There is no cover here other than the ruins. The quicker we reach them, the better. We won't speak again unless someone is in trouble. Are we clear?"

"Clear," said Harlan, adjusting his backpack. Bernard nodded, and they both fell into step.

Despite Lefarr's warnings, the pathway had enough grit mixed with the mud to make sure their sandals made a good, sound purchase. There were imbalances, but no embarrassing falls, and the party moved ahead in open file, at reasonable pace. All around them the sky was gravid with rain, which did little but inflate the dark character of the land and kept "sightseeing," as Bernard called it, to a minimum. Harlan, likewise, despite his curiosity about Agawin and the creature that allegedly guarded the tower, could find little room in his mind to think of anything other than his next sure step. But as the muscles in his thighs began to burn, announcing the onset of the final incline, he suddenly felt a swift loss of pressure in his lungs and had to drop back, a few paces off the others. He gestured to Colm that he was fine, just pausing for a drink of water. But before he knew it he was on his knees, clutching at his chest for any kind of breath. A high-pitched whine made his eardrums sing. Blood pooled against the wall of one nostril. His eyeballs felt as if they wanted to burst. He could still see Colm, but only as a hazy S-shaped line against a sky suddenly swollen with heat. He cried out to him, but the thinned air folded his words right back. And when he stretched a hand forward to signal for help, something inhuman came to meet it.

He felt nothing but the pressure waves crossing him at first. His robe billowed and his modest shock of hair fanned out. Claws with the strength to crush bones into paper took him by the shoulders and lifted him as if he were an empty shell. He was some way off the ground when he heard the muffled shouts of the men below. More pressingly, another voice was in his mind.

Beware the Shadow of Isenfier.

The next thing Harlan Merriman knew, his body was impacting on the slopes of Alavon and his consciousness was back with the other three men.

"Harlan?! Harlan?! Are you all right?" Lefarr's voice swam into play. "Colm, pick him up. Carry him to the tower. Lay him down there."

"In the *tower*?"

"On the dais itself if you have to! Move!"

And Harlan felt himself lifted again, cradled in the arms of the once-engineer.

When he did become fully awake, the rain had slowed to a creeping mizzle. He was lying by a curving wall of stone that reached for the sky like a funnel to the stars. "The tower," he whispered.

"Yes," said Bernard, kneeling beside him. He rested the back of his hand on Harlan's forehead.

Lefarr swept up, offering a vessel. "Drink," he said.

Harlan shook his head. With Bernard's help, he managed a sitting position. Once again his back was wracked with pain. His left ankle was a bloated ball of bruises.

"What happened, Harlan?" Lefarr asked urgently.

"I don't know," he muttered.

"You were floating," said Bernard.

Harlan coughed a little. "Floating?"

"You were ten feet off the ground when we reached you," said Lefarr.

Harlan looked all around him. For one moment he experienced a quieter repeat of the singing in his ears. "Where is it? Where did it fly to?"

"Where did what fly to?" Bernard asked.

"The creature. The dragon that picked me off the hill."

Bernard and Lefarr exchanged a glance. "All we saw was you hanging limply in the sky. There was no dragon."

Harlan stared at the dais. There was blood in his mouth and fear in his heart. He touched the stones he was propped against and said, "It goes by a name, this invisible thing. This creature that drives your men to madness."

Lefarr ran a thumb across his drying lips. "You commingled with it?"

335

"It with me."

"Was it Agawin?"

Harlan looked at the shifting clouds, framed by the circle of stone above. "No," he said. "It called itself Gawain."

5.

We should return to the Shelter," Colm Fellowes said, letting his gaze roam slowly across every patch of sky. He was standing with his back to the other three men, just beyond the arch-shaped opening that would have brought him into the tower proper.

"Harlan is in no state to travel," said Lefarr. "He may have broken his foot."

Colm turned, imploring Mathew to look at him. "Two men, in turns, could carry him down with ease. If nothing else, let me go back for Terance."

"No one leaves yet," Harlan said quietly. "Bernard, help me up." He put out an arm. Using Bernard's shoulder as a crutch, he struggled to his feet, holding his swollen ankle off the ground.

Colm strode up to the archway, placing his hands on the walls to either side. The surface stonework crumbled against his palms, echoing, perhaps, the feeling in his heart. "That thing is all around us," he whispered darkly, hoping to induce some sense into Mathew. (He had not even bothered to question Harlan's statement.) "Night will be upon us within the hour. If we don't go now, it may be too late. We cannot fight what we cannot see."

"We're not here to fight it," Harlan said. He grimaced as he tried to put pressure on his ankle. "We're here to solve a riddle. Besides, it could pick us off at any moment. An invisible being has no need for the cloak of darkness. Relax, Colm, it means us no harm."

Colm struck a hand against the wall and stepped back. "Men have been known to put a knife through their heart after they've encountered the soul of this beast. How can you speak of it in gentle terms when it picked you up and cast you aside like a leaf?"

"It needed to prove something to me."

"And what was that?"

"That it's real, not imagined."

Colm threw up his hands in despair.

"I understand your anxieties and I'm not trying to belittle them," said Harlan, "but I'm certain that this dragon has never intended to prey on the tribe. Its

338

auma is at such an intense vibration that it simply overwhelms the minds of most men. It's the fear of what they don't understand that kills them, not the fire of the beast."

Lefarr regarded Harlan thoughtfully, tilting his head in a searching manner. "What exactly did you learn from it, other than a name?"

Harlan hobbled over to the dais. He brushed some loose dirt off the circle of symbols and asked Bernard to clear the far side as well. "As you know, in the commingled state it's possible to assimilate something of the cohost's nature. This dragon is a trans:dimensional being. A wandering spirit, lost in time."

"It's seeking our help?"

"Possibly, yes."

Colm let out a hopeless sigh.

"It gave me a warning," Harlan said.

Now Colm turned and looked sharply at Lefarr.

"It was telling me to beware of something. Have you heard of the Shadow of Isenfier?"

"Ice? What is ice?" Colm lifted his shoulders. "We know of fire, but —"

"Not a conjunction of words," said Harlan. "I heard just one. I'm sure of it."

"Izenfire?" Mathew tried.

"Close," said Harlan. "It means nothing to you?"

"Nothing."

"Me neither," said Bernard, shaking his head.

Harlan tightened his lip. "Then all we're left with is this." He laid his hands flat on the dais. "Tell me, Mathew, why does the tribe 'follow' Agawin?"

Lefarr came to stand beside him. "The legend was in place well before I arrived." He pointed to the center of the dais, where there was indeed a worn-down image of a winged man. "In the early days of Alavon, when the tower was first explored, a superstitious conviction began to grow around this figure. Its basis was simple enough: If we demonstrated enough belief in our winged man, he would protect us from starvation and the stuff of nightmares."

"A *religion*?" Harlan looked up in surprise.

"Not a word you hear every day," said Lefarr, "on any part of Co:pern:ica. But when a man is stripped of his fain, he sometimes turns to faith as a substitute. The men of Alavon found their comfort in the myth of Agawin, even though nothing was known of his life, perhaps *because* nothing was known of his life. I should

340

explain, by the way, that in some men the superstition runs so deep that they dare not even look upon the figure in front of you."

"I'm afraid that might have to change," said Bernard.

Harlan raised his eyes to meet the tech:nician's. "You've spotted something?"

"These signs have been carefully arranged," said Bernard. "At a casual glance, they appear to be just an irregular jumble. But they're actually a complex of four overlying patterns."

Lefarr murmured in agreement. "Yes, I see it. Could they be star maps — or constellations?"

"Not from any system I know," said Bernard. He stretched his fingers over the carvings and made a few comparative measurements. "Do you see the small depressions where some of the 'stars' would be?"

Lefarr nodded.

"Put your fingertips into them."

"It's a key," breathed Harlan, his excitement growing. He placed all ten digits into the patterns. "Colm, come inside. We need four to complete the circle."

Colm Fellowes hovered in the doorway still. "This is madness," he hissed at Mathew. "Who knows what dangers the dais holds. We've already had a warning. We should leave, Mat. Now."

"No," said Mathew. "I believe in these men. If you abandon this, Colm, we three will simply return tomorrow with another volunteer. We need to resolve this. We owe it to the tribe."

Colm Fellowes ran a hand across his shaven face. He and his conscience fought for a moment. Then he stepped across the threshold, into the circle. The natural ruddiness of his cheeks began to blanch as he saw the symbol of the winged man, but he set his fingers down where shown.

"What now?" said Lefarr, as Harlan filled the last ten spots. His gaze jumped from hand to hand. Nothing was happening.

"We must commingle," said Harlan.

Colm gritted his teeth. "You know that's not possible in the Dead Lands."

"It may be enough to show like intent. Close your eyes. Concentrate on knowing the meaning of the dais."

But still nothing happened, though a gentle vortex of air was beginning to strafe the inner walls of the tower. It rippled the loose parts of everyone's clothing and stirred up the dust around the base of the dais. And though it did not have the strength to move a man, its agitated wail was enough to worry Colm.

"This isn't working," he said. "We should leave, while we can." He pulled his fingers away.

"No, wait," said Harlan, his eyes racing over the patterns again. "Colm, come back. I think we need to overlap hands. Like this." He demonstrated quickly to Lefarr, placing his right hand where Mathew's left would have been.

"Yes," said Bernard. "Yes, that could work. Our arms will mimic the crisscrossing theme."

"Colm, come on," Mathew implored him. "One more try, then we go."

Colm took up position and closed his eyes again.

Almost immediately, the vortex was back and building in strength.

"Hold fast!" yelled Harlan as it started to yowl like a creature trapped. It tugged at the pouches of skin on his cheeks and evaporated most of the moisture from his eyes. The ground was shaking, and so, too, the tower, throwing loose mortar from between its joints.

Suddenly, Mathew Lefarr cried out: "Harlan, look up!"

There, in the circle of light above, was the apparition they had all imagined but never made flesh. A terrifying beast with wings like giant sheets of canvas. Eyes of yellow oil. Teeth like daggered rocks. It twisted and hissed and roared at the men, all the while lashing its dark red tongue. Colm Fellowes screamed and ran out onto the hillside. Bernard, likewise, fell against the wall, burying his face in a huddle of fright. Only Harlan and the valiant Mathew Lefarr bore witness to what happened next. The creature twisted its ingenious neck (every scale readjusted in one flowing arrow) and aimed its snout downward. Squeezing its nostrils tight, it sent forth a column of blue-white fire. The point of the flame struck the center of the dais. It burned for a sec in a crown of light, then was sucked back into the nostrils of the dragon. In its wake, something extraordinary followed. There was a grinding noise at the center of the dais, and the spot marked by the image of Agawin began to turn and work its way upward. At first it appeared that a plug of pure stone had lifted from the structure. But as Harlan's eyes readjusted to the light, he saw that it was a receptacle of sorts. A cylinder, about the length of a man's hand, made of a glistening, trans:lucent matter. With cinders in his hair and uncomfortable traces of singeing in his nostrils, he took a breath and closed his hand around it. The outer structure vanished as if it were dust, but when he pulled his hand away, inside it was something from another world.

Lefarr was too awestruck to speak at first. "What is it?" he asked eventually.

Harlan ran his thumb along the curved and jagged surface. "Something beyond our reality," he whispered. "I believe it's the claw of a dragon."

6.

Once again, at midmorning on the day after the climb, the Tribe of Alavon gathered in a circle in the clearing by the huts. The claw lay on a stump of wood at the center, for all the men to see. Mathew Lefarr told the story of the journey, setting out all that had happened. When he was finished, he invited every man to examine the claw and hold it if they wished. None did. Instead, they turned to the man who had discovered it and asked him what was to be done with this wonder.

That question had been on Harlan's mind all night. "First," he said, "let us be clear about one thing. I've spoken with our medic, Terance Humbey, and he agrees with me that the claw is not of human origin. It therefore cannot be the remains of Agawin."

"Agawin was a winged man," Hugo reasoned. "Is it not possible that he evolved claws like a bird?"

The men murmured in agreement.

"That's not the feeling it gives me," said Harlan. He spoke boldly, aiming his words around the circle. "I was one with the dragon for long enough to know that the claw came from its kind, not from ours."

"Very well," said Hugo. "This we must accept. But why was it placed in the dais at all? What significance does it have?"

"Aye, and what power?" said one of the men, which raised an even louder hubbub of voices.

Hugo clapped his hands for silence. "Friends, Bernard Brotherton will speak on this matter."

All eyes turned toward the tech:nician.

Bernard, the bottom half of his face now shaded with a jet-black stubble, said this: "The claw was not placed in the dais, it was hidden. It was meant to be discovered by someone with the capacity to understand complex math:e:matical patterns. What this tells us is that whoever set the key was intelligent themselves."

Roderic raised his hand. "Could it be that the claw was secreted in the dais to protect it when the land was re:duced?"

"Very possibly," said Bernard.

"Who by — Agawin or the beast?" Colm said.

"That we don't know."

"Well, we have it and that is that," said Hugo. "Harlan, as its finder, you must be accountable for its safekeeping. The tribe will aid you and protect you in any way it can, but I urge you to keep the discovery hidden — at least until we ascertain what it might be used for. We are now in the dangerous position of knowing something about the Dead Lands that the Aunts don't. The meeting is closed."

Harlan looked at Hugo and nodded. He slipped off his seat, wincing as his injured foot touched the ground. It had been strapped with rough bandages by Terance that morning, after the painful descent from the hill. He hobbled into the circle and picked up the claw. "Before we disperse, does any man know the word Isenfier or the name Gawain?"

The men glanced at one another and shook their heads. "Why do you ask?" said Thomas Spilo, whose whole face was surrounded with dark curly hair.

"The words came to me when the dragon commingled, though in what capacity I couldn't be sure." Harlan looked at Lefarr, who cast his eyes down. He slipped the claw into his robe and limped away.

"That was dangerous," Mathew said, when they were back in his hut. "Why didn't you tell them that Isenfier was a warning?"

Harlan threw the question back. "Why didn't *you*?"

Lefarr sighed and sank into his cross-legged pose. "I didn't want to alarm them. But Colm knows the truth. He may not keep it to himself for long."

"Then we'd better do as Hugo implied," said Bernard. "And find out what that thing is for."

Harlan held the claw up to his face, massaging the tip between his thumb and forefinger. "There's something fluid in here that I can't squeeze out."

"Is it wise to?" said Lefarr. "What if it's toxic?"

Harlan clicked his tongue and thought about it. "Do you have anything clean and white I could shake a droplet onto?"

"Actually, I do." Mathew took a sheet of paper from his robe, which he unfolded in front of the others. "It's a letter — from my grandmother to my grandfather, just before he died. She liked the old-fashioned permanence of writing. I managed to smuggle it out of my pod when the Re:movers came for me."

Harlan pushed his tongue between his lips and grimaced. "Mathew, I can't use that."

"It's all right," he said. "My grandmother would have been proud to know that her words were being mixed with the essence of a dragon."

Harlan smiled and took the letter from him. "I'll aim at a corner," he said. Yet, no matter how hard he shook, nothing would leave the tip of the claw. "This is bizarre," he said, looking at it straight on. "I'm convinced I can see a tiny aperture with the fluid welling up behind. It ought to come out."

Before Bernard could reply with a swatch of phys:ics, Mathew said, "What happens if you touch the tip to the paper?" He looked at the scientists and shrugged.

Harlan tried it. He scratched the claw down a margin of the letter and a thin vertical line was produced. "That's extraordinary," he breathed. But there it was: a line, colored green.

"Then it can be used as a *pen*?" Bernard queried, craning his neck to see it.

"But why?" said Lefarr. "Why hide away a pen?"

"Maybe," said Harlan, looking at the letter and its beautiful script, "it's not the pen that matters, but the words it writes." And he applied the claw to the bottom of the paper and wrote *Isenfier* in small block letters.

For two heartbeats, nothing happened. But Harlan was sure he could feel the world turning. Whatever force his mind was resonating with suddenly moved his gaze to the door. "Firebird," he whispered, just before the cry went up outside.

"Firebird! Firebird!"

And then the world was indeed turning.

And the first jet of flame hit the roof of the hut.

7.

Within moments, the calls had changed in both frequency and length. "Fire!" the men were shouting wildly. The accumulated thunder of their running feet shook the ground on which Harlan was sitting. A small portion of the roof cover crackled. Cinders fell from its disappearing edges as the fire took hold and the weave was eaten up in a running line.

Mathew leaped to his feet. "Quickly. We have to get out before it collapses." He came over and shouldered Harlan upright, then ran into the daylight, shouting for help.

By the time Bernard and Harlan had joined him, most of the men were grouped together, busily watching the sky. Some were helping others to clear what they could from the huts on fire. Harlan counted five in total. No one was running for water, he noticed. But then, what good would it have done? The fires were raging too fast to be contained. And even if sufficient water could be brought, the men had no means of spraying it onto the flames.

"There!" cried a voice laced with resentment. Thomas Spilo pointed upward through a break in the smoke.

"Where? What are we looking at?" Harlan said, spinning.

"Black firebird, right overhead," whispered Mathew. He stepped sideways to gain a better view.

"*Black?*" said Bernard.

And then Harlan saw it, partially eclipsed by drifting smoke. "It's coming down," he said. "It's going to attack."

"It's dilating its nostrils," someone shouted. A sign that the bird was making fire.

"Run!" barked Lefarr.

The men scattered. All except one. In three quick strides, Colm Fellowes was at the nearest hut. In a display of brute strength, he ripped away a piece of wood used to frame the door. Yelling a ferocious challenge, he came back into the clearing. The bird angled its descent path toward him. The whole tribe was urging Colm to stand away. But Colm, his hut destroyed, his life undone by Aunts and Re:movers, his mind addled by what he had seen in the tower, was determined to stand and fight. He swung out as the bird swooped low. The bird made a strange kind of *caark*-ing noise and the clearing was lost in a brief flash of orange. No scientist had ever been able to explain how a creature half the size of a small child was able to produce such a vigorous burst of expanding flame. But Harlan would witness it twice that morning, in all its terrible glory. The blow Colm Fellowes had been trying to land spun him around in an arc of fury. So feral was his lunge that the wood slipped tamely out of his hands and fell to the ground with a meaningless *clunk*. The bird rushed by, unharmed. But Colm's robe had taken fire from the hem to the belt. He held out his arms and screamed.

Mathew and Terance were the first to reach him. They brought him down and rolled him across the earth in an attempt to smother the worst of the flames. Then Hugo was there, beating Colm's legs with another robe. By the time that water had been brought and the fire stopped, Colm had passed out in a shaking fit. Most of his robe had disintegrated. What was left was welded to his blistered skin.

Thomas Spilo thundered, "Why is it doing this? What does it want?"

But it was Bernard who suddenly claimed everyone's attention. "Look there!" He pointed toward Lefarr's hut. The firebird was perched on what remained of the badly scorched walls, eyeing the tribe with malevolent interest.

"It's scanning us," said Bernard.

And as usual, he was right. The bird's fain touched the mind of every man present, but its gaze came to rest on only one of them: Harlan.

Hugo Abbot spread his hands and urged the men to be silent. "It seems to want you," he said to Harlan, "or what you found in the tower. We can't defend ourselves against such a force. Whatever it wants, I beg you, give it up. Don't let another man be burned."

Mathew Lefarr drew alongside Harlan. Speaking quietly, out of earshot of the others, he said, "Is this the Shadow you were warned of?"

Harlan made no reply. He stepped forward until his image had filled the bird's eye. He drew the claw from his robe.

The bird hissed and laid its ear tufts back.

"It's frightened of it," Mathew muttered.

Harlan tightened his grip. Right away he achieved what no one else on Co:pern:ica ever had: a mental link with a firebird. But as his consciousness jostled with that of the bird's, he was horrified to find that he had actually commingled with something alien. The bird — or rather its mind — was dead. Another entity was using the body as a vessel. It was quick to identify itself.

We are Ix, they said.

"We." Not "I," Harlan noted.

They swarmed around his mind. Probing. Dangerous. *We are a Cluster,* they said in response to his thought-wave. *You are the one who opened the portal.*

Harlan's mind flashed to his experiment. This thing had come through the rift?

You will guide us to a fire star, the Ix said coldly, applying themselves to indiscriminate parts of Harlan's brain and tormenting his neural network in the process. Externally, the watching men saw him quake, but no one dared interrupt. The involuntary spasm of muscles forced his hand to close tighter around the claw. A fresh wave of energy surged through his mind. To his surprise, the Ix Cluster was suppressed a little. Now Harlan seized the chance to interrogate them.

Kill me and you'll never get back, he said. *Where are you from?*

The Cluster welled up in a flare of resistance. *We have traveled from Isenfier.*

Isenfier. A planet? Another dimension? No, Harlan realized. It was neither of those. The site of a conflict loomed in his mind. Isenfier was a battlefield. He shuddered and let this pass. *Why are you here? What led you to the portal?*

We are following the beacon, they said.

In that instant, Harlan's heart nearly stopped as images of David swarmed through his mind, most notably of the night terrors at the therapy center. So this is what had been coming for his son. With fierce intent, he drew upon the strength of the claw again. His consciousness powered through the heart of the Cluster, dividing the Ix and weakening them. Aware he couldn't hold them in this state for long, he sought a small colony and separated it out. *Why are you trying to reach this boy?*

The colony said: *The beacon resonates in him.*

What is the reason for the beacon?

To seek help from this world.

Who is sending the signal?

357

His dragon, they said, re-Clustering with such malevolent purpose that Harlan's body collapsed to its knees. Through sheer strength of will, he raised a hand to keep the tribe back. It was vital not to break the link with the bird. For in the instant the Ix had spoken of the dragon, they had also shown Harlan an image of it. A tiny creature, almost a caricature of its kind. Small, green, trumpet-shaped nostrils, oddly spiked scales, large flat feet. There was infinite kindness in its oval eyes. Strangest of all, it was holding a pen (or maybe a pencil). But what connection could such a thing have with David?

They are one, said the Cluster, reading Harlan's thoughts.

Across worlds?

Across time. You will show us the location of a fire star. Now.

Harlan sank farther, grimacing in pain. The muscles in the arm that held the claw felt as if they were raw and bleeding. He bravely resisted letting go. *Tell me about the dragon. Why does it carry a pen?*

This time, there was a pause before the Ix replied. *You will drop the creat:or. You will give the claw to us.*

Creat:or. Harlan measured the word carefully. He thought about the talk he'd been having with Mathew just before the fires were set. How he'd written *Isenfier* on the paper. Had he brought this devastation on them? Was it possible the universe acted on the words that were written with the claw, or brought about a close response to them? Was it possible that dragons could shape dark matter? He let the last of these thoughts leak out and sensed anxiety throughout the Cluster. Mathew was right; the Ix *were* frightened of the gift from the tower, wary of what it could do. Harlan decided to put it to the test. Leaning forward, he stretched out his hand as if he were going to lay the claw on the ground. But at the final moment, he flipped it and tried to write *Gawain* in the dust. His intention was to call up the creature from the tower. But the Ix were quick to spot the danger. Harlan had managed no more than the *G* when the bird descended with its claws outstretched, ripping at his hands and arms and face. In the melee, Harlan dropped the claw. At the same time, a knife flashed through the air and struck the bird in the side of the neck. An accurate throw, but not a perfect one. The knife jiggled in the wound and fell out in a splash of bright green blood. The firebird screeched, more annoyed than hurt. It turned to see Mathew running toward it, wielding a rock. But by then it had snatched the claw from the ground and was able to defend its prize with fire. Mathew hurled his rock through a wall of flame. It missed the bird by several feet. But the fire did not miss him. It caught hold of the arm of his robe and forced him to spin away, crying out in pain. He was surrounded by men and doused right away, lucky to escape with only superficial burns.

Once again, the bird flew to the walls of the hut, where it rested, holding the claw in its beak.

Harlan pressed his lips together, knowing he had lost. But there, in the shadow of the Isle of Alavon, a pact was struck. "Wherever you go, I'll find you," he said, staring at the bird with as much raw malice as it was reserving for him. The bird tilted its head and made a record of the face. Then it spread its wings and was gone.

"Brave words, Harlan, but hard to follow through." Lefarr sidled up to him, clutching at his arm. "We'd be old and ugly in the time it would take us to journey back to Central — always assuming we went the right way. What did you learn?"

"It's alien. It's going after my son."

Lefarr shook his head. "There's nothing we can do."

But Harlan Merriman had other ideas. Without another word, he walked across to Colm.

The engineer was still laid out on the ground, surrounded by a group of concerned-looking men. A light blanket had been draped across his body. Terance was offering him sips of water. But Colm was barely breathing. He was going to die.

Harlan knelt down. "Colm," he whispered.

"Harlan?" Terance frowned. "What are you doing? He can't speak. The pain would be unbearable for him."

"Please, let him try," Harlan said. He touched Colm's shoulder. One of the few parts of his body that still looked human. "Colm, do the Re:movers have any weaknesses?"

"Harlan, in the name of Agawin, let the man rest." Hugo Abbot had joined in the argument now.

Colm opened his mouth and made a gurgling sound.

"He wants to say something," Mathew said.

Colm nodded his head a fraction.

"This had better be good," Terance growled. He moved aside to let Harlan kneel closer.

"Colm, is there any way to defeat the machines? You worked on them once. Can they be disabled?"

A slight moan left the engineer's mouth. "Water," he croaked.

"Water. He wants water," Hugo said.

Colm shook his head painfully.

"No, he *means* water," Mathew said. "Water: That's what we attack them with."

"Attack?" said Terance. "What are you talking about? Why are you even asking him this?"

"How, Colm?" Harlan asked. He bent his ear to the dying man's lips and listened for a good half minit. By the end, Colm's body was shaking badly and his lungs were making a dreadful rasp.

"Enough," Terance said, pulling Harlan away. Within moments, however, the rasping had ceased and Colm's head fell sideways. And then he was still.

The men lowered their heads.

After a respectful period of silence, Harlan said, "Call a meeting, Hugo. Now. The whole tribe."

"What did Colm tell you?" Mathew asked.

Harlan looked at the burning huts. "How to make our way out of here," he said.

8.

This is madness! Madness, I say!" Terance Humbey struck his fist into his open palm and stared at the tribesmen around the circle. "We have just buried one of our strongest men. How many more are likely to die if we try to fight the Re:movers?"

"I agree, it's dangerous," Harlan said. "All the same, I ask the tribe to consider it. The bird is possessed by a creature of darkness, an entity from another world. It has gone to Central with the claw of a dragon. Who knows what evil it might do there?"

"So you are asking us to put our lives at risk to help those who've sent us here?" said Hugo.

"Let us not forget that our wives and children are in Central," said Roderic.

"And the birds," said Bernard. "Don't we owe some allegiance to them?" He made a slight gesture over his shoulder. The closest of the green fields was right behind him.

Several men grunted their approval for this.

"We should at least hear Harlan's plan," said Mathew. "Then we vote. Harlan, if the vote goes against you, this is done. Are you agreed?"

Harlan chewed his lip. "Agreed."

"Then tell the tribe what you propose we do."

"We light a fire," Harlan said, without a moment's hesitation. "A big one. High. On the Isle. In the tower."

"That would be a sacrilege," Hugo said.

"No," said Harlan, turning to face him. "Agawin was born of fire. Even Colm sensed that when we gathered around the dais. Fire is the medium of the legend, Hugo. Agawin, or his dragons, will aid us. I'm sure."

"Fine sentiments," said Terance, "easily forgotten in front of a Re:mover. You plan to use the fire to draw them here?"

"Yes. They'll come in a taxicar. We set a trap. Disable them. Steal the car."

Murmurs started up all around the circle. Hugo immediately called for quiet. "Tell us what you learned from Colm at the end."

Harlan pressed his hands together for a moment. "If the Re:movers are immersed in water and held there, they will malfunction."

"Well, thank goodness for that," declared Thomas. "For a sec, I thought it was going to be dangerous!"

The circle exploded in a riot of laughter.

"I've always wanted a pond. I'll get to it right away."

"We don't need a body of water," said Harlan, raising his voice above the guffaws. "We have the marshes."

The laughter trailed away into silence.

Hugo nodded thoughtfully. "How would you get them to it?" he asked.

"Please tell me you've got something clever," whispered Mathew.

Harlan shook his head "One of us, maybe two, needs to lead them across the most treacherous of the bogs."

Among the grunts of incredulity Roderic said, "It's not possible, Harlan. Even if you didn't put a foot out of place, their scanners would bring you down."

"Not if the distance was right," said Bernard. "The scanners are short-range devices. Harlan's plan could work, but the timing would need to be perfect."

Terance Humbey sighed and slapped his hands to his thighs. "If we fail, we all die. You realize that?" He flicked a stone into the circle. No one made a comment.

"Then we vote," Mathew said. "Those in favor of Harlan's plan, stand up." Mathew was off his tree stump first. Then Harlan. And Bernard. Until eventually, every man present was on his feet.

"Carried," Hugo said, with a nervous gulp. "I move we draw lots to determine which men will run from the machines."

"I volunteer," said Mathew. He raised his hand quickly to quash the muttering. "I'm the youngest and the swiftest. I know the marsh well. It would be foolish to send in anyone but me."

"And me," said a quiet voice. Surprisingly, Terance stepped forward.

"But you're our medic," said Harlan.

To which Terance replied, "A medic who will be of no use to anyone if the Re:movers survive. I ran for pleasure before I was sent here. I'm fitter than most. Like Mathew, I've studied the layout of the marsh. We might as well make use of that."

"Then it's settled," said Hugo. "Harlan, our lives now rest upon you. What would you have us do?"

Harlan pointed to the Isle of Alavon. "Gather dry grasses. As many as you can carry. Take them to the tower. We need to make a beacon. A light that can be seen all over the Dead Lands."

"It's going to take several days," said Roderic.

"Time is not something we are short of," said Hugo. "Begin."

The men peeled away, leaving Mathew to speak alone to Harlan and Bernard. "You realize the Re:movers might not come? And even if they do and we get our ride back, this alien creature you speak of may have done all it needs to by then."

"At least we'll know that we tried," said Bernard.

Harlan nodded and clapped a hand to Mathew's shoulder. "Have faith, there may be a twist to this yet. Now, let's find something that will burn."

9.

Little did Harlan Merriman know that there would indeed be a strange twist to come. While he and his tribe were building their pyre, the black firebird was flying in haste through the night, crossing over the Dead Lands and the imagineered security zone around Co:pern:ica Central, back to Bushley and the librarium there. It was an exhausting flight; the firebird was hampered by the need to take in air through the nostrils while the beak was clamped around the dragon's claw. It could, of course, have carried the claw in its feet. But after days of occupation and lack of vital nutrients, the muscular structure of the body was fading. The risk of losing the claw was too great. The answer, the Cluster told itself, was to fly through the physical discomfort, find another stupid bird, and take control of that. Fresh wings would take it anywhere it needed to go, and there were plenty of those in the aerie.

As it approached the colossal building, stabbed like a giant spike into the earth, it was surprised to see a room on the lower floor on fire. Higher up, a dozen or more birds were beginning to flock, possibly getting ready to deal with the flames. The black bird tipped a wing and circled a moment, using the clouds to keep itself hidden. This could be a useful distraction, it thought. An opportunity to scrutinize the roof of the building where the auma of this world seemed to radiate from. Then again, how much effort would it take to glide down to that room and see what was happening? This failing body still had strength enough for that.

So it landed on the sill and immediately observed three prominent life-forms: the girl who seemed to inhabit the building and two more firebirds, including one that spoke. *Aubrey?* it said in a questioning manner. The black bird *caark*ed in its throat, and quickly wished it hadn't. It had made itself known. That was foolish. This cream one was clever. It was sure to come looking. Unless it could be the Cluster's new body . . .

But just as the Ix prepared to transfer, one of the transport vehicles appeared. Out of it jumped the life-form, David, who had sometimes lived in the building, too. The black bird cursed and took to the sky, hiding itself in the plumes of smoke. It landed on another sill twelve floors up. From there it watched the flock come swooping down and follow David into the burning room.

It was a trivial setback. Nothing more. Rest, recover, relocate. The Ix prepared themselves to fight another day. But as they folded down the firebird's wings, the Cluster grew aware of another presence. A potent source of fain, looming right behind it. The bird whipped around, with every intention of flaming the stalker, but the claw it was carrying in its mouth prevented it. *(Design!)* By the time the claw had been spat, it was too late. A sack, imagineered from the strongest fireproof material there could be, was over the bird's body, knotted with rope of a similar strength. And though the Ix Cluster tried to escape and overcome its captor's mind, the captor had prepared for that, too. A powerful neural emission put the creature's fain into immediate stasis.

Aunt Gwyneth bent down and picked up the claw. *Dragon.* It spoke to her from every fiber. Not a bad result at all, after the disaster with those useless twins. Extending her fain, she lightly probed the consciousness in the sack.

"Well, well," she whispered. "So, that's what you are." Pure fain, inverted. Wickedness — in a bag.

She pulled back as the creature tried again to possess her. She must be careful. This thing was clever. And strong. Already she could sense it splitting and regrouping, trying to find any source of weakness in her mind.

Trust me, that won't work, she told it. A somewhat hollow threat as it happened. In truth, it was all she could do to maintain the delicate balance of power. If she let down her guard, this being would kill her. A tricky situation. Her only option was to negotiate.

Keeping up the arrogant front, she said, *I'm prepared to make you . . . an offer.*

What is your proposal? the Ix replied.

Aunt Gwyneth turned to the daisy fields. Not since her time in the Aunt Academy, learning what was right and what was wrong, had she been so entranced by the concept of power. *A union,* she said.

A commingling?

A union. Under my command.

There was a pause. The Ix said, *We agree.*

And the most unholy alliance in the history of Co:pern:ica began right there.

Though it nearly didn't.

As Aunt Gwyneth slackened her grip and let the Ix merge with her neural pathways, an almighty struggle began. The Ix was a thing that possessed no conscience. What else could they do but betray her trust, even though that trust was admittedly misplaced? They swept through her mind and tried at once to assume control. It was a close-run thing. Her assessment of the Cluster had been quite accurate. Powerful. Ingenious. A dedicated killer. But she, an Aunt Su:perior, *the* Aunt Su:perior, had not risen to that rank through kindness and courtesy. She had power — and cunning — in abundance, too. Turning her fain to near maximum, she broke the Cluster, as Harlan had done, and subjugated the Ix in different parts of her mind. *Try that again and I'll eliminate you, colony by colony,* she told them.

Wisely, the Ix flattened off a little.

Now you will tell me why you are here.

We seek control of the nexus, they said.

Aunt Gwyneth relaxed her fain into theirs. A nexus. An entanglement of time. How interesting. *There is a time point, here? Where to?* she asked.

The Ix floated into her consciousness. *The nexus triangulates between three worlds. On Co:pern:ica, within this tower of stone. On a thought dimension called Ki:mera, colonized by the spirit of dragons. And on a low-level physical plane, where it resolves at the battle of Isenfier.*

What is the name of the last world? said Gwyneth.

The Ix pulsed and seemed unwilling to answer. *A blue planet of rock and water,* they said, *once used as a dragon breeding ground. Its name is Earth.*

PART FOUR

WHICH HAS ITS

BEGINNINGS — AND ITS PECULIAR

ENDINGS —

IN A REMARKABLE

REORDERING OF

THE BUSHLEY LIBRARIUM

MARCH 11, 032

1.

In the aftermath of the librarium blaze, David carried Rosa into the daisy fields to make sure she was able to breathe clean air. The firebirds, their job complete, dispersed. As she watched them heading back toward the upper floors, Aurielle glanced at Azkiar and saw the despondency in his eyes. He needed a task, she thought, to take his mind from the lingering smell of burning paper. She fluttered to his side and suggested he fly off in search of Aubrey. Azkiar crossed the tips of his beak. He was keen to make amends for the damage he'd caused, but he could see no point in scouring the aerie looking for Aubrey.

So Aurielle told him what she had seen. The black firebird. The blood. The distance in its eyes. *Firebirds are never black,* said Azkiar. Aurielle recalled the image on the sill. *I know — but it looked like Aubrey,* she said.

Azkiar blew a heavy sigh. Aurielle's visual sensors had surely been smoke stained. She'd seen a silhouette, nothing more, he thought; it happened in a window in the aerie every day. But she had that fretful look in her eye, the one that always made him want to *do* things for her. He preened a loose feather and said he would try, even though he was sure that Aubrey had simply fallen into hibernation somewhere. A firebird could sleep for half a spin, if it wished. But it would do no harm to run a quick check of the lower floors. Especially if it stopped Aurielle pitying him.

He found the body on Floor Twelve. On the floorboards, underneath the window, lifeless. Dropped there like a discarded rag. For several moments, Azkiar couldn't approach it. He had seen a dead firebird twice before, but never in a state like this. Carefully, he tottered up. He extended a foot and tilted the flaccid head toward him. He studied the glazed and faraway eye. The ducts had opened, the tear had discharged. Some days ago by the look of things. The blood mark was recent (and a concern), but it was the condition of the plumage that made his toes curl. The feathers lacked color, just as Aurielle had said. But they were a uniform gray, not a midnight black. Their shine had disappeared, leaving them brittle, ugly, and dry. He rocked the body lightly under his foot. Even with pressure, it did not break down. That puzzled him deeply. Normally, a firebird's body would disintegrate shortly after its tear had been shed. Something was preventing that from happening here. It was as if poor Aubrey had been frozen in a kind of undead form, hovering, as it were, between two worlds. Azkiar took a pace back. His first impulse was to burn this abomination flat. But Aurielle would have his ear tufts for nostril cleaners if a fire kicked up again as a result. So, with a gentle *rrrh* of respect, he left the body where it was and spiraled to the ground again to make his report.

By now, the girl Rosa had started to recover. She was sitting up against the wall of the librarium, being closely attended by David. Aurielle and Aleron were perched on a window ledge nearby. Azkiar landed in the daisy field, staying well away from the man he'd once attacked. *Rrrh!* he called, to get Aurielle's attention. *I've found Aubrey. He's dead. Upstairs.*

"Uh?" The sound of Rosa's voice made all three firebirds look her way. Pushing David aside, she scrabbled to her feet and took a pace toward Azkiar. The red firebird poddled back, looking confused.

"Hey, Rosa. Sit down. What are you doing? You need to rest." David was at her shoulder in a moment.

"I heard it," she said.

"Heard what?"

"Heard it talk."

David glanced at the birds. All three had taken off by now and were flying for a window ledge higher up the building.

"Floor Twelve," Rosa muttered, counting the floors. She turned toward the librarium door.

"Rosa, wait. Slow down." David twisted her around.

"Get off," she responded, flinging him aside. "Did I ask you to come back and start interfering?"

"Look," he said, pushing his hands into his pockets, "I know you hate me for running off, but I *had* to leave the way I did. My father passed me secret information, something I could only see on his com:puter. If the Aunts had found it, I would have been sent to the Dead Lands with him."

"And this is a bad thing?"

"That's not fair." He took an angry step forward. It brought him closer to her than he'd meant to be. So close that his breath made waves in her hair. "I care about the librarium, just as much as I care about . . ." But there the sentiments seemed to fail him and his words trailed off into silent ambiguity.

Rosa gulped and turned her face a little farther from his. After a pause that seemed like forever she said, "One of the birds is dead."

"How do you know?"

"The red one told the others. I understood what it said."

"How?"

"I don't *know*. But I'm going in to find them whether you come or not."

And so together, they hurtled through the librarium, letting it guide them straight to Floor Twelve. As they burst into the room where Aubrey lay, the firebirds scattered away from the body. Azkiar was quick to spread his muscular wings and make himself look as fearsome as possible.

"It's all right," Rosa said, raising her hands for calm. She made a *rhhh*ing noise in the back of her throat. All three firebirds sat up straight, their ear tufts springing out like antennae.

"Well, that got their attention," David muttered. He knelt by the body, keeping a wary eye on Azkiar. "Ask them how this happened."

"David, I'm not exactly fluent."

"Just try," he said, checking Aubrey's eye.

What followed was a kind of birdcall at dusk. For several moments the room was filled with every manner of click and rasp. When it was done, Rosa pressed her fingertips together and said, "They don't know. But it's very unnatural. The cream-colored one is frightened. She says the last time she saw this bird it was black."

David raised his gaze toward Aurielle, who spoke to him.

"What did she say?"

"She wants us to go upstairs with her."

Rrrh!

"She's got something important to show us."

Rrrh-rruurr-rrrh!

There was a pause. David said, "That sounded intense."

"She was just asking . . . if my arm was all right."

"And is it?"

Rosa let her fingers hover over the scars. They were raw, but healing remarkably quickly. "Just sore," she muttered.

"You should get to one of the rest rooms and treat it. How did it happen?"

She told him briefly — all that she remembered.

He took her hand a moment and looked at the pattern. "This is what we saw in your dragon book. Did the Aunt do it deliberately?"

"I don't know," Rosa said, and took her hand back.

David slipped his arm under Aubrey's body and lifted the firebird off the floor. "Tell these guys to organize a watch. Until we know what killed this bird, we should be on our guard."

Rosa looked to one side. While she didn't like the way he'd assumed command, she had to agree that his motives were right. She communicated his words to Aurielle. Azkiar and Aleron were immediately dispatched from the room.

"Tell her we'll come upstairs, but not until we've taken care of this." He showed Aurielle the body and gestured to the window.

Aurielle chattered a short response.

Rosa said, a little huffily, "She wants to know if she can stay with us."

"She's got wings. We can hardly stop her."

"She was being polite, David. She wants your permission. The birds are calling you the new curator."

"Me? How did I get elect . . . ?" He stopped there, knowing that nothing he could say would come out favorably. "Fine," he said finally, and turned toward the door.

The descent to the ground was slower than usual. When David stepped out into the sunlit daisy fields, he looked for a spot where the flowers were plentiful and pretty, then dropped to one knee and put Aubrey down. As he stood up he imagineered a spade. In one movement he swung it around and started to dig. When the hole was made, he laid the body in it and stood back so that Aurielle could see. The firebird made a little croaking sound but did not seem to object to the ritual.

"Do you want to say anything?"

Rosa was standing a couple of feet away. She shook her head and couldn't speak.

"Will you ask her what color he was?"

Another short dialogue established that Aubrey had been blue, like the sky.

David nodded. He filled in the hole and de:constructed the spade. During the dig, he'd been careful not to crush too many of the daisies. When he laid the main sod back, most of the flowers were still intact. As the first breeze took them, the petals rippled and changed their color from white to sky blue. He glanced at Rosa. There were tear tracks on her cheeks. He went over and slipped his arm around her.

And there they stood, completely unaware that from a window on the ninth floor of the librarium, Aunt Gwyneth was watching.

"Tell me," she said, to the Ix she was hosting. "What happens if David dies?"

The Ix will gain control of the nexus.

"So why haven't you done it? You must have had countless opportunities to kill him?"

He is strong, said the Ix. *The time point protects him.*

"In what way?"

He can call upon the power of dragons — and other beasts.

Aunt Gwyneth pondered this carefully. She ran a finger along the claw. "Tell me more about this artifact. What use is it to us?"

The creat:or can only function truly in the hands of those who resonate with dragons. It must be destroyed.

"I will be the judge of that," she said coldly. "What if he was to get it — David, I mean?"

There was a pause as the Ix swam around her mind. *All of the nexus would be visible to him. He would see the other time points to Earth and Ki:mera.*

"And thereby hold the balance of power," mused the Aunt. "Well, we can't have that."

Kill him, said the Cluster, trying to assert itself. *The Aunt:Ix could neutralize David now.*

"Not yet," she growled, beating it down. "Let the boy work for us first. He will show us to the upper floors and *The Book of Agawin.* When the moment comes, he will be no match for me."

He is strong, the Ix repeated. *How will it be done?*

"He's a construct," she said. "And the one thing constructs have is a template. I treated the boy once. I flowed into his auma. I know his strengths —

which are considerable, I admit — but I also know his weakness."

You will share this, said the Ix.

"And you will be quiet!" the Aunt hissed loudly. She pulled back from the window, fearful that her outburst might have been heard. Tossing her head, she hissed once more. An irritating tic had developed in one eyelid. A result of fighting for dominance with the Cluster. To punish the Ix, she morphed into the black-and-white katt again, a form they considered agile but vulnerable. "His weakness is love — for the girl, for his father, even for his own imperfect katt. The way to defeat him is to squeeze his heart. And there is no one better at that than an Aunt. . . ."

2.

From his position by the grave, David turned and stared at the librarium windows. "Did you hear something then?"

Rosa followed his gaze. "What kind of something?"

"A hiss, like someone being shushed?"

"There's no one here but us and the birds."

All the same, David squinted hard at the windows. He had scrutinized a dozen or more when Rosa grew tired and poked him in the ribs. "What are you doing?"

"Probing for traces of anything irregular."

"Such as?"

He clicked his tongue and looked at Aurielle, who was waiting patiently for whatever happened next. "I told you Dad gave me secret information?"

"Yes," she sighed, not wanting to be reminded of that parting moment.

"It was a film of his time rift experiment. You remember the portal he told us about?"

"Vaguely."

"I'm pretty sure something came through it. Not a physical entity, more a surge of fain. I'm concerned it was responsible for the bird we just buried."

Rosa looked at the building again. "Alien *fain*? In the librarium?"

"Something turned that firebird black. For all we know, it was —"

"Is that a katt?" Rosa gasped suddenly.

David panned his gaze sideways and saw it sitting as calmly as a cloud, on a ledge some nine floors up. The black-and-white katt from Bushley Common. "Oh, no," he groaned. "I thought I'd left that on a bench in Bushley. It must have followed me off the common and hid itself under the seat of my taxicar."

"I don't care how it got here," Rosa said. "It's a *katt*, in a building full of birds. Now we know what happened to the one we just buried! If the red one sees that, there's going to be carnage." She looked at Aurielle, who was already sitting up, puffing out her feathers. With an uncomfortable *rrrh!* she took off and flew away.

"Oh, great!" Rosa threw out a hand. "I think that cancels our trip upstairs."

David sighed and looked at the katt. It was washing its paws, totally unfazed. "OK, I'll deal with it. Upstairs can wait. We need to clean up after the fire anyway. I'll see you in that room. Five minits, max."

"Why did you *ever* come back?" she grumbled.

He chose to ignore that and hurried on inside.

When he caught up with her at the scene of the blaze, he was holding the katt against his shoulder, gently stroking the back of its neck. It was purring loudly, shut-eyed, content.

"David, get that out of here," Rosa said at once. She had found a broom in one of the utility closets and was brushing loose debris and ash into a pile.

"Don't you like them?"

"That's hardly the point."

"I'm not convinced it killed the bird. I know they like to chase them, but there are no signs of feathers or blood in its claws. It's such a friendly little thing. Probably quite old. I bet it's . . ."

Rosa rested her weight on the broom. She was glaring at him now, her whole body language telling him he was wasting his time.

"All right." He sighed. "I'll take it away. But it's tired. At least let it have a sleep first." In a blink he'd imagineered a comfortable basket. He placed it on the single bed that hadn't been burned, where it could catch the rays of the sun. He put the katt into it and told it to behave. The katt stretched, arched its back, and spiraled down. Before long it was curled up with its tail around its nose.

"If it acts up, I'll put it in a cage," he said.

Rosa shook her head and continued sweeping.

For the first time since he'd been back, David let his gaze wander around the room. It was in a terrible state: charred shelves, smoke-stained walls, remnants of book covers everywhere. Rosa winced as he crouched down and crumbled what remained of a once-thick paperback. "So, what happened?"

In one breath, she brought him up to speed, telling him how the fire had started and the Aunts had been stealing the auma from the books.

"So Strømberg was right," he muttered. "He told me the Aunts were planning something. I'll send him a

:com. He'll want to see this. It has to be illegal, what they were doing. Aunt Gwyneth will probably be out-lawed for it."

Brr-up, went the katt.

"What happened to the device they were using?" He walked around, sifting the debris with his feet. All of a sudden he spotted something and pushed aside the frame of the other, damaged, bed. "Is this it?" He held up the pad. The casing was warped and split along one side. At one end, its pink neural circuit boards were visible.

"Yes," said Rosa. "Useless, right?"

He brought it over, smearing cinders off the screen. From its audio slot came a weak kind of *whirr.* He tapped it against his palm. Nothing happened for a sec. Then two orange lights flickered on.

Rosa sucked in sharply and let go of the broom. Despite the clatter as it hit the floor, David didn't look up right away. He was trying to read something off the screen. Eventually, he turned it around and showed it to her.

Au a suc ess ul y tr nsf rred

"Auma transferred," he said. He brought his gaze level with hers.

She shrugged. "So?"

He glanced at her arm and seemed to know. "It's gone to you, hasn't it?"

(In the basket, the katt pricked an ear.)

Rosa gulped. She picked up the broom and started pushing again. "I didn't know until Aurielle told me upstairs."

"Aurielle?"

"The cream-colored bird. That's her name. Aurielle, Azkiar, Aleron. Cream, red, green. She saw the auma go into my scars. I didn't tell you right away because my head was still dizzy from the input of knowledge."

"Do you feel OK now?"

"*Mmm*. Fine. Ask me anything you like about furniture design in the forty-ninth spin — it was one of Mr. Henry's favorite topics."

David smiled and looked at what was left on the shelves. "I worked in this room with Mr. Henry once. There was nothing in these books about language or the birds. So how are you able to talk to them?"

(The katt raised its other ear at that.)

Rosa tidied up the ash and put the broom aside. "I don't know. When I came around I was just aware that I could, as if it had been imprinted on me. But there's more to it than just being able to talk. I've been picking up on something more . . . elemental."

"Go on," he said.

She shook her head. "It's just an instinctive feeling, but I'm convinced there's a spiritual link between the birds and the books. It's got something to do with the history of the building. When I try to home in on it, though, all I see is fuzzy pictures flashing through my head."

"Of what?" David asked.

She sat down on the bed with her knees turned in. "Dragons," she said, so quietly that the katt arched up in its basket. "And there's a name. It comes like an echoing drum."

"Agawin?"

"Yes. You've heard it, too?"

He sat down beside her. "Counselor Strømberg told me there's a book I need to check."

"I know it," Rosa said. "He showed it to me. It's hidden in the room where you woke up. It's full of weird symbols. Dragontongue and stuff. I was supposed to be finding a way to translate it when it all kicked off with your dad and the Aunts."

"Can you take me to it?"

"Yes," she said, and was about to jump up when Azkiar appeared on the window ledge. His gaze swept the room and settled on the basket — and the katt.

"Uh-oh. This doesn't look good," said David.

There was menace in the red firebird's eyes, the kind of look that suggested he held the katt responsible for Aubrey's death. But Aunt Gwyneth was not at all troubled. Indeed, her devious mind had swiftly conjured up a way to turn this situation to her advantage. As Azkiar flew in, a bizarre thing happened. The ash pile erupted and re-formed into a dark-winged creature. It appeared in front of the startled firebird as a hissing, ugly ball of venom. Before he could change course or think to draw flame, the creature had attached itself to his chest and exposed a wide array of needlelike teeth, ready to sink them into his neck.

Rosa screamed. And David was on his feet in an instant. But even before his amazing mind could imagineer a suitable form of defense, the katt had come bounding across the room and in one leap taken the creature down. As they hit the floor together, the creature broke free and turned to look its assailant in the eye. What followed wasn't pretty. With a flash of claws that saw dark-colored blood and minor body parts sprayed against a wall, the katt brought the fight to a swift conclusion. When it was done, it stood over the corpse for a moment, threw a dispassionate glance at Azkiar (dazed and confused, but otherwise OK), then turned and climbed back into its basket. What was left of the strange black creature dissolved into a puddle and drained away through a knot in the floorboards.

Azkiar, his pride dented, glared at the katt, then left the room on a powerful wingbeat, undoing Rosa's efforts with the broom in the process. Shaking her head at the mess he'd created, she asked, rather fearfully, "What *was* that thing?"

"Our mystery fain, hopefully," David muttered, though there was nothing left to commingle with or probe. Even the wall stains had withered away. And how, he wondered, had a simple katt, someone's long-discarded construct, been able to deal with the threat of an alien life force? He turned and walked back to the basket, running a knuckle between the katt's ears.

Its left eye was twitching, but it seemed unharmed. Once again, as he'd done on the common, he extended his fain and probed its mind. Nothing. A katt, full of vague daydreams. But of course Aunt Gwyneth had prepared herself for this. It had taken little effort for the Aunt Su:perior to cloak her true identity.

"So," David said, "does it stay or does it go?"

Rosa watched the katt settle down as if it had done nothing more than knock a small ball around the room for several minits. "I guess it's earned its place," she murmured. "But I still don't know what we should do with it."

"Well, we could give it a home — and a name." (*You'd better make it a good one,* Aunt Gwyneth was thinking darkly.) "I reckon it's a male. What about Felix?"

Male? Aunt Gwyneth almost bit into his finger. (Though the irony of the last two letters did amuse her.)

Rosa shuddered. "Whatever. I just want to get out of this room now. Do you still want to see the book?"

"Of course."

Meow! went Felix, reaching out a paw.

"All right, you can come, too," David said. And resting the katt against his shoulder, he followed Rosa out of the room, Aunt Gwyneth dribbling on his jacket for good measure.

In Mr. Henry's favorite reference room, the one in which David had recovered from his coma, Rosa slid the ladders along the shelves, riding them just like the old curator would have done. "This panel is false," she said, banging it at roughly the same place she thought he had. After three attempts, the panel swung open.

David looked into the ˚secret — but empty — compartment.

"Oh," Rosa said. Her shoulders sagged. "That's weird. He definitely took it from here."

David put the katt down and strolled around the room, running his fingers over similar panels. "He must have put it back somewhere else. There could be any number of hiding places in the building."

"There's one here." Rosa went to the cupboard that held the animal book. It was still there, but *The Book of Agawin* wasn't.

David took it out and flipped through the pages. "Wow. Have you seen this?"

"Yes," Rosa said. "Strømberg showed me. All those creatures died out ages ago. The one you're on is called a 'squirrel,' I think."

David stared at the picture for the longest time.

"What's the matter?" she asked.

"I've seen these creatures before," he muttered. He took the auma pad out of his pocket.

"David, what are you doing?!"

"I can feel the pad humming."

"What? Well, switch it off. Just smash the thing, will you?"

He held it in the air as she tried to grab it. "No," he said. "You don't understand. The book wants this. I can sense it in my fain. It's putting some of its auma into the pad so I can absorb it, just like you did. All it's doing is . . ." He blinked and cut off.

"What?" she demanded.

The auma pad buzzed. "It's telling me something."

Rosa spread her hands, inviting him to say what.

"A squirrel is going to come to the librarium."

"A *squirrel*?"

"Yes." And he stared at the bushy-tailed mammal again.

And in his mind, it sat up — and smiled.

3.

Aunt Gwyneth said, "Tell me about the creature."

The Ix Cluster swelled at the forefront of her mind. *The construct we created to deceive the humans?*

"There was no 'we' about it. That was all your doing. What *was* that vile abomination?"

A darkling, the Cluster replied. *A form the Ix take on a physical plane.*

"Are there darklings on the planet you called Earth?"

There was a violent pulse of energy behind the katt's ear. *A colony was defeated at the battle of Isenfier, but the Shadow will bring them back. We will take the Earth and the fire at its core. The Ix will be victorious. The Inversion will succeed.*

Miarrrgh! went the katt and threw his head to one side as he fought to stop the Cluster surging again.

David stopped what he was doing and came over to the basket.

"Is it all right?" asked Rosa.

"Just dreaming, I think." He put a finger beneath the katt's chin and stroked it. Aunt Gwyneth responded by bubbling saliva over his knuckles.

"Nice," David said and wiped his hand on his jeans.

For the past two days, he and Rosa had been hard at work cleaning and restoring the burned-out room. No firebird had visited in that time. And they had still to locate *The Book of Agawin*. Nothing more had been said about the animal book or David's prediction about the squirrel. Life was back to normal, it seemed.

None of this was sitting well with Aunt Gwyneth. Tired of her confinement in a basket, and a form that continually made her want to kick the scruff of her neck, she had resorted to interrogating the Ix. This was a dangerous practice. For if she opened her mind too widely to them, the struggle to maintain dominance usually resulted in a physical outburst, and that drew David's attention. But if she kept her mind in stasis, she learned nothing of the alien life-forms either. When they did speak, the dark beings kept no secrets. Even she was chilled by their sweeping arrogance. So confident were they of ruling the nexus that they always spoke openly of their battle plans. Isenfier. The Shadow. What they called the Inversion. Aunt Gwyneth was as much confused by these terms as the firebirds were after centuries of guarding the tapestry on Floor One Hundred and Eight. But she was in the unique position of commingling with the beings, who not only knew of the connection between three worlds, but had visited time points on two of them at least.

She chose one of the terms and asked about it. "Tell me about Isenfier. You lost a battle there?"

No, the battle is suspended in time.

"Suspended? How is that possible?"

It was done with a creat:or.

Aunt Gwyneth thought about the dragon's claw, which, for safety's sake, she'd hidden. "Those things can control *time?*"

The creat:or can shape dark matter, but those who wield the creat:or must resonate precisely with the nexus and the universe.

"Who could wield such a thing?" (*Apart from David,* she added as an afterthought.)

The Ix fizzed around her mind like water molecules coming to a boil. She could sense their resentment well before they said, *There are dragon elementals on Earth, responsible for aiding the protection of the planet.*

The katt twitched a whisker. "Explain the term 'dragon elementals.'"

Humans born of dragon auma, able to create the living likeness of a dragon from the physical crust of Earth. It was a creature such as this that wielded a creat:or at Isenfier.

Crust of Earth? Aunt Gwyneth thought of Eliza in the Dead Lands and what David's mother had done with clay, particularly the birth of Penny. So intense was her musing that she let her attention slip for a moment, almost allowing the Ix to re-form. For a second time the katt let out a violent hiss as Aunt Gwyneth forced the Cluster back into submission.

"It's doing that ripping thing again," Rosa said as Felix dug his claws into the base of his bedding.

Once again, David stopped what he was doing. "Maybe it needs some thera:peutic input. When Counselor Strømberg arrives I'll ask him to check it over. I'm going to send that :com today, whether we've found the book or not."

That, thought the Aunt, was all she needed. Strømberg picking her up and stroking her. Once again she intensified her auma, smashing the Cluster into scraps temporarily. She picked on a scrap and neutralized it. It left a burning hole in her mind, a void in her memory she knew she would never be able to fill. But as a demonstration of power it was quick and effective. The Ix took the hint.

We will answer your questions, they said weakly.

"Very wise. Tell me more about David Merriman. How can he have the auma of a dragon when no such thing exists on this world?"

The Ix paused. *He is between worlds,* they said.

"There are *three* Davids?"

Negative, said the Ix. *There is one entity, varying at quantum speeds between the time points. His auma alternates across the planes. This is a primary condition of the nexus.*

"Is his life on Earth different — when he's *there?*"

Yes, but his purpose remains the same. Only the connections vary.

"Connections? What connections?"

The Ix took a moment to consider this question. *The mammal in the book is one.*

"The squirrel? Why would an insignificant creature mean so much to someone like him?"

On Earth, he has resonated strongly with them. We do not know what their function is.

"And where do I, Gwyneth, fit into this?"

You are another connection.

Suddenly, the tic around the eye was back. "Are you telling me that *I* have another life — on Earth?"

We must Cluster to answer that.

"Do it," she snapped, flashing the katt's tail. "Try anything and I'll neutralize you all."

We accept this, said the Ix.

She let them regroup. After several moments of neural activity, they reported they had an answer.

"Well? What is it?"

At the time of Isenfier, Gwyneth does not exist.

"What?" The katt's teeth began to chatter fiercely.

On Earth, you are called Gwilanna. You die before Isenfier begins.

"How? In what circumstances?"

Fear, they said, buzzing around her brain. *Fear of the Shadow. Fear of the Ix.*

"Fear of *you*?" she spat. "Then —" *Die yourself,* she was about to say, when a light began to flash in a corner of the room and a strange combination of clangs and whistles and hoots and bells went off all over the building. The katt leaped to his feet and jumped around to look at David and Rosa.

"Well, *that* doesn't happen every day," David said.

There was someone at the librarium door.

4.

Maybe it's your squirrel," Rosa said drily.

But when David popped his head out of the window to see, he was even more surprised than he might have been if Rosa's suggestion had been correct. He dashed to the front door and flung it wide. "Mom!" he cried in delight. "And . . . Penny," he added, as his grinning sister popped out from behind their mother's back.

"We've come to see you," Penny said, waving a hand.

He smiled to see her holding a daisy to her chin.

"Is it a bad time?" Eliza asked. She flicked a look beyond him, into the librarium.

"No," he said, "but . . . erm?"

"Why are we here?"

"It's 'cause I want another *book*," chirped Penny.

She stepped up and punched him lightly in the ribs. (Why did sisters *do* that? he wondered.)

"And we miss you, of course," his mother added.

"And we want to see *Rosa*," Penny said, putting so much slant on the name that she almost curtsied. She jumped up straight and put her head back. "Wow, it's big, isn't it? Can I go in?" This turned out to be a nonquestion. Before David could speak, she'd dashed past him into the foyer.

"Penny, come back. You'll get lost!" he shouted.

"I'm in here," she called faintly. "Wow, there're books *everywhere*, Mom!"

Eliza stepped forward and took her son's hands. "You OK?"

"Sure."

"What's the burning smell?"

Even now, the aftereffects of the blaze still lingered. "We had a fire —"

"A fire? *Here?*"

"— and a bit of trouble, but everything's under control now."

Eliza looked at him as if she suspected that the "bit" of trouble was really rather serious, but she let it pass. "Were the birds affected? I don't see any."

"Slight misunderstanding with the birds. I'll explain later. Come on in, I'll show you around."

He stood back and let his mother go past. As she entered the foyer she paused to listen to a rustling sound. "What's that?"

"That will be the books saying hello. It means they like you."

"The books do?"

"*Mmm*. You'll get used to that." A slight breeze found its way down the stairs to caress the ends of Eliza's hair. It was as if the building had sighed with joy to see her. "So, would you like a cup of tea before your tour? Or do you want to meet Rosa first?"

Suddenly, there was a thumping clatter from one of the rooms and a voice went, "Ow!"

"Oh, Penny," Eliza tutted. She set off in the direction of the sound, only to have David stop her and say, "No, it's this way, Mom."

"But?" She pointed to the left of the stairs.

"Doesn't work like that. You don't go where you think you ought to, you go where the building tells you you should. The two things often coincide, but it's always best to put your faith in the building." He gestured for her to follow.

They found Penny on Floor Five, standing sheepishly beside several piles of books that had collapsed in a slicing domino effect. Rosa was there already, silently picking them up.

"I didn't mean it," Penny whispered, hiding her face behind her knocked-together fists.

Rosa lifted a dark eyebrow.

"Rosa," David said, taking a book from her hand and separating her from the clutter. "This is my mom and my, erm, little sister. They've come to pay us a visit."

Rosa tossed her hair. Just for a moment she was twelve again. "We've met," she said to Eliza.

"Yes, but you're rather different now," Eliza said. "You're very beautiful, Rosa." David switched his gaze between the two women. Though neither of them wanted to break their proud stares, he was confident his mother's remark had softened the tension. And he couldn't fault her observation. Since Rosa had acquired the mark on her arm, she seemed to be even more striking than before, in a darkly intense and moody sort of way.

Penny tugged her brother's sleeve. "Honestly, I didn't mean it."

"I know," he said. He gave her a quick hug.

"It was the katt," she said.

"You've got a katt?" said Eliza.

"Unfortunately, yes." Rosa glanced at David. "It shot out of the basket when the room alarms went off. I thought it was with you."

"It made me jump," Penny said. "It gave me a funny look."

"I doubt it," said Eliza, flicking through a gardening book. "Most katts have got one look: permanent confusion."

David saw Rosa's mouth twitch into a smile. It was brief. Almost negligible. But there all the same. It was surely only a matter of time before she and his mom became friends. "So, shall we go to a resting room?"

"OK, I'll do these later," Rosa said.

"She'll help you," said Eliza, nudging Penny (who grinned as if she'd got something stuck in her teeth).

"She can't," Rosa said. "Only David and I know exactly where the books need to go."

Before Penny's lips could thicken into a sulk, David brought his hands together in a clapping motion and said, "Right. Let's . . . go and relax then, shall we?" And he turned his sister around and marched her

411

away. (This time when she socked him in the ribs, she meant it.)

Thankfully, Penny had brightened up by the time they'd reached the room where Mr. Henry had kept his favorite reference books. The table Thorren Strømberg had constructed there was a fading shimmer. David reimagineered it, adding cups and saucers. While Rosa set about preparing drinks, Penny squirmed into a chair and said, "Shall we give David his present now, Mom?"

"Present?" He brushed Felix off a chair so his mother could sit down.

"It's something for the building, really," said Eliza. "Don't take this the wrong way, but I didn't have you in mind when I made it. Well, no, that's not strictly true. I was *thinking* about you — because you'd just gone away — but I'd intended to create a more natural dragon —"

"Dragon?" Rosa said, suddenly becoming interested.

"— and it just came out the way it did. It was as if it already existed somewhere and I just gave it . . . form."

Eliza reached into her bag and put a sculpture on the table. It was about twice the height of a cup (in its

412

saucer) and made of solid clay. It was sitting upright on two flat feet, balancing on a tail that swept out behind it and curved up at the end in a triangular point. The scales were crosshatched over its back, but arranged in a pattern of crescents on its chest. The wings were half-folded down. Apart from the general form, two things really stood out for David. The whole profile of the head was far gentler than the images of dragons in his mind, mainly because of the oval-shaped, violet-colored eyes, which inspired warmth and kindness and trust. And secondly, it was holding an open book.

Eliza turned it so that Rosa could see. "I made it from earth I brought back from the Dead Lands. I imagineered the color" — green, with turquoise hints — "but the book just appeared out of nowhere, like I'd blinked and continued sculpting unawares. It seemed appropriate to bring it to a place full of books. I hope you can find a shelf for it."

"Of course we can," said David. "What do you think, Rosa?"

"It's not what *I* think," she muttered. "Look at the katt."

Felix was up on a chair again, completely transfixed by the dragon. He put his front paws on the edge of

413

the table and got into crouch mode, ready to spring. "Ah-ah, I don't think so," David said, and picked the katt up by the scruff of the neck. He meowed loudly and struggled in his grip, but reserved his worst moment for Eliza. As David turned, the katt hissed and spat at her. She jerked back, looking more confused than frightened.

David carried Felix across the room, constructed a cage of metal bars, threw the katt into it, and locked the door. Felix hissed and growled and paddled and spat. More worryingly, he kept throwing his head from side to side as if he were quarreling with himself.

"That katt gives me the creeps," said Penny, moving to another chair farther from it.

"Where did you get it?" Eliza asked, staring intently at the cage.

"Stowaway from Bushley Common," David answered. He tracked her gaze. "Why, what's the matter?"

"The eyes," she said. "They remind me of someone."

"Who?" said Rosa.

Eliza shook her head. "Forget it. It's ridiculous. Let's enjoy our tea."

David pulled up a chair and quickly changed the subject. Pointing at his mother's sculpture he said, "I've seen one of those before."

"That's funny, Penny said the same thing."

"Told you," Penny piped up in triumph. "She wouldn't believe *me*," she said to her brother. "It was in the tunnel, wasn't it, when we looked through the glass?"

"Tunnel? Glass?" Rosa lifted her shoulders.

David briefly explained about animating the *Alicia* story. How, he wondered, had his mother come to make a dragon just like the ones they had seen? He was still musing on this when Penny cupped her hands around his ear to whisper something.

"What? No," he said.

"Go on," Penny tutted. "Please, just for me."

"We don't like to imagineer here — unless strictly necessary."

Eliza tucked her hair behind her ears and said, "Are there laws against using your fain in the librarium?"

Rosa said tautly, "Mr. Henry used to say that the contents of the books were this building's constructs. The words, when read, are a natural form of imagineering."

"But words can't make things *move*," Penny argued. (On a shelf to her right a book fell over. She noticed it but rattled on regardless.) "If David makes the dragon *read*, we can see what's written in his book, can't we? Oh, *please*, David. Do it. For me."

"All right," he said, avoiding Rosa's eye. "We'll try it, but I can't guarantee the results. We should commingle — me and Mom."

Eliza smiled. "That would be fun. We used to do it when you were little. Do you remember?"

"Oh, spare me," Rosa muttered, under her breath.

Penny mouthed at her brother, *Is she always this grumpy?*

He wagged a finger. Penny sat back and folded her arms.

"Ready, Mom?"

"Yes," she said, closing her eyes. "You do the intending, I'll support."

David focused his gaze onto the dragon.

In the blink of an eye, it gave itself a shake. This set its scales rattling from top to toe, ending with a *ping* at the triangle on the tail.

Penny gave a squeal of delight. Even Rosa, leaning back against the rest room countertop, had to smile when the dragon sneezed a big puff of smoke and blew fine ash across its book. It frowned and busily dusted the pages.

"Is it a storybook?" Penny asked excitedly. "Can the dragon talk? Will it read something out?"

David didn't reply. The animation, nevertheless, was unaffected. Drumming its slightly webbed toes on the table, the dragon began to flip through the pages of the book at a speed that produced a noticeable draft. It flicked forward and backward several times, even turning the book upside down once, before it settled on a page it wanted to show. A single letter was written there: G.

"G? Is that all?" Penny said.

Hrrr, went the dragon, and hurriedly flicked through the pages again to show an A, then a D, and a Z.

"It's spelling something," Penny said. "GADZ . . ."

By now, however, the dragon was looking nervously over its shoulder as if it were concerned that it might be in danger. It became so flustered as it searched for the next letter that it fumbled the pages and dropped the book. Rosa, seeing this, stepped toward the table. "David, can you hear me? Are you all right?" She waved a hand across his eyes. There was no response.

"Eliza, what's the matter with him? Why is he shaking? Eliza? What's —?" Suddenly, a high-pitched, muted wail drew her attention to the cage across the room. Felix was staring at them, trembling with intent. His ears were pricked. His eyes, stone black.

"David, stop this!" Rosa shouted. "Stop the commingling! There's something wrong!"

"Look at the book!" cried Penny. "What's happening to the book?"

It was shining like a four-pointed star. All along its vertical axis, a rip was appearing in the fabric of space. The dragon covered its eyes and went into a crouch, mimicking Eliza, who was doing the same thing.

"Penny, get out of the way," cried Rosa. With one heave, she pulled the girl off her seat and dragged her back, away from the table, just as two streams of glowing black light stretched out of Felix and flowed around the dragon. The dragon was spun about and thrown to one side. But the light continued on its way, acting as if it had entered a prism. It split into a host of finer rays and melted into David's vision. The Ix were inside him, seeking to kill.

But David was not about to die that day.

What happened next would be written in the librarium's history forever. With a *bang*, David's chair hit the shelves behind him, bringing down a shower of books. At first glance it appeared he had stood up too quickly and merely kicked his chair away. But in fact he was going through a physical transformation of immense proportions, enough to move a mountain, never mind a chair.

Penny screamed and buried herself against Rosa's shoulder as a great white beast emerged in place of her brother. The animal, which he would later call "bear," opened a pair of ferocious jaws and roared at the time rift, flashing five hooked claws at a finger of darkness trying to billow through it. That was all it took to seal the danger. The rift closed and compressed to a single point. But the Ix inside David were committed to fight. The Cluster roared through his cerebral cortex, confident of early supremacy. In truth, it had little chance of ever gaining control. The walls of the great librarium shook as the huge bear roared again. Every point of its white fur tingled black. Then a blue-white halo lifted from its body and in one expulsion of pure white fire the Ix Cluster was dispersed into harmless microdots of ineffective energy. Gone.

When it was done, the clay dragon was lying on the table, unharmed. Eliza was still in her seat, recovering. Rosa and Penny were cowering together on the far side of the room.

The bear snorted and swung its head toward the window. It grunted at a pair of firebirds that had just come in to land. Then, as if a cloud had drifted past the sun, the bear morphed back into David. He staggered for a moment, catching his balance. He looked at Rosa. She was too stunned to speak.

The first words came from Aurielle. Spreading her fabulous, apricot-tipped wings, she glided into the room and landed on the table. She stared long and hard at Eliza's dragon and even longer at Rosa's arm. *Rrrh-ruurr-rhhh!* she chattered.

"What did she say?" asked David, still nursing a growl.

Rosa gulped and pressed Penny's head to her chest. "She wants us to follow her to Floor One Hundred and Eight. We're to bring the dragon with us."

Rrrh! went Aurielle.

"'Now,' she says."

5.

But first, there was the little matter of Aunt Gwyneth to attend to. And it *was* a little matter.

Raising a hand to acknowledge Aurielle's request, David walked over to the cage he'd constructed around Felix. The katt was no longer there. In his place was a groggy (and somewhat perplexed), miniature version of Aunt Gwyneth.

David quickly extended his fain and probed her mind. It was still the dreaded Aunt all right, but not so superior anymore. Her fain was in tatters, like a punctured cloud. And whatever she'd done to disguise herself as Felix had backfired in the most spectacular way. She had lost her ability to imagineer — at least for now. But she still had a tongue and a temper. And she used them.

"You! Get me out of here. Now!" she squeaked. She gripped the bars of the cage and tried to rattle them.

David sat down cross-legged on the floor. "I don't think so," he said. "I like you just where you are."

Aunt Gwyneth scowled furiously as Rosa, Eliza, and an openmouthed Penny all came crowding around. "And what are *you* looking at?" she hissed at Aleron.

He was at the window, awaiting instructions from Aurielle.

"Careful, Aunt, he might just eat you," David warned. "Your kind are not popular in this building, remember."

"David?" His mother touched his shoulder lightly, holding her fingers there a moment to convince herself that this . . . man was still her son. "I have no idea what just happened in this room, but that — I mean, she — is still an Aunt."

"Finally, some respect," Aunt Gwyneth railed, blowing a sprig of hair off her cheek.

Rosa crouched down and put her face to the cage. "Need a hairpin, Aunt?" She produced one she'd found when the twins had disappeared. It was half the length of Aunt Gwyneth's body and twinkled keenly when Rosa rolled it through her fingers.

Aunt Gwyneth actually *gulped*.

"David, please stop this," his mother said.

He gestured to Rosa to back away.

With a snort, she jabbed the pin at the bars for good measure. "Is she harmless?"

"Yes."

"Good. Let her stew. You and I need to have a serious talk."

But Aunt Gwyneth was not about to give up easily. "I demand that you release me at once. I am not a criminal. I was invaded by the Ix and held hostage to their plans."

"Ix?" said David, in a level tone.

Aunt Gwyneth leaned forward. Her wrinkled face looked like a piece of dried mud. "That's what you destroyed with your clever antics. A Cluster of Ix. An alien danger your fool of a father introduced to this world from a place called *Earth*."

"Our father?" Penny looked up at her mother.

"Later," said Eliza, stroking Penny's hair.

"Whatever that thing is — or was," said David, "my father was trying to protect Co:pern:ica from it." He reached into his pocket and brought out the tangled auma pad.

423

"What's that?" Penny asked.

"A nasty elec:tronic device that sucks the life out of things, Penny — especially books."

"Why would anyone do *that*?"

"So they could build up their fain and become the most powerful force on the planet. Isn't that right, Aunt Gwyneth?"

"You've no right to interfere with my projects," she snapped. "Co:pern:ica needs leadership. Discipline. Strength. Only a su:perior Aunt can provide that."

"Not anymore," David said, standing up. He put the auma pad back into his jacket. "I think we're on the brink of discovering what this building really means to this world. We're going to blow your system apart. Thanks to you, the Aunts' grip is about to weaken."

"And you think *you* could do better?" She banged the cage door to keep his attention. "You think Co:pern:ica will place its trust in a freak that can't decide if it's a human construct or a roaring animal? I know what you are, *David*. I know why the Ix were coming for you. I know why Isenfier was stopped."

Rosa threw him a sideways glance. "What's she babbling about?"

"Release me and I'll talk," Aunt Gwyneth said. She clamped her mouth shut and smirked.

David was having none of it. "Tell Runcey to guard her," he said to Rosa. "Mom, Penny, come with me."

But Rosa was having none of *that*. Slamming two hands against his chest she said, "Stop right there. You don't just float off upstairs without explaining what happened just now. What are you? How did you morph into that . . . thing?"

"I don't know," David answered her plainly. "I was attacked; I responded. That's all there is to it. I know as much about that animal as you do at present. It's been in my dreams since I was twelve years old."

Picking at her nails Aunt Gwyneth said, "He's out of control, Rosa. How long do you think it's going to be before the Higher step in to re:move him for good?"

"Shut up," Rosa growled.

The Aunt flared her nostrils. "I'll remember your insolence when I'm out of here, girl."

"Look," said Eliza, stepping in to make the peace. She put herself between Rosa and her son. "Why don't you two go upstairs and Penny and I will stay here and . . . look after things?"

"No. I want to be with David," Penny said. She ran up and grabbed her brother's hand.

"She can't come with us," Rosa said to David. "We can't take a kid above Floor Forty-Two."

David switched his gaze to Aurielle, who was hopping impatiently from foot to foot. He said to Penny, "Have you brought *Alicia* with you?"

The girl heaved the storybook out of her pocket. "Can I swap it for another?"

Rosa said, bluntly, "The books belong here."

David glanced at the shelves all around them. The librarium was whispering as it sometimes did. Outside, in the fields, the daisy leaves were fluttering. "Actually, I think the building would like it if Penny borrowed another book."

"Yes!" went the girl.

Rosa threw up her hands. "This is crazy. We don't know what we'll find on the upper floors, David. She's just going to be a burden to us."

"I am n —" Penny was about to say, but her brother raised a hand to quiet her. "We'll take her to the fiction department and let her look around. What harm can that do? The danger's passed. We'll take Runcey with us. He can keep an eye on her."

"It's *Aleron*," Rosa said, taut and grumpy. "I'll be waiting on the stairs. If you're not out in one minit, I'm going up without you." She snapped a *rrrh!* at Aurielle and marched away. The cream-colored fire-bird flapped out after her.

"Mom, will you be OK with her?" David nodded at Aunt Gwyneth. She had settled down on the floor of her prison and assumed a haughty, meditative pose. "Don't believe a word she tells you. And under no circumstances let her out of that cage. I'll :com Counselor Strømberg when we get back. He'll know what to do."

"You'll regret this," said the Aunt. She closed her eyes and went, *Ommmm.*

"I'll be OK," said Eliza. "Go and be nice to Rosa."

Beckoning Aleron to join him, David drew Penny away. But at the door to the stairs he stopped for a moment to pluck a book off one of the shelves. It had a thick, red spine and a well-worn look, as if it had been used many hundreds of times. He opened it about a third of the way through, turned two pages, then settled on one, carefully tracing his finger down it. At the point where his finger stopped moving, he frowned.

"David? Is everything all right?" his mother asked.

(Aunt Gwyneth opened one eye.)

"Yes," he said, but he didn't sound convinced. He pushed the book back, then guided Penny out.

Aunt Gwyneth opened both eyes and said, "Well, Eliza, how pleasant to have some time to ourselves. What shall we do? Sing songs? Play a game?" She folded her hands into her lap and began to chant a rhyme that children were often taught: "*I fain, with my little brain, something beginning with . . .*"

"Aunt Gwyneth, I'm not in the mood for games." Eliza was staring intently at the shelf where David had checked the book.

The Aunt slid her gaze in that direction. "Stop prevaricating, girl. Go and take a look."

"At what?"

Aunt Gwyneth sneezed. It sounded as if a small bomb had suddenly gone off. "The book, of course. It's probably a reference volume, like all the others in this disgusting arena of floating dust. I'd say he was hoping to discover what your dragon was spelling out. The sculpture was trying to tell him something. Something that caused the Ix that took me hostage to break away and attempt to kill him. Aren't you curious? You saw how troubled he was."

Eliza squeezed her hands together. "If he'd wanted me to know, he'd have said something to me."

"*Pah!* How weak and pathetic you've become. I had such hopes for you."

"Aunt Gwyneth, let's get one thing clear: If you try to turn my mind, I'll . . . imagineer a blanket over your cage."

"*Tch.* So disrespectful, too."

"Me?" Eliza turned to the captive and scowled. "You falsely banished my husband to the Dead Lands and abandoned me there without a shred of help — and given half a chance you'd destroy my son. I don't think I owe you any respect."

"I beg to differ," Aunt Gwyneth snarled. "Open this cage at once."

The command was persuasive. Very persuasive. A sign that the Aunt Su:perior might be regaining her powers. Eliza could feel herself wanting to reach forward. In the nick of time, she snatched her hand back. "No. You're wicked. You're staying where you are. Don't make me put a cover over you."

Aunt Gwyneth breathed in sharply. "How *dare* you treat me like this? You, of all people."

"What's that supposed to mean?"

And then the Aunt did something completely out of keeping with one of her kind: She introduced a note of sorrow to her voice. "I wasn't going to tell you this. But as Strømberg will have me sent to the Dead Lands and we'll never see each other again after that, then you might as well know the truth. I was talking about the bond of family. You rage at me, throw taunts at me, and all the while speak ill of me. If anyone is wicked, it is you, Eliza. I didn't bring you up to lock me in a cage! Is this really any way to treat your *mother*?"

6.

My—? No!" Eliza stood up, wagging a finger. "No," she said again, "that's just plain ludicrous."

"Is it?" said the Aunt. "You freely admit you know nothing of your life before Harlan Merriman — but I do. How many constructs have you met, Eliza, that can't recall anything from their childhood? I closed you down and erased your memories for one reason only: You would have been de:constructed if the Higher had known what you were capable of."

"Penny . . ." Eliza felt her mouth growing dry.

"Quite. The ability to reproduce the way you did is indicative of your ancestry. Your father was descended from Agawin himself. He was taken from me and re:moved by the Higher when he was no older than your son is now."

"How did you meet him?"

"How did *you* meet Harlan? These things just happen, girl. He was a man, tall and clever, with magick in his fain and . . . and wings on his back."

Eliza drew closer to the bars. *"Wings?"*

"Don't shout," the Aunt said, shying away. "When you're this size, the air pressure really isn't comfortable." She stood up and adjusted her clothing. "The wings were stubs. Never fully developed. But enough to set him apart from any other suitor — of which there were many, I might add." She put a hand to her bun and fluffed it up. "I was quite something — when it mattered. I'm glad to see you've inherited my . . . splendor, though the hair is a little odd, it must be said."

"I fail to see the likeness," Eliza said sharply. She pulled back from the cage and went for a walk around the room. She took a book off a shelf and pushed it back again, as if she needed to exercise her arm. "If this is true, what became of him — my father?"

Aunt Gwyneth cracked her knuckles like a row of seed pods. "I don't know," she said (with a credible degree of regret in her voice). "I tried many times to discover that myself, before I was taken into Aunthood.

After that, a certain bitterness entered my soul. Even you, his daughter, I had to denounce, though I couldn't bear to see you fully de:constructed. My Aunt Su:perior took pity on me. She put your template into stasis until I was ready to accept you back. By then, you had no need to know your mother. So you were reintroduced as an orphaned young woman. And I remained silent and merely observed you."

Eliza touched the spine of a book, enjoying the curvature of it and the way the author's name was faintly embedded in a deep shade of blue two-thirds of the way up. Books were beautiful, she thought, arranged like this. Like a kind of sleeping ornament. And despite her dismissive attitude when she had first come to the librarium, she rather liked the deep, rich smell of them, too. There was nothing quite like it on all Co:pern:ica. "How do I know you're not spinning me a tale so I'll break that lock and let you out?"

"I would have thought the answer to that was obvious. It's running around upstairs by now, looking for another book to read. Penny is only alive because I'm protecting her. Come to that, my dear, so are you."

Eliza walked to a chair and slowly sat down. "Tell me about Agawin. Was he man or construct?"

"Try enigma," said the Aunt, going on a little walk herself. "Had you continued your training you would have studied this myth in full."

"Myth? He's not real? But if he never existed, how could I be descended from him?"

"Oh, *something* existed," Aunt Gwyneth said, trailing her fingers over the bars of her cage. "There are documents, drawings, etchings in stone. Most of it cached with the Aunts, of course. There are rumors that artifacts exist in the Dead Lands, particularly at a place called the Isle of Alavon, but none of it is conclusive and his origins are merely speculative at best. Some scholars have suggested he was not of this world. That he traveled across time and created Co:pern:ica to his own template: part man, part firebird, part fain. Others claim he was simply a man who found a way to look into the face of all creation and was driven insane by what he saw."

"And what did he see?"

"Dragons," said the Aunt, quite matter-of-factly.

Eliza felt her heart stop beating for a moment.

"You have something to say about this?"

"I saw dragons. I think I saw him, too — or the spirit of him. A flying man with sunken eyes. He, they, were there — in the Dead Lands."

"They were not."

"But . . . they led me to the cave."

"They did not," Aunt Gwyneth insisted. "Your need for survival led you to shelter. What you saw were projections, images pooled from the collective consciousness of the Co:pern:ican race. There's a word for it, Eliza. It's called 'superstition.' It is natural for any living beings to question the origins of their existence. Over thousands of spins, our fain has been seeded by the romantic notion that Agawin commanded a legion of dragons and used their power to create this world. The only reason the Aunts have not erased this myth is that it acts as a kind of comfort to us. Everyone wants to believe in something that will make their mundane lives more bearable and their inevitable death less . . . final. The truth is, we do not know how we came to be. There is no proof of anything, although . . ."

"What?" asked Eliza. She leaned forward, making her chair lift.

Aunt Gwyneth tapped her fingertips together. "The general consensus of Aunt opinion is that Agawin was merely a renegade ec:centric — the first, of course — able to imagineer well beyond the capabilities of other Co:pern:icans. The Grand Design was introduced because of him, to prevent any sweeping acts of adverse creativity. In that sense, you and your remarkable son are perfect examples of his line. But if there is any substance at all to the more fanciful stories, we believe this building holds the key. It *is* a remarkable source of fain."

"Which you tried to steal."

"Conjecture," snapped the Aunt. "I was searching for answers, nothing more. It was important to keep the project secret to maintain my credibility as an Aunt, particularly in front of counselors like Strømberg. But I did it for one reason only — to monitor and protect your son . . . my grandson."

Eliza relaxed her body shape a little, but hardened her green-eyed gaze. "What did you mean when you said you knew what David was?"

"You've seen the time rifts around him," Aunt Gwyneth replied. "He is the focus of an invasive force called the Ix. I managed to . . . intercept an Ix Cluster and keep it at bay for a while. As you can see from my physical appearance, I have paid a wretched price for my heroism. Something which should not be disregarded when Strømberg arrives to gloat over me. The Ix are pure fain, but a negative strain."

Eliza gulped as she took this in. Negative fain was something never talked about. To imagineer catastrophe or hatred or terror was unthinkable in Co:pern:ican society. She stood up and went to the window. So peaceful. So beautiful. The flowers. The sky. The odd droplet of rain, falling. Why did that always lift her heart so: the presence of rain? "What do these beings want with David?"

"They believe he is some kind of time agent, which adds substance to the idea that Agawin was borne from another world. It would all be rather exciting if it wasn't for the fact that the Ix intend to destroy David. Without me, that's a distinct possibility."

Eliza whipped around to face the cage again, this time with anger bubbling through her veins. "How can you be so hypocritical? You wanted him de:constructed."

Aunt Gwyneth laughed this off. "I could have re:moved him many times over, especially when he was in stasis in this very room. One day you'll understand that everything I've done was meant to test him or guide him or strengthen him. He needs me, Eliza. If you want to help the boy, let me go."

"No," she said, after giving it some thought. "For all your pretty words, I still don't trust you."

"Well, if nothing else, look at the book!" the Aunt fizzed. "All the time we spend dithering together extends the possibility of another time rift opening. We could at least find out what made him so anxious." She pointed at the bookshelf again.

"Oh, very well." Eliza marched to the shelves and drew the book down. It was a dictionary. (One of Mr. Henry's favorites.) It was heavy and she needed to support it carefully as she searched for the letters her dragon had revealed. There was only one entry that began with the sequence G-A-D-Z. It chilled her to see it, though she couldn't say why. A word she was unfamiliar with, but that seemed to shine a light in the back of her mind: Gadzooks.

"Gadzooks?" said Aunt Gwyneth when she heard it read. It seemed to set a nerve alive in her mind, too. "What is its meaning?"

Eliza put a finger on the page. "It's an archaic expression, a contraction of the phrase 'claws of

Godith.'" She turned a few more pages. "That's very strange. Godith is a mythical dragon that was supposed to have created the universe with her breath. Do you know anything about that?"

"No," said the Aunt. She narrowed her gaze and studied Eliza carefully. "Listen to me, girl. This is important. Hidden in a room upstairs is a claw. I cannot say for certain it came from a dragon, but if you insist in believing in these creatures, it would be most unwise to say that it didn't. We must recover it at once and take it to David. In the wrong hands, such a thing would be deadly."

Eliza put the dictionary back — and sighed.

Aunt Gwyneth slammed her fists against the bars. "This is not a ruse, you stupid girl. You have the evidence there in front of you. Your sculpture was clearly issuing a warning. You must have felt it when you commingled with David? You heard what Rosa said. They don't know what awaits them on the upper floors. Your son's life and the future of Co:pern:ica might be at stake. Are you going to act or not?"

"All right," Eliza said, spreading her hands. "Tell me how you know about this claw in the first place. If you can convince me, I *might* let you go."

For once, Aunt Gwyneth pumped for the truth. "When I first encountered the Ix, they had taken the form of a black firebird."

"Go on," Eliza said, remembering Penny's claims in the gardenaria.

Aunt Gwyneth's mind began to calculate — fast. "It was tracking David's movements, I suspect. I followed it here and did battle with it. It had the claw then, but hid it when it forced me to turn into a katt."

"And you know where it is?"

"I'm not familiar with this building, but any descendant of Agawin ought to be able to extend her fain and tune in to its whereabouts."

Eliza tapped her toe. She counted to three, then marched across the room and yanked up the cage (throwing Aunt Gwyneth onto her bottom). "All right, I'll do it. But you're coming with me. I'll carry you, *Mother*, but I won't let you out."

Aunt Gwyneth stood up and dusted herself down. She made a promise to herself that when she got out of this embarrassing cage she would make the girl pay for that bout of heavy-handed brutality. For the moment, however, things were well enough. The Aunt Su:perior raised a smile. Despite the annoying swing of the cage, she put her hands behind her back and fiddled with the hairpin she'd taken from her bun a few minits earlier. It had been a long time since she'd picked a lock. But even in her fainless state, such a task was not beyond her capabilities. All that mattered now was to have the dragon's claw. The natural order would then be restored. And she, Gwyneth, would at last become the most powerful woman on all Co:pern:ica.

7.

Gadzooks. 'David carried the name with him all through the lower floors of the librarium. And each time it formed its shape on his lips, an image of a dragon floated into his mind. Another like the one his mother had made, a cousin of the sculpture in Penny's hands. But unlike the book-reading dragon, Gadzooks carried a pen (or possibly a pencil), and a notepad, presumably to write things down. David thought of Mr. Henry then, and how the curator had always held the view that if books were windows onto the world, writing was the latch that opened them — in short, the centerpoint of all creativity. Words made the universe turn, he said. Somewhere within that revolving world, as distant but as vibrant as a shining star, David knew he shared a place with the dragon Gadzooks. He simply did not know in what sense yet, though it felt as natural as the air in his lungs and as permanent as the creases in the center of his palm. He looked at the dragon in Penny's hands, solid now, inert, holding its book to the fore like a sail. To the untrained eye it was a model, nothing more. And, like everything else on Co:pern:ica, from the lowliest button to the puffiest cloud, it had a certain level of auma — to the casual observer, a fairly low reading. But there was something strange about this creation, which Eliza herself might not even be aware of. There was a spark inside the sculpture, right at its middle. A glint of white fire. A *fire* within. How could a creature created from earth, with the properties of earth (its solidity, basically, was just a disguise), hide such powerful auma inside it? How could something made of clay be *alive*?

"Will you tell me about our father?"

"*Umm?*" David said.

Penny rolled her eyes sideways. "I didn't know we had a father. What's he like? Why isn't he at home — with us?"

From the head of the party Rosa called out, "Get ready. We're going in."

"Later," David whispered, patting Penny's arm.

They had reached the corridor on Floor Forty-Two, approaching the door to the fiction department. This time there was no need for passwords or codes; they simply sailed through on Aurielle's command. Azkiar was waiting on the other side, perched, half-asleep, on the swinging sign.

"Wow, I like that one!" Penny said.

But he clearly did not think the same of her. His ear tufts swiveled so far forward that the feathers above his eyes were nearly ejected like a row of arrows. Filling the space like a bloodred stain, he glided onto the librarium floor and began a heated exchange with Aurielle. Aleron, ever calm, fluttered to a shelf and blew a snort of air.

"Rosa, what are they saying?" David asked.

She pinched her lips together as if she'd been expecting something like this. "He wants to know what took her so long and what the kid is doing here."

"*Tch!* Why doesn't anyone *want* me?" Penny tutted. She stuck out her tongue, which only made Azkiar glare at her — hard.

"And there's been a development upstairs." Rosa cocked her head to listen. "I'm not sure I've got the translation right, they're speaking very fast, but I think he just said that something's got away and he can't find it." She leaned closer to David so Penny couldn't hear. "What was that about the danger being over?"

"All right, I'll deal with it," he said. *"RRRH!"* he went loudly.

Aurielle and Azkiar immediately stopped arguing and turned in unison to look at him.

"Impressive," said Rosa, folding her arms. "You've learned enough of their words to be able to say, 'Hey.'"

"Tell them I want Aleron *and* the red one to guard Penny while she searches for a book. They're to stay on this floor and take her back to Mom as soon as she's done."

"Oh . . . ," Penny started.

"No arguments, Penny. Something's going on upstairs. It would be better if Rosa and I dealt with it alone. Here, come with me a moment. Let me show you where I found *Alicia*." He guided her to the space where the book belonged and slid it back into place. "I'm sure any of these stories would be very entertaining. What about this one, *The Twonks*?" He pulled it down off a shelf her height. "Look, it's got a silly picture of a man with food in his beard."

Penny gazed at it without much enthusiasm. "Maybe," she said. It did *look* funny.

"Well, it's here, if you want it," David said, leaving *The Twonks* on the shelf. "He's done a lot, hasn't he, Roland Darl? Take your time looking through them. Borrow any you like."

"David." Rosa came up and tapped his shoulder. "Azkiar — the red bird — doesn't want to stay. He wants to be upstairs when we see the 'sheet' or something. I can't make out what he's trying to tell me."

David sighed and flicked his gaze toward Aleron. "Can you get him to stick really close to Penny?"

Rosa thought for a moment and tried a few words.

The next thing Penny knew, she had a green firebird sitting on her head.

"Not *that* close," David said. All the same he turned to Penny and said, "That means he likes you. Have fun. He'll look after you. I've got to go."

Too startled to argue, Penny merely waved good-bye.

The journey picked up speed. Azkiar flew on ahead and was out of sight by the time they had reached Floor Fifty-Two. There was little time to stop and look around properly, but David was soaking up the rooms as they went. None was shaped quite the same as any other, and many had chairs and lounging areas, but the one thing they all had in common was books. Shelf after perfect shelf of books. All in order. All the spines level. Every row the exact same distance from the edge. This was repeated all the way up to Floor Eighty-One, where the pattern suddenly began to change. On some shelves, gaps began to appear. Only a few at first. But by the time another four floors had been climbed, the lines were radically broken. The books were now spread out in irregular groups, as if they had chosen to huddle together by common acquaintance or kin. At first David simply assumed that whoever had done the ordering here had left (or even died) before they could complete their task. Then he noticed something very unusual. The books had no titles or authors — or words. When he took one down and opened it, the pages were blank. And yet he could feel more auma in his hands than would be present in a whole roomful of books farther down the building. He shouted to Aurielle to slow down for a moment, so that he might investigate further. But the female bird was so close to her goal that she simply squawked and pushed on. David put the book back, in not quite the same place — and saw it move to its correct position. If ever he needed proof that the librarium was alive, there it was.

He caught up with Rosa and Aurielle on Floor One Hundred and Eight. The firebird had perched on a tall wooden pedestal just to one side of a closed arched door. Above the door was a large old clock with a carved wooden face. Dragons decorated all the numerals. David turned and walked a few paces in reverse, so that he might look back the way they'd come. The shelves of books seemed to blur and stretch, way out of proportion to the distance they'd traveled. Yet the way through the arched door was simple enough. Aurielle tipped her beak toward a twisted cord of rope suspended from the ceiling. When Rosa pulled it, the clock hands began to spin and the sound of chiming spread through the building.

The door swung open.

The room was large and rectangular and long. It smelled of old feathers, which was hardly surprising as the floor was ankle-deep with them. Unusually, the windows were set very high and most had their shutters half-closed. This did not prevent sunlight angling through the slats and lending the room a dappled golden hue. From a circle of plaster at the center of the ceiling hung a large chandelier, in which an untidy nest had been built. Azkiar was sitting in it. Loose books were everywhere, of course, stacked in piles, or strewn untidily on dusty shelves, or lodged in a heap on a chair in the corner, or spread out on the table that ran the entire length of the room. David felt the urge to start checking them at once, but a call from Aurielle made him look up.

She had landed on her "tower" and was urging the humans to come and see something pinned to the wall behind her. David left Rosa admiring a couple of candlesticks and waded through the feathers to investigate.

He must have studied the tapestry for all of a minit before calling out to Rosa that she needed to join him. But Rosa was still occupied halfway down the room. She was holding two halves of an eggshell in her hands and had a strange, otherworldly look in her eyes.

"I got it wrong," she muttered as he returned to her side.

"Got what wrong?"

"My translation downstairs."

"Never mind," he said. "You really need to come and look at —" The faint noise of humming suddenly drew his attention. It was coming from a large old book on the table. He turned it over. This one *did* have a title: *The Book of Agawin.* "Wh — ? How did this get here?" he said.

But Rosa wasn't listening. "What I took to be 'got away' was right," she muttered, "but only in a general sense. 'Broken free' would have been a better translation." She fitted the halves of the shell together, then slowly opened it again. "This is what Azkiar couldn't find. Something's hatched."

8.

Penny," David whispered, fearing for her safety. In one stride he'd started to run for the door, much to the consternation of Aurielle. The bird flapped and squawked in such an agitated manner that her centuries-old book tower finally collapsed and she was forced to take to the air. The crash displaced a dust cloud as high as the shuttered windows. For a while the chandelier was lost from view, though Azkiar could still be heard coughing out words that Rosa probably wished she couldn't translate. When Aurielle emerged, her dismay was barely camouflaged by the dirt patches clinging to her grubby feathers. Despite this, there was a positive outcome. The accident had made David hesitate and look back to see if Aurielle had been injured. While he was still batting feathers from his face, Rosa had come up with her own reason to dissuade him from leaving.

"There's no need to go," she said. "Whatever was in the egg won't harm Penny."

"Uh?" he spluttered. "How do you know?"

"I can feel your auma all over the shell." Bizarrely, she could feel hers on it, too, though she chose not to admit that to him. Instead, she looked at Aurielle and asked, "Where did the egg come from?"

Aurielle shook her tail feathers out, sending two more spiraling to join the others. She pottered toward the center of the table (steering a course around *The Book of Agawin*), leaving a trail of prints in her wake. Briefly, she explained how she'd found the egg in the Dead Lands and how, during the time jolt, it had merged with David's tear and Azkiar's fire and —

She never got as far as the daisy chain because David pointed at Azkiar and said, "His fire was trapped inside my tear?"

The red firebird spat out a dry feather shaft.

"I saw a flash when he attacked you," Rosa said urgently. "That must have been what it was."

"So what's come out of it?" he said.

Rosa stared at the shell and laid it back on the nest where she'd found it. "I don't know. But all I'm getting from it . . . is love."

"Well, I need to be sure," said David.

"No," she said angrily. "You can't go. Not again." Two small words that ripped into his heart.

A moment or two passed. Glances were exchanged all around the room. High above, a window shutter creaked. Azkiar, who had flown to a shelf to shake himself down, looked up from his preening, perhaps wondering if there was something he needed to investigate. Aurielle, meanwhile, had let out her own jittery plea for David to stay. For once, it needed no translation.

"Anyway, the book's here," Rosa said, hoping that would reach him if her heartbreak couldn't. "This is what we were looking for, isn't it?"

"All right," he said. "But first, tell me what you make of this." Gripping her by the elbow, he plowed through the feathers and maneuvered her toward the far end of the room. Aurielle skittered down the table after them.

"It's called a 'tapestry,'" said Rosa, already study-ing it as they approached. "I read about them once when I was ordering books on Floor . . . Hang on, is that . . . ?"

"You and me? Yes. And that figure in the corner, cradling the katt, looks like an older version of Penny. I don't know who the guy standing next to her is. But you see the little girl in white who's kneeling? You see the dragon she's holding, the one that has a pencil?"

"It looks like one your mom might have made."

"*Um.* It is. Its name is Gadzooks."

Rosa looked sideways at him and frowned. "How do you know?"

"I've been seeing him in my mind — ever since I got the name. Think about what happened with the reading dragon."

"*G-A-D-Z* . . . ooks?"

"Exactly. And that shadow coming out of the big hill in front of him is probably the daddy of the Ix Cluster I fought."

Rosa ran her gaze across the tapestry again. This time there was a glint of fear in her eyes. "Is he controlling it?" she asked. "Or creating it?" There was a spike of darkness extending from the tip of the dragon's pencil back into the body of the shadow.

"I don't know," David said. "See what she says." He gestured at Aurielle. The firebird clicked her tongue and stepped forward.

And so began a long discussion, in which Rosa learned that the tapestry predicted a battle called Isenfier and that firebirds had always protected it. How long it had been there Aurielle couldn't say. But she was clear about who had made it.

"Agawin," David guessed.

Rosa nodded. "She says it's a vision of his future."

"And we're in it?"

Rosa lifted her shoulders. Her beautiful face was blank for once. "Maybe we'll learn something from the book."

"Did you ask about the little girl holding Gadzooks?"

"Yes. She doesn't know who she is. They just call her the 'angel.' Oh, and there's something else. She wants you to look at the dragon's notepad."

David squinted at the tapestry. "I can barely see it."

"Apparently, she knows a way." She gave a quick nod to Aurielle. The excited firebird flew to a panel beside the tapestry and struck the tail of a small dragon that had been carved out of the wood. Immediately, a door slid open and a brass-colored tele:scope sprang out on a long and wobbly crisscrossing extensor. David took hold of it and drew it to his eye, adjusting the rotating lenses until their focus was on the dragon's pad. Amazingly, he *could* see something on it. He studied it for a moment and extended the tele:scopic arm toward Rosa.

"The sign," she breathed. It was the same three-lined mark that had opened the door to Floor Forty-Two. The one she also seemed to carry on her arm. "He's writing 'sometimes' on his pad. Why would he do that?"

David sighed and shook his head. "I wish Dad was here. He'd love all this." He bounced the tele:scope back toward the panel and walked down the room, drumming his fingers on the tabletop. Remarkably, *The Book of Agawin* had escaped the fallout of dust. Laying his hands on the table beside it, David stared at the book for a few slow heartbeats, as if he knew that once these pages were opened, his life would never be the same again.

Rosa, sensing the enormity of the moment, stroked a hand down his arm and said, "Strømberg told me you have to read it from back to front."

David turned the book over. He ran his fingertips across the title, letting them trace the indents of the words. The book seemed to hum in appreciation. The sound it made reminded him of a lullaby his mother used to sing to him when he was a child. "Time to wake," he whispered, and opened the cover.

The paper was the color of Aurielle's feathers and felt pleasantly warm to the touch. The upper half of the opening page was covered with a host of unfamiliar symbols — all manner of curving marks with wild strokes and dashes flying off like sparks from the centers of the characters. And something Rosa hadn't noticed before, maybe because of the light downstairs.

"It's all in green," she muttered.

David nodded. He could sense the auma of dragons in the script. "Ask Aurielle if she knows how it got here."

"Does it matter?"

He found her inquisitive eyes. "You thought Mr. Henry had hidden it. So who put it on this table if we're the only humans to break the code to Floor Forty-Three?"

This made Rosa look over her shoulder, as if she half-expected the ghost of Mr. Henry to glide out of one of the shadowy alcoves. She passed the question on to Aurielle. The firebird chattered a strange reply.

"She says it came by itself. It appeared a few days ago. She thought we'd sent it."

David thought about the book he'd seen moving on the shelf, but chose to say nothing.

"What's that?" Rosa asked. She pointed to a solitary word at the bottom of the page. (Aurielle tilted one eye toward it.)

"His signature."

"That squiggle says 'Agawin'?"

"In dragontongue, yes. And this" — he waved a hand at the denser text — "is a summary of what the book's about. Do you want to hear it?"

Rosa put a fingertip to her lips. "No, I think I'll go and count the daisies." She thumped his arm (hard), making Aurielle clatter back. "Of course I want to hear it, dummy."

David looked down again. The reflected symbols danced like flames as his eyes scanned the page and he started to translate. In a quiet voice he read, *"We come from a world of fire."*

"We? Co:pern:icans?"

"Not sure. It doesn't say." He read the line again. *"We come from a world of fire. This I have witnessed in the beauty of creation. This I have beheld in a . . . glint — I think — of time. All that is, is within us and without us. The fire of the dragon. The eternal breath of life."*

"Is that it?" Rosa screwed up her nose in disappointment.

David turned to the next page, where there were two large symbols about a third of the way down.

"What does that say?"

" 'The Flight of Gideon.' "

Rosa did her best to translate this for Aurielle. It clearly worked, for the firebird paddled her feet in excitement and responded with a whole flurry of words. (Azkiar gave a squawk of annoyance as yet more dust floated into the air.)

"She knows of him," said Rosa, interpreting the squawks. "A golden firebird they're all descended from. She wants to know if it's true that he came from another world."

David let his gaze come to rest on Aurielle. She looked so comical, her body still blotched with choking dust and one rogue feather attaching itself to the side of her neck. "Let's check on Mom and Penny, then I'll read it all, OK?"

Rosa passed this on.

"I can tell you one other thing," David said. He flipped to another page like the last. "It's split into parts. The Flight of Gideon, The Battle of Isenfier, The Isle of Alavon, The Icelands of the North, and . . ." He practically heaved the book over to reach the last part. "The Ark of Co:pern:ica."

"Ark?" said Rosa. "What's an 'ark'?"

The words had hardly left her lips when the building responded with a shuddering lurch, as if something had suddenly struck into its base.

Both firebirds were in the air in a moment.

Rosa spun around. "What happened? What's that noise?" From deep within the body of the librarium they could hear the grinding shift of stone, as if some sleeping giant had woken. Rosa put her hand on the tabletop and felt it vibrating. One of the candlesticks toppled over.

"The windows," David said. "Look at the windows." The shutters were banging back and forth, in danger of breaking free of their fixings. Suddenly, a jagged light ruptured the clouds, lighting up the room in bright blue flashes.

Then the rain came down, like a volley of roaring drums. Rain in quantities that no one living on the world of Co:pern:ica had ever witnessed before. A phenomenon way outside the Grand Design. The plausible impossible. A tempest.

A storm.

David was staggered. He had once discussed storms with Mr. Henry after coming across some scenes in a book of meteorology. The curator, while admitting that his knowledge of atmos:ferics was limited, had reassured the boy that storms could not happen on a world where there were no great bodies of water (he called them "oceans" or "lakes") and so much of the surface was devoid of plants. (The daisies, he told him, were a small miracle of something he called "nature.") Nevertheless, David had carried the pictures with him and seen, on paper, what a bad storm could do. It could lead to devastation, homelessness, and fear. And the single most striking image of all.

Flood.

9.

Both humans immediately ran to a room where they could peer straight out of a window. Rosa arrived half a sec before David and was first to see the impact the rain was having. Far below, at a frankly dizzying drop, the daisy fields had turned dark green and sodden, their flower heads swaying in a current of rising water. The speed of the transition was staggering. And although it was impossible to see or measure, Rosa formed the idea that the rain was falling considerably farther than the limits of the Bushley librarium. Where was all this water *coming* from? And how high would it ultimately go? A great spume suddenly erupted from the well, spraying the southern face of the building. Rosa squealed and jumped back in shock. "What's happening?" she cried. "David, what's caused this?"

He truly had no idea. But he could feel a growing

tremor in the boards beneath his feet and a fundamental change in the auma of the books. Something monumental was about to happen. And Penny and his mother must be right at the heart of it.

"Come on. We've got to find the others," he said.

But the librarium had its own ideas about that.

As they dashed for the lower floors, Rosa stumbled (for the first time *ever*) on the laces of her boots and happened to look back toward the tapestry room. To her astonishment, the arched doorway had changed. It was taller. Greener. Its frame sweetly dressed with twists of leaves. The old wooden clock had disappeared from view, replaced by a kind of rotating vent through which a dial of sunlight was passing (sunlight, yes, despite the rain). The fraying bellpull was no longer hanging from the ceiling. But in the place where it would have made a shadow on the wall, something *organic* was moving. A small and incredibly beautiful creature with patterned yellow wings as fragile as paper was fluttering about there. Rosa beckoned David to come and see, unaware that he'd taken off in the opposite direction. Suddenly, the building lurched again and she was thrown, facedown, to the floor. It seemed to take an age to complete the fall (she had the strange impression she was gliding through a rainbow made of stars) and in the time that it did, many things changed. She would have been expecting, for instance, to collide with a hard, unforgiving floorboard. Instead, the blow was cushioned by a thick expanse of flower petals, dried leaves, moss, and twigs. Scent and taste were the first two senses she recovered and both of them told her she had struck earth. As she rose to her knees she understood why. The whole structure of the room — the posts, the shelves, certain parts of the ceiling — had merged together and morphed into an area of *woodland*, a landscape Rosa had seen (and admired) in several books. As if this weren't strange enough, the marks on her arm, the scratches inflicted by the cruel Aunt Petunia, were glowing blue and drawing the rotating light toward them. Through the doorway, she heard a neighing sound. A spiraling breeze stirred up the leaves. And from their dappled center came a pure white beast that tore Rosanna apart with love and wonder in equal measure. She cried out for David to come. But David was long gone by then.

He was calling out to her, in fact, wondering why she wasn't at his shoulder, all the while trying to make sense of the changes taking place around *him*. He had just burst into a room where the shelves had formed an assembly of crisscrossing branches. Among the finer branches, an animal was hiding. It had a gray furry body and a comical face. The patches of black around its slightly bugged eyes made it look as if it were wearing a mask. Dropping down in a long J shape behind it was a tail composed of equal-sized rings of black-and-white fur. The animal's keen eyes took David in, then darted toward another room, in a direction he hadn't thought to go. The sounds of heavy purring were drifting out of it. His nose was also quick to detect a strong variation of the ripe deposits that Boon left in the gardenaria at home sometimes. He stepped toward the door and looked in. Prowling a floor of sawdust and bark was the biggest katt he had ever seen. It was the color of sand (another lesson of Mr. Henry's) and had a mane of brown hair around its head, which ran in straggles down its shoulders and back. Another katt, of similar size, but maneless, was lying on its side in the corner of the room, licking its paws. The katt on its feet grunted and raised an imperious gaze. It flicked its tail and allowed a low growl to escape from its throat. Then it snorted and padded toward the visitor. David stood quite still. The big katt twitched its nostrils twice, then let its head rest against his hand, pushing against his palm just as Boon would have done. David cupped a hand around its soft, warm ear. "Where did you come from, eh?" he whispered. But in some ways the question was no longer relevant. He was deeply aware by now that he was not in control of his destination or of the changes taking place in the building. He had run away from Floor One Hundred and Eight with the sole intention of heading downstairs. But one glance through the window of the room he was in told him he was being taken higher. Far below, even the daisies had joined the transition. They were collecting into groups, describing unusual shapes in the water. Streamlined bodies with triangular fins. Tails as flexible as a man's hand. Creatures that moved as easily through water as firebirds could zip and pitch through air. Amazing. And so David acknowledged the presence of the animals and surrendered his consciousness to the librarium. All he could do now was follow its will — and pray that Rosa and his family would be safe.

As it happened, his sister was more than safe. Indeed, Penny would later come to learn that it was *she* who'd been the catalyst for the transformation about to rock the whole of Co:pern:ica, not merely the great museum of books at the center of it.

Shortly after David and Rosa had left her, she had set about finding a new book to read. (She had looked again at *The Twonks* and laughed at the pictures, but had left the reading dragon on the shelf as a marker while she examined the other books.) It was a daunting proposition. There were thousands to choose from. More than Penelope could possibly count. So for a while she'd done nothing but roam back and forth, reading the titles of any that looked interesting. (Aleron had wisely jumped off her by now because he kept sliding every time she tilted her head.) In time, not surprisingly, her neck began to ache. The titles blurred. The sheer quantity of them began to overwhelm her. That became a barrier to making a choice. She sighed, wishing David could be there to do the choosing. It was surely more fun, when you knew nothing about books, to have one recommended by someone who did. Strangely, as this thought drifted through her mind, she felt that the books were responding to it. Two or three times she glanced nervously around her, thinking she could hear them murmuring something. But that was just silly (*wasn't it?*). More likely she was hearing a breeze from the window, stirring up the ancient dust. She went over to the window and leaned forward on tiptoe, supporting her body on the deep recess of stone so she could get a good view out. A few light raindrops were falling. Her eyes grew wide with delight. Rain was something she had never seen before, though her mother had taught her how in certain areas of Co:pern:ica water fell from the sky sometimes. Penny stretched a hand and caught a cool drop. It twinkled in the center of her palm for a moment. Then with a gentle *pop!* it burst and its light traveled over her shoulder, flaring as it entered the darker librarium. She whipped around to see where it had gone. And there, to her astonishment, three-quarters of the way down the aisle between the shelves, stood a little girl, slightly more than half her own height.

"Hello," said the girl, and waved a dainty hand. She was wearing a pretty white dress, white ankle socks, and red buckled shoes. Her hair was the dark flowing color of Rosa's. Her eyes were the striking blue of David's. Around her wrist was a bracelet of violet daisies. The raindrop was glittering brightly in front of her, like a star in the center of her chest.

"Who are you?" Penny gasped.

The child tightened her lips as if she weren't quite sure what name might be appropriate. Her eyebrows came together in a sweet sort of frown. "I'm . . . Angel," she said at last, as if she'd solved a riddle.

Penny glanced sideways at Aleron. The firebird was awestruck, barely breathing. He was perched precariously on one of the shelves, trying to get his left foot to take a hold. Eventually, his balance gave out and he had to make a semicircular flight to regain his position. He closed his wings in a fluster as he landed, before resuming his mesmerized pose.

"Do you live here?" Penny asked.

The girl swung her body and thought about this. "Sometimes," she answered. "I like it here more than anywhere, I think." She glanced along the shelves. "Are you looking for a book?"

"Yes," said Penny. "But I don't know which to choose."

"I'll help you," said Angel.

"Have you read them?" Penny said. She couldn't keep a mild squeak out of her voice. She was, of course, a tiny bit put out by the thought that someone much younger than herself might have more knowledge of the books than she did.

But the little girl shook her head and said, "No — but I know which one you'd like. I'll show you where it is. It's been waiting for you for quite a long time."

That was an odd thing to say, thought Penny. All the same, she gave a grateful nod.

From the center of her back Angel put out two wings. "All you have to do is believe," she said.

Penny's mouth opened as wide as any book. Aleron's reaction was a little more pronounced. With a drowsy *rrrrrrhhhh,* he fell off the shelf and thudded to the floor in a faint. Penny gasped and gathered him into her arms. To her relief, she could still trace air in his nostrils.

Angel seemed unconcerned. "Leave him on a shelf. I'll look after him," she said. She flipped her hands and set the raindrop floating. It swerved left and right in a wavy line, before it whizzed past Penny's head. She turned to see it sparkling at the end of a row.

"How did you . . . ?" *Get wings,* she wanted to say. But when she looked back, Angel had disappeared.

So Penny set Aleron down as requested and hurried off in pursuit of the raindrop. It wasn't difficult to follow, but it *was* quick. She was nearly out of breath by the time she'd skidded to a halt in a section marked Animal Stories. The drop was hovering beside a row of books where the authors' names all began with an R. At first there seemed nothing remarkable about that. Then one name suddenly stood out from the rest.

Rain.

David Rain.

Penny felt her senses whirl. The only feeling she could liken it to was the moment during the *Alicia* story when she and David had looked through the window at the end of the tunnel and peered into the room that had seemed so very familiar to her, yet she had never seen before. If her father, Harlan, had been at her side, he might, with a little more knowledge, have postulated that the name "David Rain" was a product of the time nexus linking Co:pern:ica, Ki:mera, and Earth. As potent in its way as the dragon word "sometimes." As meaningful as anything in Penny's life. And then there was the title: *Snigger and the Nutbeast*. That seemed to set off a second wave of giddiness. Penny read it over and over until her head began to feel as huge as a cave. *Snigger. Nutbeast. David.*

Believe.

She shook herself and made a decision. This was the book she wanted, for sure. She hooked a finger over the spine and tilted it toward her. At the same time, just as if a switch had been thrown, the building seemed to shake very gently. Penny paused. She hadn't caused that — had she? She waited half a sec, then dragged the book again. With a *swish*, it slotted out of its position. Once again, she felt the librarium react. It seemed to yawn (distantly) in every direction. Somewhere far below, maybe at ground level, she heard an almighty drawn-out creak.

She gulped and looked at the book. On the cover was a quirky illustration of a hunched-up figure in a long black coat. It was skulking beside a large old tree, being watched from one of its branches by a tiny gray animal with a curving bushy tail. Penny opened it using just one finger. Right away, the whole book altered its shape and the animal on the cover grew out of the pages. Penny squealed and let it go. The animal landed on all four feet, flicked its bushy tail, and with great agility climbed the shelving up to Penny's head height. There it stopped, twitched its whiskers, and gave a happy chirrup. Then it sat bolt upright with its tail held stiff, staring at something at Penny's back.

"Well, well," said a voice. "What *have* you done?"

Penny gasped and flattened herself against a wall. The speaker was Aunt Gwyneth, fully grown once more. In her right hand she was holding the dragon's claw. In her left was the cage she'd been imprisoned in. Inside it now was Eliza Merriman.

10.

Hhh! YOU!" Penny cried. Her eyes darted wildly toward the cage. Eliza was trying to call out a warning, but her voice was weak and did not carry far. She raised her arms and tried signaling instead, but Aunt Gwyneth shook the cage from side to side, sending its occupant crashing back and forth like the clapper of a bell.

"What have you done?" screamed Penny. "Let my mom go!"

"Oh, spare me your emotional blather," said the Aunt. "Did you really think I wouldn't get free? Your mother won't be harmed. She's being taught a lesson. She has to know who is in control, that's all."

A lively flash of blue light paused the argument. Penny jumped a little and glanced through the window. Suddenly, the rain was pelting down. Another long, low creak rose up from below and the building swayed in a circular motion, as if it had been cast adrift from the ground. From deep at its roots came the sound of grinding stone; farther forward, the groan of stretching timber. Too confused to take it in, Penny returned her thoughts to her mother. After the battering she'd taken, Eliza was sprawled over the floor of the cage. Not injured, but very dizzy. "How did you grow big and put Mom in there?"

"Ah, well," said the Aunt, sounding rather smug. "I'd love to be able to claim that I did it, but it was really the influence of this little gem." She twiddled the claw in front of her face, admiring its slender outline and strength. "Before you ask, it's a dragon relic, put here by a seer called Agawin. Don't pester me with questions about him; I really don't have the time. I think he intended that your brother should find this. I propose to deliver it to David — for a price."

"What does it do?" Penny growled. To her relief, her mother was beginning to sit up.

"Well, if I remember my training correctly, most Aunts would have called it a 'wand.' You wave it, you wish, and it performs certain magicks. Something you're quite good at, it seems." She circled a hand, inviting the girl to observe the changes taking place around them. The bookshelves were slowly reinventing themselves into a network of planks and ropes. A long-armed creature with drooping eyes and scratchy, golden fur swung across the room and entered a box-shaped compartment in the corner, giving a whimpering call as it went. The whole librarium was coming alive with hoots and calls and screeches and chirrs, not unlike when someone pressed the doorbell. And all the while there was the sense of movement. A slight pitch sideways. A mild tilt. Buoyancy.

"Oh, yes, this is all your doing," said the Aunt, picking up on Penny's bewilderment. "The book you just transformed was a key. A trigger to a complex feat of metamorphosis. Once activated, the whole building displays its true purpose. Do you know what you've begun here, child? The rain should give you a clue. It's a boat. A very large boat. A floating sanctuary called an 'ark.' A refuge for animals stripped from the Dead Lands during the time of the Great Re:duction. Clever, I must admit, to disguise it as a museum for books — a dreary place that no one would think to show interest in. I wonder how he worked it out? What arrangements he made? What lengths he went to? What sacrifices he endured?" Her gaze fell solidly on the claw again. "What help he had? I sense the involvement of dragons in this. And did he take in *all* the species, I wonder? Or did he leave out some of the uglier ones? I do hope he's housed a giraffe. I always loved the old digi:grafs of —"

Her musing stopped abruptly. For the last few moments of her lumbering lecture she'd been talking to the air in front of her. She was about to whip around when Penny knocked into her from behind. With a rush, the girl wrestled the cage free and set about making her escape. Ordinarily, this sort of behavior would not have troubled the Aunt Su:perior, for it was no effort for a woman of her capabilities to track down a frightened, desperate child. But the kick that Penny had administered to the old woman's bony kneecap did madden her and hinder her response. The reprisal, when it came, was swift — and savage. A stake of wood, ripped from the still-growing edifice around them, flashed through the air and speared the floor in front of Penny. It was as tall as her chin and landed so close that she could almost scent the individual splinters as it quivered underneath her nose.

"The next one goes through your foot," said the Aunt. "Now come back here, before I run out of patience."

"Penny, do as she says," squeaked a voice.

The girl looked down in anguish at her mother. "But you were warning me to get away," she whispered, remembering the flapping of arms.

"I know, but she'll hurt you if you try again. She needs us. The claw won't work without our auma. She tricked me into finding it and turned it against me. But I'm alive and so will you be if —"

"What are you whispering?" snapped the Aunt.

Penny turned around, her breathing loud and heavy in her chest. She felt the ark rock again and suddenly an idea came to her. She blurted out, "Is it true you need us to work that thing?"

"It *helps*," Aunt Gwyneth said scornfully. "Now get over here."

"I know something you don't."

"Penny, what are you doing?" Eliza hissed.

The Aunt sighed and tapped her fingers against the claw. "You're deluding yourself, child — but do go on."

"I saw a flying girl."

478

Eliza said, "*What?*"

Aunt Gwyneth's face darkened — but with interest, not malice.

"She brought me here," said Penny. "She showed me the book. She said her name was Angel. I know where she is." These last five words were an outright lie, for Penny had no idea where Angel had gone to, and would never have given the girl up if she did. Her plan was simply to make the Aunt curious and gain a little more time. The room had completed its transformation. And the *chaka-chaka-chaka* noises coming from next door were an indication something was happening there as well. How long could it be before David or the firebirds came to check on her? Or the magical Angel herself?

In four strides, Aunt Gwyneth was at Penny's side. She took the girl by the hair and yanked her closer. Penny's face screwed up in pain.

"I'm glad you think it hurts. It's meant to, child. Don't ever disobey me again. If you're lying about this Angel girl, I'll make you so small you'll only be fit for spider food. Oh, silly me. You don't know what a spider is, do you? Think of a creature with spindly legs and a hairy body and an ugly mouth that would trap you and starve you and use its saliva to soften your body before it digests you. They will be running all over this ark. There might even be one or two in this *room*." She rolled Penny's hair a little tighter in her fist. "Where is this flying girl?"

"Be-behind you," Penny rasped.

There was a pause. The Aunt read her captive's eyes. Surprisingly, the girl was telling the truth.

Well, almost the truth.

She threw Penny aside and spun herself around, hopeful of seeing a phenomenon that was only ever talked about in the most secretive meetings of Aunt Su:periors. Instead, she came face-to-face with another kind of wonder: three dragons. Or to give the species its correct name: "dragonets." Each was roughly four times the size of a firebird. One green. One red. One a soft cream color. The latter was exceptionally beautiful. The sleek lines of her face, from her sweetly sculpted ears to the tips of her exquisite nostrils, were so perfect they might have been imagineered by light. She was enjoying the fact that by moving her wings far quicker than her heartbeat she could hover in midair. She seemed particularly proud of her arms, especially the dexterity of movement in her five hooked claws. By that same token, however, she looked acutely upset to see a single dragon claw in the hands of an enemy of the Ark of Agawin. Her jeweled eyes shone in the semidarkness, sparkling through a rich kaleidoscope of colors before settling on a single color: crimson. Her companions adjusted their irises likewise. On a single command (a *hrrr*, not a *rrrh*) they opened their jaws and made fire in their throats. And before Aunt Gwyneth could quicken her thoughts to imagineer an escape, she'd been doused in flame from head to toe.

11.

But, amazingly, it did not kill her. Her body pitched and jerked within its sleeve of fire and she screeched as loudly as any creature on the ark (setting off an echoing cacophony throughout), yet when it was done she was still standing. The only indications of any kind of burning were the crackling frizzles at the ends of her hair and the lingering smell of charred carbons (mainly motes of wood that had settled on her clothing during the transformation). She lifted her gaze toward her attackers. "Thank you," she said to them, rolling the words together in a growl. "I feel so much *better* for that." And here was a lesson for Aurielle to learn: A dragon cannot flame its own kind. All their combined assault had achieved was to energize the claw and make Aunt Gwyneth stronger. She was not slow to explore her new potential either. Aleron and Aurielle wisely backed away from her furious glare, but Azkiar, ever the impulsive one, bared his fangs and made a lunge for her. With one flick of the claw, she sent him tumbling backward. He crashed into a wooden post, bringing down a section of the structure that housed the gibbering animals. The same impact scared away a small collective of dark-colored birds that had been strutting about on one of the beams. They scattered in front of Aurielle and funneled through the window. When they had cleared, Aunt Gwyneth was nowhere to be seen.

At that point, Penny came bounding forward and said with some urgency, "She flew away! She made herself into a bird!" She put the cage aside and flapped her arms. Aurielle, who had settled on the floor by now, blew a smoke ring and flexed her optical triggers. Although she did not understand what had happened to the aerie or the exciting transition the firebirds had gone through, the advantages of it were plainly felt. One was improved vision. She let her gaze stream into the misty sky. The birds were dark specks, not much bigger than swollen raindrops. One had separated off from the group and was spiraling up the side of the ark. Aurielle let her eyes zoom in on it. Despite reaching the limits of her sight, she was able to verify Penny's account. The black bird had an arrogant glint in its eye — and one of its claws was colored dark green.

"You've got to go after her!" Penny gabbled on. "She's going to hurt David. I know she is."

"David." The one word of human-speak Aurielle understood. She flipped a worried glance at Azkiar. He was winded and had suffered damage to a wing (one of his balancing stigs had sheared). He would not be flying anywhere quickly — at least not in a straight line. And all this time the Aunt was escaping. Aurielle knew she must act. Telling Aleron to guard the humans (and to please keep Azkiar *put*, for once), she lifted off and arrowed her body through the window. She rolled twice in the rain before opening her wings with a satisfying *phut!* And away she went in pursuit.

Aunt Gwyneth meanwhile — or the raven she'd become (a deliberate low-level transformation to preserve the capability of the claw) — was also enjoying the wonders of flight. She was soaring through the air, angling her head both left and right, taking in the changes to the librarium. Her dialogue with Penny had not been overstated. The giant stone building had metamorphosed into a colossal floating vessel, with a bloated wooden hull and a sturdy prow. It sat upon an ocean (there was no better word) of clear blue water still being patterned by tumbling rain. A host of creatures, some in shoals, some individual giants, swam alongside as it bobbed through the water. What powered it, who could say? Where it was going, the Aunt could not tell. But it was all the while being joined by an increasing number of smaller boats, imagineered by bewildered Co:pern:icans who had adopted the ark as their template for survival. They could be seen lining the sides of their vessels, aiming eyeglasses and tele:scopes at the leviathan dominating the rising water. None of the supporting boats was any taller than the ninth row of planking in the ark's strapping hull. And none were within the shadow of its girth. But all of them were going where its bow wave pointed. What other choice did they have?

Aunt Gwyneth banked to one side and turned her thoughts to the structure of the craft. The "rooms" of the librarium were still plain to see, though their famous square windows were now uniformly arched and the rooms were arranged not in recurring even-sized floors, but in a series of concentric oval decks. An animal's head could be seen poking out of a window here and there. (The long-necked giraffes were at midterrace level about halfway back.) Walking the main deck were two enormous beasts with wrinkled gray skins, huge flapping ears, and the longest nasal attachments the Aunt had ever seen. But where, she wondered, was David Merriman? Her dark raven eye swept upward. Like the building before it, the highest stories of the ark were hidden under lines of frothy cloud. Her instincts told her that this was where she would find her quarry. So she set a course for a point just above the top level of white, thinking she would swoop down and surprise any creature concealed within it. But the higher she climbed, the thinner grew the air and the thinner grew her blood and the less appealing this plan became. Of greater concern was the sight of Aurielle coming after her. The cream dragonet was gaining fast. Cursing the raven's pitiful shortcomings, Aunt Gwyneth dipped, early, into the cloud. There was no point challenging a creature better adapted to altitude than she. But the use of guile was another matter. Inside the mist, the advantage would swing the way of the opponent most cunning. The raven gave out a condescending *caarrk*. The stupid dragon bird would be dead within minits.

But what awaited Aunt Gwyneth inside the cloud was something far stranger than condensed water vapor. As she burst through the outer layers she emerged onto a bright white world that bore no resemblance to any landscape she had ever seen before. It stretched for miles in all directions, mostly flat, but with occasional knots of jagged white blocks, all made, she thought, from the same crystalline "matter" as the general surface. What struck her most of all was the intense cold, which seemed to parch the blue sky of half its oxi:gen. She could feel it stinging the linings of her nostrils and tightening the feathers at the edges of her wings, hampering her ability for fine changes of direction.

But there was only one direction the Aunt was headed in. And it was soon very plain to see. Sitting on the surface of these hostile surroundings was the animal David Merriman had changed into to destroy the Ix Cluster. Aunt Gwyneth circled it. Twice. It didn't move or attempt an attack. Was it him? Was it David? Was he imagineering all of this? The cold was biting at her legs by now, and the lubricant that swiveled the raven's eyeballs seemed to have turned to splinters of glass. So the Aunt set down at a comfortable distance from the great white beast and transformed once again to her natural self. This, she quickly realized, might not have been wise. For if the cold felt harsh against the raven's feet, it scratched like a katt on her exposed face. Whatever would be done here must be done fast. She raised the claw and, pointing it, said, "Identify yourself. What is this place?"

"I am an ice bear," the creature replied, in an unhurried voice so thick with pride that it seemed to curve the air around it. "These are the Icelands of the North."

"Cut the twaddle. Are you David?"

The bear blew a stream of air from its snout. "Sometimes," it said. It tilted its commanding head toward the claw.

"Move and I'll turn you to dust," spat the Aunt. (Another poor decision: The spittle quickly hardened to a spike on her lip.) She whipped around, hearing wingbeats overhead. Aurielle had just ripped through the cloud. But instead of swooping down to strike, the dragonet just streaked by as if nothing below her even existed.

"She cannot see us," the bear explained. "From this time point on, the firebirds play no part in your destiny."

Aunt Gwyneth flashed the claw again. "And what would you know about my destiny?"

The ice bear lifted its chin. Suddenly, the space in front of it was filled with flakes of twinkling ice. "It's here. In the 'Is.' All around you, Gwyneth. Each flake is a fire star, a portal to a probable future. Only one of them leads to your survival."

Despite the plethora of stabbing pains it caused, Aunt Gwyneth furrowed her brow. The fire stars shimmered, each one offering a tantalizing glimpse of a choice she might have made or a thought she might have had or a villainous plan she might yet hatch in some darkened recess of her scheming mind. Fire stars. Is. Futures. Time. She risked extending her fain for a moment and realized she was standing (floating, maybe?) in a limitless matrix of pure fain. At last, she had found the Higher. Now all she needed was to take command of them.

"For as long as I have this," she sneered, aiming the claw at the ice bear's forehead (several hundred flakes immediately twinkled), "*I* will be in control of my future." She let the threat seep into the matrix. Again it was the bear, not the Higher, that replied.

Closing its eyes to concentrate, the Higher said, "Any act of aggression would lead to your death. The claw is about to turn against you, Aunt. Give it up with grace and you may survive."

"May?" she snarled.

The bear's ears gave the tiniest of twitches. The ice flakes flurried and one seemed to separate out from the rest. "This star guarantees your existence. Touch the claw to it and you will be safe. The creat:or is needed at the Battle of Isenfier. Join us and it will let you live."

"Us?" Aunt Gwyneth scoffed.

The bear opened its haunting eyes. At the same moment, the figure of a child appeared. She came from a space just beyond the bear's head and flew down to the world of ice at its feet. Rosa emerged on the other side, sitting on the back of a stunning white horse. When the horse shook its mane, beads of white and violet light spiraled along the length of its horn. And all around, as far as any human eye could see, there appeared a multitude of bears.

Aunt Gwyneth stood back. "This is a trick," she hissed. "A clever projection, nothing more."

The little girl sighed, as if she'd lived through this many times before. "Aunty, I think you should believe us," she said. "I think you should be *good* this time. I really want to help you."

But, like the cold creeping into her knuckles, badness was ingrained in Aunt Gwyneth's soul. Disregarding every warning she'd been given, she attempted to draw upon the power of dragons to destroy the solitary flake in front of her. A loud crackle of energy lit up the claw and produced a phenomenal surge of power. The impulse sent the Aunt flying backward as if she'd been hit by a speeding taxicar. Issuing a ghastly scream, she blasted through the cloud and shot into the air surrounding the ark. Several hundred tele:scopes followed her flight. They saw her go spinning beyond the first line of boats to end with a thumping splash in the water.

And *still* her life was not quite done with.

The three occupants of the boat she'd fallen nearest to hooked her toward them and hauled her in. When they turned her over, one would have gladly thrown her back.

"Harlan, what is it?" Mathew Lefarr said. "This woman's going to die without our help — if she isn't already gone."

Harlan Merriman kept his distance. "How in the name of Agawin did *she* get here?" Despite the patch he now wore across one eye (a painful reminder of their clash with the Re:movers), he would know this face anywhere. "That's the Aunt who sent me to the Dead Lands. She's evil, Mat."

"She might be; we're not," said Bernard. Taking care to protect a large swelling in his ankle, he knelt down beside the Aunt and held his ear close to her blue, wet lips. Under a nearby bench was a rolled-up blanket that he yanked out and spread across the quivering body.

"He's right, Harlan," Mathew added. "We can't come back and put aside the spirit we found at Alavon. If nothing else, we owe our dead friends that. Whatever this woman has done to you, we must show her some compassion in what might be her final few secs."

Harlan swallowed hard. For a strange, otherworldly moment, his conscience wrestled with his feelings of vengeance and the entire universe seemed to turn around him. He snapped out of it and made his decision.

"I'll find something she can rest her head on," he muttered. (He had tried to imagineer a pillow, but the creation of the boat had sapped the last reaches of his fain.) He disappeared into the cabin at the prow.

The moment he was gone, the Aunt's lungs gave a hideous rasp and she spat a small fountain of water over Bernard's knees. "Please, try to be calm," he said. He thought to hold her hands, but they were under the blanket.

The Aunt stared, half-lidded, at death, but still had time for one last pronouncement: "My bo-dy is bro-ken, but . . . nnn . . . my will . . ." And it seemed to both the onlooking men that a slight smile was playing across her lips as she said it.

Mathew saw her hand moving under the blanket. "Bernard, what's she doing?"

Bernard drew the cloth back. On the floor of the boat, in a thin, green scrawl, was a message:

I, Gwyneth, also known as Gwilanna, l

"Goodness," he said. "She must be writing a will." (One of the few times on Co:pern:ica that the traditional skills of writing were properly employed.) He

493

looked at the unfinished word. "What is it you want to write? Is it 'leave'? What do you want to leave — and to whom?"

"Why is it green?" Mathew muttered. "Bernard, show me the pen."

But Bernard, still concerned with his act of citizenship, leaned closer to the Aunt and repeated loudly: "*I, Gwyneth, also known as Gwilanna, leave* . . . what?" Shaking wildly, her hand began to echo her body's distress. "Please, let me help you," Bernard said. He tried to steady her wrist. All he received for this act of goodwill was a spiteful hiss and a spray of saliva across his robe. He jerked back, bumping Mathew and blocking his view.

Harlan's view was not impeded, however. As he stepped out of the cabin he not only saw the words but what was creating them. "Mathew, stop her!" he shouted and picked up a boat hook. For all his willingness to show the Aunt mercy, he would gladly have plunged the hook into her just then. But as the dragon's claw at last fell out of her hand there was no more need for violence. Aunt Gwyneth had departed the world of Co:pern:ica with a glazed look of triumph etched on her face and one last trick in her miserable heart. Bernard had been wrong about the next word in her will. It was not "leave." The full message was this:

I, Gwyneth, also known as Gwilanna, live. . . .

PART FIVE
WHICH SPEAKS OF MANY
FUTURES — PROBABLE
AND OTHERWISE — AND LOOKS
BACK UPON
TRAGEDY AND FORWARD
ON TO CHANGE

1.

Via a winch on the lower decks, they brought Aunt Gwyneth's body onto the ark and laid her out in a manner befitting a woman of her status. In a room not inhabited by any of the animals, David imagineered a suitable bier and an open casket in which to place the corpse. Around it he created an auma field that would preserve the remains and alert him to any form of tampering. As an extra precaution, he placed two able firebirds on watch. The window was shuttered. The lights kept low. Somehow, the chatter of animal noises respectfully managed to bypass this room. Only the gentle creaking of the boat accompanied the Aunt on whatever journey her soul had now taken. It was, as Harlan Merriman would comment, a most bizarre situation. Hardly the ideal circumstances in which to stage a family reunion. Yet everyone present, young

Penny included, was powerfully drawn to that gray, austere face. Even in death, the Aunt Su:perior exerted an unprecedented level of control.

Almost as an afterthought, the greetings began. First, the relief of a battle-scarred husband reunited with his adoring wife (now returned to her normal size following the demise of the Aunt's powers). Then the slightly lost-for-words delight of an eight-year-old child meeting the father she never knew she had, and the pride of that father for the son who stood at the helm of the greatest revolution in Co:pern:ican history — an *ark*, transformed from a structure made of stone. Much wonder was expressed about the boat and its cargo, and the floodwater, which still continued to rise. Then there was the grateful presentation to the Merriman family of Mathew Lefarr, the brave and noticeably handsome young man who had risked his life to bring Harlan and Bernard back from the Dead Lands. Plus Bernard himself. Half-crippled. Exhausted. Not a little traumatized. But there. Forever at Harlan's side.

Only one person failed to find any real joy in the gathering. Rosa swept in late and was mortified to see the pale-faced corpse of their worst adversary back on the boat. Turning to David she immediately railed, "Why is she here, wetting my ark? If she's dead, dump her in the ocean and be done."

"That's not a good idea," said Harlan.

Rosa turned and glared at David's father. And perhaps there was some hint of lingering angst about the way Mr. Henry had passed away that made her say, with more rancor than necessary, "This is my home. I don't want that mangy old witch on show, *thank you*."

"I completely understand that," Harlan said, raising a hand to keep Penny and Eliza at bay, "but we need to watch her, Rosa. She may not be dead."

"What?" said Eliza, covering her throat.

Penny stood on tiptoe and peered at the body. "She looks sort of dead to me."

Rosa clearly agreed. She stared at Harlan Merriman as if he had just jetted in from another universe and had no understanding of the biology of this world. Muttering something only she could hear, she bent down and picked up a small stake of wood and ran forward to drive it through the Aunt's sodden heart.

She would have succeeded if David hadn't caught her and wrestled her, kicking and punching, off the ground.

"Let go of me," she argued.

"No," he said, holding on tight (very tight). Penny looked on openmouthed. A smile lit the face of Mathew Lefarr. "Just listen to what Dad has to say, will you?"

Harlan pulled the dragon claw out of his robe and recounted all that had happened on their boat.

Rosa dismissed his concerns in an instant. "It hardly matters what she wrote, does it? Look at the evidence." She pointed in the vague direction of the casket to illustrate the fact that the Aunt had clearly failed.

But Harlan would not give up. "The claw is extremely powerful. We found it in the Dead Lands, hidden in a stone dais, guarded by a secret key. I believe it's a relic from a dragon called Gawain, during the era of a man called Agawin —"

"Agawin?" To everyone's surprise it was Eliza who'd interrupted Harlan's flow.

"You know this name?" asked Mathew.

Eliza said, "Aunt Gwyneth spoke of him once."

"We know of Agawin, too," said David. "From Mr. Henry, the old curator." He looked at Rosa, who kept silent, for once.

"Anyway," Harlan continued. "The claw is not to be taken lightly. I tried to call upon its influence myself and it brought" — he glanced at Penny and chose his words carefully — "great unhappiness upon us." His eyes sought David's in a clear appeal for a confidential meeting.

Penny pushed her thumb against her upper lip and looked for the longest time at the coffin. "It is magick," she said, wide-eyed, to David. "She used the claw to make Mom small."

Harlan felt for Eliza's hand.

"Long story," she whispered. "I'm OK now."

"Let's just finish her off and be sure," growled Rosa. Although physically calm by now, she was still a whirlwind of vengeance. "What are you looking at?" she suddenly snapped at Mathew, though it was clear to everyone else in the room what his mesmerized gaze of admiration meant. And she, for all her puffed-up stances, had taken more than one extended glance at him.

Mathew turned to Harlan and set his face straight. "I agree with Penny — and Rosa. She looks gone, Harlan. Not even an Aunt Su:perior cheats death."

"I would like to say something." A new voice rose above the rest. Eliza approached the casket and took Aunt Gwyneth's hand. "Everyone, this is my mother."

"*What?*" said Rosa.

Harlan was horrified. "No. Eliza, that's not possible. You . . . you can't be part of *her*."

And Penny, growing more puzzled by the minit, looked at the adults around her and said, "So, I've got a grandma *as well* now?" A dead one, granted. And evil to boot. But a grandma all the same (who might yet return to life, apparently). She squinted at the face, looking for some family resemblance. (There was none.)

Eliza continued, "Whatever else she is, and whatever she's done, she brought me into this world and I owe her some small respect for that. It's my wish that she lies here in peace, as David has arranged."

At this point, Bernard Brotherton stepped in. In a few hushed, well-chosen words he advised Harlan not to let doubts or prejudices come rising to the surface.

Harlan should rejoice. Let him not forget what his heroics at Alavon had achieved. Even if there was a question mark about Eliza's heritage, the fact remained that he had been returned to the woman he loved — and to his children. Let a light shine on his fortune now. It was time for the Merrimans to be as one. Turning to the rest of the room he announced, "I agree with Eliza, but for slightly different reasons. The death of an Aunt —"

"Even a 'mangy' one," said Mathew, smiling at Rosa. (She turned her face away.)

"— needs to be properly reported and catalogued. It's traditional to show them lying in state after death, which satisfies the needs of both sides, does it not?"

"It doesn't satisfy mine," said Rosa.

Bernard finished what he had to say, regardless. "Their role on Co:pern:ica is sure to be re-evaluated because of this incident. I recommend we seek professional advice. A counselor would know how best to deal with it."

"What about Strømberg?" Harlan said. "Do you have :coms on the boat, David?"

"I don't know," he said. Since the change, everything was different. "He's bound to see the ark and come looking, though. The firebirds could find him. What do you think, Rosa?"

She sighed heavily. One dark, temperamental boot tapped a disgruntled rhythm on the floor. "I need to talk to you about Aurielle and Azkiar."

"Who?" said Penny (ears the size of . . .).

"Shut up," Rosa tutted, "I'm talking to David."

"You — !"

"Penny, be quiet," her mother said.

"Not here," Rosa said to him, flicking her head to suggest they meet on a higher deck.

Where are they? he commingled, which only made her frown.

She responded with a little guile of her own. *"Rrrh!"* she went. *Right now, I don't know.*

Is something wrong?

She rolled her eyes in exasperation. *"Rr-rrrh!"* she replied. *We can't find the tapestry.*

At this point, Mathew knocked on Aunt Gwyneth's coffin (to gain attention, not entry) and said, "Erm, is this a private conversation or can anyone with feathers join in?"

"It's private," said Rosa, very moody, very definite. If she had possessed feathers, they would have been somewhat ruffled just then. Once again she looked at Mathew and said, rather cryptically, "*You* need to shave."

"What?" he said, a little taken aback. Why throw such a remark at him when Harlan and Bernard were equally unshaven?

But Rosa would offer no explanation and her brief conversation with Mathew ended there. Laying her fingers over the marks on her arm, she made a sharp whistling noise. Within moments, a white light at the doorway heralded the arrival of her unicorn, Terrafonne.

Everyone present, David excepted, stood back in awe of the perfect white horse.

With a snap of her fingers, Rosa bade the unicorn kneel to let her mount him. "Talking of flying things," she said, "I haven't seen Angel since . . . the Icelands. You might like to tell our guests what to expect." She turned Terrafonne through a half circle. The horse reared up and drummed his hooves on the boards. "I'll do what I can about Strømberg. Come and find me." And with that, she whooshed away on a trail of stars.

Mathew whistled. "Wow, she is some girl."

Just for a moment, a hint of resentment might have entered David's eyes. Harlan, trying to avoid any trace of bad feeling, directed his son to another topic. "Who's Angel, David? What was that about?"

"*I* know! I've *seen* her," Penny said, bouncing. "She's a little girl. Littler than me. She wears a white dress and a daisy chain on her wrist."

"A little girl?" Eliza looked shocked. "Well, where is she? And who's looking after her?"

"Angel kind of takes care of herself," said David.

"She's got wings," said Penny.

"*Wings?*" said the travelers from Alavon.

To which Penny added, rather pointlessly, "She flies." Just another everyday occurrence in the librarium of many surprises, was it not?

The ark rocked a little, left to right, which seemed to set the mood even again. A trumpeting cry in the distance prompted Bernard Brotherton to ask, "Who tends to the animals, David?"

"The ark also looks after itself," he said. "I've only been through a small part of it so far, but it seems to be providing for the animals in every way. If you treat them with respect, there's no reason you shouldn't move safely among them."

"So it's a living entity," Harlan said in wonder. "The quan:tum mech:anisms controlling it must be —"

"Harlan, stop," said Eliza. "We don't want any seminars. We're agreed that Aunt Gwyneth isn't . . . going anywhere. So I suggest we all get some rest. That eye needs redressing, poor Bernard is exhausted, and, frankly, you all need a bath. Can we get hot water, David?"

"And food?" said Bernard, who looked ready to eat an ark.

David said, "The boat responds like the librarium, Mom. Let it guide you to where you need to be."

"Thank you," she said, drawing Penny to her side.

"So, are we leaving Grandma here?" said the girl.

Eliza tidied a sprig of the Aunt's brittle hair. "Until Counselor Strømberg arrives, yes."

"So be it," said Harlan. He looked up at David and noticed that his son's gaze was deeply focused on the dragon's claw. Tapping it lightly against his palm, he walked over and pressed it into David's hand. "Meet me here at dusk. We must speak privately."

"Are you going to write something?" Penny asked her brother, pushing her tongue between her lips (a trademark trait of concentration in the family).

"I need to understand this first," David said. But already it was singing to him of long-forgotten histories and dangerous futures — and a deeply tragic present. He could feel Harlan's auma imprinted on the claw, echoing with unresolved grief. But now was not the moment to delve into that. Placing the claw into his jacket he said, "Mom's right. Relax and enjoy the voyage — wherever it is we're going."

With that, he began to make his way from the room. Somewhere near the doorway, his mother bade him stop. "Is everything all right — with Rosa?" she asked quietly. "You looked a bit concerned back there."

"Everything's fine," he told her, and felt the claw buzz against his heart. Was it reacting to what it knew was a lie? "She's . . . misplaced something. I need to help her find it." Thankfully, Eliza didn't pursue this, and David was grateful for that. For it would have been hard at that point, trying to explain to his mother what the *Tapestry of Isenfier* was, and why Penny Merriman was pictured on it.

And why Mathew Lefarr was, too.

2.

Despite the scale of the transformation the librarium had gone through, there were a large number of rooms that did not house animals but still contained books. It was in one of these that David eventually tracked Rosa down.

She was sitting alone in the middle of the floor, forlornly clutching a book to her chest. "Look at them," she said, as David stumbled in. "What are we going to do about this?"

He crouched down among them, shaking his head. He picked up a book, but having nowhere to put it simply tossed it aside again. "Is it the same in other rooms?"

"The ones with books, yes. If Mr. Henry saw this, he'd be so unhappy. If someone had put this room into a sack, shaken it up, and spilled out the contents, it couldn't have ended up in a worse mess. It'll take forever to sort out. I love the animals, but the books are my life. And now . . . well, we don't even have a librarium anymore."

"I s'pose not," David said, just as his gaze was taken by a movement outside. Through the window he could see a bright orange firebird circling in the sky. Quite a number had appeared since their aerie had changed. They were mostly seen hunched up together, perched on the deck rails, or occasionally exercising their wings in flight. Like the books, their future seemed undecided. "How have the birds reacted?"

"How do you think? Aleron is miserable. I've sent him looking for Strømberg, just to take his mind off it."

"Tell me about the tapestry. When did you know it was missing?"

Rosa tilted her head. Her dark hair fell forward in an unwashed bundle. "After we zapped Aunt Gwyneth, I rode Terrafonne back to where I thought One Hundred and Eight would be. I found Aurielle flapping about in a panic. The whole floor's been transformed into a woodland glade. It's beautiful, but the candlesticks, chandeliers, and feathers are all gone. And there's no sign of the tapestry, anywhere. Aurielle and Azkiar are searching for it."

"What about Agawin's book?"

"Gone."

David clapped his hands around his nose and sighed. "I don't understand this. How can we have come this far and have both these things go missing? This can't be what Agawin intended."

"Maybe they transformed?"

Perhaps they had. This was an outcome David hadn't considered. It would have needed some powerful auma to create the glade and its organic plant life. What if that was now hiding the mystery of Isenfier? Or Terrafonne, for instance, was *The Book of Agawin*?

For a moment, the only sounds that filled the room were the creaks of the ark as it sliced through the water far below. Then Rosa moved the dialogue sideways, saying, "It's Mathew on the tapestry, isn't it?"

David took his mind off the transformation theory and stared at the books around his feet. "I don't know. He looks more handsome than the image I remember."

"Da-viiid . . . ," she said. "Come on-nn. Even with

the fuzz on his chin, he's *clearly* the man shown standing next to Penny. Are you going to tell him?"

He shook his head. "It's a bit pointless without the evidence in front of me. I might tell Dad about the tapestry later."

Rosa rocked back and forth, rubbing her arms. "I think it's spooky that everyone who was in that picture is turning up on the ark. Who is Angel, David? Where did she come from? It doesn't bother me that she flies like a bird or talks to Aunts as if she's known them for hundreds of spins, but it does make me weak to see her wearing the daisy chain I made for you. She's got your eyes."

"She's got your hair and mouth."

"Er, yeah. And the *wings*?"

"Azkiar."

"What?!"

"His fire. My tears. Your daisies — your love. She's part human, part fain, part firebird — oh, and part clay. That was Mom's doing. The little girl we call Angel is Agawin's vision of the perfect species. She's more advanced than any of us."

Rosa screwed up her face. "And how do you know this?"

514

"I absorbed it — from the Higher. A lot happened between the start of the flood and us facing Aunt Gwyneth. While you were discovering Terrafonne, I was being drawn toward a perception matrix called the Is."

"You *met* the Higher? *Here?* On the ark?" She pointed vaguely upward.

David glanced into the middle distance. "The Higher can exist anywhere," he said, "here, there, the spaces in between. It's just easier for us to think in terms of 'up.' In Central, they massed in a dome on the roof of the librarium because the air was clear of other traces of auma."

"What do they look like?"

"They don't look like anything. The Higher are a strain of humans that evolved beyond the need for a physical body. They're a collective of pure fain that oversees Co:pern:ica and has influence in other areas of the universe as well. Sometimes they simply call themselves The Fain. They taught me a lot of interesting things, mainly to prepare me for the confrontation with Aunt Gwyneth."

"Why did they put us in the cold like that?"

"They imprinted the Icelands of the North

around us so that I could appear in a more favorable environment."

"You — or that bear thing?"

"Me and the bear 'thing' are one and the same. If it's any consolation, I don't fully understand it either. When I asked the Higher to explain it to me all they said was, 'The bears are a story waiting to be written.' Maybe Dad will shed some light on it. He's itching to tell me something. He was holding back downstairs, because of Penny. I'll find out later. Right now, I'm going to take a look around. Let me know if Aurielle comes back or Strømberg turns up."

She looked him up and down and nodded. "David?"

"Yeah?"

"Can that dragon claw do anything about this?" She swept a hand across the jumble of books.

"I'll think about it," he said. And right there and then, he did. As his positive intent poured into the claw, an idea immediately came to him. He glanced through the window at the boats dotted on the water and said, "Don't touch the books. Leave them where they are. They don't need to be in order anymore."

"Why, what are we going to do with them?"

"I'll tell you later."

"David, you're being annoying. Tell me now."

He backed away. "Uh-uh. Not until I've thought it through. Get the firebirds together. As many as you can."

"Firebirds? Why?"

"It's what Mr. Henry would have wanted," he said. And he walked out of the room, whistling a tune — much as the old curator would have done.

3.

Later that day, on his way to the rendezvous he'd planned with his father, David had a surprise encounter with Angel. He had spent most of the afternoon checking the animals, eventually going right to the top of the ark where the air was cool and the horizons were large and the Higher were easy to commingle with. On the way back down, he found himself being taken through the glade that had once been Floor One Hundred and Eight of the librarium. And there, beneath the canopy of a beautiful old tree, he saw her.

She was sitting on one of the exposed and mossy roots, quietly reading a book.

"Hello, Angel," he said.

She looked up and smiled. A miniature Rosa in a plain white dress. "Have you come to read to me, Daddy?"

"If you'd like me to," he said. "What book is it?"

"Yours, silly."

"Mine?" he said.

She nodded freely. "One day, you'll remember." She held it out for him to take, the daisy chain prominent on her wrist.

"*Snigger and the Nutbeast?*"

"You're the nutbeast." She laughed.

"And who is Snigger?"

Angel thought for a moment, then snapped her fingers. A confused gray squirrel appeared at her feet. It saw David, did a double take, sat up on its fluffy tail — and smiled.

David opened the book and read the first line. "*It was a beautiful autumn morning in the library gardens. . . .*"

From the trees, several red leaves fell.

"Yes," said Angel, paddling her feet.

Chuk! went Snigger.

'*Library.*' Not '*librarium,*' David thought.

The same, but different, Angel commingled. "Read some more, Daddy."

David blinked and his thumb slipped off the first page. He pried the book open at a dedication. *For*

Lucy Pennykettle (aged eleven today). "Lucy?" he muttered. He felt the dragon claw buzzing against his heart as the name began to resonate with him.

Angel pointed down the clearing. Among the falling leaves, a floating image of part of the *Tapestry of Isenfier* appeared. It was Penny, kneeling down.

The same, but different, David thought.

Angel smiled. "Snigger's got something for you," she said.

The squirrel was digging frantically in the dirt, uncovering what appeared to be a small piece of bone. Angel jumped off the tree root, picked up the bone, and handed it to David in exchange for the book. He cleaned the bone against the edge of his jacket and looked at the now-familiar markings. "Sometimes," he said.

Angel put out her wings. "Sometimes it will be Lucy," she said.

And sometimes it will be Penny, David thought. "When is it Gadzooks?" he asked.

Snigger leaped off the ground and dissolved with a spray of stars into the book.

"When the bears come," she said, with a glint in her eye. "I have to go now, Daddy."

"Angel, thank you for this." He held up the bone. "What does it do?"

"That will help you find Zookie," she said. "But only when you're ready to see him."

And in a flash of light she was gone.

A few minits later, David swept into Aunt Gwyneth's room. It was not quite dusk, but his father was already there. "Any change?" he asked, peering at the body.

"None, as far as I can tell," Harlan said.

David sent a quick *rrrh* to the guarding firebirds. One of them reported no activity, the other just jolted itself out of sleep.

"Where are the others?" David asked his father.

"Mathew has set off on a tour with Penny, to map the ark's layout and log as many species as they can. She's found a delightful book, a guide to animals great and small. I've no idea where it came from, but she's thrilled with it and it's given her a much greater interest in the boat. Bernard is hobbling about on the middle decks somewhere observing the movements of some small buzzing creatures Eliza calls 'bees.' He developed a fascination for them after one landed on his collar while we were eating. A small swarm went past while he was cleaning his dish and that was it, he was away. Eliza is relaxing at the prow of the boat, reading. I haven't seen Rosa, but then I've been asleep for a while."

"How's your eye?"

"Improved, thank you."

"Good. I'm glad to hear it. Now, what is it you want to tell me?"

Harlan slipped his hands into his pockets. During the day, all the men of Alavon had changed out of their robes into more conventional clothing. For Harlan, this meant a pair of casual pants and a white collarless shirt. The look, though relaxed and informal, appeared to have done little to stabilize his nerves. "I'm still concerned about our corpse. On the boat, Mathew heard her say that her body was broken but not her will. She knew exactly what she was doing when she wrote that message, David. She aims to survive. I used the claw myself in the Dead Lands. Its effect was immediate. So why isn't something happening with her?"

David drew up a chair, and sat astride it with his arms resting on the back. "The wisdom from the Higher suggests that Aunt Gwyneth's auma has been successfully reassimilated into the dark energy of the universe, where it should have no ill effect — though they still recommend we observe her, for reasons I'll come to in a moment.

"Everything you've said about the claw is correct. It is a relic from Agawin's time, torn from the foot of one of the most potent dragons known to the Higher, the creature you called Gawain. Strictly speaking, anyone can wield it, but the greater the individual's resonance with dragons, the more dramatic the outcome will be. It's capable of complex acts of creation."

"Like the ark?"

"Exactly."

"Can it be used to manipulate negative intent? The last time I saw the claw before Aunt Gwyneth got it, it had been stolen by a firebird possessed of an alien force called the Ix. Eliza told me how you dealt with that danger by the way. That must have been quite impressive."

David smiled wistfully. "Something to discuss with Strømberg," he said, "the transformation into the bear. To go back to your initial question, because dragons were essentially spiritual creatures — Gawain, in particular, was highly revered — the claw would react against any form of direct malice. This is how Aunt Gwyneth was defeated. She was attempting to destroy a sensory matrix called the Is, which the Higher control. The claw rejected her harmful intent. That's how she ended up in the water. But the message she wrote in the boat is different. Any malevolence there was hidden in ambiguity. The claw would respond to a positive plea for life."

"But it hasn't," Harlan said, looking her way. The Aunt's eyes were wrinkled but firmly shut. "Perhaps her fain was so weak as her life began to slip that she wasn't able to realize her intent?"

"Perhaps," said David. "But there's another, more worrying, possibility.

"The Higher were eager to impress on me just how the claw works. I'm pretty sure Agawin knew about this when he sealed the claw away. Agawin learned the truth about dragons. He knew their origins, their whereabouts, and their gifts of prediction. But the part that would fascinate the phys:icist in you is their link to time, consciousness, and matter. The claw draws upon the energy of universal flux and the principle of describing order from chaos. If that was applied over a time nexus, such as the one you tried to link to in your lab . . ."

"Its effects might be delayed," Harlan muttered. He

turned away, feeling the dressing at his eye. This wasn't what he'd wanted to hear. "So she could keep us guessing for another twenty spins and still give us a nasty surprise one day."

"That's about the size of it, yes."

"So what do you plan to do?"

"Hand her to Strømberg and leave it to him. We have the claw now. We can be ready for her if she turns up again."

Harlan walked to the window and opened the shutters. Darkness had fallen and the water was calm. The many hundreds of boats that now accompanied the ark could only be identified by the colored lights strung from their tipping masts. The heavy rain had given way to a sturdy breeze, which swept in to refresh the atmosphere in the room. One of the firebirds gave a grateful *rrrh* and looked pleased to have some air running through its feathers. Harlan drummed his fingertips against the shutters. "There's something else you have to hear. Does the term 'Isenfier' mean anything to you?"

Not wishing to mention the tapestry yet, David just said, "In a reference book Mr. Henry used to have, Isenfier is mentioned as the site of a battle. How did you learn of it?"

"In the Dead Lands I had a vision of Gawain. I was warned about a Shadow, which I took to be the Ix. When the black firebird came, I commingled with the Cluster that had got into its mind. The Ix were following a signal from Isenfier, hoping to track you down and kill you. When I asked the Ix why you were being targeted, they identified you as some kind of champion or savior. With you gone, it was clear they thought they could win the battle — or that the battle could continue. I wasn't sure."

"What was sending the signal?" David asked. His tone was noticeably quieter now.

His father turned to look at him. "A dragon. A peculiar little thing. It held a pen — or possibly another claw. The Ix had a name for it. Creat:or, I think." He paused a moment. "You know of this, don't you?"

David pushed himself upright and came to the window. "I've seen an image of the dragon you're talking about." And he told his father then about Agawin's tapestry, and how it described the battle of Isenfier, apparently suspended in time. For the moment, to preserve the calm, he said nothing about Penny's presence on it — or Mathew's, for that matter.

"Where is the tapestry? Can I see it?" Harlan asked. Even with just the one eye frowning, he looked every bit the devoted scientist.

David shook his head. "It disappeared during the change. Two of our firebirds are searching for it. I don't want to upset Mom with this, so it would be best if you kept it to yourself for now."

"Can you draw it? Or imagineer something from memory?"

"I can try."

"Good," said Harlan. "Do what you can. If this really is Agawin's creation, we must show Mathew and Bernard at least."

David half nodded. "I'd like Counselor Strømberg to see it as well. Can we wait till he arrives?"

"Yes."

Just then, the faint clang of a bell reached their ears. Both men instinctively looked up. And though there was no real change to the scene, another bell was struck slightly nearer the first, then another and another. Until the ocean was ringing with sound. And closer to the ark, voices were shouting. And they were all saying one thing only.

Land.

4.

Leaving orders with the firebirds to come to him at once if there was any change in Aunt Gwyneth's condition, David and his father headed for the nearest deck. Along the way, David imagineered an eyeglass. As soon as he was out in the cool night air he trained it forward. Far beyond the leading line of boats (scores of them had now got in front of the ark), he thought he could see a faint wave of light. In the darkness, at this distance, it was impossible to confirm that it was land based, but there was little reason to doubt the message chain. Within the hour they would know for certain. By morning, they would see the land clearly.

Before he closed the eyeglass up, David swiveled it toward another light at the very prow of the vessel. Rosa was there, sitting astride a glowing Terrafonne.

Her hair was being pulled back by the wind, accentuating the delicate curve of her jaw and her long slender neck. She looked stunning.

"Anything?" asked Harlan, cupping his eye (to no effect).

David took the glass away. "Too far to tell." He sat down on the deck with his back against a cabin wall. "Dad, can I ask *you* something now?"

"Anything."

"How did you escape from the Dead Lands?"

Harlan sat down a little more slowly and a little less comfortably. There was a gnawing pain across the center of his back and a chafing scanner burn above his left knee that even Eliza had not seen yet. "Are you sure you want to know?"

"I think you need to share it. Your sorrow was all over the claw."

Harlan nodded. "It wasn't pretty," he said as he stretched out his legs. "But your sister's heard it and so should you."

"You told *Penny*?"

"Only the bones," Harlan chuckled. "If you'd been around at dinner, you would have heard Mathew

529

pepping her up. He managed to describe to her, in exciting detail, how we lit a huge fire to lure the Re:movers and steal their transport."

"Is that true?"

"In essence, yes. We set the blaze in a ruined tower on top of a hill called the Isle of Alavon. It must have been seen across half of Co:pern:ica. We also arranged torches in the shape of a letter A on the wetland where the Re:movers make their drops, to get them precisely where we wanted them. The marshes in that region are perilous. In daylight, because of the abundance of grasses and the fact that the water is so shallow and still, the land appears flat and walkable. But the entire morass is a giant pit of unfaithful ground and evil trenches. One false step and you're sucked into slime, where all you can look forward to is slow suffocation. It's quite horrifying.

"We trained on the marsh for three or four days, flagging up pathways and running them constantly, especially at night or when rain was in the air, until we were confident we knew the topography and could change direction at will — and survive. We dug make-shift hideouts in the driest ground so we could launch simultaneous attacks from several directions. In those final few days we ate communally, so we could talk through the problems and dangers — and fears. When the chosen night came, we shook hands and wished each other brave fortune. Then we lit the beacon and waited. Twenty-one men. Armed with nothing but sticks, stones, and grim determination. And it worked — if anything, a little too well.

"We had made preparations for two Re:movers in one vehicle. In the end, three came in two. Craft very similar to penal taxicars, but sleeker models, refitted for combat. Fearing we were out of our depth, I wanted to abandon the attack. I formed an idea to explain to the machines that we had lit the fire in praise of Agawin. There would have been reprimands, some splitting up of the tribe, perhaps, but they probably wouldn't have punished us too harshly. But before I could get the message out, a stone flew through the air and struck the first car, leaving one of its windows shattered. After that, we had no choice but to fight.

"The first maneuver went much as we'd planned it. Mathew leaped up, hurled another stone at the second taxicar, shouted some abuse, and took off across the marsh. Two Re:movers immediately went after him. We knew they would have some basic capability for adapting to the poor conditions, but we were gambling on the fact that the marsh is unpredictable. Sure enough, one of them plowed straight in and went down to knee level while it was opening fire. In our hideouts, we tightened our fists in triumph. But our elation was short-lived. From that moment on our plan was exposed. While the sinking machine struggled, the other opened its wrist :com and asked the taxicar for assistance. We knew their databases were bound to be inadequate because there are no comparable conditions in Central. But those things learn fast. There was a beep and the standing machine swept another device across the marsh. I realized it was some kind of densito:meter, highlighting areas of solid ground. It took it less than ten secs to work out a route to Mathew.

"It went straight for him, covering the terrain at remarkable speed. Meanwhile, the sinking one had applied a kind of anti:G:rav to its body and was beginning to overcome the suck of the marsh. Bernard said into my ear, 'We need the weights.' We had roped together lines of stones, each just heavy enough for a man to carry. The idea was to loop them around the Re:movers at close range, hopefully to pull them down.

I gave the order and eight of us ran forward. We came at it from behind in two groups, not expecting a great deal of resistance. But we were in for a serious shock. None of us knew that the machines can dislocate their joints. The Re:mover unhinged its knees, swiveled a few degrees, and opened fire. Our leading attacker, a huge hulk of a man with wild curly hair, was cut down in a moment. He fell heavily to the marsh, creating a dense spray of mud and water. Bernard stumbled into him and only survived the next blast because he tripped and fell, injuring his ankle. The flash that was intended for Bernard struck the man behind him, searing his robe and the length of his arm. He cried out in agony and staggered sideways, losing his footing. He fell, facedown into the marsh. There was no hope for him. Two dead and one crippled. And we were still some fifteen paces from our target.

"But we had the darkness and a medic called Terance Humbey, who knew the best ground and had the speed to cross it. As the rest of us threw ourselves flat, Terance got around the side of the thing, swung his rope in both hands, and landed a powerful blow to the side of the Re:mover's head. I saw the head tilt as it wrenched from the shoulder. A bunch of wires sprang out. The

Re:mover jerked and began to fire at random, lighting up the night with its scanner flares. Terance swung again, catching it with another powerful blow. This time there was a crackle. The smell of burning circuitry. By then I was on my feet and hoping to get my rope around the thing. As I closed in, the scanner flare that dazzled my eye went off and I lost my aim. The rope flew over the Re:mover's shoulder, but one of the smaller stones lodged in the damage Terance had caused. The rope was left dangling down the Re:mover's back. It wasn't weight enough, but it *was* working. The machine had gone in to thigh level.

"It took another two ropes before it went under. We lost one more man and another was scalded from his hip to his heart before we dealt the blow that took out the scanner. Terance helped the machine on its way with another heavy swing, and the three of us still able to fight — myself, Terance, and a man called Hugo Abbot — turned our attention to Mathew and the other groups hiding on the marsh."

Harlan paused here and massaged the skin of his temples. "Forgive me. This next part is very difficult. I may stumble over the words."

534

"Take as much time as you need," said David. "You're doing just fine."

Harlan nodded and removed his bandage, holding it as if it were a cherished souvenir. Around the socket of his eye, dark scanner burns were visible. In his own words, not pretty. "By now, the second taxicar had taken off to go to the assistance of the Re:mover on the marsh. I was watching its flight when I heard Bernard yelling out an urgent warning. I turned and saw an arm rising out of the mud. The Re:mover had a circular device in its hand. I knew straightaway it was a bomb and I was doomed. But before I could even close my eyes, Hugo had pushed me aside and thrown himself over the hand. This brave, peace-loving, elderly man moved me as if I were his only child and sent himself to a certain death. The weight of his body carried the hand down just far enough to deaden the explosion in the mire. But I can feel it now just as much as I felt it then. A man's life, shuddering away inside me. A scar far worse than anything visible on my skin."

"And the other men?" David prompted gently.

Somewhere behind them an animal gave out a plaintive cry. A slender creature called a "ferret" sniffed at

535

David's feet, slipped under his knees, and continued on its way.

Harlan looked up at the stars. "The Re:mover chasing Mat was avoiding the wet areas with ease. But what its scan had failed to tell it was that some solid areas were not reliable. So when it tried to cross a bridge that we had built of light wood and marsh mud, it went in and its momentum took it under easily. That one didn't respond. But by now we had a greater threat to deal with — the taxicar. It was equipped with a laser head and infrared detectors. The detectors picked up any signs of body heat and the lasers did the rest. I hope I never live to see another man fatally shot by a weapon like that. The body blanches before it disintegrates. I can't begin to tell you what it's like to see the victim's horror frozen in mono:chrome on their face before they die."

"How did you defeat it?"

"I stole the other car. I'd driven them manually in the days when you still could. It was equipped with a laser as well. I simply blasted the first car out of the sky. Nothing so destructive has ever filled me with such satisfaction.

"So we had our victory and we had our ride home. It took some time to work out the navigational aids because the routers for the cars are implanted into the Re:movers' heads. But eventually we were able to set a course for Bushley. By then the flood had started and we could see the ark on all our displays. I knew it had to be connected with you. On the approach we began to lose G:rav. So I ditched the taxicar onto the water and we pooled our auma to make two boats from it. Myself, Bernard, and Mathew took one. Terance skippered the other. And that was that. The next thing we knew we were trying to save the life of that evil witch, Gwyneth. Of all the boats she could have landed beside, it had to be ours."

David raised his head and looked into the night. "I think you'll find that wasn't a coincidence."

His father threw him a quizzical glance.

"It was a test to see if you'd show her mercy."

"Test? Who could set a test like that?"

"She could."

Angel suddenly appeared before them. Wings spread, she glided into view and landed softly on the deck beside David.

Harlan stared at the girl in awe. It was the first time he'd seen the mysterious flying child who Penny had not stopped talking about. She walked up and studied the burns to his eye. He held his breath as she reached out a hand and placed it over his thumping heart. Her blue eyes sparkled. "Hugo is very happy," she said.

And for the first time in his life, Harlan Merriman unleashed his emotions and cried. And as the tears rolled out of his damaged eye, so it healed and he could see clearly once more.

"I thought you had to go?" David said to Angel.

"I did," she said brightly. "But I came back again, because we're almost here."

"Here?" said Harlan, looking for a landmark. "Where are we heading?"

Angel pointed to a light in the distance. David stood up and went to the rail. Farther along the deck, several animals had come out of their compartments to stare across the water just as David was doing now.

"Do you recognize anywhere?" Harlan asked him.

David chewed his lip. "If ever we're separated, I want you to pass on a message for me, Dad. When people talk about this flood, they will say that it's come to destroy us. It hasn't. It's here to make us think about a better way of life. One in which we can still imagineer, but where our ability to do so is balanced by our willingness to care for the creatures on this ark. This is the new directive from the Higher. Wherever these animals choose to land, wherever they migrate to, wherever they settle, the humans will respect them and their habitats, or lose their power to create form from thought. And it all begins here — in what used to be called the Dead Lands."

Harlan got to his feet and squinted at the light. "Is that —? No, it can't be. It surely must have gone out by now."

David put an arm around Angel's shoulder. "There may be dark days ahead of us. More conflict with the Ix. Maybe a twist or two with the Aunts. But the only thing that matters for now is that beacon. This is the legacy your tribe left behind. Welcome back to Alavon, Dad, where the fire of Agawin will never die out. . . ."

5.

By morning, the ark had drifted alongside the southern edge of Alavon and found waters deep enough in which to anchor. In keeping with its program of self-sufficiency, a sturdy wooden drawbridge swung out from the central section of the hull and dropped down to make firm contact with the land. The great *whump!* brought scores of animals to the windows and all the humans, bar Rosa, to the decks. David, giving orders to monitor the animals but not impede them in any way, hurried down to check it out. He arrived at the opening to find Rosa on the drawbridge sitting astride Terrafonne. A little posse of animals had already stacked up in the hold behind her. "What's this place?" she asked.

"The Isle of Alavon."

"Isn't that where . . . ?"

"Dad was taken to, yes. See the beacon?"

"It's kind of hard not to." Even in daylight the flames were inspiring.

"Strange to think Agawin lived there once."

Rosa gulped and steadied Terrafonne's head. The unicorn, his hooves clip-clopping on the bridge, seemed anxious to explore the land. She looked back over her shoulder at the hold. "The animals are restless. Are they allowed off to exercise?"

"Those that need to leave at this point, will."

"Leave?"

"It's part of their program of survival and the people's, too — to return to the land, where they can thrive."

"That's the Dead Lands they're going to. There's nothing out there."

David squinted at Alavon's kind green slopes. "They'll have water. And there are lots of willing hands on the boats. The followers are looking to the ark for guidance. It just needs someone to show them the way." He reached out and stroked the unicorn's neck.

"Me?" Rosa said, pointing to herself.

"I want to mark this occasion with an image the people in the boats won't forget. We both know Terrafonne is quite a performer."

Rosa guided the white horse farther onto the bridge and looked around at the bobbing boats. Nearly all had a lens trained on the ark. "You could always waddle ashore in your ice bear form and show them some flakes of . . . what was it you called that white stuff?"

"Snow."

"That would be pretty."

"It would, but it wouldn't be right. It's not time for Co:pern:ica to learn about ice — or the bears just yet. *And*," he stressed, before she could follow up the point, "this will launch my idea about the books."

"Go on," she said, "I'm all ears."

"How many firebirds were you able to call?"

"A few." She pointed to the upper decks. Several hundred were perched on the rails.

"Perfect."

"For what?"

He looked into her spirited eyes and smiled. Despite the air of indifference, he knew she was curious. He raked his fingers through Terrafonne's mane and said, "Do you remember how Mr. Henry used to tell us that books were our truest, most dedicated friends? How one well-written passage of words could not only melt the heart of a reader but stay with them forever?"

"Of course I do," she said. Her gaze began to soften as her eyes grew moist.

"I think if the circumstances were right, Mr. Henry would have liked everyone on Co:pern:ica to experience that feeling. We could start it, Rosa. Here. On the waters of Alavon. Today."

"Start what?" she said. "I don't understand."

"Start sharing the books."

"Sharing them? How?"

"We ask the firebirds to pick them up and fly them to the boats —"

"David, don't be dumb. We'd lose them all."

"Not as gifts, as *loans*," he said, "to be read and brought back and freely exchanged for others. In that way, the books belong to the librarium *and* to the people. And the really sweet part is this: As the people return them, you'll be able to put them in order and keep them in order — until they're ready to go out again."

"Me?" she said. "What are *you* going to do?"

David smiled and thought about the claw in his pocket. "I'm going to write new books," he said.

Over the next few days, a steady stream of animals disembarked just as David had predicted and began to meander across the land. There was no selection process. Those that chose to go simply stepped onto the bridge or flew across the water or, if they were already in the water, swam away from the vessel. None, Harlan noticed, climbed the hill where the tower stood and the beacon still burned. But it gave him an enormous sense of pleasure to watch two animals that Penny described as "cows" grazing on one of the bright green fields.

Many boats, by now, had moored themselves at imagineered jetties or been driven aground by the lapping tide. And thanks to Rosa, who had ridden Terrafonne ashore in a spectacular leap full of rainbows and stars, people were testing the land as well, following her to Alavon in small parties. By the afternoon of the third day, the first simple dwelling place had sprouted from the minds of those able to imagine a life among the minimal crops they'd found. For Mathew Lefarr, this was difficult to watch. The more he saw of the infant colony, the more he knew he ought to be a part of it. And so, at a carefully selected moment, he approached his fellow travelers and made an announcement: "Friends, I will be leaving you here."

"Oh, Mathew!" said Eliza.

"What?" said Penny, who looked as if a limb had been torn from her body.

Even Rosa cast her eyes down.

He raised a hand before anyone else could speak. "I'm going to go ashore. Much of my time in the Dead Lands was invested in making the Isle of Alavon a comfortable place to live. This is a new and exciting development. It casts no reflection on any of you when I say I want to be part of it. There is probably about a minit before the ark moves on and one of you tries to change my mind. So I will wish you all safe travels and slip away before the drawbridge lifts. Come and find me when your journey is done. Wherever I make my home, any of you will be welcome in it."

Penny rushed forward and clamped her arms around him.

"Be a good friend to the animals," he whispered. "One day, I'll breed you a goat." (Out of all the many animals they'd logged, the goats were Penny's favorite.) He planted a kiss on the top of her head before moving her into Eliza's care. He shook hands firmly with Harlan and Bernard, both of whom were swift to pledge their allegiance to any just cause he might fight for again. He turned next to Rosa. Poor Rosa, she had no idea what to do. She liked Mathew, though she had made a deep secret of it. She admired his honesty and hard work and plain-speaking ways. True, she had hardly said a kind word to him, but that was because his good looks unnerved her. She stepped forward and offered her hand (from a distance). He picked it up and kissed it. She almost melted.

And lastly there was David. No doubt everyone present expected a brief, if well-meant, thank-you from the son of Harlan Merriman before he all but imagineered Mathew to a distant place. Instead, David asked Lefarr to stay. This might have been taken as a gesture of friendship were it not for the slight cut of authority in his voice. When challenged, David would only say that the ark had gathered Mathew in and a greater purpose awaited him. Harlan, well aware of Mathew's disappointment and David's abruptness (and the creak of the closing drawbridge), drew his son aside and quietly asked him to reconsider. The argument was weak, he said. Mathew had an independent, pioneering spirit.

It was poignant that he should desire to have a foothold in the reborn farmlands of Alavon. There was no better place for him to form a new tribe. Also, on a more personal level, surely David had noticed the way Mathew admired Rosa? Granted, he had made no move on the girl for he clearly saw her fondness for David. But it was a possible source of tension all the same. Mathew was young, intelligent, and not exactly "unhandsome." Even Penny, of all people, had remarked as much.

David accepted this advice, which he knew was well intended, but then revealed to his father the real reason he had asked Lefarr to stay. He described the missing detail from the *Tapestry of Isenfier*. Mathew, he said, was the man seen standing in the corner — with Penny.

Harlan turned away, angry that this had been kept from him. "Penny?" he hissed. "She's part of the battle?"

"Yes," David said.

Harlan closed ranks again. "Have you found the tapestry?"

"No, not yet."

"Have you completed the drawing?"

"No, not quite."

"When it's done, promise me you'll show it to me, David."

"Yes," David said. "Yes, I promise."

And Harlan gritted his teeth and walked away.

And so Mathew, along with the Merriman family, and Bernard Brotherton, and the beautiful Rosa, stayed with the ark as it journeyed around Co:pern:ica, shedding its animals. Mathew, to his credit (and Rosa's further admiration), did not question David's decision but simply accepted that his future, for now, was tied up with this journey. He helped out where he could — even cooked sometimes — and played games with Penny (who clearly adored him), and chatted with Eliza while she continued to explore her creative gifts, and aided Bernard in his quest to harvest the sticky-sweet foodstuff his bees were producing, and spoke of universal mysteries as he walked the decks with Harlan, and even monitored the stationary Aunt Gwyneth now and then.

And sometimes, when a chance presented itself, he would find himself in a room of books, working on the scheme that David had suggested. All this time, under

Rosa's instruction, the firebirds had been faithfully dis-
tributing the books and had now reached the stage of
bringing some back when they returned from a drop.
Sometimes notes would accompany them.

Thank you, this story has enriched my life.

Do you have anything on weather?

Is it possible to come aboard and browse?

One afternoon, Rosa was cataloguing a number of
returns when Mathew suddenly burst out laughing.

"What?" she said. He was across the room, reading
a note.

"You've received a proposal. Someone wants to
marry you."

"What? Don't be silly."

"Honestly, it's real." He came a little closer and
showed it to her. In a striking hand it said, *To the
pretty book girl. Will you marry me?* "You've been
spotted in someone's eyeglass," he said.

She cocked her head and thrust the note into his
chest. "Very funny."

"What?" he laughed. "You don't think *I*
wrote it?"

She looped her hair behind her ears and went back
to her work.

For a moment there was silence. Then the floor echoed several times to his footsteps and he went to stand by a window, looking out. "If I *had* written it, what would be your answer?"

She put down her book. "Mathew . . ."

"I'm serious. When I go back to Alavon, you could come with me."

"And break Penny's heart?" she said, trying to keep the conversation light.

"I'd look after you," he said. "I could build us a home."

She swallowed hard and nodded. She knew this. She did. Sometimes when she looked out on the land, she thought of it. A life elsewhere. A life with Mathew. "It wouldn't be the same," she said.

"As the ark? Why not? We could have books there. We could build a new librarium."

She raised her head and looked at him. Her eyes were glazed with tears. "I know," she said, "but we couldn't have David."

A sea of thoughts hovered between them. And then he simply accepted her statement with the quiet grace she expected of him. And had they not been separated by an awkward arrangement of chairs and books and the corner of a table, she might even have run to him with a hug of consolation. As it happened, he was the one to suddenly become animated. He backed away from the window and set off for the door.

"What's the matter?" Rosa said.

"There's a stranger coming up the bridge."

He was gone before she could reach the window. And that space was quickly filled by a firebird anyway. "Runcey!" she gasped. (In times of excitement, this was always his name.)

The emerald green bird sat up brightly.

Rrrh! he said to her. *Strømberg is here.*

6.

Thorren Strømberg joined the ark when the last of the animals (two goofy-looking creatures with huge tails and enormous silly feet), had just walked (or rather bounced) onto the parched yellow soil at a landmass called Ozralia. Mathew challenged him on the bridge. Throughout their journey, no one had attempted to board the ark or even formally communicate with it. Yet here came this tall, wild-haired man striding up the walkway as if he owned the whole thing.

"Mathew, it's all right, let him on." David patted the young man's shoulder as he stepped past to greet their visitor.

Strømberg opened his arms and welcomed David with a hug befitting a bear. He looked up at the enormous vessel and said, "Now I see what your

552

dreams were truly made of." And together they strolled aboard.

Whether it was due to his counseling skills or his general charismatic demeanor, Strømberg quickly became a unifying presence. David took him first to see Aunt Gwyneth. The dead Aunt, still attended by the guarding firebirds, was, as expected, unchanged. David told the full story of their conflict, including her attempt to attack the Is and her ambiguous parting message. Strømberg took it in but made no comment. He approved of what had been done, he said, and would make arrangements for the disposal of the body. The casket could now be closed.

After a short tour of the boat, chairs were arranged on a shaded lower deck and everyone gathered to hear what news the counselor had. Harlan was eager to know what the people of Co:pern:ica were making of the ark.

"They see it as a miracle," Strømberg said.

"What's a 'miracle'?" asked Penny.

"An old word for a spectacular phenomenon," said Bernard. A bee was crawling on his nearly bald head. That was the kind of phenomenon Penny liked.

Mathew put a glass of water on the deck. He had made his peace very quickly with Strømberg and was stoically showing no emotion toward Rosa. "Is there panic in the community? Disorder? Chaos?"

"Far from it," the counselor replied. He sat back in his chair and crossed his long legs. "The ark is being seen as a gift from the Higher, a gesture of extreme benevolence. There's a genuine sense of excitement in the air. People may have lost their homes and their routines — and some of their ability to imagineer — but their minds are opening up to fresh possibilities."

Eliza leaned forward and said, "Thorren, did anyone die in the flood?"

"I've heard of no reported cases," he said. "That, of course, just adds to the wonder."

"And the Aunts?" asked Harlan, pacing around with his hands in his pockets.

"Re:structuring — for the better, I might add. Just before the librarium transformed, I circulated the rumor of wrongdoing there and named Gwyneth and her followers as the perpetrators. The story was still growing when the waters came and the ark appeared. The timing could not have been better. People initially saw the boat as an angry response from the Higher. At that point they really did fear for their lives. Since then, as I've said, their perception has changed and the quiet revolution we've all been hoping for has begun to happen. A young Aunt named Agetha quickly came to prominence and introduced a number of altruistic changes. Thanks to her, confidence in the Aunt network is slowly being restored."

"David," said Harlan, coming to sit, "I think it's time you told Thorren, and the others, about the tapestry."

"Tapestry?" said Eliza.

David let his eyes come to rest on his mother, who realized immediately what was wanted of her. "Penny, let's go for a walk," she said.

"Now?" said the girl.

"I could do with some air."

"We're *in* the air!"

"*Now*, Penny."

The girl stood up, pouting furiously. "You're going to talk about . . . secret stuff, aren't you?" She frowned harshly at her brother who said, "I'll come and read to you later."

But even that sweet promise couldn't lighten Penny's

mood. Slamming a hand against the midriff of a bemused Mathew, she stomped away ahead of her mother.

David imagineered a low table and asked the others to gather around. He unrolled a piece of paper and pinned it at both ends by imagineered weights. On it was a detailed drawing of the *Tapestry of Isenfier*. Rosa folded her arms and felt her mouth grow dry. All of a sudden, Ozralia felt awfully chilly.

"This is a reproduction," David said, "drawn from memory, of a tapestry Rosa and I found on Floor One Hundred and Eight of the old librarium. Generations of firebirds have protected the original. Ironically, I can't show it to you because we can't find it, but I think I can tell you what it means and who the people are." He pointed them out. "Me, Rosa, Mathew —"

"Me?" said Lefarr. He sat up, looking shocked.

David nodded. "Yes, with a teenage Penny. The kneeling child in the foreground is Angel."

"What's she's holding?" Bernard asked.

"A small dragon," David said.

"This is a battle scene," Strømberg muttered, carefully running his gaze over it.

"It's called Isenfier," Harlan said, sounding grim. "And it's happening — or rather not happening — somewhere in time, on another world."

"On the opposite side of your rift, I imagine?" Strømberg raised his eyes toward David.

David nodded. "Aunt Gwyneth called it Earth."

"Not happening?" Bernard repeated. "You mean there's an inter:rupt in the continuum?"

Harlan said, "David, show Thorren the claw."

David pulled it from his pocket. "The dragon in the tapestry is holding this — or something equally as powerful. It's writing an ancient symbol, capable of suspending the time point."

"But how are we involved?" Mathew said. "I mean, we're here, not there."

"Dad?" David said. "Do you want to explain?"

Harlan blew a short breath. "I'll try. Time, as you know, is a strange concept. Though it may appear to us that it always advances in a linear fashion, we can't really prove it. That feeling of moving forward may be nothing more than an intuitive notion. Some theorists even suggest that what we perceive as the past, the present, and the future are gathered into one eternal 'now.'"

"Which is constantly changing," Bernard chipped in.

"Quite," said Harlan. "This means there may be infinite possibilities to the course of our lives, which supports the idea that we might exist in alternative realities, on the *same* time point. Hence the battle is happening or not happening." (A confused Rosa shook her head and walked away.) Harlan went on: "It's important to understand that the people represented on the tapestry are not the David, Rosa, and Mathew gathered here, even though they may look like them, but probable variations of them. The truly interesting character, of course, is the dragon."

Strømberg hummed in thought. "Given that your theories are correct, why would this dragon suspend this particular incident in time?"

"They're in danger," Harlan said. "The people in the tapestry. They're being threatened by a force you saw glimpses of in David's dreams. The dragon has used its own kind of claw to stop the battle at a crucial moment and throw out a distress signal over a time nexus. Agawin somehow had a vision of it and realized that one day the right David would see the tapestry and —"

"Ride to the rescue?" Rosa said.

All the men turned their faces to her.

"How does that happen?" she said, looking worried. "How does my David go there and save them?" She gestured toward the drawing.

"I assume he writes with the claw," said Harlan.

Or uses the bone, David was thinking, remembering now what Angel had said about finding Gadzooks.

"I have a question." Mathew sat forward with his elbows on his knees. "If it's true — about alternative realities and stuff — then I have a problem."

"What's that?" asked Harlan.

"Gwyneth."

David raised his eyes.

Mathew went on. "Maybe the counselor can answer something for me: Did she, Gwyneth, ever use another name?"

Strømberg tapped his fingertips together. "Another name?"

"Gwilanna, for instance?"

David noticed Bernard rubbing his chin in thought.

Strømberg replied, "No. When inducted, an Aunt's name is always fixed to her parents' choice. It's part of a strict verification process."

Mathew tightened his lips and said, "Then why would she use the claw to write another?"

"Oh my goodness," Bernard said suddenly. "She must know herself — in the other world."

"How?" said Rosa, from the far side of the deck.

Harlan narrowed his gaze. "The Ix traveled here from Earth; she could have learned of it from them."

"So where does that leave us?" Mathew asked.

The sound of wingbeats made everyone look up. Aurielle and Azkiar, in their firebird form, were descending from the upper decks. They were flying side by side, carrying a rolled-up cloth between them.

"The tapestry," Rosa said. "They've found the tapestry." She pushed away from the rail and hurried to their landing site farther up the deck. As David and the others came to join her she was already deep in conversation with Aurielle. "They found it in the glade," she communicated to David.

"The glade? But why didn't they find it earlier? They must have searched there lots of times."

"Angel told them to look again. It was there, in the leaves. Rolled up, like this."

"Unroll it," David said to Aurielle in dragontongue.

The two firebirds pushed with their feet until the picture was laid out fully on the deck. Aurielle sat at one end and Azkiar at the other.

Mathew Lefarr was the first to comment. He looked at the tapestry, then at David. "That's not the same picture you drew, is it?"

Rosa shook her head. "This is wrong. What's happened? We're in different places. And why is the sky filled with ugly flying creatures? They look like that thing we saw once in the librarium. And who's that *boy*?"

"This is Gwyneth's doing," Harlan breathed. "She's given herself up to the nexus and realigned the time line. If she died on Earth where she was known as Gwilanna, the events on the original tapestry were true, but if she continues to live . . ."

". . . It all changes," David said.

Suddenly there was a bump, followed by an elongated grinding noise as if the keel of the ark had plowed into several acres of mud. Both firebirds took off and Rosa rushed to the deck rail again. "David!" she screamed. "The water! Look at the water!"

At the same time Harlan Merriman was shouting, "The bird. David, she's caught."

Aurielle was flapping wildly, trying to release a thread of the tapestry caught in her claw. But the harder she tried, the harder she pulled. And with every fresh pull, the image was changing. David was being drawn into the Shadow of Ix. And a new figure on the hill, who he knew must be Gwilanna, had her hand twitched forward and her face slightly pinched as if she were smiling and waving good-bye.

And all around the ark an orange light was growing.

And there was no water.

There was only fire.

Chris d'Lacey is the author of several highly acclaimed books for children and young adults, including the other titles in the Last Dragon Chronicles, *The Fire Within*, *Icefire*, *Fire Star*, *The Fire Eternal*, and *Dark Fire*. He has also written The Dragons of Wayward Crescent books, including *Gruffen* and *Gauge*. Chris lives with his wife in England.

To learn more about Chris and his dragons, visit *www.scholastic.com/LastDragonChronicles*.